KINGDOMS
OF THE
FROZEN
DEAD

MAP OF KEPLER
THE ATLANTIS OCEAN
NEW PARIS
WEST COAST SHORES
LOCKHEED
FORMER WESTERN REPUBLIC
MENDELTON
MORKUM
GALILEO FIELDS
IMMORTAL EMPIRE
N
W
E
S
THE MEDICI OCEAN
POLITICAL BOUNDARIES

FORT AURORA BOREALIS
THE ASIMOV STRAITS
NORTHERN KINGDOM
CERULEAN
SEA of DAO
SILVER ORCHID
MOUNTAIN OF PERIL
HYPATIA
KOCHU AZHI
EINSTEINIAN
NEW AMERICA
DESERT OASIS
WATERTON
EASTERN RIDGE TRAIL
GREAT CRATER LAKE
SHADOW OF THE MOUNTAINS
EASTERN DESERT
GANDHI
CLEMSON
GUARNERI
NATIVE LANDS
FORMER EASTERN CONFEDERATION
SOUTHERN KINGDOM
NOVI DUPREE
ALIGHIERI
CAPE GREGORY
THE AURELIAN GULF
KILOMETERS
0 200 400 600 800 1000 1200 1400 1600 1800 2000

MORTAL HERITANCE | BOOK TWO

KINGDOMS

OF THE

FROZEN

DEAD

SANDRA L. VASHER

MORTAL
INK PRESS

KINGDOMS OF THE FROZEN DEAD
Copyright © 2021 by Sandra L. Vasher.

For information, please contact Mortal Ink Press LLC, PO Box 30811, Raleigh, NC 27622-0811, USA.
www.mortalinkpress.com

Library of Congress Control Number: 2020920582
ISBN 978-1-950989-02-7 (paperback)
ISBN 978-1-950989-10-2 (ebook)

Cover design copyright © 2019 by Jennifer Zemanek / Seedlings Design Studio.

In memory of Mary Cantrell.
May your soul fare well until we meet again, my beautiful, feisty friend.

ROYAL CHURCH OF SOUTH KEPLER
PRAYER FOR THE DEAD

May your voyage to heaven be swift,
as you find eternal grace;

While your body returns to dust,
may your soul evermore be free;

May you glorify Creation,
and your spirit be made anew;

Then beyond the known universe,
into the starry space,
may you fare well, friend,
until the day we meet again.

So be it.

CHAPTER ONE
THE SURVIVING PRINCE

Prince Bastian's caravan was slaughtered. Dead. Everyone. There had only been twenty or so guards left, but it still came as a shock to see them that way, slumped over prone horses, bullet holes through their jackets, bloodstains on their shirts.

The sight sickened him. Not the sight of death. That itself never bothered Bast. It was the echo of pain and suffering that came *with* death when it happened this way that got to him. The Immortal way of killing Mortals was ugly, atrocious, cruel.

When Bast killed Immortals, he did it the least painful way possible. Freezing was numbing and nearly instantaneous. The victim's brain halted so fast it hardly had time to send a pulse of conscious pain to the dying Immortal. A piercing pang in the front of the brain—not enough to compete with a migraine—then the body would let a final breath go as organs ceased and stopped in time. It was benign. They never saw it coming, and there was no suffering. It was far better than the heartless Immortals deserved.

And again, Bast didn't have a problem with death. Death made him Mortal. Mortality gave him a reason for morality, and magic was the God-given gift bestowed on him for both. Magic flowed through Bast's blood like a miracle made personally for him. Magic made him feel alive. He thus felt that without death, he would barely *be* alive.

Pain and suffering, though …

Of course, he understood why God gave *him* pain and suffering. It was what made Bast smart, gave him depth, helped him distinguish between good and bad. Without pain and suffering, Bast wouldn't have the wisdom necessary to be powerful with true purpose.

But *he* was royalty. He had more power than most and significantly more responsibility. He needed that wisdom, so he needed pain and suffering. The same wasn't true for most of the people in the Kingdom of South Kepler, who were good people who didn't need more misery than that which life brought by chance. As he looked around at his dead— people he'd had little regard for in life but who were still *his* people, still *his* innocents—he felt bile in his throat.

He stared down at the body of a woman whose name he didn't know. Her eyes were open, head tilted to the side, skin still fading from pink to gray. If it hadn't been for the singed holes—a line of six running from her hip bone to her left breast—and the blood that drenched her uniform, she might simply be resting with her eyes wistfully set on a man nearby. The man wasn't looking back because his eyes were closed in death, but perhaps they'd been something to each other. Lovers maybe.

A single line of bullets delivered a senselessly gruesome death. Bast forced himself not to vomit at the sight.

Immortals had done this, and it was despicable.

He crouched down and closed the woman's eyes before whispering the Prayer for the Dead. *May your voyage to heaven be swift, as you find eternal grace …*

"Prince Bastian?"

He looked away from the corpse to the only other person who had survived this attack.

Brandon Thurlow.

What a joke.

Thurlow had followed Bast like a mangy dog from the top of the Mountain of Peril down to where these brave soldiers had put up their last fight in service of the kingdom. The filthy, duplicitous scoundrel cried like a weakling while Bast led the way. He asked aimless questions meant to mislead Bast. "How did it happen?" "Was it the Guru?" "Did she suffer?" "Where's Nate?" "What happened, Prince Bastian?"

Bast hadn't yet responded to the idiocy. He knew Thurlow's decision to hike the Mountain of Peril rather than stay with his own people was calculated. Bast's sister, Vivian, had been too weak to see the manipulation. She thought the captain had *feelings* for her. Well, now the captain was looking suspiciously not-dead standing here while Bast prayed over another fallen soldier.

"Prince Bastian, I understand your desire to pray, but this attack was clearly planned. The Immortal Empire doesn't conduct these operations lightly. We *must* find Prince Nathanial and return you both to safety."

Disgraceful. This man was walking amongst people he'd pretended to care about, and he felt it appropriate to tell Bast to *rush* the prayers?

"I believe God will give us adequate time to put these souls to rest, Captain," Bast said, putting as much ice into his voice as he could without reaching the point where the air would actually freeze.

Thurlow knelt beside him and had the nerve to put his hand on Bast's shoulder. "Sir, you're in shock. Perhaps if we could find your brother, you would feel some comfort."

Bast laughed nastily. As if Thurlow hadn't manipulated *that* part of this whole nightmare as well, making friends with Nate the moment Nate pulled rank. Not that Nate could ever *really* be more powerful than Bast. But whatever. Nate was a fool. Thurlow had fooled him. Now Nate was dead. When Bast had time to think about it, he would probably miss his brother. It wasn't the same as with Vivian …

Vivian.

A wave of darkness fell over Bast.

"Prince Bastian, where is Prince Nathanial? I don't see his horse. Please, sir. We must find him. Were you separated on the mountain?"

Nate's horse was missing? Bast couldn't tell the horses apart. But no matter. Nate had always said his horse was smart. Maybe it had managed to get free somehow. Poor beast. Nate was the best thing in that horse's life, and that wasn't saying much. Bast hoped the horse wouldn't wander the planet Kepler for the rest of its miserable years looking for his master.

"*Where* is Prince Nathanial, Your Highness?" the captain asked again. "If Vivian is … if she's … we *must* find Prince Nathanial. He's … he's the *crown* now. It is *imperative* that we protect him."

Bast despised the sincerity in Thurlow's tone. It was beyond frustrating that his telesthesia gift was failing him with this piece of trash. Normally, Bast could tell when someone was lying. He hadn't caught Thurlow in a lie yet. That didn't mean the guy *wasn't* lying, though. Bast's magical power to hear a lie in someone's voice only worked when the liar knew he was lying. The most manipulative people could lie so well they believed their lies were true. Even when her words were not truthful, Bast hardly ever caught his mother lying. That didn't mean she didn't lie. She lied easily, especially to herself. It seemed Thurlow was so tangled in his own game that he thought he was still loyal to Nate.

Bast turned from the dead woman and met Thurlow's eyes steadily. "Is Prince Nathanial who you're really worried about? Because if so, there's no need to worry anymore."

Thurlow's face seemed almost to age as he formed his next sentence. "Why don't I need to worry?"

Perhaps the man *had* genuinely cared about Nate. Sure. It was rational. Nate would have been far easier to control than Vivian. It made all the sense in the world that Thurlow would have ingratiated himself to Nate. Nate was valuable to Thurlow.

So maybe this news was actually going to hurt poor Brandon Thurlow, but Bast felt like teaching the guy a lesson. Thurlow might have seduced Vivian and slipped Nate into his back pocket, but Bast wasn't anyone's pawn. He relished the hurt that flashed over Thurlow's face as he said, "Prince Nathanial is *dead*, Captain."

Thurlow almost fell back. "Nate's dead, too?"

Bast stood up and walked to another soldier, pausing to pray for this one as well.

"Yes," he confirmed after, as he moved on to yet another of his dead. "I suggest you adjust your priorities. *I* am the crown now. I am the one you protect. I am the one you take orders from. And I say God will give us time for fifteen or so more prayers."

Thurlow gawked at him.

"Or do you think you can manipulate me, too?" Bast asked. "Because I can assure you, I never fell for your act with my sister."

Thurlow made an over-dramatic, choked noise. "I *loved* Vivian."

Bast was on to a seventh soldier, another whose eyes were open. "And I'm sure that's why you only showed back up after she was dead."

"You *disappeared*. I searched for you. For *all* of you. I searched for hours. *You* were the first person I found."

Did Bast detect a note of accusation there? What gave this guy the right to act as though any blame could possibly be placed on *him* for this mess?

"Oh, really, Captain? You searched and searched and somehow *missed* the hoard of Empire Immortals on their way up the mountain to kill us? Your only job was to protect the queen. I put up with you for her."

The captain's face paled, but he was more stubborn than Bast gave him credit for. He stood his ground while Bast continued to pray. "Sir, you've been through a terrible ordeal today. As you said, you … are the crown now. I must suggest again that we move as quickly as possible to relocate somewhere you will be safe."

"And *I* must *insist* you hold your tongue."

Finally, the captain managed a moment of silence while Bast completed the task at hand. When he was done, he stood up, slowly, with a plan that had come to him while he finished commemorating the dead.

"We will leave now," he told Thurlow.

"Don't we need to recover the … Nate's … and Viv's …"

The idiot made a noise like a dying cow.

"You will please be more respectful," Bast ordered. "*Prince* Nathanial and *Queen* Vivian."

"I'm sorry," Thurlow blubbered. "I'm so sorry. I ... I ..."

"Yes, yes, you're sorry, I'm sorry, our whole caravan is dead, and I have two siblings on that damned mountain that I can't bury because if we take time to go back now, we won't find safety."

"You're going to leave *them*? Without giving them the rites? But you—"

"Do not question me." There were still a few horses harnessed to the coach. Why the animals were left alive, Bast couldn't fathom. He did not like animals himself. If he were ruthless enough to kill as savagely as the Immortals, he'd definitely have killed the horses, too. "We will go to the nearest outpost, secure reinforcements, and return as soon as possible to retrieve the bodies for proper funeral rites and later burial in Alighieri. Where you will stand trial."

Thurlow couldn't have paled further, but he took two steps back, tripped, and fell to the ground. "Stand trial? For what?"

"Conspiracy," Bast said crisply. "To kill the queen. Unless you can get on my good side before then and convince me you weren't involved in this." He narrowed his eyes at the cowering man. "You *could* run. If you are guilty, you probably should. It's not going to be a pleasant trial. Very public. My mother will be there. I'd run if I were you."

"I *didn't* do this," Thurlow said. "I would *never*—"

"Oh, because you loved my sister?" Bast laughed. "*I* loved her. You tricked her. You barely knew her. If you defiled her, you are a monster worse than—"

The captain seemed confused. "How can you talk about your sister that way?"

"How can *you* talk like you don't know what's going on here?" Bast swept his arm around them. "Look, Captain. What do you see? I see a slaughtered crew, a single surviving prince, and a lone captain who conveniently disappeared down the mountain just before the dead queen was taken to her place of doom. God saw fit to save my life for reasons I do not understand. Prince Nathanial and Queen Vivian were taken for other reasons I do not understand. And *you* ..."

The captain's mouth gaped ridiculously, and Bast assumed his point was made. He walked toward the coach that had been Vivian's, wishing for the first time ever that Nate was around to help with the horses. The captain started crying noisily again.

Bast, this wasn't his fault.

Why had Vivian been so smitten by him? Bast was going to find evidence against this man. He was sure of it. But for now, while he needed help with the horses ...

He threw Thurlow a disdainful glance. "Oh, stop being so pathetic, Thurlow. Queen Vivian wouldn't have wanted you executed immediately. She would have begged me to give you a second chance."

Thurlow's tears were even uglier with fear in his eyes.

Bast despised Thurlow the whole way to the closest town where South Kepler had members of the Southern Guard stationed. There, Bast got a night of sleep he desperately needed, and he didn't suffer from any nightmares. The next morning, he had Brandon Thurlow arrested and stripped of his title as "captain." Then Bast personally selected a new team—guards chosen by him alone, who he knew would be loyal either because they had an innate sense of honesty or true fear of power or, preferably, both.

He ordered his new team to return to the mountain to recover the bodies of his deceased family, buried in rubble now thanks to an attack followed by an explosion no one had anticipated.

Remembering the innocent Mortal sisters who died in the explosion as well, Bast also asked the team to watch for the bodies of two girls. He couldn't even imagine the terror the youngest, who'd caused the explosion, must have felt in her last moments. To cause that kind of destruction. Poor child.

As for the other girl—Carina—he regretted how his interactions with her had gone. Perhaps if they'd told her exactly what they needed her for, she would have attempted to help. Whatever secrets she was keeping, and Bast had theories about *that*, she plainly wasn't cooperating with any Immortals, or she and her sister would still be alive.

He asked the team to make sure that when the two girls were found, they were given proper rites as well and buried somewhere nice on the mountain. A sunny place near the top would do.

After that, Bast had work to complete. It was abundantly clear now that the Immortal Empire was actively threatening South Kepler. Vivian's assassination needed to be further investigated, as did the attack on the Mountain of Peril. Bast would have to tell his mother everything, and he needed to assume his new duties as the crown prince.

His team set up a temporary station for him at the base of the Mountain of Peril, then he busied himself with mounds of correspondence while the team handled the search for bodies. Given the trauma Bast had sustained less than forty-eight hours ago at this very mountain, he felt calm. Calm enough not to look up from the letter he was writing to his mother when a shadow darkened his desk.

"We found it, sir."

"Found what?"

"The … the body, sir."

Bast shoved the contents of his stomach down, though there couldn't have been much left in his weak-willed gut. He'd barely been able to swallow for the last two days. That gut was the only part of Bast's body that he could not overcome with mental strength. Nate wouldn't have had this problem. Nate would have been able to eat as long as he knew whatever he was eating had never been conscious. If their situations were reversed, Nate would probably have been sad about Bast's death for about a minute before he'd started thinking about lunch.

Nate. Who was dead. Whose *corpse* had just been located.

"Is it intact?" Bast asked the guard.

The guard flinched. "It was covered, sir."

Obviously. The whole *house* had come down. What Bast wanted to know was whether he needed to do something to protect his dead brother's dignity. If Nate's head had been severed, Bast might have to go for a closed casket at the memorial ceremony, whereas a little post-mortem flesh healing could probably fix any limbs hanging askew.

"Do you want to do the rites here?"

"Yeah, that makes sense," Bast said absently. "It's a long trip home. I'll do the prayers myself. Nate deserves at least that. He did die trying to save …"

The guard cleared his throat and shifted from foot to foot.

Bast paused and looked at the guard, who he did not recognize. The man had dark stubble on his face, and his skin was overrun with blackheads. His jacket was wrinkled, and his boots looked dull. Bast instantly disliked the guard and further disliked his wavering. What, was Nate in some kind of embarrassing position? Did it look like he'd died doing something idiotic? Running into danger like he had to rescue Vivian? It *had* been stupid. There had been no way to save her. If there had been, Bast himself would have done it. Nate still deserved the prayers, though. His death was *honorable*. Tragic and meaningless, unfortunately. Quite diminished Vivian's sacrifice. But still—

The guard cleared his throat again and tried to say something Bast couldn't hear.

"Pardon me?" Bast stood up, and the guard shrank. Bast noticed the guard's collar wasn't buttoned properly. He tried not to snarl as he asked: "What are you trying to tell me, soldier?"

The guard shivered.

Oh, he was cold? Bast didn't care. "What the hell is going on with my brother's body? Is it in pieces? Is it impossible to retrieve? Did you find a hand and nothing else?"

"It's … not Prince Nathanial," the guard stammered.

Bast resisted the urge to clutch his stupid, rebellious gut. "It's *not* Prince Nathanial?"

The guard shook his head rapidly. "No, sir. I mean, yes sir. We combed through the rubble twice looking for your brother, but—"

Bast interrupted impatiently. "Fine. Whatever. Whose body did you find? I told you to bury the girls if you found either of them. There is no need to bother me with trivial matters."

The guard's voice quivered like a child's. "No, sir. We haven't found any other Mortals. Only—"

Bast considered freezing the man to death. This incoherent idiot was testing his nerves.

"Whose body did you find, soldier?" Bast asked the oily guard.

"Queen Vivian's, sir," the man croaked.

"I'm sorry, *whose?*"

"Queen … Queen Vivian's, Your Highness," the man practically sobbed. "Please … I'm sorry, sir. She's … covered. With a blanket. Her arms are folded, and her eyes are closed … but it's … definitely her."

Bast was going to be extremely sick.

"She's the only Mortal body we recovered."

Bast's sister had died on that mountain, and he'd ordered his team to recover the dead queen's body. But he realized now that his mind had not yet connected that body—or any body that was not a living, breathing body—to his sister.

His sister, who he *hadn't* been able to save.

"Please, sir, we are all devastated by this loss. I cannot imagine how hard—"

Bast ignored him. "Where is she?"

"It's … a long climb, Your Highness."

His breath became visible as mist despite the late summer heat as he issued an order. "Take. Me. To. Her."

"Yes, sir," the man said, and so, Bast began his second climb up the godforsaken Mountain of Peril.

ARTICLE IN *THE ALIGHIERI POST* DATED MONDAY, AUGUST 39, 881 AAH

Queen Vivian Eliza Andrea Wellington, the fifteenth Queen of the Southern Kingdom of Kepler, died on Thursday, August 35, 881 AAH, on the Mountain of Peril, during a brutal confrontation with a battalion of Empire Immortals.

Queen Vivian was previously the victim of an assassination attempt, made at her coronation and leaving her infected with the Immortality Virus. Queen Vivian was eighteen years old. She is the fifth monarch to be killed in service to the Crown since the rise of the Immortal Empire.

The Queen's brother, Prince Nathanial Herschel Xavier Wellington, also perished during the attack. The Queen is survived by Prince Bastian Cassius Davis Wellington, now the Crown Prince of the Southern Kingdom of Kepler.

The royal family requests privacy during this time of deep trouble and sadness. The kingdom mourns the loss of its young queen.

God save the Crown.

—Immortal Empire raids continue to be reported in small villages across the North, devastating an already crumbling Northern infrastructure.

—Southern Guard recruitment efforts are stalled as the royal family diverts forces to the border to fend off Immortal Empire encroachment.

—Immortal Empress Hildebrand refuses to claim responsibility for the assassination of Queen Vivian but calls the death "convenient"; threatens attack on the castle at Alighieri to topple the last remaining Mortal monarchy.

—Queen Constance vows not to set a date for the memorial service for Queen Vivian and Prince Nathanial until all those responsible for the deaths of her two eldest children are brought to justice.

—Rumors of Prince Nathanial's possible survival denied by Crown Prince Bastian, who commented, "I only wish the rumors were true. Unfortunately, my brother did not survive. The heavy burden of the crown is mine to bear alone."

CHAPTER TWO
THE DEAD PRINCE

Nathanial Herschel Xavier Wellington was the crown prince of the lustrous, mighty Kingdom of South Kepler. So, he was drinking tonight.

Nothing with alcohol in it. He had turned seventeen three months ago, but the bartender didn't believe him when he said he was eighteen. He apparently looked pathetic enough to earn as many free coke-and-no-rums as he wanted, though. He'd accepted the non-alcoholic drink (and five refills) on the grounds that he at least wanted to sit in this dingy bar and *try* to let himself feel miserable in an appropriate way. But truthfully, this wasn't the misery Nate had hoped for—caffeine did things to him, and by now, his hands were shaking and he was kicking the bottom rung of his barstool so hard his heels hurt.

A large man with bright red eyes, bad breath, and a front knuckle the size of a baby's fist sat down next to Nate and jostled him hard enough that Nate inadvertently tipped over his fifth refill. The bartender eyed Nate like he thought maybe he was *on* something and came over with a rag to mop up the mess.

"You got anywhere to go tonight, son?"

Nate hated when people called him "son." It was the epitome of patronizing. What gave every man who got old enough to have a beer gut and a bald spot the right to call any man who looked at least five years younger "son"? Nate hoped he'd die before he reached that stage of regret. Thankfully, his current position made it so that wouldn't be that hard to achieve. At the rate he was going, he'd likely be dead before he reached eighteen.

The bartender clanked a glass of water down on the bar in front of Nate and leaned toward him. "There's a men's shelter down the road. You look like you could use a clean bed and a shower."

Nate resented the implications of that statement and also wanted to sniff his armpits to see if he smelled. He thought he'd showered yesterday. It could have been the day before. He definitely hadn't shaved all week. Which he could normally get away with—he was fair enough—but even he looked scuzzy eight days out from the last time he'd bothered to groom himself. Bast would have died.

No, wait. Bast wouldn't have died. Bast understood the concept of self-preservation. Bast was going to live a long, clean-shaven, well-dressed life, probably as the king of South Kepler, since Nate, regrettably the rightful heir, was presumed dead, and his brother, Bast, was not.

Nate took a swig of water and managed to miss his own mouth. Water dribbled down his chin. He was very suave. Who the hell cared about a clean bed? Why waste the sheets anyway? Nate hadn't slept through the night in six months.

"Long live the king," he muttered, drawing the attention

of the big Immortal next to him, who gave him what was probably meant to be a friendly punch on the shoulder.

"Buddy, you look like you need some fun." The Immortal sounded gruff, but Nate couldn't detect anything lethal coming off the guy. Nate was still getting used to this kind of thing—Immortals who weren't specifically talking to you to threaten you or someone you cared about. Turns out all kinds of Immortals were hanging out in tiny nowhere towns in the North like this one. Hypatia. Pretty name, but not one the town deserved. The whole place was coated with grime, and half the town worked the coal mines nearby.

Nate thought his family was a little extreme about the Kepler Declaration of Mortal Commitments, but this place was everything the Fourth Commitment meant to prevent. Or maybe it was the Second. Nate didn't exactly have the Mortal Commitments memorized. Whatever. There was definitely a commitment related to environmentalism somewhere in there.

"Forget the shelter. I know a place you can take your mind off *everything* if you got enough money."

Oh right. The grimy Immortal was still talking.

The guy grinned. "You got any money? I got time to take ya' there if you do."

Nate had no money. Or rather, he had plenty of money. Heaps of it. He had more money than a hundred men would need to live lavish, spoiled lives (in the South, because Nate didn't think it was even *possible* to live lavishly in the North). But that money didn't mean anything since he couldn't get to any of it right now without drawing attention to the fact that he was still alive.

Also, he couldn't respond to this lunk. Not because Nate wasn't interested in taking his mind off everything. He just couldn't say a lot to *anyone* here. If he talked too much, his accent would give him away. He'd learned recently that he sounded "fancy" when he talked with these rogue Immortals who mostly just wanted to get drunk and play cards in dive bars until they were too stupid to know who'd won.

"That was a kind offer if I ever heard one."

Nate closed his eyes and let his head sink into his shoulders. Great. Franklin had shown up. No one was going to be doing *anything* interesting tonight. No alcohol. No more coke. Did anyone in this place even have a deck of cards?

"This one yours?" the bartender asked Franklin. Nate had not yet turned around. He didn't feel like it. The big Immortal had, though, and he elbowed Nate and said: "Your dad's a badass. Where'd he get that scar?"

Nate hopped down from the stool, dug around in his pocket, found a single quarter, and set it on the counter. "That's all I have," he said to the bartender. "Thanks for the drinks. And he's not my dad."

Franklin followed Nate back through town silently, allowing Nate to stalk in front of him like an angry teenager. Who cared? He *was* an angry teenager. He was perfect for the stereotype. Seventeen years old, messy family, recently deceased sister, constantly underestimated, low self-esteem to prove it, on the run hundreds of kilometers away from home, keeping a secret no one would have believed he was keeping.

And there it was.

Whenever Nate got unjustifiably pissed at Franklin, he remembered that secret and all his rage transformed into guilt. Franklin had saved his ass more than once. After Nate and his siblings, Prince Bastian and Queen Vivian, were forced to flee from Alighieri, the capital city of South Kepler, Franklin was the only person on all Kepler who'd chased them down for the sole purpose of making sure Nate was okay.

He'd gone through hell doing it, too, and at a time when he was trying to avoid arrest himself, and Nate *hadn't* been okay when Franklin finally found him. Not at all. He was buried alive under a pile of rocks on the Mountain of Peril, being hit hard by the realization that his sister was dead, his brother was gone, and *he* was the new heir to the throne of South Kepler. If Franklin hadn't been there …

But Franklin was there. Just like he'd been tonight. Just like he always was exactly when Nate needed him. Nate *shouldn't* have been keeping any secrets, and he *should* have felt really frickin' grateful. Emotions weren't things you could demand yourself to feel, though. Franklin was the one person Nate could count on to be there for him, but Franklin was *also* the one person preventing Nate from getting home. Franklin had been barring Nate from home for six months now, in fact.

Six months. That's how long all of South Kepler, including the rest of Nate's family, had thought he was dead. And that was a major problem, because whether the kingdom thought Nate was alive or not, Nate was currently the crown prince of South Kepler, and until he returned home, he couldn't tell Bast he was still alive and he couldn't abdicate the damn throne.

So, Nate *wasn't* grateful. He was an angry, selfish, grieving, *un*grateful teenager with unresolved conflict, a little secret, a whole hell of a lot of guilt, and a problem the size of a *kingdom*. If Franklin wanted to put up with him like that, then it wasn't Nate's fault that Franklin made poor life choices.

Franklin didn't say a word to Nate until they were back at the house in Hypatia, where they'd rented a room from an old lady. The place was smaller than anywhere Nate had ever lived. Only five rooms: a kitchen and living room downstairs, and upstairs, the woman's bedroom, a bathroom, and a spare room the woman rented out to sketchy strangers.

Nate thought of himself as the only member of his immediate family capable of "roughing" it. But as it turned out, he didn't love living in cramped quarters, and the spare room was creepy. It had once belonged to the lady's son, a boy she only talked about in past tense. There were about a dozen pictures of the kid hanging in the hallways, but none where he looked any older than twelve. Nate assumed that meant the boy was now dead or Immortal.

The Immortal Empire used a raid-and-snatch strategy to increase the Immortal population, and poorly defended towns like Hypatia were perfect targets. Nate couldn't stomach the thought of all the kids who'd been stolen and infected with the Immortality Virus. Awful.

But still, he wasn't about to dredge up trauma that had happened forever ago to a woman who was old enough to be half-deaf and practically blind. Um, no thanks. Franklin could have that conversation if he wanted. Nate was avoiding it at all costs in every way. Though Nate knew Franklin didn't care that much about the old lady's kid either. Franklin had chosen to rent from her *because* of her visual and hearing impairments, which made her easier to fool.

Franklin was a nice guy.

"You know you shouldn't drink that stuff," Franklin said as they climbed the creaky, carpeted stairs to their room. He handed Nate the key.

Nate took it reluctantly. Franklin did things like this. Subtle stuff to teach Nate lessons he was supposed to learn without Franklin saying a word.

In this case, Nate's hand shook as he tried to put the key in the lock, and that was the lesson. His hand wouldn't be shaking if he hadn't just loaded his body with sugary shit and caffeine. Never mind that *all* the good stuff was sugary and caffeinated. One glass of coke could hype Nate up enough to make him a fast talker and a dangerous Mortal to pick a fight with. Five drinks made it embarrassingly difficult for him to unlock a door.

Also gave him an urgent need to pee. Urgent urgent. The kind of urgent that made unlocking a door *especially* difficult. It must have taken him a full minute to unlock the stupid door, then he plowed in, threw his jacket down on the narrow cot he'd claimed, and immediately bolted for the bathroom.

Sharing a bathroom with an old lady meant flowery soap and a toilet with a carpeted lid. The woman thought Nate had good manners because he knew better than to leave the seat up. That was not good manners. That was a habit he had picked up thanks to sharing a bathroom with Bast for years. Bast said it was sloppy to leave a toilet open after you used it, and whenever Nate had forgotten, he'd pitched the kind of fit only an obsessive-compulsive-perfectionist-neat-freak could pitch.

But Nate put down the seat and the lid anyway and returned to the room, and by then, Franklin was lying on his back on the room's second cot with his arm covering his eyes. He hadn't bothered to take off his shoes, and he didn't bother to uncover his eyes before he started laying into Nate.

"What you did tonight was irresponsible. What if that guy next to you hadn't been in such a friendly mood?

The last thing we need is for you to get in a bar fight with an Immortal."

Nate sat on his cot. It was pushed against a wall painted a dirty shade of yellow. He noticed a crack in the wall across from him, which Franklin's cot was pushed against. There was a dusty, framed cross-stitch of a kid kicking a toggleball hanging crookedly to the left of the crack.

"You mean the last thing *you* need is for me to get in a bar fight. Because you're the one who's in trouble, right? I'm already dead. Who would care if someone killed me? A bar fight would be a quick, satisfying way to go."

Franklin uncovered his face and turned his neck toward Nate. He had a long scar that covered his face. The dingy light caught the shiny skin, and Nate felt just bad enough that he almost said "sorry." He chose to pick lint from the blanket on his cot instead. Franklin didn't like being pitied.

Then Franklin said, "I'm not worried about someone killing *you*. I'm worried about you setting the bar on fire and killing someone else."

Nate flicked lint at the floor. "Thanks for your overwhelming care and concern."

Franklin rolled away from Nate. "It's almost two in the morning. Turn the lights off. I need sleep."

If Nate hadn't been so high on caffeine, he could have flipped the switch telekinetically. But with all this energy in his system, trying that would have risked breaking the switch off the wall. He got up to do it. The lights flickered out. He heard Franklin shift on his cot like he was settling in, but Nate was too amped up to lie back down.

He walked to the one window in the room. It was frosted over, which probably meant it was cold outside. Nate wasn't sure how cold. With one or two exceptions, the only times

Nate had ever felt cold were when he'd gotten the worst of Bast's temper in a thermodynamic magic match. (The three times the crazy ice girl they'd met over the summer had managed to make him cold did not count. Because that would have required Nate to acknowledge that she'd existed and was now dead. And it wasn't good to think badly of the dead.)

This early February cold barely bothered Nate at all. If anything, it was probably good for him, since his hot tendency had been on overdrive recently. The old lady's steam heaters barely worked, but Franklin had asked Nate several times over the last week to open the window when the spare room got unbearably hot for both of them despite the chill outside.

If he'd been Bast, Nate would probably have concluded that his ability to overpower the weather meant he was getting close to god status. Since he was Nate, all he could conclude was that there wasn't anything about his life that was predictable, and he sucked at controlling his own magic.

"Go to bed, Nate," Franklin said wearily.

"I don't feel like it," Nate said. "Maybe I should take a walk."

"Maybe you should strap yourself to the bed."

"I can't sleep."

"I don't care. Lie down and try to meditate or something."

"Why? Big plans for today?"

Franklin didn't answer.

"Are you going to help me find a job so that we can rent a better place in the next town? Are we enrolling me in a university course? How to Be a King for the Woefully Unprepared?"

No response.

Nate glared at Franklin's back. "Think we could go to a library, so I'd have something to read? Boredom is bad for me."

Franklin grunted, and Nate took that as a maybe. He flopped down on his cot and listened to Franklin's breath become deep and heavy. It was unfair that Franklin could sleep so easily when Nate couldn't sleep at night *or* focus during the day.

This was one of the reasons Nate *couldn't* rest. How was he supposed to sleep when Franklin was dead out? One of them should always be keeping watch. Franklin thought they could trust the old lady, but Nate had a few good reasons to think she was shady. Not that he could tell Franklin his reasons. Still.

He tried to "meditate or something," and when that didn't work, he opened his eyes and thought of stripping the blanket off the cot. He should *not* have ingested that much caffeine tonight. Franklin was right about that. Nate was never going to sleep this way.

Or maybe Franklin was wrong. Because just as Nate was starting to truly regret those five cokes, he heard something. People. Coming into the house. Coming up the stairs.

He jumped out of bed. "Franklin, get up," he said sharply.

Franklin sat straight up like he was always prepared for a military emergency, listened for two seconds, and leaped off the cot.

"Guess the old lady couldn't be trusted after all," Franklin said while Nate grabbed his bag. Thank God they traveled light—Franklin insisted they always be packed and ready to run.

"Window?" Nate asked.

"Yep." Franklin agreed. "Window it is."

Nate jumped, slowing his fall from a second-story window with well-aimed telekinesis, and then got out of the way as Franklin jumped and rolled into a smooth landing behind him. No telekinesis needed. Franklin had warrior skills.

"Now what?" Nate said to Franklin as they saw lights flash on in their room in the old lady's house.

"Now run," Franklin said.

BROADCAST OF THE NORTHERN MILITIA
DATED SATURDAY, AUGUST 37, 881 AAH

Attention all stations, attention all stations. Security clearance level blue, message follows. Repeat, security clearance level blue, message follows. As of Saturday 37 August 881, both princesses of North Kepler, repeat, zero-two princesses, have been reunited with their father at Fort Aurora Borealis after search and rescue efforts were resumed following reliable reports of sightings and verified by Sergeant Mishe Lovric of the Northern Militia.

Units dispatched by the Northern Militia were able to locate, identify, and safely recover the princesses in the Red Ridge Mountains. Both princesses are alive, well, and unharmed.

Reminder, this message is security clearance level blue. Do not discuss with any persons not cleared. Failure to follow clearance requirements is considered treason and will be met with the full force of the law.

The king is delighted with the return of his daughters.

CHAPTER THREE
THE PRINCESS LIFE

Carina Lucia Esmeralda Garcia was the Crown Princess of the Northern Kingdom of Kepler. It was an idea she was still getting used to. It was a whole new *life* she was getting used to. So, she was running right now. On a treadmill. In an enormous, solar-powered training center situated at the edge of a steep cliff overlooking the dauntingly dark waters and ship-defying blocks of ice of the Asimov Straits.

"Not that the ice will bother *you*," Glory-Jane said with a tittering laugh during the Fort Aurora Borealis tour Carina's dad didn't give her himself. "But the tundra up here is chilly enough for the rest of us!"

In Carina's first letter back to Sister Agda, she described Glory-Jane as an "unnecessarily cheerful woman." In her letter to Sister Elizabeth, she added that the head of her new personal staff looked "like a soggy dumpling." Sister Raji, who had obviously been privy to both letters, wrote back that Carina should give the cheery, soggy dumpling a chance.

She was trying, but *nothing* about her life here on Aurora

Borealis Isle resembled anything like life with the Sisters at Novi Dupree Sanctuary. The crisp morning air of the Red Ridge Mountains never burned her lungs like the near-frozen air here. There was enough work to be done at the sanctuary that Carina never needed a run on a treadmill there. She certainly wouldn't have needed four guards to stand by while she ran.

Four guards. Before dawn. On an island surrounded by water so cold, icy, and dangerous that you could only get here on a special ferry operated by a crew of telekinetic oarsmen, thermodynamic engineers, and a captain with a convenient telesthesia ability to alter what people thought they were seeing.

Carina's full "staff" included twelve guards plus six attendants who rotated in and out. *No one* else had a larger staff, including the king himself, who refused to reassign anyone when Carina asked.

"Not an option," her dad had said. "Those people are in place to protect the crown of North Kepler, and you are the single most important resource the crown has. If anything, we should reassign people to you."

Her dad, King Reginald of North Kepler. Because Carina Garcia was one of *those* Garcias. The Garcias who made up the Cardinal Family of the North. The Royal Family of the Kingdom of North Kepler. The Northern Royals. The family who had been responsible for ruling North Kepler for hundreds of years thanks to the extra powerful native abilities that all First Degree Cardinals in the family were supposed to have.

Speaking of which.

Her newest magic trainer, Terrance Hess, had just sauntered into the training center.

Carina slowed the treadmill to a walk and took a quick drink from her water bottle. Then she redid the thick ponytail she'd wrangled her hair into. There was sweat forming on the back of her neck, and Carina never sweat from overheating. Only from nerves.

Terrance Hess stopped by the treadmill. "Looking good, killer," he said. "Ready for your next lesson?"

An alarm beeped on Carina's new, solar-powered watch, which had been calibrated specially for her by the master timekeeper who kept North Kepler's official atomic clock. The watch was a gift from her dad, who was trying to make up for all the times he'd failed to tell her before she and her sister Miguela got separated from the rest of the family that they were royal princesses with super special magical abilities. His other gifts so far included a diamond brooch, a fountain pen, and a signed copy of *Error, A Northerner,* by Heathrow Princeton, an extremely successful young writer and mathematician her dad wanted her to meet.

As if *any* of that could make up for what happened. She'd had no idea that the brutal attack on her childhood home, which left Carina and Miguela thinking they were orphans, had anything to do with the brutal attack on the Royal Family of the Kingdom of North Kepler. She hadn't known she and Miguela were princesses at all.

You didn't just miss something like that, either. Oh, no. Carina's parents had put effort into keeping that secret. No one had ever referred to their dad as "King Reginald" when she and Miguela were kids. Their mother had called their dad Julian, and it had never occurred to Carina to connect her dad to the King Reginald William Julian Garcia she read about in her school books.

Since the Northern Royals never made the names of

their royal children public until the kids became teenagers, and Garcia was a common last name, there had been no hints there, either. If her dad had ever called her or Miguela "princess," Carina always assumed that was only a pet name. The same as calling your daughter "honey" or "sweetie." As a result, six years passed from the attack to when they learned the truth. That was *sixteen* years of Carina not knowing she was a princess, all because the Northern Royals didn't think kids should be raised in castles. So. Not. Cool.

In the meanwhile, the Immortal Empire, who seemed never to have given up looking for the lost princesses, found Carina and Miguela at Novi Dupree Sanctuary, forced them on a run through half the Red Ridge Mountains, and nearly managed to kill them on the Mountain of Peril in a terrible confrontation that ended in so much death and destruction that Carina was still having nightmares about it months later and Miguela was in a deep dark depression.

It was sheer *luck* that the Northern Militia happened to find Carina and Miguela right after that attack. Because unlike the Immortal Empire, the Northern Royals *had* given up their search for the princesses. Carina and Miguela were assumed dead until an anonymous tip came in suggesting otherwise. If that hadn't happened, Carina and Miguela might never have known their father, mother, and brother were still alive. The Northern Royals kept their survival, their location, and even their leadership that well-hidden.

That was a lot to make up for.

But Carina had a lot to make up for herself. Which is why Terrance Hess had his wolfish eyes all over her as she got off the treadmill.

Hess was the third magic teacher her father had acquired for her since she'd reunited with her family six months ago.

Carina's magic abilities were woefully lacking compared to where she should have been as a sixteen-year-old First Degree Cardinal. She'd tried working with her brother Eugene and his teacher—since she and Eugene supposedly had the same abilities—but that only held Eugene back. Then her dad switched her to a woman whose specialty was adult magic education, and Carina nearly froze that poor woman to death during a remedial frost lesson. Luckily, Eugene was around to heal the woman. Carina didn't know how to use *her* healing abilities to help her frozen teacher.

"It just goes to show you *aren't* remedial," Dad had said. "And as I've explained to you *multiple* times, that was *my* fault, not yours. I made a mistake selecting a teacher who couldn't handle a First Degree Cardinal. But we *learn* from our mistakes here in the North. Your new teacher has experience working with recruits who have unrefined magic. And he'll only be working with you on telekinesis. We'll find someone else for the thermodynamics."

So at least Carina was unlikely to accidentally almost kill Hess, but the arrangement still wasn't working for her. Hess had perfect tawny hair, a dimple in his chin, and almost as much arrogance as a certain prince she'd met last year.

He put his arm around her shoulders as she got off the treadmill and began walking her toward the fitness center exit. Carina saw her top guard, Mishe, scowl at Hess on the way out, but it didn't help. Mishe was too professional to openly question any of the king's decisions about Carina's teachers. Honestly, Mishe's professionalism was a little too much sometimes. He had at least as much muscle as Hess, plus trimmed dark hair, soulfully deep black eyes, and ears that easily turned adorably pink. This is not to say she wanted to date Mishe or anything, since he was at least ten years older than her, eye contact for more than a couple seconds would have been nice. Then again, Mishe never put his arm around Carina's shoulders, and that she appreciated.

Hess took Carina to the special gymnasium in the training center designed for magic training. It had padded walls and shellacked wood floors with black, blue, and red lines painted on the wood. There were platforms of varying heights on one side of the gym, foam mats stacked on the floor, and a couple of benches. Mishe and the other three guards followed her and Hess into the gym. Which was good. That meant only five people would get to see how much she sucked today.

Hess stopped in the middle of the freshly waxed floor, where a set of colorful balls of varying sizes were clustered. He put his hand lightly on Carina's lower back. "Alright, Princess. Today, we're working on telekinetic force. These medicine balls are all different weights, and the heaviest ones aren't necessarily the biggest. I want you to use telekinesis to line them up in order of weight. Most people can only telekinetically lift about double what they can lift with their arms, so if something's too heavy, just leave that one out."

Carina stepped out of Hess's reach and focused on the medicine balls. She'd only learned last summer to pick up anything telekinetically at all, and she was still a little clumsy with telekinetic magic. But she went to work lifting the medicine balls and trying her best to line them up by weight. She could lift all of them, but she could barely tell which were heavier.

When she was finished, Hess said, "Not bad. You have to be lifting at least quadruple what I expected. Unless you have more muscle than I realize."

"I have some muscle," she said, thinking of the gazillions of crates of beer she'd loaded onto wagons for the Sisters of

Novi Dupree over the years.

He came close again, put his hands on her upper arms, and squeezed like he was testing that assertion out. "Some," he said. "But we can work on that. Now let's try a different exercise. This time your goal is to throw each ball as far as you can." He pointed to a yellow one. "Start with that. It's the lightest. Throw it against one of the padded walls."

The yellow one was the biggest. She'd been sure it was also the heaviest. She picked it up telekinetically, though, and attempted to throw it. It hit the wall with a satisfying thud.

"Very good," Hess said. He pointed to a blue one. "Now that one."

It was one of the smaller balls, but when she picked it up telekinetically, she discovered that it was far heavier than it looked. She could only throw it a meter or so.

"Was that the heaviest?" she asked.

He frowned. "That was one of the middle weights."

"Oh." Carina couldn't hide the disappointment in her voice, and the whole morning proceeded like that. Hess wanted to try agility exercises, but she was still incapable of rolling a ball across the floor. He showed her a dexterity exercise, but trying to spin a ball in the air only ended with her flinging it accidentally at Mishe. Then Hess moved on to a multifunctionality exercise, and she accidentally slammed two of the balls into each other so hard that one cracked and the other split down the middle.

Hess whistled at the damage while Carina groaned and put her face in her hands. Whenever her lessons went this way, it reminded her of the run-ins she'd had with the Southern Royals last year. The whole reason she'd recently decided to become a runner was because of them. The stationary bikes would have been easier, and there was a heated swimming pool in the greenhouse on top of the fitness center. That place was beautiful, toasty, and serene, and Carina actually liked it up there.

But shortly after the queen of South Kepler gave Carina the only truly effective magic lesson she'd ever had, one of the princes had chased her through a whole village, and she had not enjoyed being slower and unable to defend herself with magic.

Luckily, Prince Nathanial was dead now. Unluckily, his brother, Prince Bastian, who was the scarier and more talented of the two, was very much alive. *He* was the new crown prince of South Kepler. A kingdom that didn't exactly get along with North Kepler.

"I am doomed," she grumbled to herself.

Hess put his arm around her again. "Don't be so hard on yourself. You have some catching up to do. And you did well today. Let's spend the rest of the morning strength training."

"Isn't that what we've been doing?" Carina said, trying to politely shrug him off. "I've been lifting everything you told me to lift."

Hess moved behind her, put both hands on her shoulders, and began kneading. "*Relax.* We can work on this. You know, for most people, what they can do with their mind has a lot to do with what they can do with their body." He intensified that kneading. "There's a real mind-body connection when it comes to magic."

Carina did not want a magical mind-body connection with Terrance Hess, and it occurred to her that maybe if he'd stop touching her, she'd be less agitated and more focused on her magic abilities.

He shivered and removed his hands from her shoulders. "Hey! No need to freeze out the teacher. Don't be so discouraged! I promise you're going to get better."

She doubted that. So she and Hess moved on to the weights room, and instead of thinking about how Hess was watching her performing weighted squats, glute bridges, and chest flies, Carina let her thoughts wander to other creepy things that haunted her mind.

Like how Prince Bastian tended cold like her, had drop-dead-gorgeous, crystal clear, blue eyes, and was willing to threaten an innocent girl until she died or gave up the information he wanted.

She switched to heavier kettlebells at that thought.

But then she was thinking about how the prince's sister, the late queen of South Kepler, had died in Carina's arms, right after telling Carina that when she saw Prince Bastian again, she should tell the guy that his sister had always loved him most "if it came down to that."

Oh. Right. Because *that* was a conversation she wanted to have. She switched to even heavier weights, and Hess said, "Are you sure you can handle those?"

She ignored Hess. And side note: all those books where the oblivious princess falls for the drop-dead-gorgeous prince even though she knows he's actually a cruel jerk? Those were ox beast shit. Carina was *never* reading one of those again. No matter how great the guy looked on the cover. Cruel was not something you overlooked for the sake of gorgeous. Gorgeous only made cruel a million times worse because it made you feel like your eyes had tricked you. "Hey, look, super-hot boy, right here! Royal! Charming! Not at all concerned about the ethics of torturing you! Wanna hook up with him?"

No way in hell. Stockholm syndrome wasn't her thing. Though she *had* been dumb enough to date an *Immortal*, who was probably still alive. Carina hoped she *never* ran into

Max-the-Lying-Immortal again. And she probably didn't have to worry about running into Prince Bastian anytime soon, either. Diplomacy with South Kepler couldn't happen as long as the king of North Kepler thought it was better to be dead than face up to the evil empire that had it out for them.

So, on the upside, Carina wasn't going to have to talk to the crown prince of South Kepler for years. On the *down*-side, she herself was the crown princess of a crumbling kingdom. She was isolated from that kingdom in a heavily guarded, highly classified military complex built around the Northern Royal's "summer" home. She could barely move a stupid medicine ball with magic. She never knew when she might accidentally give someone frostbite. She'd spent the summer traipsing around Kepler like an idiot, dragging her sister through hell, and putting *all* of Mortal Kepler at risk because she was a stubborn, naïve, spoiled brat who wanted to hang out with a boy who was actually *hundreds* of years older than her. And—

"Whoa, Princess," Hess said as Carina chucked a kettlebell into the air with gusto, only barely managing not to hurl it at Hess. "Are you okay?"

She set down the kettlebell and noticed that it and everything within a three-foot radius of her was covered in frost. Hess had even backed away, though Mishe was jogging towards her with a wool coat. He walked right over the frost and handed Carina the coat, which she gratefully put on because even though she'd been lifting twice as much weight as she normally did, she was freezing right now.

"That's enough for the day, Hess," Mishe said to her trainer with a sharpness that only chilled the air further. "The princess will meet with you again tomorrow morning."

Then Mishe escorted Carina out of the training center

and back to the summer house, where there would be attendants waiting to run her a warm bath, work her tangled hair
into pretty princess curls, dress her in designer jeans and furry
Prada-Gabbana boots, and ask her if she'd like a cup of hot
tea while someone did her makeup.

As they walked, Carina wondered for the hundredth time
what would have happened if she'd never left Novi Dupree
Sanctuary. The Sisters had assured her that her embarrassing
little sassafras stealing incident had nothing to do with the
Immortals who'd shown up at their door last summer. It was
a fantasy to think that staying safe at Novi Dupree had ever
even been an option. But oh, what she would have given to
be back there in that quiet, peaceful place she'd never quite
appreciated enough.

Carina Lucia Esmeralda Garcia was the Crown Princess
of the Northern Kingdom of Kepler. And it sucked.

$1,000,000 REWARD WILL BE PAID FOR THE
CAPTURE, DEAD OR ALIVE, OF

LORD FRANKLIN LEONARD WELLINGTON

Age, 48 years.
Weight, 82 kilos.
Height, 1.8 m.
Build, broad.
Color of hair, light brown.
Color of eyes, hazel.
Marks, scar on face from lower left
lip to upper right eyebrow.

LORD FRANKLIN LEONARD WELLINGTON is known as a CRIMINAL and has a history of dangerous conduct, as well as a DISHONORABLE DISCHARGE from the Southern Guard.

Last seen in the Red Ridge Mountains, somewhere near Shadow of the Mountains. Wanted for assassination of the queen, conspiracy to assassinate, treason, resisting arrest, aggravated assault, aggravated battery, and tax evasion.

Lord Franklin was formerly a general in the Southern Guard and is a SECOND DEGREE CARDINAL with a KNOWN TELESTHESIA GIFT. He should be considered SKILLED, ARMED, and DANGEROUS.

September 881 AAH

CHAPTER FOUR
WE WERE FUGITIVES

Nate ran every morning, not because he especially liked running, but because he had an excessive amount of energy to burn. Franklin ran in the mornings, too, but usually refused to do it with Nate. Which was stupid because they'd have been safer running together.

"You're twenty years younger than me," Franklin had said the last time Nate pestered him about it. "I don't run as fast as you."

"You are a *fugitive*," Nate had reminded Franklin. "You need to be fast."

"I need to be *strategic*," Franklin—who habitually drove his wagon faster than anyone Nate had ever met—said. "And I'm the one on the poster. I'll decide how fast I need to run."

Nate hadn't thought that was a smart attitude toward being a wanted fugitive, and he knew Franklin wished he'd been running with Nate in the mornings now.

"Damn it," Franklin said, sounding out of breath as they dashed down an alley. "I thought the old sow was trustworthy.

And blind. How'd she recognize me?"

"Maybe she didn't." Nate had slowed down for Franklin, so carrying out a conversation was easy for him. "Or maybe not even an old blind woman could miss the posters the Southern Guard put up, oh, I don't know, *everywhere*."

"That was rhetorical. Just shut up and run," Franklin said.

It was good to see that Franklin understood the stakes here, so Nate shut up, ran, and fantasized about returning to South Kepler and clearing Franklin's name. That was the only way to keep Franklin from ending up on Queen Constance's chopping block. Which was an actual thing in South Kepler—the chopping block—and it was a place to which Nate's mother had no problem sending enemies like Franklin. That's just what you got when you were wanted for assassination of the queen, conspiracy to assassinate, treason, resisting arrest, aggravated assault, aggravated battery, and especially tax evasion.

Franklin wasn't guilty of the first three, but he *had* resisted arrest by the Southern Guard, and the guy could be menacing when he was pissed, so the aggravated assault and battery charges were going to be easy to prove, too. Nate had thought the tax evasion thing was bogus. Then Franklin confessed that he "may" have forgotten to file his taxes a few years in a row after he got kicked out of the Guard and became a washed-out alcoholic. Point being: Nate's mentor was now considered one of the most dangerous people on Kepler. A downright terrorist. Probably just below Empress Hildebrand and right above Lord Godric.

It was all rank Kepler sludge, of course. Franklin was completely loyal to the crown. He was more loyal than Nate, and Nate was supposed to be the next king. Franklin would never have hurt Vivian or any other member of the royal family. He wouldn't even speak badly about Queen Constance, because she was Nate's mother and, therefore, according to Franklin, a member of the royal family who deserved respect.

Nate respectfully disagreed. His mother was a wicked, evil bitch who had no remorse for hurting or killing Mortals or Immortals if it forwarded her agenda: to destroy the Immortal Empire. Which she assumed was the best agenda for the whole kingdom. Nate had some thoughts about that himself, though, and let's just say that being inclined to seek peace with the Immortals rather than demolish them was exactly why no one in his family thought he was equipped to be royal.

So back to the fantasy. Happily, Nate could fix things for everyone. After all, Constance's allegations against Franklin were clearly motivated by one thing and one thing alone: Franklin was the only person alive who thought Nate *should* be the next king of South Kepler. Thus, he was the only person blocking Constance from putting her favorite pawn—Bast— in play instead. But all would be well if Mom and Bast both knew that Nate officially had zero interest in any throne. If Franklin would just let him go home and give up the crown, this could all be over.

"Nate! Watch where you're going!" Franklin shouted, and Nate looked just in time to avoid tripping over a bucket of slosh.

Right. Okay. Focus, Nate. Franklin couldn't get caught today. The Guard was probably on orders to kill him on sight. Nate flung the bucket of slosh back and heard someone trip on it. He hoped it was rotten slosh. Or sewage.

"For the love of Sam, Nate, put your head on! They … don't know who you are! And take the next … left toward the market."

"The market?" Nate sped up the pace and started looking

for the left despite his misgivings about Franklin's direction. "That place will be full of people. If you want me to stay dead, we should not go there."

"It is … the middle … of the night." Franklin sounded like he needed to stop for air or death as the distance between him and Nate grew. "The market will be abandoned … can you slow down?"

"No!" Nate yelled. "Pick it up, old man! Or you might as well turn yourself in."

"I don't … give a damn if they catch … me … you're the one … I'm … worried about … you're the crown … prince … hell, Nate, slow the …"

The rest of that was all f-bombs, which Franklin only dropped when he needed it to count. Nate slowed slightly.

"How many times do I have to tell you I don't *want* the crown? I am *not* supposed to be the damn king of South Kepler."

"The person … who is … *not* supposed to be the … damn king … is your brother … you … wait, no, don't go left, go right!"

"Why?"

"Because I just saw something."

"Like, saw something or *saw* something?"

"*Saw* something."

No one ever thought Franklin had any useful magic. Especially for a Second Degree Cardinal. The cardinal system was a little complicated. You were a First Degree Cardinal if you were born a child of a king or queen, and almost all First Degree Cardinals had three magic gifts: telekinesis, a thermo-dynamic tendency, and some kind of telesthesia.

But farther away from the direct line of succession, the magic dwindled. If you were a prince or princess, but you never became the king or queen, then you were a First Degree Cardinal, but your kids would be Second Degree Cardinals, and they would likely only have two magic gifts at most.

Franklin's mother, Princess Erline, had been a First Degree Cardinal, and a sister to Nate's grandfather, King Cassius. That made Franklin a Second Degree Cardinal, but he didn't have the two gifts he should have had. He only had one, and it wasn't even telekinesis or a thermodynamic tendency. It was a telesthesia gift.

Bast sometimes said this meant God didn't like Franklin.

Nate thought Bast underestimated telesthesia gifts.

To be fair, most people did. Telekinesis and thermo-dynamic abilities were showier gifts. And telesthesia was normally limited, so it made sense that the other two types of magic were perceived as superior. Most telesthesia gifts were glorified parlor tricks anyway. Like Viv's gift, which had given her the ability to see connections between people as colors. What was the use in that?

King Herschel, Nate's dead father, had been a silver tongue, more useful since it meant he could subtly influence others to do what he wanted them to do. Bast was a lie detec-tor, something that was considered incredibly powerful.

And Nate …

Anyway. Franklin's telesthesia was an uncommon proph-ecy gift. Periodically, he had brief flashes of insight into the future. The gift was random and limited; he could only see things that related directly to people he cared about now or would someday care about. He couldn't see anything certain about his own future.

Still, he could see flashes of the *future*. Nate thought that was an exceptionally useful gift, even if he didn't appreciate that Franklin saw things about *him* from time to time and didn't see fit to tell him what most of those things were.

"What did you see?" Nate called back as he turned obediently down an alley that looked like a dead-end. "Something good or something bad? Because it looks like you're running us into a wall."

Franklin's steps fell hard behind Nate. "Keep going."

That didn't seem like the right choice. The wall at the end of the alley was approaching fast, and when Nate took half a second to look behind, he could see Guard soldiers not too far back. He didn't recognize any of them, but he never did anymore.

Which was probably good in this instance since Nate and Franklin had reached a dead-end and it was time to stop "flight" and start "fight."

Why did Nate's sword have to be hundreds of kilometers away in Alighieri? Why was Franklin refusing to travel with swords? If they'd been armed, at least there might have been *survivors* after this. Now all they had to fight with was Nate's magic. Which wasn't exactly defensive. More like tremendously offensive and dangerously explosive. Franklin was right that if anyone saw it, they would probably report back to Bast or Constance, who would know right away who the guy with the fugitive was.

All of which meant that Nate couldn't simply incapacitate these soldiers. He was going to have to *kill* them or risk Franklin's life. He tried not to think about that as he waited for his victims to get closer, but Nate had never killed anyone before. Not even an Immortal. He'd seen Bast kill Immortals. He'd seen Vivian incinerate a whole group. But he had never done it. And the thought of killing a *Mortal*, especially one pledged to protect the crown, made him sick.

"I don't know if I can do this," he admitted nervously

to Franklin, who was right by his side now, eying their oncoming guests.

"This way."

Nate whipped around. Someone *behind* them had said that, even though that wasn't possible, since behind them was a dead end.

Or not.

Where there *had* been a dead end, there was now a door-sized opening in the wall and a stranger standing in the doorway.

No, wait. Not a stranger.

That was the Guru-who-had-no-magic.

"Not leaving it open all day," the guy said.

The last time Nate had seen this man, he'd been abandoning Nate and his siblings on the Mountain of Peril, leaving them alone to handle a slew of Empire Immortals coming up the hill to slaughter them. They'd spent *weeks* trying to find the Guru on the slim hope that he could *help* them, and he'd just left them there like that. A bunch of kids to face Immortals with assault rifles.

The Guru was not trustworthy.

Franklin pushed Nate toward the door. "Go," he urged.

"No," Nate said. "I know him. He's not a friend."

"*Now*, Nate."

The Guru tapped his foot. "Time is *not* on your side, Mortals."

Franklin grabbed Nate by the shoulders and shoved him physically toward the door, forcing Nate through the opening, then following after. The next thing Nate knew, he was on the other side of the wall, running with Franklin and the Guru.

Nate didn't run nearly as fast when he wasn't sure if he was running to or away from his imminent demise. Right now, he felt much slower than Franklin.

"This way," the Guru was saying.

"Uh, why are we following him?" Nate said while they ran.

Franklin huffed. "Less questions, more running."

"How about more answers, *then* running? Why are we following an Immortal to get away from the Southern Guard?"

"Just do it," Franklin ordered, and to the Guru, he said, "How far to shelter?"

"Two blocks," the Guru said. "But we're already in Immortal territory. And that door doesn't open from the side you were on. It'll take them ages to figure out how to get in."

"Maybe not ages," Nate said. "There weren't that many places for us to go."

"If they make it through on their own, they're going to run into the neighborhood patrol fast. And your guys have medieval swords. Our patrol has the weapons of the future."

The Guru was in fairly good shape for someone who was supposedly a couple thousand years older than Nate. Better shape than Franklin. He said all that without losing any breath. "We can make it another two blocks down the road, and then we'll be there."

Nate began looking around while they ran. As far as he could tell, they were still running down an alley, not a road. The doors he could make out in the dark *did* seem more like front doors than back doors, though, and he noticed a few bicycles here and there, alongside a flowerpot or so.

"By the way," the Guru said, altering his pace to run by Nate. "Congratulations on making it out of that mess on the mountain. Didn't think you'd survive that."

"I almost didn't survive," Nate said. "No thanks to you."

"I know. But self-preservation is a strong instinct for an Immortal, and you're not my problem."

Nate felt the need to run a little faster. "So, Franklin and I should be following you through Immortal territory because …?"

The Guru ran faster, too. "I told you I owed a friend of yours a favor."

Nate almost stopped dead in his tracks. "*Franklin* is that guy?"

"Lucky for you. Right, kid?"

"Less talking, more running," Franklin reminded them from a few steps behind.

"Keep up, Grandpa," the Guru said, though he and Nate both slowed down. "We're almost there. Half a block more and we'll be scot-free."

"What does that mean?" Nate asked. "And where exactly is 'there' again."

"Old Earth phrase. And there it is." The Guru stopped at a darkened door. Franklin stopped and started heaving in air, and Nate looked around anxiously while the Guru pulled a keycard out of his pocket and smacked it against a lock Nate couldn't see. There was a click, then the Guru pushed the door open and swept his arm out "After you."

Franklin and Nate walked into a dimly lit hallway, and the Guru closed the door behind them. Franklin leaned over his knees and wiped sweat from his brow while Nate observed his surroundings warily. The Guru switched on a light, and Nate's first thought was that the place was very white. His second thought was that the Guru had helped them escape the Southern Guard, so maybe he wasn't as bad as Nate thought.

Then this guy with bright red eyes, out-of-control eyebrows, and serious bedhead appeared in the hallway, drew a gun, and pointed it directly at Nate.

"Drop your weapons," he said.

Nope. This was not "shelter." The Guru had run them into a trap. Because another Immortal who Nate was unfortunately already acquainted with was here. It was the guy who'd left the Mountain of Peril with the Guru. The guy the ice girl had been dating. The guy who'd *shot* Nate at All Saints' Cathedral.

Nate felt his hands get hot. "Franklin, step back." He locked eyes with the Immortal, who glared back. "This guy's trouble."

The Guru shoved by Nate in the hall and flipped on a second set of lights. "Kozlov, drop your gun. How many times do I have to tell you? The last thing we need around here is a hothead with a trigger finger."

The Immortal did not drop his gun. "But Myles, that guy is *dangerous*," he said, using the gun to gesture at Nate. "We should dispose of him."

The Guru (Myles?) sighed. "Maybe in the morning, okay? For now, he's traveling with a friend of mine."

Franklin stood up straight. He seemed to have more or less caught his breath, though Nate was still concerned. Men that age had heart attacks sometimes, and Nate could not afford to lose Franklin.

The Immortal's eyes dulled. "Leo? What are you doing here?"

"All will be explained, Max," Franklin said wearily. "For now, how about a glass of water? And maybe lower the gun?"

The Immortal looked suspiciously at Nate.

"I can vouch for him," Franklin said. "We're not here to hurt anyone."

The Immortal slowly lowered his gun.

"Well," the Guru said to Nate and Franklin, "welcome to Hypatia Safe House."

CHAPTER FIVE
THE HYPATIA SAFE HOUSE

The Guru led Franklin and Nate like prisoners through the safe house with The Immortal Who'd Shot Nate walking right behind. Nate was not comfortable having that guy with his *gun* right behind him.

Not. Comfortable.

He busied himself checking out his surroundings. The safe house, he decided, had an institutional feel. The hallway opened to a living space with an orange couch, a few metal chairs, and a coffee table. Three books were stacked neatly on that table. Nate recognized the first one because he'd read it last year. *A History of Human Power and Politics.* It struck him as creepy that he and any Immortal were reading the same book, but this one made sense. *A History of Human Power and Politics* went all the way back to ancient Earth history. Probably felt like a memoir to some of them.

Off to the side was a kitchen with white countertops, cupboards, and an unremarkable table. The Guru retrieved a glass of water for Franklin and offered Nate the same.

"No, thanks," Nate said. He wasn't drinking or eating anything here until he knew this wasn't some elaborate trap. Also, Immortals had *no* sense of sustainability. They had an *electric* stove. Why waste electricity when gas was such a good alternative on Kepler? Irresponsible. That's what that was.

Thankfully, there didn't seem to be much else to the place. Beyond the kitchen and living area, there was a bathroom and a hallway of closed doors. The Guru took them to a room where four beds were lined up against the walls. There was a backpack leaning against one of the beds and a duffel bag slouched by the other with a rifle nearby.

"Good for you I do my stargazing at midnight." The Guru eyed Franklin. "I suppose it wasn't entirely random that we ran into each other? But I'm going to have to do some fast talking in the morning to explain to the others why we're letting Mortals into an Immortal safe house. Royal Mortals in particular."

"If we're not welcome, we can leave," Nate said.

"You're not," Ice Girl's Immortal said. "Leave."

Franklin threw the bag he'd been traveling with on one of the beds. "Thanks, Myles. We appreciate the help."

"What are you *doing*?" Nate hissed to Franklin. "I am not sleeping here."

"I don't care." Franklin could do apathy like no one else. "If you want to sit up, you can. Everyone else is sleeping."

"Oh, I'm not sleeping if he's not sleeping." The Most Obnoxious Immortal on the Planet swiped his hand—the one with the gun in it—toward the floor as he spoke. "Not a good idea. Awfully bad plan."

"No one's sleeping yet," the Guru said. "I'm going to need to get caught up first. Should we expect Southern Guard idiots blowing up half of Hypatia to try to find you?"

Franklin looked longingly at the bed, then sighed. "I could use more water. Myles, why don't you take me back to the kitchen, and I can give you the short story?" He tilted his head toward Nate. "Without them."

The Guru grunted a yes, and Nate was alarmed.

"You're going off with the Guru and leaving me here alone with *him*? The Immortal with the *gun*?" he yelped to Franklin.

"His name is not *the Guru*. It's *Myles Kayes*, and my name is Max Kozlov," the Very Stupid Immortal said to Nate. Then to Myles, he said, "And you're not leaving us alone unless you want carnage."

Myles cussed under his breath, and Franklin rolled his eyes dramatically. "You two evidently have some tension to work out. Make it happen while we're gone."

"But Franklin!" Nate protested.

"But get over it," Franklin said. "You're going to be the king of South Kepler. Learn who your real enemies are. It's not these guys."

Nate was already used to not sleeping, so he was ready to stay up the rest of the night watching Max if that's what was necessary to prevent Max from killing him. As Max sat on the bed across from Nate, staring with his eyes wide and his gun sitting on his lap, Nate sat on another bed, staring back.

Staring contests weren't Nate's thing—they required so much attention—but he understood that in this instance, he could not be the first to blink. Still, he was being an idiot about this. Magic always trumped a gun if you had time to think about it.

Nate magicked Max's gun to himself, then magicked the

rifle by Myles's bed to himself, too, just to make sure he had his bases covered.

"Hey!" Max said, but Nate channeled Bast and raised an arrogant eyebrow as the guns landed smoothly in his hands. If Max made a move to retrieve his gun, Nate would light the whole place on fire. See how the Immortal liked *that*.

Max didn't make a move to reclaim the guns. Twenty minutes passed that way before Nate had to shift on the bed because his butt hurt from sitting still that long. Another twenty minutes passed—how much was Franklin telling Myles?—and the Immortal shifted like *his* butt hurt, too. Nate thought that was a win.

When an entire hour had passed, Nate got shifty again, but not without noticing that Max was also shifty. Good. Let the guy be uncomfortable. Let him suffer. Let him—

"Shit. Don't magic princes ever sleep?" Max said scornfully, ruining the competition all at once. "Are you some kind of vampire?"

"Are you some kind of zombie?" Nate retorted. "Because you're barely even blinking."

"Blinking hurts my eyes."

"Hurts your *red* eyes."

Max flinched, and Nate wondered if he'd finally instigated the fight he realized he wanted. It would be so satisfying to punch Max in the nose. Unfortunately, the door opened before anyone could initiate a blow. Myles was there with Franklin right behind.

"Is this still going on?" Myles flung himself down on his bed. "Doesn't testosterone peak at nineteen? You should both be past temper tantrums."

"I'm only seventeen," Nate said.

"I was talking in Earth years." Myles waved his hand

carelessly at Max. "And he's hundreds of years older than you, even if he only looks like a seventeen-year-old because of the age inhibitors. He should be more mature than this. Life experience should matter for something."

Max huffed. "I am not a *child*, Myles. This rash Mortal took both the guns, and I've seen what he can do. He is *extremely dangerous.*"

"Thanks," Nate said.

Franklin plunked down on the fourth bed. "Nate, give them back the guns and let the rest of us sleep."

Nate clutched those guns. "No way! I've never shot anyone! And I can't sleep because I can't trust him!" He pointed at Max. "He might have another gun!"

Max leaned forward with a nasty scowl. "I *don't.* But now you have two guns *and* magic, and I've seen you set a *church* on fire. Who can't trust who here?"

Franklin stood up. "Give them to me, Nate."

"What?" Nate gripped those guns. "No! You'll give them back to the Immortals!"

Franklin pulled his hand down over his face, which had the effect of tugging his scar down grotesquely. It made him look older than anyone in the room. "Fine. We'll put them in the kitchen or something. No one in the room needs a gun tonight, but everyone needs sleep, and no one will get it if you two keep acting like nuclear proliferation personified."

Returning the guns was a horrible idea. What was to prevent either of the Immortals from just getting up and grabbing them after Franklin was asleep? Nate was not good with the idea. Nate was not good with any of this.

Max wiped sweat from his brow with the back of his arm while Myles shook his shirt away from his skin.

"Is he always like this?" Myles said to Franklin, whose

forehead was starting to glisten as Nate wondered why Franklin wasn't on his side right now.

Franklin took a labored breath. "Nate," he said through gritted teeth. "You need to calm the *eff* down."

"I *am* calm," Nate lied, even though he could feel his heart pounding through his chest and yeah, fine, the heat was his fault. So, what? He continued sarcastically: "You only want me to sleep in a nest of Immortals with a guy *who shot me*. I am one-hundred percent *calm*."

"Wait, are *you* doing this?" Max asked. "Whoa. I thought it was scary that Carina could make things kind of chilly. But she never wanted to hurt me." He lowered his voice. "Or at least she didn't *initially* want to hurt me."

"Oh, but Icy changed her mind?" Nate said. "Good to know she had one sane quality."

Max stood up from the bed. "Unlike *you*, Carina was a good, kind, smart—"

"Crazy, stubborn," Nate added.

"*Beautiful* person," Max finished.

Honestly, though, Nate couldn't really think straight when it came to Icy because whenever he thought of her, he thought about how she could have helped Vivian and she'd *refused*. Of course, they'd gotten off to a terrible start, but that wasn't the point. Nate's family was royalty. They had the right to be difficult. Saving Vivian's life wasn't just personal. Without Vivian, Mortal Kepler's wellbeing basically came down to Nate and Bast alone. So just Bast, really. And Nate *had* tried to be nice. Icy was the one who'd been unwilling to listen to reason.

"Is it possible for someone who leans hot to spontaneously combust?" Max asked while Myles unbuttoned his collar.

Franklin answered like Nate wasn't sitting right there. "Some of it he can't help. There's no one balancing him out. Nate's not used to being the only person around with a thermodynamic tendency."

"What do we do?" Myles said, also speaking as though Nate wasn't there. "Because I hate agreeing with my ignorant mentee, but I agree with him on this. Your prince is getting ready to incinerate us. If he can't stop, you can't stay here. This is supposed to be a safe house."

They were all whiny babies. Nate was a little worked up, yes, but things weren't *that* hot. No one was going to be incinerated. Unless they all kept talking like he wasn't here.

"Nate, I need you to focus." Franklin was right in front of him now, though Nate didn't remember him moving. He was talking in a low, firm voice. "You are becoming dangerous to everyone in this room, including me."

Franklin only talked like this when Nate became legitimately dangerous—as in thermodynamic overdrive dangerous. Nate tried to pay attention, but his vision was swimming weirdly.

"We are safe here," Franklin went on.

Nate got stuck on that. He wasn't truly safe anywhere. Never had been. Not even at home in South Kepler. And Franklin was less safe because of him. Always had been. Even in South Kepler. And the guns felt heavy. *Everything* felt heavy. Nate reluctantly handed one gun over to Franklin, then the next, but it didn't help.

All of Kepler was squashing him.

Vivian would never have been in a mess like this. She was so much better at tending hot. She was better at everything. Why had she been the one to die? She was the ruler South Kepler needed. No one needed Nate, especially not as the ruler of anything.

Nate couldn't hear what Franklin was saying anymore. He tried to find Franklin's face in a blurry haze, but he couldn't. Then Franklin put his hand on Nate's shoulder.

"What are you thinking about?" His voice made it sound like they were underwater. And that was a personal question Nate didn't feel like answering.

"Are you thinking about your sister?"

He was *always* thinking about Vivian. Which would have made her smile, and her smile had scared Nate a little. It was like their mother's. Powerful and terrifying. When Vivian smiled, it always seemed like she was planning to destroy something.

She didn't, though. Destroy things. And he'd looked up to her. And she'd cared about him. Which is more than he could say for most of his family.

"Do you think Vivian wanted to die?"

A huge ball of hurt expanded in Nate's chest. No, she hadn't *wanted* to die. She had wanted to *live*.

"Do you think she wanted *you* to die?"

The ball got bigger. He shook his head again. Vivian would *never* have wanted him dead.

Franklin's voice wasn't as muffled anymore, but it was still low. "Would Vivian have wanted you safe now?"

Yes. Obviously. Nate nodded feebly.

"Then would she have wanted you flying off the handle like this?"

"I'm not … flying," Nate managed to say.

Franklin almost smiled. "Fine. Would she want you burning down a safe house?"

Nate tried not to stay in touch too much with his feelings—God knew that was a terrible idea for someone who'd lived the kind of life he'd lived—but he knew what it was like to feel tears choking you. The sensation came over him now. It was hot and humiliating as he realized that if he cried, there would be three witnesses. That was three more than he *ever* wanted to watch him cry over his *feelings*. Which were almost for sure the result of exhaustion and nothing else.

"Nate?"

He forced out an answer. "I don't know. She's dead."

"Nate, don't you think it's time for you to grieve your sister's death? Because it's been six months, and your inability to control your emotions is threatening people who had nothing to do with her death."

"They didn't help."

"They couldn't help. She was sick. She was going to die, no matter what."

"She might have lived longer if—"

But Nate didn't actually have an "if." If *what?* If Myles had been mythically magical as everyone hoped? If he'd had a cure for the Immortality Virus when they found him at the Mountain of Peril? If he and Max had stayed when the Empire Immortals showed up?

"*No one* could have saved her, Nate. She was infected with the Immortality Virus. There is no cure for that. Not for people like you who have too much magic to be compatible with the virus. You know that."

Nate's vision finally focused. Franklin was a soldier. A good one. And he was the kind of person who didn't go soft. But all those things aside, he looked sympathetic now. Like he knew something about what Nate was going through.

Max—still sitting across from him, though partly behind Franklin—had averted his gaze. Myles had sat up and was taking off his shoes with significantly more care than necessary to remove shoes.

Nate hastily wiped his face with his sleeve. It was a wasted effort. He shouldn't have bothered, and he already wished he could forget this moment had ever happened. He didn't need anything more to feel bad about. He had plenty.

His sister most of all. It hurt deeply that he was never going to get to see her again. Never talk to her. Never piss her off. Never make her think he was hopelessly flawed. Never be defended by her. Never hug her. Never even just sit next to her and think about how lousy it was that when two people who tended hot sat in the same room together, everyone sweltered.

And that was just what *he'd* lost. Nate also grieved for what *she* was missing. For life stolen from her. Mistakes she'd never make. Promises she'd never have a chance to break. Love she'd never experience. It wasn't fair, and it all made Nate feel so sad and tired.

Franklin squeezed his shoulder lightly. That was about as affectionate as Franklin got, and it pulled Nate out of himself a little. It wasn't his problem if he was making the Immortals uncomfortable with his miserable emotions but making them uncomfortable with thermodynamic magic … that was something he *was* accountable for.

Nate wasn't great at controlling his hot tendency. Still, he knew a few things to try. Starting with one long breath, sucking in as much air as possible and trying to let it expand not into his shoulders but into his gut. Letting it out slowly, shakily. Knowing Bast could have done this better but trying it a second time anyway and feeling the air reach deeper and flow out smoother while the tension in his body started to drain away.

His eyelids felt weighed down. He took another deep breath. Lifting a single finger would have taken more energy than he had left. It was all he could do to breathe.

The heat in the room was dissipating. Nate knew because Myles was looking at him again, curiously this time, like he was some kind of science experiment, and so was Max. Not okay. But better than them looking away like watching Nate break down was worse than talking with Franklin about sex or something.

He tried for another breath and to actually look at Franklin again. At his eyes. They were sad and tired, too, but not displeased. Not apathetic. Franklin squeezed Nate's shoulder one more time and let go.

"That was good. We're safe here. You need to rest. I'd like for you to sleep."

Nate didn't trust the Immortals, but he did trust Franklin. He curled down to his side on the bed, wished again he had his sword so he could cuddle with something, eyed the evil Immortal, and considered shutting his eyes as his head hit the pillow. It wasn't a comfortable bed, but he was so so so tired.

"Sleep, Prince Nathanial," Franklin said.

"Don't let the Immortals kill you," Nate mumbled.

"As if *he's* the one in danger here," Max said.

But Nate heard it in a distant voice, and then he was out.

STATEMENT FROM THE ROYAL SOCIETY OF NORTH KEPLER (ABOUT THEMSELVES)

The Royal Society is a fellowship of North Kepler's most eminent scientists and scholars, dedicated to promoting science, recognizing excellence in science, supporting outstanding science, and fostering education and public engagement around science.

Since 550 AAH, our fellows have met at least annually to discuss the most important scientific advances of our time. The Royal Society's motto, "leave no hypothesis untested," is an expression of our determination never to shrink in fear of progress. North Kepler can only improve through learning. It is in this light that we take our best steps forward, never hiding in the darkness of ignorance.

The Royal Society is graciously funded by foundations, businesses, individual donors, legacies, and Royal Patronage, through which the Royal Family supports leading research and scientific discovery.

CHAPTER SIX
PANCAKES AND FROST

Carina did not have training with Hess this morning. She had something much worse: her first Royal Society meeting. Her nerves woke her so early that she had extra time to stand in the shower, trying not to fret about whether she'd do something stupid at the meeting. The Royal Society mattered in the North. This wasn't something she could screw up.

Miguela was curled in Carina's bed when she emerged from her shower, though all that gave it away was the tippy top of a ball of bedhead on Carina's pillow. The rest of Miguela was a lump under an enormous amount of bedding.

When she and Miguela had lived at Novi Dupree, they'd always slept in the same bed, under one blanket. Now, they had their own princess suites and their own beds. Carina needed a heated blanket and multiple quilts to make up for the loss of the little human furnace she'd slept with for six years.

She climbed onto the bed and patted the lump that definitely hadn't burrowed under those covers for heat. "Hey. Bad dream again?"

Miguela's muffled voice said something that sounded like an affirmative, and Carina rubbed her sister's back. Her sister had two recurring nightmares that Carina knew about. In one, Miguela blew up an old barn, killing her entire family, including Carina. In another, Miguela blew up a cottage at the top of a mountain, killing all the Southern Royals and Carina.

"Which one?" Carina asked.

A small opening for Miguela's nose and mouth appeared. "New nightmare. Bounty hunters corner us in New America and take us to Empress Hildebrand, who can't decide whether to kill us herself or make us duel each other."

"Huh. I had a dream just like that," Carina told Miguela. "She decided on duel-to-the-death in mine, but then Ivan showed up and helped us escape."

Miguela's entire head finally emerged. She was flushed and sweaty, and there were tears streaked down her cheeks. "Do you have a thing for Immortal guys?"

"Maybe," Carina said with some fake haughtiness. "Do you want to get breakfast with me and lecture me about my terrible taste in boys?"

A dark look appeared on Miguela's face. "You're trying to manipulate me."

That was not true. Carina was *way* beyond attempting to manipulate Miguela. She was blatantly trying to help now. Because if Carina was transitioning badly to princess life, Miguela was in total shutdown. For the most part, Miguela spent her days in her princess suite, hidden away from everyone. She wouldn't eat with the family, comb her hair, bathe, put on pants …

It was a complete free fall that had started right after the whole mess at the Mountain of Peril. Miguela had woken from three days of unconsciousness on a bench seat in an extravagant coach with her head resting on Carina's lap, and the first thing she'd said to Carina was, "You're alive." Then the second thing was, "I killed the queen and her brothers."

It didn't seem to matter what Carina said after that. It didn't matter that no one would be alive if Miguela hadn't done what she'd done. It didn't matter that the queen was dying anyway. It didn't matter that one of the princes had escaped. ("I *still* killed Prince Nathanial," Miguela had wailed when Carina said that.)

Things only got worse when they arrived at Aurora Borealis and Miguela learned that the family she thought she'd killed years before was still alive. Carina was mildly pissed off at her dad, nervous around her mom, and uncomfortable with Eugene. Miguela had no problem with Eugene. But their parents? Them she was *furious* at.

Red. Hot. Furious.

Enough so that Mom and Dad had mostly decided to give Miguela space, something Carina didn't think was helping. She'd written to the Sisters about it. Sister Elizabeth said, "Give her time." Sister Raji said Miguela would "eventually buck up."

Only Sister Agda had anything sensible to say, which was, "Wallowing is a poor coping strategy. Find something to keep her busy." Except, there was nothing to keep Miguela busy up here. Unlike Carina, who was already enrolled in a ton of classes, working hard on her magic, and being taught royal protocols and etiquette in her free time, their parents hadn't felt it was appropriate to burden Miguela with any of that.

"Trust me, Carina," Dad had said. "Your sister can't be allowed to bury her head in work, or all that rage will build up inside her like a pressure cooker. That's how it is for someone who tends hot. She has to process it."

Carina respectfully disagreed.

"Are you *sure* you don't want to have breakfast with me?" she tried again. "I'm going to the mess hall, so we won't run into Mom or Dad."

"Can I just stay in your room for a while?" Miguela begged pitifully.

And the thing is, Carina got it. If she felt like her magic was out of control, Miguela must have felt like *she* was a ticking time bomb. If Carina was scared of being a royal, Miguela must have been terrified. After all, Carina was the kind of girl who, at one point, would have swooned over a princess suite with a walk-in closet full of garments shipped in from Gandhi. Miguela had never been like that. She'd thrived on the simplicity of Novi Dupree.

Carina gave up and kissed her sister's forehead. "As long as you want."

There were only a handful of other people in the mess hall when Carina got there, so she picked up a tray and a copy of *The Cerulean Times*, filled a plate, and sat down by herself. The guards who'd followed her sat elsewhere, and she tried not to notice them chatting amongst themselves. They never ate with her.

She picked up the *Times*, and an ominous article caught her eye. "Empress Hildebrand Announces Plan to Infiltrate New Paris with Empire Immortals."

"Carina? Can I sit here?"

She looked up from the news. She hadn't even seen Eugene in the mess hall before, and now he was right in front of her, holding his own breakfast tray.

The little brother Carina remembered from before was

five years old and chubby with baby fat. He had big brown eyes full of wonder, and he was easy to make laugh. She'd tickled him, held his hand on wagon rides, and shared green apple ice cream with him.

This Eugene was not the same. At eleven years old, he was tall and paper-thin. His eyes had a bronzed cloudiness to them that made him difficult to read. He was pensive and serious, and she hadn't heard him laugh since she and Miguela arrived. Which is probably what happens in *any* family when one dead sibling comes back to life to usurp the other's position as crown heir to the throne. Carina was resentful herself over the switch. Especially because he'd learned *years* before she would have that he was a magic prince. Hard to hide that kind of thing when your family gets rushed off to a secret military base and you suddenly need a million more guards.

His shoulders curled in, and he began to turn away. "Sorry. It's okay if you want to sit alone. Mom says I should give you and Miguela space."

Mom says. Because Eugene could still spend time with Mom, while Carina couldn't. Because Carina's magic wasn't controlled enough not to put Mom in danger. Not when Mom—

Eugene began walking away.

"Eugene, wait." Carina stood up and tipped over a glass of juice. Eugene was quick with telekinesis, though. Juice and the glass were both magically righted before any spill occurred. She grabbed the glass anyway and reddened as she met his eyes. They had the exact same magic—telekinesis and a cold thermodynamic tendency with healing abilities—but Eugene was leaps ahead. He was so good with cold magic that he had his own office in the infirmary. When someone got badly hurt on Aurora Borealis, *Eugene* treated them.

His eyes flashed with discomfort, and he looked away like he was embarrassed, too.

"Um, thanks," she said. "You can sit here if you want. I'm sorry I didn't answer right away. I'm … not a morning person."

He hesitated at her poor excuse, which wasn't even true, so it was probably lucky for Carina that Eugene wasn't a lie detector. Or at least she didn't *think* he was. Some First Degree Cardinals were.

"Are you sure? Because if you're not a morning person …"

"I'm sure. You can sit with me."

He stood for a second longer, looking at her like he expected her mind to change. He had a tray of healthy choices: fresh fruit, goat's milk yogurt, and long grain granola with only the slightest dribble of honey. But he also had a mug of the same rich hot cocoa she had.

She lowered herself back onto the bench seat. "Please sit?"

His eyes flickered again, but he set his tray down on the table and stepped over the bench one lanky leg at a time. "Thanks," he said.

"Sure." She forked up a bite of her own breakfast, pancakes with peanut butter and nectar syrup, and discovered that her pancakes were now cold. Sister Lindy would never have served cold pancakes at Novi Dupree.

"How are things going with Terrance Hess?" Eugene asked. "I dug around for information about him. The militia guys like him. They say he's down to Kepler."

Carina didn't want to discuss Hess with Eugene. She picked up her cocoa and took a sip. She set the cocoa down immediately. It, too, was chilled.

"Huh. I thought maybe it was just me," Eugene said. "Mine's cold, too."

"But you just got yours," Carina said. "It should

still be hot."

He bit his lip. "Yeah, but we're both sitting here, so …"

Was she *that* upset by her brother's presence at breakfast? That was … unpleasant.

"I think it's something we're doing together," he said. "We're out of balance when it's just you and me. Especially if we're both—"

"Both what?" she prompted.

"In a shitty mood," he said with a wry smile.

She stared at him.

He dropped the smile.

"Sorry. I think we're both fighting the climate up here. And Miguela's hardly around, and dad spends all his time in his library, so we're too cold with nothing to tip the scales."

She pushed cold pancakes around on her plate.

"But I don't think unbalanced has to be bad. I mean … we could play with cold magic sometime. We could probably make it snow together. Or make an ice castle outside." He attempted a smile again, this one timid but more genuine. "There's no one else around who's powerful enough to do anything cool with me."

"I don't know how to do any of that," Carina said. Not that she'd never made ice. She could ice over all kinds of things. She just couldn't do it intentionally.

Eugene got up without finishing his breakfast. "I hear you're going to a Royal Society meeting today. I've never been allowed."

Was there a note of bitterness in his voice? Probably. But she understood why he didn't want to eat with her anymore. She got up, too. There was no sense in staying. Her pancakes were completely frosted over.

Carina's empty stomach growled an hour later while Glory-Jane and two other attendants tutted around her, generally making Carina feel pinched and uncomfortable.

Though that could have been the outfit itself. Maybe gowns and tiaras had gone out of style. Carina's official royal attire was a version of the formal Royal Militia of North Kepler uniform. Sort of. The soldiers wore charcoal gray trousers and long, matching jackets with practical zippers and clasps, plus a high-collared, navy-blue thermal shirt, sturdy black boots, and black leather gloves.

Carina's uniform was much flashier. An unnecessary tuxedo stripe adorned her precisely tailored trousers. Her jacket reflected light and was lined with bright blue silk. She wore it over a navy vest and a starched white blouse with the heavy diamond neck brooch her dad had given her. Her gloves were a shimmery silver. Her boots had three-inch heels, and she had *not* needed that height.

For today, her attendants had also teased, twisted, and sprayed her normally wild, curly hair into a stiff helmet, and they'd chosen a color scheme of silver and icy blues for her makeup. It made her cheekbones look cut from glass, and her eyes were so dark compared to her silver eyeshadow that she barely recognized herself in the mirror.

She looked high fashion.

And *brisk*.

"I believe your first Royal Society meeting will be a success," Glory-Jane said, looking at the final product like all Carina needed to survive the meeting was the proper physical appearance. They were in Carina's dressing room, a space large enough for a huge three-way mirror, three attendants, two guards, and a princess on a pedestal. Her attendants, who were constantly threatened by Carina's wild curls, continued spraying back stray locks of hair.

"I'm worried," she said while the attendants fussed. "I need to make a good impression, and I think this might make me look …" She waved her hand at herself in the mirror but couldn't think of how to describe it. Terrifying? Evil? "And I don't understand anyway. If we want to stay hidden up here, why let a bunch of old scientists come visit? I know all the members of the Royal Society swear an oath of loyalty and all, but it still seems risky."

Glory-Jane patted Carina's shoulder. "Heathrow Princeton is only seventeen, and you have an appointment with him for twenty minutes after the meeting adjourns. Or longer at your preference if the conversation is agreeable."

That was not something making Carina less nervous. Why was her dad so keen on her meeting the youngest member of the Royal Society?

"So, if I like him, I suggest lunch, but if he turns out to be a toad, I'm free after twenty minutes?"

Glory-Jane laughed. "Time to meet with the king for your pre-meeting briefing, Princess. Mishe will escort you there."

King Reginald's real office was located in a governance building everyone called "the assembly," and the assembly was where the Royal Society meeting was taking place. But the king mostly worked from his private library, a small room off the side of a building everyone called "the lodge." Her dad was sitting on a fancy blue couch, sipping coffee, and writing something on a notepad in his lap when she arrived.

Carina remembered her dad from Before as someone with a *presence*. He was tall, and he had ringing, loud laughter and a confident gait. There was fire in his eyes—bursts of color spiraling out like flames from his pupils into rich brown irises. She hadn't known that her father tended hot or that he was the King of North Kepler, but it hadn't mattered. *Before,* he'd always made her feel safe.

Now, King Reginald's cane was leaning against the armrest of the couch—a remnant of injuries he'd sustained during the attack that separated their family six years before. It was still difficult for Carina to understand how he, mom, or Eugene were still alive. She had seen what happened. One minute, they were all in an old barn, and an Immortal was threatening Mom and Eugene with a sword. Carina and Miguela were watching. Dad was too far away to get to any of them.

Then it looked like the Immortal was going to kill Mom, Miguela screamed, and the barn exploded. Carina had not understood until recently that Miguela was the one who caused that explosion or that she and Miguela both survived because Carina tended cold enough to reflexively produce a defensive telekinetic shield with some magic push-back. When everything was over, Carina had been left in the eye of the destruction with Miguela by her side, unconscious but unharmed.

Since Eugene tended cold, too, he could also produce a defensive telekinetic shield. That is what had protected him and Mom back then. As a baby, he wasn't quite as strong as Carina, though. He and Mom were still buried alive.

As for Dad, he was a First Degree Cardinal, but he tended hot and he was already injured. Defensive telekinetic shields weren't in his wheelhouse, so it took all his magic to create any shield at all. He still ended up buried alive and uncon- scious for long enough that when someone came to Carina and Miguela's aid, it looked as if the girls were the only survi- vors. That was what caused the years of separation, and the family had reunited but not yet recovered.

This wasn't the same as Before.

King Reginald smiled as soon as he saw Carina enter the library, and he said, "Good morning, Princess." But his smiles always seemed forced now, and the bursts of color in King Reginald's eyes were dim these days. Also, his guards were immediately outside the door. She couldn't help but wonder: if he needed guards for himself, how could he keep her safe?

She perched on a chair across from him, unable to slouch thanks to the thick fabric of her jacket. King Reginald seemed to know what she was thinking. "Fabric's like cardboard, right? It'll soften after a few washes. You'll get used to it."

She nodded without smiling. "You wanted to brief me?"

He leaned back again seeming disappointed. "Straight to business, then? Coffee first?"

She didn't need anything that would agitate her empty stomach. "No, thanks."

He paused. "Did you have breakfast?"

She thought of the pancakes she'd never eaten and shook her head.

He promptly picked up a mobile com from a side table and dialed a number. "Yes, this is the king," he said into the com. "We need breakfast for two delivered to the library, please. Yes ... yes, tea and cocoa would be good ... extra fruit, too. Yogurt ... and muffins ... Thanks." Then he set down the com with gusto and looked at her like he'd solved intergalactic peace. "There. Breakfast will be here in a jiff."

She'd been hungry. Why did she now feel annoyed?

"Thanks," she said. "So, the meeting—"

"Will be boring, but the Royal Society will love you." He lounged on the couch and snorted. "You represent extra funding to them."

She didn't appreciate how casually he was taking this. Major decisions were made based on the Royal Society. That included decisions like whether it would be best for the Cardinal Family to stay hidden after a brutal attack on the king's family. Eugene had mentioned at dinner a few nights ago that the Royal Society actually ran some huge risk analysis related to that after the attack. Many of the district reps privy to the knowledge that the Northern Royals were still alive disagreed with the decision. But you can't argue with numbers, can you? No. You can't. Not in the North.

"I don't understand, though," Carina told her dad. "These scientists are going to present a bunch of research projects to me, and I'm supposed to choose one to 'patron.' But what exactly *is* a patron?"

"It means you become the champion for the project," Dad said. "It's a longstanding tradition. Every member of the Cardinal Family of the North patrons at least one project. As the crown princess, you'll eventually patron a dozen or so."

"Yes, but *how* do I do that?"

He answered offhandedly, sipping what must have been cold coffee by now. "Mostly, patronage is about money and moral support. The research team will give you updates about the project, and when the district reps hold their meetings here, you stand up with the project lead and you're a mascot with money."

She fussed with the diamond brooch at her collar. "But what if the Royal Society doesn't think I can do it?"

"They will. All you have to do today is look and act like the crown princess of North Kepler." He gestured at her. "And you're doing just fine."

There was a zipper jammed into her side. She tried not to squirm.

"Anyway, I want to talk about your training. I know things went poorly with the last two, but I'm hoping Hess—"

Carina cringed. 'Poorly' wasn't the word for it. 'Disastrous' was more like it. "I'm sorry," she said hastily.

A tiny spark picked up in his eyes. "You don't *need* to be sorry, Carina.

"I know." She did. Sort of. But she hated this conversation, which they'd had too many times. "If we hadn't been separated, I'd have started magic training as a ten-year-old, because that's how the Northern Royals do it."

"Well, it's *absurd* how they do it in the South. Those poor kids. Magic royals from day one. They end up completely out of touch with the commoners."

Having met a few Southern Royals, Carina didn't disagree, but she wasn't sure *he* was more in touch with the *commoners* himself.

"Honey, you have to stop beating yourself up over—"

The door to the library opened. A man with a cart loaded with breakfast foods was there. "Your Highness, you requested a second breakfast?"

Her dad's face lit up. "Ahh, yes. Thank you. What do we have? Are those pearberry muffins? The ginger sprinkles on those are pure sugar." He hobbled over to the cart and began loading a plate with food. "Do you want a pearberry muffin, Carina?"

He said it like maybe he could make up for her magic problems—and for everything separating them now—by offering her carbs. Carina liked pearberry muffins. The ginger sprinkles *were* pure sugar. But still, she specifically ignored the damn muffins and went for a savory tart instead.

As if she could be bribed with sugar.

CHAPTER SEVEN
A QUESTION OF ETHICS

An hour into Carina's first Royal Society meeting, she wished she'd eaten two or three pear muffins for breakfast. It took *energy* to tolerate a bunch of overly intelligent people talking about stuff no one else cared about. She was grateful for the stiffness of her uniform now because it was the only thing preventing her from fidgeting, and Carina was currently on display. She and her dad sat with the society's chair—Doctor Robert Friedman—on a special raised platform while a sea of scientists looked up at them throughout the whole meeting.

And Carina's need to fidget wasn't just because the meeting was boring. She'd had high expectations for the Royal Society, but so far, not a single speaker had covered anything that truly mattered. The current speaker was droning on about the study of a fossilized triple-eyed lochswine herd some farmer had discovered north of Orchid Lake. How was that subject relevant with the Immortal Empire moving into New Paris? The triple-eyed lochswine had gone extinct a million years ago. North Kepler's magical population was at risk *today*.

She'd felt the same about the last speaker's topic: the fight between the Association of Fruit Sugar and a team of researchers studying the effect of beet apple sugar on intestinal cancer in obese mice. How had *that* been worth twenty minutes? North Kepler didn't *have* an obesity problem. It had a dead king problem.

She shifted uncomfortably as a third speaker got up to discuss a study on the correlation between depression in the elderly and pet rattycat ownership.

"There's a break after this," Dad whispered to her.

"How long?" she whispered back.

"Ten minutes. And the real meeting starts after that."

"Isn't *this* the real meeting?" she hissed.

"No, this is just announcements and updates."

Doctor Friedman cleared his throat loudly, and Carina's dad threw her a guilty look. Carina schooled her face in an attempt to make it seem like she was focused on rattycat ownership. But she couldn't help but think that if this is what the Royal Society was all about, it was no wonder North Kepler had fallen.

When the updates were finally over, her dad slipped away "for a bio break," and Doctor Friedman started to chat with her. Friedman had the waistline of a man who hadn't seen hard times, a forehead so oily it shined, and a self-righteous chortle that made Carina feel judged. Chair of the Royal Society of North Kepler was a Very Important Position, and this was the doctor's fifth consecutive year in the position. Presumably, his track record meant he was inspiring at *something*, but so far, she couldn't tell what.

He patted his stomach with both hands and said, "Princess Carina, I hear you have some scientific inclinations.

Shame you can't enroll at Cerulean Technological Institute next year."

"Uh, yeah," she said. It *was* a shame. She'd have liked very much to go to school like a normal teen. But there was something about the way he'd said it that bugged her.

"Nothing like the intellectual intersection of top-notch minds at a quality institute of learning," he continued. "And we *do* like our Northern Royals well-educated, don't we?"

Carina was currently enrolled in six correspondence classes at the University of New Paris under a fake name. Organic chemistry, anatomy, human physiology, general microbiology, calculus, and Kepler history 201. She'd chosen those classes with her dad, then sent the list to Sister Rachel, who'd handled Carina's education at Novi Dupree. In return, Sister Rachel sent back a list of twenty books to supplement for the lack of literature and arts in this semester's curriculum. Carina was now diligently working through *Excerpts from Influential Genre Fiction of the Pre-Galactic Age*. The chapters from *Twilight* and *Great Expectations* were killing her.

Point being, she may have been behind in magic, but she was not behind in the rest of her studies. "Actually—" she began to say.

"Oh, don't worry. Our research teams always brief their patrons about the subjects of their studies. Have you looked through the agenda?"

She had tried, but the words were printed so small and tight—and she was still so hungry—that reading the agenda made her head hurt.

Friedman chortled. "Never mind. The teams all prepared detailed summary reports for you. You can read through those later."

"Looking forward to it," she lied, hoping her face wouldn't

show it. She lied so much more here on Aurora Borealis Isle than she ever had at Novi Dupree. But then the auditorium lights flashed, indicating that break time was almost over, and this saved her from additional conversation with Friedman.

Her dad returned just in time. Almost like he knew exactly how long he needed to be gone to avoid the risk of small talk himself.

"Now the *real* show begins," Doctor Friedman said to them, puffing out his chest as Carina and her dad sat down. "Reggie, are you and the princess lunching with us after this thing wraps up? She was just telling me about her passion for science."

Carina started to say, "I was?" but her dad cut her off.

"Sorry, Friedman," he said jovially. "Heathrow Princeton is taking the princess to lunch."

Carina flushed while Friedman wagged his eyebrows. Was it not bad enough that her dad was apparently trying to set her up on a date? Did Friedman have to know?

"Oh, I see where *I* am in the pecking order." Friedman chuckled. "Though I suppose it only makes sense for the princess to prefer the company of an attractive mathematician over—" he patted his belly again "—me."

"It's only a twenty-minute introduction," Carina said.

"Oh, sure," her dad said. "But Princeton is in residence at the Center for Mathematical Possibility and Probability at CTI. You'll like him. He's about your speed."

Meaning he was behind in magic, too?

"I should think so," Friedman said. "He's the smartest mathematician of your generation. And we *do* want you meeting the right people, Your Grace."

So, it wasn't *just* that her dad was trying to set her up. This was about her dating someone the Royal Society approved of.

Which might be for the best since Carina felt her choice in boyfriends so far had been the worst. Her insides *still* burned in shame when she thought about Max.

"Just wait," her dad said. "Heathrow is giving one of the patron presentations."

Princess life was so weird.

Luckily, Carina was distracted from her royal love life by the pageantry that followed. The lights dimmed as Doctor Friedman walked to the podium. A hush fell over the audience. The center platform lit up with a dramatic spotlight. Then an illuminated Friedman paused with his hands out before bellowing, "Welcome! To the two-hundred-and-thirty-first meeting of the Royal Society of North Kepler."

And oh, the *applause!*

"*This* is the real meeting," the king told Carina while they clapped.

Friedman led a pledge to uphold North Kepler's "rational" governance. A woman in a lab coat sang North Kepler's national anthem. A cellist played something a comprehensive study had deemed the most beautiful piece of music ever composed.

When that was over, the king himself got up and gave a long, repetitive speech about the importance of the Royal Society, especially to the Northern Royals, who were, "phenomenally lucky to have the support of such brilliant and talented professionals" all of whom he "truly admired, respected, and relied on" for "policy guidance of the utmost importance."

Carina was introduced by a woman she'd never met who somehow had *ten minutes* of stuff to say about what the Royal

Society hoped her return would mean for the kingdom, which was confusing because how could she mean anything when her family's existence was being kept secret?

Then, *finally*, it was time for the main business of the meeting: the patronage projects. But to Carina's great disappointment, the first team's project was just as irrelevant as everything the pre-meeting speakers had discussed. It was a study of possible methods of communicating with neighboring planets. Did these people *not know* that North Keplerians were being *reclassified* as South Keplerian citizens? That the Immortal Empire was *infiltrating* the North? That villages were being raided? That magicians were being kidnapped and sold to the Immortal empire? On *Kepler*?

"Oh, she's a live one, isn't she?" Doctor Friedman said, his chortle breaking Carina from her thoughts as she realized with horror that the whole stage had frosted over.

She hadn't even known she was doing that.

"I … don't know what happened," she stammered, trying not to make it worse as the audience stared at her with concerned, frightened faces.

Her dad put his hand on her shoulder. "It's only first-time jitters," he said. Then he waved his hand in front of him, and the frost on the stage slowly melted. But shame pitted in Carina's gut, and she could see the muscles bulging in her dad's cheeks as if his jaw was clenched tight.

"Sorry," she whispered to him.

"It's fine," he whispered back. "Just try to relax."

Right. She would just do that.

Doctor Friedman introduced a second research team, which was debunking a myth about the relationship between the gravitational pull of Kepler's two moons and native Keplerian magic. Then the third team was researching sonar waves emitted by certain breeds of giant Kepler beetles.

Giant Kepler beetles. Because that mattered.

Carina began mentally reciting a serenity mantra Sister Rachel had taught her several years back. This is how she managed not to ice anything over when the fourth team got up to talk about a study of the phylogenetics of aquatic Kepler species and she was reminded of Max telling her he was in the mountains to "study the frogs." Though Carina's dad glanced sideways at her when that presentation was over, and she wondered if she was making it chilly anyway.

But no. The guy that got up to give the fifth presentation looked at least a decade younger than any other Royal Society member. So *that* was Heathrow Princeton—her dad was probably looking at her because he wanted her reaction—and actually, Carina didn't hate Heathrow's project. It centered around a learning method his team was developing to help children connect their magic abilities to math and science education and thus develop both areas of aptitude earlier.

That sounded useful to her. Though honestly, there could have been some bias there. Because to her enormous surprise, Heathrow Princeton was easy on the eyes. Way too easy. No one who'd gotten his doctorate before seventeen should have the good fortune to be so symmetrical. She even missed the last points of his presentation as she became occupied with the color of his eyes. They were partially hidden behind heavy-rimmed, nerdy-hot glasses, and she couldn't decide if they were more the color of the amber ale the Sisters made in the fall or closer to their summer honey mead.

Her dad elbowed her lightly. "Possibility?"

Heathrow's presentation was over, but he was standing there by the lectern, now looking at her with a close-mouthed smile as she assessed him. Was he attractive? Yes. Smart?

Clearly. Mortal? Well, that was the benefit of the guy being vetted by her own dad.

And she *did* want the Royal Society to like her.

She smiled back.

"Thank you, Doctor Princeton," Friedman said jovially. "On to the next presentation."

Carina's thoughts followed Heathrow Princeton off the stage, and if the meeting had ended there, she might have considered it a relative success. Except, it didn't end there. The next presenter got up, popped a picture of some microscope slides onto a screen, and started his presentation with, "These are photos of the blood and tissue samples from Queen Vivian's body."

Her attention immediately snapped back to reality. "From Queen Vivian? How did we get those?" she asked her dad.

"Recovery team took them," he explained quietly. "Standard protocol for anyone who dies of the Immortality Virus."

But Carina had a *very* vivid memory of Queen Vivian's death. She'd used her own sleeve to wipe away the blood that had bubbled up from the queen's mouth. *Why* hadn't the Southern Royals told her the queen was dying? If they had, she would have tried to help regardless of how much they'd scared her. She'd felt terrible for the queen.

Carina had requested that the militia soldiers treat the queen's body with as much respect as possible. She had personally arranged the queen's hair, folded her hands, and draped a wool blanket over the body. She'd *specifically asked* some guy taking blood samples from the dead Immortals to leave Queen Vivian alone. It only seemed respectful.

The presenter was still talking.

"We've now prepared the samples we extracted from Wellington's body to add to our catalog of—"

Wellington? Like the girl hadn't had a first name? Carina interrupted him without thinking. "Vivian Wellington was the *queen*."

The presenter stopped, looking a little bewildered.

Doctor Friedman intervened. "Ah, Princess, if this project interests you, I'm sure Doctor McIntosh will take questions after he finishes his presentation."

Carina's throat felt tight, and her dad looked alarmed, but she had questions now. "I don't understand," she said. "Why do we have samples of the queen's body? Do we have permission from the Southern Royals to study those samples?"

Doctor McIntosh—a small man who had smeared blue ink on his cheek—answered like he was flustered. "She was deceased. Consent wasn't applicable."

Carina was sure it *was*. Or at least she was sure Prince Bastian would have thought it was. But everyone was looking at her now. Did she want to make this a massive issue?

Friedman, perhaps sensing that "she was dead, we didn't have to ask" wasn't acceptable to Carina, tried to smooth things over.

"Princess Carina, while I am sure we all appreciate your sense of ethics, the Immortal Empire used the Immortality Virus as a weapon to kill the queen of South Kepler," he said. "Honorable as it would be to seek express permission from our ignorant Southern counterparts to study the queen's blood, it is of far greater importance to study the strain of the Immortality Virus the queen was attacked with. It's an issue of safety for your own family. *Our* royal family. Our position is ethically defensible."

But not *diplomatically* defensible, she thought while she sank in her seat as much as her uniform would allow. So much for making the Royal Society like her.

The king interjected. "Also, the Southern Royals sent blood samples to New Paris Medical School long before the queen died. They have, essentially, already provided us with consent to study her illness. But you could patron this project, Carina. That would allow you to have a firsthand look at how samples like this are treated."

"A fantastic idea!" Friedman said. "The princess will patron Doctor McIntosh's Immortality Virus research project. I'm sure the team will be thrilled to have her support."

Carina felt a bit dumbfounded over the whole meeting after it ended, and it wasn't exactly the moment she would have chosen to talk to a guy she might like for the first time. But Heathrow Princeton caught up with her just as she was walking down from the stage, and there was no easy way to get away.

"Princess Carina," he said with soft eyes and a voice that was far too polished, and he must have seen the uncertainty on her face because he continued with, "Ahh, sorry. Do you still have time for lunch?"

She hesitated.

"It can be a quick bite if you want," Heathrow added quickly. "I'm supposed to meet up with Bob—Friedman— later to discuss my newest theory on imaginary infinite numbers on the Zodiac Curve."

"I really don't know anything about the Zodiac Curve," Carina said.

Heathrow had very white teeth. "I can tell you about it at lunch."

Carina wasn't sure what part of her statement he'd interpreted as wanting a math lesson, but she was too mentally fatigued to come up with another excuse. She prepared herself to say "no."

He stepped a little closer, glanced at her dad and Doctor Friedman still talking on stage, and lowered his voice. "*Or* we can talk about the consent issue if you want. I agree with you, by the way. Gutsy move to call it out. Especially in front of Bob. He's not the easiest person to face off with."

She could now see that Heathrow's eyes were precisely the color of that amber fire ale Sister Raji always liked so much. Copper marbled with flecks of bronze.

"It's because I tend hot," he told her as if he knew what she was thinking. "My eyes. The orange flecks. There's something about the hot tendency that fragments the melanin in our eyes. It's the opposite of what makes the brown in your eyes so steady."

Compliments. That's what had gotten her with Max. She was not going to let herself get carried away making too much out of a compliment. But she *did* like that he'd chosen first to tell her he agreed with her on a more substantial thing.

"I guess I have time for lunch," she said.

He grinned at her. "Lucky for me you're willing to overlook the fact that the Royal Society is trying to set us up, huh?"

It was infectious, that grin mixed with that honesty.

"Lucky," she admitted, and she appreciated that her guards followed at something of a distance while she walked to the mess hall with Heathrow for lunch. Princess life was still so weird. But there *were* worse ways to meet a guy.

EXCERPT FROM *ERROR, A NORTHERNER*
BY HEATHROW PRINCETON

Statistically speaking, one in every seven Northerners is gifted with an extrasensory ability, but it is well-documented that extrasensory abilities run in families. A child with one parent who has an extrasensory ability is twice as likely as a child whose parents do not have any extrasensory abilities to have an extrasensory ability himself. If both the child's parents have extrasensory abilities, the child is three times as likely to inherit an extrasensory ability.

Extrasensory abilities correlate directly to a North Keplerian's level of education, household income, career opportunities, access to medical care, life satisfaction, and so on. The most privileged Northerners are those who wield the most powerful extrasensory abilities. A Mortal man who possesses either a telekinetic or thermodynamic ability is, on average, five times as wealthy as a Mortal man without either such ability and ten times wealthier than Mortal women lacking extrasensory abilities. This gap is astonishingly overlooked in socioeconomic research.

CHAPTER EIGHT
THE PATRIARCHY NEVER DIES

Carina hadn't thought the com in her suite was particularly useful until Heathrow called her that night on it. "Hey, Princess Carina," he said. "There are some papers you might be interested in about the Immortality Virus. Do you want me to send them to you?" Then he chatted with her for an hour about the leadership vacuum in North Kepler and how crazy it was that so many of the research teams seemed out of touch with Kepler reality.

So, she liked him, and she liked the com, and she didn't mind when Heathrow called again two nights later. By the time her first patronage meeting came around, she'd read dozens of articles and studies about the Immortality Virus, the research that had been done on it in Gandhi, the vaccine that had prevented it from killing off the Mortal population, the deadlier strains of the virus, and the ongoing efforts to come up with a cure. All courtesy of Heathrow Princeton.

Thanks to Heathrow, she was also far more aware of what life was like in North Kepler these days. Despite South

Kepler's encroachment on Northern land at the borders and despite repeated threats from the Immortal Empire, some places, like Cerulean and New Paris, had large enough independent militias and savvy enough governors to hang on to local rule. But some, like Mendelton, a small town near the southwestern border of North Kepler, were completely under South Keplerian rule.

"What happens when the Immortal Empire takes over one of our towns?" Carina asked Heathrow one evening. "Do they kill all the Mortals?"

"No," Heathrow said grimly. "The Empress is power-hungry, but she's supposedly incredibly intelligent. They kill or capture anyone with magic, the city's resources become the property of the Empire, no one can leave, and all the kids are injected with the Immortality Virus. But the Immortal Empire hardly ever decimates a whole city. She only kills enough rebels to take control. The border skirmishes between North and South Kepler are far more violent."

Somehow, that did not surprise Carina.

In any case, by the morning of her first official patronage meeting—a small group meeting with just her, Doctor McIntosh, Doctor Friedman, and her dad—she thought she was prepared. She was thankful for her attendants that morning, who dressed her up in a woolish business suit, a silky ice blue blouse, and heels she never would have chosen because they made her two inches taller than necessary. But still, the ensemble made her feel like she had it together. She showed up early to the small conference room feeling confident.

Doctor McIntosh was there already, answering questions from Doctor Friedman, her dad, *and* Heathrow. She checked her atomic watch to confirm she wasn't late. She wasn't. So why had they started without her? Wasn't this supposed to be *her* meeting? She tensed as the conversation halted, but Heathrow broke the tension.

"I hope you don't mind a guest," he said. "Friedman's my mentor. He invited me to come along for the educational experience of attending a royal patronage meeting."

That was maybe the only good thing about what she'd walked in on. She thought she could use an ally in a meeting like this. She graced the room with a cautious smile.

"Lovely to see you again, Princess Carina," Doctor Friedman said. He pointed to an empty chair at the head of the table. "Royal patron always gets the seat of honor. Doctor McIntosh was just showing us some of the preliminary results of the team's research."

Doctor McIntosh, who had red ink smeared on his cheek today, cleared his throat and said, "Um, yes, that's right, Princess. As I was saying, the early results of our testing indicate that the strain of the Immortality Virus Vivian Wellington was infected with is significantly mutated from any typical strain."

Heathrow lifted his pen. "Ah, excuse me, Doctor McIntosh? What degree of variance is there between the typical strains on the Perrywinkle scale?"

"The differences are statistically significant but—"

Carina's dad interrupted. "The Perrywinkle scale? I thought the Royal Society deemed that outdated five years ago."

Friedman chuckled. "Keep up, Reggie. Princeton's talking about the *new* Perrywinkle scale."

"That's right," Heathrow said. "And it's at least ten times as accurate as Brown's test of limits, which is what had been in place after the old Perrywinkle scale was questioned in 834." He looked specifically at Carina and winked. "But I think we can forgive the king for being a little behind in his studies. Right, Princess?"

Carina had no knowledge of the Perrywinkle scale, and she'd only vaguely heard of Brown's test of limits. Was *she* that behind? She thought she'd come prepared.

She smiled again anyway and said, "Right," but as the conversation continued, she felt as if the men in that room were speaking another language. Nothing she knew seemed relevant. At some point, she stopped trying to understand and started just trying to make it *look* like she understood, nodding along with whatever sounded right until Doctor Friedman addressed her directly a few minutes later.

"Then you think McIntosh's team should test the samples against the outliers we collected and froze in 702, Princess?"

Carina had no idea how to respond.

Heathrow rescued her. "I'm sure the princess agrees there's no need to go so far back," he said, and she was grateful for the save until she noticed that the men stopped directing *any* questions at her after that, speaking to Heathrow instead, like *he* was the patron. The longer the conversation went on, the less anyone even bothered to look at her. By the time Doctor McIntosh put a photo of eleven people in gray jumpsuits on the conference table, Carina felt entirely removed from the discussion.

"This is something we're very excited about," McIntosh said. "The militia captured these Immortals while searching for the princesses this summer. They've been in a prison facility in Cerulean since."

Carina squinted to look for red eyes in the photos. "Were these the Empire Immortals who tried to kill Miguela and me?"

"No, honey," her dad said. "These are probably just Immortal bounty-hunters. None of the Immortals the team captured were officially affiliated with the Empire."

A feeling like a balloon in her chest, preventing her diaphragm from moving, made it more difficult for Carina to respond. "These Immortals were hunting us down as hired guns?"

"Probably not *these*." Her dad patted her hand. "We found them weeks before we found you, and you don't need to be concerned. No one can find you here."

The balloon expanded.

Doctor McIntosh carried on. "They were sentenced to execution, Princess, and now they're in a very high-security facility. But the king approved a stay of execution in favor of what we believe is a far better use of these Immortals. In lieu of execution, we'll be testing potential treatments for the strain of the Immortality Virus the queen of South Kepler was infected with—"

Carina interrupted. "I'm sorry … we were going to *execute* them?"

Her question got met with four confused looks.

"I mean … have we actually *convicted* them of anything?"

"They're Immortals, Carina," her dad said, overly-gently. "The militia soldiers who picked them up had the option of executing them on the spot."

Carina, however, was thinking about how she'd been arrested a few months ago by the Southern Royals just for having magic. Was this different? Except for maybe being *worse*? She thought of Max. She was still furious at him, but did he deserve to die just for being Immortal? What about those kids who were forced into immortality when the Empire took over their towns?

"Shouldn't they be given trials?" she said.

Heathrow spoke up. "If I may, I think the Princess is concerned about consent again." He turned to Carina's dad.

"Your Highness, I'm sure you can see where she's coming from. We all understand that Immortals lack the cognitive ability to act with ethics and morals, but they are still human. Perhaps we should ask the prisoners to sign consent forms."

"Actually—" Carina began to say.

But Heathrow went on like he hadn't heard her. "May I suggest that the princess and I personally visit these prisoners? I would be happy to accompany her in Cerulean next week. I'm sure that would make her feel more comfortable with the arrangement. And she's very unlikely to be recognized."

"Yes, I think that would work." King Reginald said affably. "Thanks for raising the concern, Heathrow. I'll have a meeting set up between you and the guard staff to ensure that the princess will remain safe while she's with you in Cerulean."

Heathrow caught Carina's eye. He looked pleased with himself. "Feel like a field trip, Princess?"

The balloon in her gut had hardened like a rock, and she didn't even understand exactly *why*. But there was a touch of frost spreading from where she was clutching the edge of the table. She let go and said, "Yes, thank you," in a voice that came out quieter than she ever normally spoke.

Heathrow said, "Any time."

By the time she got to her training session that afternoon with Terrance Hess, Carina was feeling a little cold. She'd decided that the feelings she had about the Royal Society had a lot to do with a greater sense of helplessness she was carrying around these days. Why did things always happen *to* her instead of *because* of her? When would that change?

Hess fell into the category of "things that happened to

her." He was wearing an especially thick sweater this morning, though, probably because she'd become progressively cold with him as their training sessions progressed. She was hardly improving under his watch, and she spent half her lessons attempting to avoid physical contact with him.

Yesterday, things had been so bad that she threw a medicine ball extra hard during an exercise and cracked the floor where it landed. Hess responded by giving Carina another unsolicited shoulder rub. "You're incredibly tense," he said. "It's okay. I'll be gentler tomorrow."

The temperature in the gym had dropped. But Carina wasn't sure he'd noticed, and it satisfied her to see that he'd decided it was sweater weather today.

There were two colored balls on the mat near Hess. She lifted one ball, then the other, and decided they were the same weight.

"I see you've already figured out today's drill," Hess said. "Since you've conquered one heavyweight, today we're going to be doing two at a time. Did you know you could lift more than one thing telekinetically?"

Wasn't it common knowledge that she'd been holding up all the debris from an entire house that had just exploded when she'd been found?

He flashed a big grin her way. "Never mind. You don't have to tell me what you don't know. I get that we're working on your confidence." He waved his hand as if to beckon her closer. "Come over here, let me show you the right stance."

Carina was tired of Hess "showing her the right stance" with anything, but he was the teacher, so she walked over to the mat where he was standing. Then he positioned himself behind her with his hands on her upper arms and her back uncomfortably close to his chest.

"Alright, you're going to stand here. And this arm—" he slid one of his hands down her arm to her elbow and then moved her elbow up "—should be a little higher than the other."

"I've got it," Carina said, trying to move away from him. But when she took a step forward, he just clutched her arms, pulled her back, and laughed.

"Can't get away that easily," he said playfully.

"Is there a way for you to show me without touching me?" she asked.

Hess laughed again, and it made her feel like something was crawling over her skin. "You don't have to go all frigid on me." He let go of her as she slipped out of his grip. "I'm your friend, Carina. I need to show you how this stuff is done."

"Try telling me instead," she suggested from a safe meter away. "I'm not that dumb."

Something panned over his face, and he took another step closer. "You aren't dumb at all."

She could smell his breath. It was oniony.

Another step closer, and this time it seemed like he was leaning toward her. "If there's anything you need, it's for someone to treat you like the powerhouse you are." He put his hands back on her shoulders and lowered his voice. "And I didn't want to say anything before, but I think I know why you don't want me touching you."

His eyes were a dull, unmemorable blue. His nose was crooked. There was a blemish on his left cheek that wasn't attractive. He was completely ignoring her boundaries and the guards in the room, and every time he told her she was powerful or smart, he followed it up with a comment about her lack of confidence that somehow made her feel weakened.

Not in a "you're making my knees weak" kind of way, either.

"Don't worry, you don't have to say it out loud," he said, and what happened after was kind of a blur, as she realized he thought she had some *latent attraction* to him. Was he going to try to kiss her in front of her *guards*? Presumably not, but his face just kept getting closer, and then, well …

She didn't *mean* to freak out.

But she also didn't feel much remorse when Hess's face turned gray, his lips turned blue, and he collapsed to the ground clutching his throat.

Oops.

Carina's entire on-duty bodyguard came running, and it dawned on Carina that Mishe was about a hundred times more skilled than Hess as her top guard put her teacher into a hold that looked exceptionally painful. Not that it was necessary. Hess was shivering so hard he didn't even seem to be able to talk.

"You son of a Kepler cow." Mishe growled at Hess, and to her, he said, "I'm sorry we didn't step in earlier. He's supposed to be a professional. I never dreamed—"

"Me neither," she said. "But I think training is over for the day. You should probably send him to the infirmary."

"Only if you don't want to go there first, Your Grace. You're not hurt, are you?" Mishe's eyes darted down from her head and back up to her eyes in a scan so fast she almost missed it. "No. Obviously not."

Professional had just become Carina's favorite thing about Mishe. She cracked a smile at him. "Could you escort me back to the house? I think I'd like to spend the rest of the morning with my sister."

Mishe cracked the tiniest smile back. "Yes, of course, Princess Carina."

CHAPTER NINE
TOO COLD FOR COMFORT

Miguela was hanging out with Eugene in *his* royal prince suite when Carina went looking for her sister after that. This felt extremely unfair to Carina. Why did today have to be the day Miguela ventured out of her own rooms?

Carina desperately needed someone she trusted to tell her this was going to be okay, though. So, she stood at Eugene's door and tried to work up the nerve to knock while she looked at decals of fighter jets and rods of Asclepius taped all over the door. This wasn't going to work. She couldn't talk to Miguela with Eugene there. She could wait to debrief with Miguela. She could ignore the looks the guards standing down the hall would probably give her if she turned around now.

But the door opened abruptly without her knocking to reveal Eugene, dressed comfortably in jeans and a green sweater, and appearing just as straight-faced and impossible to read as always.

"What happened?" Eugene said.

Maybe she could tell him she'd forgotten where her own

room was and now, she'd realized her mistake and—

He opened the door wider. "Hey. Are you okay?"

She looked past him, and she was struck by how evident it was that this was Eugene's *place*. Framed photos of Eugene with Mom and Dad. Worn sweaters thrown over chairs. And did Eugene have some kind of obsession with aerodynamic magic? He must have had a dozen posters featuring airplanes and fighter jets, plus one of the historic Lockheed skyline, the capital city of the former Western Republic.

Miguela was curled up on a leather couch with her feet tucked under her, but she stood immediately and came to the door when she saw Carina standing there.

"What's wrong?" she said.

I nearly froze another teacher to death, and this time it was because he was a jerk who wanted to take advantage of me. Oh. No way. She was not doing this in front of Eugene. She didn't need to talk. She needed to leave and go … somewhere. To the gym, maybe to run. Or the stables. They had horses up here she was getting acquainted with and malamutes she could pet.

"I'm fine," she said, shifting her weight to back away before the word "fine" was even out of her mouth.

Miguela grabbed her arm and stopped her progress. "Please. I can practically *feel* you hurting." She tugged, and Carina followed her sister to the couch in Eugene's room. (Which was hopefully made of soft, broken-in *synthetic* leather, because skinning a cow didn't sit well with Carina.)

"You're freezing," Miguela said. She grabbed a throw blanket from the back of the couch, put it over Carina's lap, and scooted close. Eugene went to what looked like a hot beverage station permanently situated in his room. He had a huge hot water boiler, a fancy tea chest, a big canister of cocoa mix, and a whole rack of mugs there. She tried not to feel jealous while he fixed her a mug of hot cocoa.

Then he brought it to her, perched on the edge of a nearby chair, and sat facing her while she took a sip of the hot cocoa. It was the best hot cocoa she'd ever had. Just the right amount of chocolate, and he'd added marshmallows. It disarmed her enough to finally respond to Miguela with: "Not as freezing as Hess right now."

Miguela leaned away from her, and Eugene's face twisted briefly before it broke into a rare smile.

"Is he dead?" Miguela said, which prompted Eugene to begin full-on laughing.

"He is *not* dead," Carina cried. "And it wouldn't be funny if he was!"

Eugene sobered up fast. "Sorry," he muttered.

"What did Hess *do*?" Miguela said.

"Why are you assuming *he* did something?" The cocoa was already cold in Carina's hands. "Last time I nearly froze someone to death, it was completely my fault."

"No, it wasn't," Eugene said. "Dad told you. Thermodynamic tendencies are difficult to control even when someone doesn't have power like we have. It's not your fault your teacher was unprepared."

"But Hess wasn't working with her on thermodynamics," Miguela said. "He was only supposed to be teaching her telekinetic magic."

"Yeah," Carina said morosely, "And he definitely wasn't supposed to be trying to … uh … make a move on me."

Miguela bounced off the couch like she'd been bitten by a Kepler roach. "What?! He didn't!"

Carina didn't want to talk about this in front of Eugene, but she *did* need Miguela's righteous indignation.

"What *exactly* did he do?" Miguela demanded while the

room got a little hotter.

"Tried to kiss me," Carina admitted. "I think." Then she figured she was already in far enough that she might as well tell the whole story. By the time she was finished, her hot cocoa was frozen solid and Miguela was pacing around with pink cheeks.

"That is *so* not okay," she said. "Why isn't dad vetting your teachers better? How come he can't find you someone *decent?*"

Carina winced, thinking of the meeting she'd had in the morning with the Royal Society, and Miguela didn't miss it. "What *else* did he do?" she said, and she was definitely not talking about Hess.

"I had a patronage meeting before training," Carina explained. "Dad, Friedman, the head of the research team, and Heathrow were all there. They basically spent the meeting talking over me."

Miguela stopped and stared at Carina. "A bunch of men patronized you at your patronage meeting."

Eugene reached to take Carina's frozen solid hot cocoa from her. "I'll get you a new one," he told her. "Lucky we don't have to send for someone every time we freeze over a hot beverage, right?"

"I don't have hot cocoa in my room," she said blankly.

He turned back around and blinked at her. "Did the water heater not come in yet? Dad ordered it the first week you got here."

Miguela sat back down next to Carina, took her hand, and began rubbing. "You haven't *needed* water heaters in your room before. You've had a Miguela for when you get upset. And you had a bad day, but I'm proud of you for what happened with Hess."

"I almost killed him, Guela," Carina said.

"Nah," Eugene said while he stirred more cocoa mix in a new mug. "Freezing someone so solid they die is hard. You need intent to do that. They'll treat him for hypothermia at the infirmary. He'll live."

"What happens when he starts telling people about it?" Carina asked.

Miguela scoffed at the question. "What would he say? That he tried to kiss you and you almost frosted him to death? That would kill that guy's ego."

"He might lie," Carina said, and as she did, she knew that was exactly what would happen. "He'll probably tell people I tried to kiss him, and I only tried to freeze him after he rejected me. People will hate me."

Eugene came back over with that fresh cup of hot cocoa. "That's not how things work around here. Dad will boot Hess from the fort before he has the chance to say anything. He'll be tried for treason if he talks about you at all. And if rumors start to spread, all you do is ask Glory-Jane to leak the truth. She's great with gossip, and insider information about the crown princess will always trump what some fired instructor has to say."

There was a knock on the door, and Carina, Miguela, and Eugene all looked to see it open. Dad was there, with Mom right behind him, though at first, Carina couldn't see her mother. Lucia Garcia was a solid foot shorter than her husband. But her head poked around Dad's shoulder, and Carina had the thought she often had that Miguela looked especially like their mom. All three of the women shared the same heart-shaped face, big brown eyes, and wild curly hair, but Miguela also had Mom's dimples, Mom's short height, and Mom's curvy shape.

"See?" Eugene said to Carina as their parents came in.

"Hess is probably already on the ferry back to Cerulean."

Dad sat down in a chair across from Carina and Miguela. "I am so sorry, Carina," he said. "That jackass had a great reputation in the militia."

"Maybe the militia isn't the right place to check for references," Eugene said a little coldly, and he pointed to a chair adjacent to the couch. "Sit there, Mom. You should be okay between Miguela and Dad."

"Thanks, sweetie," Mom said, but this time Carina knew she wasn't the only one peeved by their strange new family dynamic because she could see Miguela tense up. Even though she and Miguela had been here at the fort for months now, the five Garcias were hardly ever in one room at the same time, and it had everything to do with the biggest reason Miguela was angry at their parents.

"Do you want to talk about it?" Dad asked Carina now, which made her want to hide under the throw blanket. Did she want to *talk* about how she'd almost let her teacher kiss her? How she'd nearly killed him for it?

"Julian," Mom said softly, "we don't need to make her tell the story again. Mishe told us enough."

Carina's mom was far better than her dad at knowing what Carina could or couldn't talk about at any time. Really, one of the worst parts about being up here was that Carina could barely spend any time with Mom. She missed her mom almost more now than she ever had before.

Dad kicked his legs and the cane out in front of him. "Well, the point is he's gone. And at least we have a few men we can trust. Like Mishe. And Heathrow. I hear they've already worked out the details of your trip to Cerulean, Carina."

He would *have* to bring up some guy he wanted her dating in *this* context.

"Wait, what do you mean *they've* worked out the details of some trip?" Miguela said, her voice tight with anger. "Why wasn't *Carina* involved in that?"

Eugene's brow mashed together, too. "You get to go to Cerulean?" he said to Carina. "For what? I never get to leave the fort."

"Heathrow is taking me to see a prison facility where we're keeping some Immortals who were captured during the search for Miguela and me," she told him.

But that only made Eugene turn on Dad. "You're letting her go to a *prison* to see some *Immortals*? I never even get to go to buy my own clothes."

Bitterness. Sharp, acrid bitterness. That was what made Carina think: *because it's been so hard for you to have all your clothes custom tailored and shipped in from designers in Gandhi.* Eugene's eyes darted to hers, and the expression of indignation there made her stomach sour.

"Carina is several years older than you, Eugene," Mom said patiently. "Which is the same reason she had to attend a Royal Society meeting and become the patron of a project. When you and Miguela are old enough, you'll have the same rights and responsibilities."

"Not really. We're completely different people," Eugene said.

"That's enough, Gene." Dad pointed to Carina's hot cocoa, which was frosted over again, and tried to speak to her in what he must have thought was a soothing tone. "Carina, can you calm down, please? We won't all be able to sit together if you get too cold. Your mother—"

"I'm fine," Mom said quickly. "Perfectly toasty over here."

Which made Dad turn his gaze on Miguela, whose whole body was coiled up like a spring and whose face was flushed bright red. Carina shifted closer to Miguela.

"We *need* to talk about this," Eugene said indignantly. "When the baby comes, we'll be totally out of balance."

And there it was. The reason Miguela was so furious. Miguela might have been able to forgive their parents for everything else, but what she could not get over was that Mom was now pregnant. ("With a *replacement* baby," Miguela had said to Carina more than once.)

"We *know*, Eugene," Dad said.

"That's *enough*, Eugene," Mom said.

But Miguela stood up abruptly, and as she fled the room, repeating, "I'm sorry, I'm sorry!" Carina was alarmed at how that movement could send heat pulsing through the air. Dad brushed sweat from his forehead while Mom started to shiver, and Eugene stood up and moved to the far side of the room, as far away from Mom as possible.

"This is so *stupid*," Eugene said. "We're a *mess*. Why can't we tell Miguela that we can't all be in the same room if she keeps running away?"

Carina had a migraine headache coming on. They couldn't tell Miguela that. The last thing Miguela needed was more unnecessary guilt, especially related to the "replacement baby." But it was still a major problem because they *were* kind of a mess, at least magically speaking.

Mom didn't have a thermodynamic tendency, but the baby apparently tended *very* cold. If Eugene wanted to spend time with Mom, Dad had to be right there to compensate for the chill. Even Dad couldn't compensate if Carina was the one who wanted to spend time with her mother, though. She'd hugged her mom once after they reunited, and Mom got so cold she almost passed out. Miguela was the only person in the family whose magic ran so extreme that it could counter Carina's. If Miguela wasn't right next to Carina, Carina couldn't be anywhere near Mom.

Which was maybe the most tragic thing about being home. Mom hadn't grown up royal or magic. She understood what Carina's life had been like for the last six years, and even if she hadn't, she just plain understood Carina better than anyone else in the family. Now that Carina knew her mom was alive, they could talk over mobile coms, but it wasn't enough.

Still, Mom caught Carina's eye now, and she knew they were thinking exactly the same thing. No matter how much it hurt that they were living totally apart in the same (large) house, correcting the situation wasn't worth making Miguela feel worse. Carina could wait for more hugs. She could handle this. After the baby was born, things would be fine.

"Carina," Mom said. "Why don't you stand over there with Eugene, and Dad can sit next to me? Then we can get a heated blanket, and we can spend time as a family."

"As a family without Miguela," Eugene said, and Carina noticed her mom shiver. A heated blanket wasn't going to be enough.

Dad tapped that cane rapidly on the floor. "We're going to fix this. I'm interviewing three more thermodynamics teachers next week."

Eugene scowled. "Why can't you just—?"

"Once Carina has more control, everything will be fine," Dad said, talking over Eugene.

Carina thought Dad was delusional. Just a little more control, and everything would be fine? Then Miguela wouldn't be furious anymore, and Eugene wouldn't be irritated, and the baby wouldn't be threatening mom with hypothermia, and the family could move back to North Kepler proper, and the kingdom could start facing the Immortal Empire?

Uh-huh.

But she nodded anyway. Because it had already been a lousy day, and she hated stirring up additional conflict with her family. "I, um, think maybe I should go talk to Miguela," she said, and then she smiled as best as she could at them all and left the room. What else was she supposed to do?

Miguela was in her bedroom, sitting near a window she'd cracked open to let in what felt like a polar vortex when Carina found her.

"Is your trip to Cerulean a date?" Miguela asked.

"Does that mean we're not going to talk about what just happened?" Carina said.

Miguela drew what looked like a firework in the frost on the window. "If it *is* a date, you should tell Heathrow how he made you feel at the meeting."

"I wasn't angry. And it wasn't just him."

"But you were hurt, frustrated, and put down, and he was part of it all. If he respects you, he'll want to know."

"Very rational," Carina noted. "I hear it's a Northern trait. Does that mean I should talk to Dad, too? Since he was also part of it?"

Miguela only grunted.

"Rational doesn't apply to our parents, then?"

Miguela swiveled away from the window. "I thought for *six years* that I'd killed them, Care. Now we know I didn't, but it's only because you and Eugene have incredibly uncommon magic defense reflexes. I still caused a massive explosion that buried half our family alive. Dad still got hurt bad enough that he walks with a cane. Now *you're* the crown princess of a whole kingdom, the queen of another whole kingdom died in your lap last summer, and *she* tended hot like me, but we didn't even know we had anything in common with her because our parents didn't bother to tell us anything important before I almost killed everyone, and since then, they've been trying to *replace* us with a new child, and I *hate* them."

Carina didn't think it would be helpful to point out that Miguela probably *didn't* hate them if the thought of being replaced made her so mad. She kept quiet instead.

"I just want to go *home*," Miguela said.

"I know," Carina said, and then she let all the problems of her own day go while she went to hug her sister, who obviously had far bigger feelings than Carina was experiencing. "Me, too."

CHAPTER TEN
SUNLIGHT AND TOAST

There was sunlight basking down on Nate, and someone was making breakfast. It smelled like bacon—which was awful because pigs were highly intelligent animals who didn't deserve to be slaughtered—but where there was bacon, there was usually toast, and *that* Nate approved of. Especially if there was peanut butter available to slather on.

He opened his eyes …

… and found himself lying under a thin, scratchy blanket on a bed with springs that were gouging his hip. Nate recalled that he was in a den of Dangerous Immortals. He and Franklin needed to book it ASAP.

Except … toast.

Anyway, Franklin's pack was stashed neatly under another bed. Not exactly a sign of endangerment. Nate decided he could prioritize breakfast over escape.

He got out of bed, stretched, yawned—not because he was tired but more as a "hello world" kind of thing—and realized his breath reeked. Franklin wouldn't care, and Nate didn't care if an Immortal got a whiff, but you never knew when you might meet an attractive girl in a new place. He dug for his toothbrush in his duffel, found it, and set off to find a bathroom.

The bathroom was unoccupied, and there was a shower in there, so Nate took it upon himself to bathe. He didn't have a razor handy, but at least he could change into clothes that seemed fresher than the ones he'd been sleeping in. As in, underwear he hadn't worn for at least a few days.

Good.

Feeling chipper, Nate then sniffed his way down the hall to the place that smelled like breakfast, where he found Franklin sitting with the Immortals at a kitchen table. Nate's mentor was drinking coffee and gnawing on a dead pig while he read a newspaper, but when he saw Nate, Franklin looked over the paper and grinned.

"Ahh … sleeping beauty awakens. And looks cleaner than he's been in a year. Do you have a date we don't know about, Prince Nathanial?"

"Only with you," Nate said sweetly. "How long was I out?"

"About thirty-six hours," Max-the-Trigger-Finger said. "You slept through all of yesterday. Didn't even wake up when Franklin rolled you over so he could get you under that blanket. Which, by the way, I wouldn't have thought you'd need given how you almost roasted us the night before last."

"Thirty-six hours?" That was a lot of sleep. But Nate had been surviving on two or three hours a night since Vivian died.

Max was eating bacon. He crunched a corner from a thick piece, and did not swallow before he said, "I was hoping it was a coma. But Franklin says it was because you overheated. It must suck to have an awesome power that puts you to sleep when it gets out of control."

"Good morning to you, too, Evil Immortal," Nate said because today he didn't feel particularly threatened by the guy, who did not have his gun out.

"His name is Max." Franklin set the newspaper down. "And he and Myles just saved our royal asses, so let's try to be civil."

Nate thought about being annoyed by that, but he'd spotted a toaster and some bread. He decided to make himself toast. "Then, what exactly is this place, and what are our Immortal saviors doing here?"

"This is one of Myles's places," Max said. "And we are here because a bunch of irresponsible Mortals blew up his actual home. Lucky he has, like, ten of them."

"Are all your homes equipped like hostels?" Nate asked Myles, who had been reading a different section of the newspaper.

"Most of them," Myles said. "I rent out the rooms. There are more Immortals than you would think looking to get away from the Immortal Empire."

"And you cash in on it," Nate said.

Myles shrugged. "It's one of the ways I make income."

Nate's toast popped out of the toaster. "Do you keep peanut butter at your rental property?"

Myles pointed to the cupboard. "To your left. Coffee's fresh, too."

"Thanks," Nate said, and then, because he was feeling appreciative of the peanut butter toast and the shower, he said, "So how much do we owe you before we check out?"

"You don't," Myles said. "This is a return favor. Franklin saved *my* ass from the Immortal Empire a few years back. And we're checking out later this morning.

Nate buttered his toast and thought about that. "*We're*

checking out?"

"Yeah," Max said. "That's what I said."

It was disturbing to Nate that Max thought they had anything in common. He turned to Franklin, who was reading the paper again. "Franklin? Explain."

Franklin didn't bother looking up. "Myles and Max are heading in the same direction we're going."

"I thought our direction was 'anywhere but here.'"

Franklin picked up another piece of bacon and bit off a piece almost as big as the barbaric bites Max was taking. He *knew* that bothered Nate.

"You thought because I don't tell you everything. We're looking for the Sisters of Novi Dupree. They run a women's sanctuary and a brewery. Ever heard of them?"

Nate thought maybe he'd heard of the brewery, but not the Sisters or the sanctuary. There was something about the sad absent look Max assumed and the way Myles gazed into his coffee cup at the mention of the place that made Nate extremely suspicious, though. He considered using his secret power to pry, then decided this was worth an educated guess.

"Novi Dupree doesn't happen to be a women's sanctuary in the Red Ridge Mountains, does it?" he asked. "Because there's this girl I met a few months ago—super skinny, terrible taste in boyfriends—and she supposedly lived in a place like that."

Max shot out of his seat. "If you don't stop speaking about Carina like that, I will kill you," he said viciously, and Nate got a look at the Immortal's eyes turning red again.

"Sit down, Max," Myles said. "You don't even know what happened to her."

Max did not sit. "We left her on a mountain to *die* in a horrible, bloody ambush. It was the *wrong* thing to do. There is a difference between avoiding interference in Mortal affairs and straight-up *negligence*."

"Were you in love with that girl?" Nate said. "Because if you were going to pick a Mortal, she was not a smart choice."

"Why do you always have to be a jerk?" Max said. "What did you have against Carina?"

Nate had lots against *Carina*, starting with: "One, she was dating *you*. Two, she had too much magic not to be registered with South Kepler. Three, she refused to tell us where she was from, so she was almost for sure a Northern rebel. Four—"

"She was an orphan from Novi Dupree," Max interrupted coldly. "She barely knew how to use her magic. She had no idea she was supposed to be registered with your evil kingdom. She wasn't a Northern rebel. Her family was killed by Red-Eyed Ones, and she was running away because they were after her, too."

"Guess she wasn't too scared of them," Nate said. "Since she was cool with dating you."

"She didn't know I was an Immortal when I was dating her." Max rubbed his eyes. "And by Red-Eyed Ones, I meant First Strain Immortals. My eyes are only red now because I'm thinking about a girl I loved and how she was on the run from some violent beasts and all she wanted was to learn enough magic to protect herself and her sister, and she … they … didn't make it."

It was weird for Nate to feel bad for any Immortal, but Max seemed genuinely upset about Icy's demise. Nate was never going to look back on his memories of Icy with fondness. Still, if she wasn't a Northern rebel, then she'd seriously been in the wrong place at the wrong time. Those Empire Immortals were after Nate's family, not some random girls with random magic. Also, the girl who'd been with Icy hadn't been hostile to anyone, and she'd tended hot and obviously had less control over her thermodynamics than Nate.

Poor little thing.

Max's eyes were red *and* watery now.

Nate brought his plate of peanut butter toast to the table where the others were sitting. "Alright, look, I don't like you," he said to Max, "but I am sorry about what happened to Carina and her sister."

Franklin reached for more bacon. "I don't think they're dead, Max. Like I told you yesterday, we didn't see any bodies. And there are some things that make me think Carina at least might be alive."

That was news to Nate, and he could not help but feel peeved about it. What did Franklin know about Icy Carina? Had he *seen* something? If so, was it related to *him*? Because that probably meant Nate was going to see her again, and he had that confrontation to look forward to.

"Or they could have been buried in the rubble," he said under his breath.

"Have you forgotten how we found your sister's body?" Franklin asked Nate with an exacting look.

Nate winced. If there was one memory he would like to erase, it was of seeing Viv on the Mountain of Peril after Franklin helped him out of the rubble. But Franklin had a point. Vivian should have been buried with Nate. Instead, she was lying in a dry, mossy area nearby, covered by a light, wool blanket.

And it got stranger. When Nate pulled back the blanket, he could tell his sister's body hadn't been damaged by the explosion or the collapse of the house. Her clothes weren't singed. She had no bruises, no cuts. She was lying with her hands folded over her stomach and her hair spread out beneath her head like someone had arranged it carefully. Her eyes were closed. Her mouth was only barely parted. She looked like she was sleeping.

She wasn't.

Nate had touched her cheek with the back of his hand, and when all he felt was cold, he had to remove his hand immediately because he had the instinct to warm her up. The hot tendency was useful for that kind of thing when someone like Bast got too cold for his own good.

But it couldn't bring anyone back to life.

At the time, Franklin had said something about Icy and her sister. Something like maybe they'd escaped and left Vivian covered that way. Nate hadn't bought into that. He'd seen a rafter coming down on those girls just before the house came down on him.

Furthermore, he didn't want to imagine anyone other than him or Bast being there for Viv as she took her last breath. He'd shut the whole memory down.

"I'm sorry, Nate," Franklin said, bringing Nate back to the kitchen and the safe house. "We don't have to talk about this right now."

Nate's toast felt like rocks in his gut. He *didn't* want to talk about this. Ever.

Still, Max was rubbing his temples with both hands and staring down at uneaten bacon on his plate. Nate doubted the guy was a vegetarian, and Immortal or not, he was still a human. He could have feelings.

"Franklin might be right," Nate admitted. "Vivian's body … well, it looked like whoever left it there treated it with respect. It was covered. Those Empire Immortals wouldn't have done that. And no one in my party would have left her."

Max looked up at him. Now that Nate was bothering to

see the guy as a person, he realized that Max was sort of gaunt. Cheeks sunk in. Purple circles under his eyes. Scruff on his face that was far nastier than Nate's scruff. The guy needed a haircut. That mane was sticking up all over the place. But his eyes weren't red anymore.

"Then you think Carina and Miguela might have done it?" Max said. "Covered your sister's body? Which would mean … they survived?"

Franklin looked silently at Nate. And Max hadn't shot him again yet, so Nate made a choice to act like a Mortal prince for the moment, not just a sarcastic teenager.

"Yeah," he said. "They might have."

"Maybe they finally made it to Cerulean," Max said thoughtfully.

"Why were they going to Cerulean?" Nate asked.

Franklin tossed the newspaper onto the table. "What's more important is that *we* are headed to Einsteinian. Because that's where Lizzy Dupree might be, and she is the founder of Novi Dupree Sanctuary."

"And we have a ride to catch," Myles added. "We should head out soon."

"We're catching a ride? From whom?" Nate said, magicking the newspaper to himself. It was local news. *The Hypatia Hype.*

"An acquaintance," Myles said, way too carefully. "She has an SUV."

Nate flipped through the paper. "Dirty gas guzzler. Doesn't sound like a good way to get anywhere. Can't we ride?"

After all, his sword might have been stuck in the castle at Alighieri, but his *horse* was exceptionally intelligent and had legs. Pepper was currently stabled with Franklin's horses in a place run by another shady Immortal who hadn't charged them much for it.

"We only have three horses," Franklin said. "And remember? We ditched the wagon."

"Because we travel light. It's fine. I'll tell Pepper to find us a fourth."

"Excuse me, but who the hell is Pepper?" Max said.

"It's his horse," Franklin—who liked to tease Nate about this, even though it was not a laughing matter—said with a dry smile.

Max's eyes got huge. "You're going to *tell* your *horse* to find us a fourth?"

"He can talk to animals," Franklin explained.

Myles fixed a keen look on Nate that made him feel edgy. "Really? That's not a very common telesthesia gift, is it?"

Max continued to gawk at Nate. "You can talk to your horse *with your mind*?"

Nate tried to ignore them and went back to reading *The Hypatia Hype*. "Magic prince. Tell me why we can't take horses again?"

"The ride I have lined up is faster and more convenient," Myles said.

"Faster and a violation of the Mortal Commitments," Nate said absently. He'd found the "mainland news" section, and his toast tasted bad again. The first headline in that section read: "Immortal Empire Threatens Crown Prince."

He skimmed the article. Increases in border skirmishes. Assassination still under investigation. Crown Prince, Bastian Wellington, personally threatened by Empress Hildebrand. Called 'The Last Cardinal on Kepler' by Lord Godric.

Nate set the paper down. "Bast is in trouble. I need to go to Alighieri."

"Absolutely not," Franklin said.

"But Franklin—" he held the article up for Franklin to see "—Bast is being threatened directly by the Immortal Empire."

"We've discussed this before. You aren't ready to go back. You can't face Prince Bastian."

"Burn," Max muttered.

"More like *not* burn," Nate said grouchily. "And I don't want to 'face' Bast."

"The issue is closed," Franklin said. "We'll stop by the stable on our way out so you can tell Pepper where we're going and he can follow."

"But—"

Franklin gave Nate his 'I inspire fear' look. Nate wasn't afraid of Franklin, but he knew when it wasn't worth trying to fight his mentor.

"Fine," he said. Just to show he was pissed off, though, he magicked the remainder of the bacon out of Franklin's reach. Passive-aggressive. It was a Wellington trait. Unfortunately, the bacon landed within Max's reach, and Max snatched a piece.

"That pig was probably smarter than you," Nate told Max.

"Not smart enough not to get eaten," Max said merrily, apparently quite heartened by the possibility that his Mortal ex-girlfriend might still be alive.

Nate, however, was not heartened. He said a silent prayer for the pig then added a real plea for Bast, who probably wouldn't have expected much to come from any of Nate's prayers. But Bast needed all the help he could get, even if he would never think it himself.

It was time for Nate to go home.

CHAPTER ELEVEN
SOUR CHERRY SUV

Myles's acquaintance met them on a corner just outside the alley. She was leaning against the driver's side door of a bright sour-cherry red SUV, wearing blue-rimmed rock star sunglasses, a stretchy taupe dress that didn't seem appropriate for much, lipstick that matched the car, and heels Viv would have liked. Probably Bast, too. He said everyone looked good in heels. Nate agreed for the moment, and he was already feeling better about riding to Einsteinian in a non-sustainable SUV.

"Whoa," Max said. "*That's* our ride?"

Myles cuffed Max on the back of the head. "You are over five hundred years old. Stop ogling Sofie like you're a seventeen-year-old Kepler Mortal." He jerked his head at Nate.

The woman boosted herself away from the car and greeted Myles with a kiss to the cheek. "Myles," she said. "You must be absolutely *desperate* to have called me!"

"Nice to see you, too, Sofie," Myles said. "And good to see you made it through the last harvest."

She lowered her sunglasses, and her red eyes flashed. "Not something we're going to talk about if you want a ride, Kayes." She assessed the rest of the group, and her eyes settled on Nate. "So, this is our young prince, hmm? The last Cardinal king?" She held out her hand to him. "I'm Sophie. Pleasure to meet you, Your Highness."

Nate patted her hand awkwardly. "It's Nate, and I'm not any king. That would be my brother, Bastian."

"But you're next in line, aren't you?"

"I'm going to abdicate."

Sofie's voice had been airy up until then, but now she dropped it to a sultrier tone. "Not interested in power? I suppose you'd rather live your life in *peace*?"

"Don't tease him," Myles said. "We need to get going."

Myles took the passenger seat, Franklin took a seat in the middle of the SUV, and Nate climbed into the back, thinking it might help him avoid further discussion about the whole "king" thing. No such luck. Max climbed back with him and immediately started asking annoying questions.

"You're really supposed to be the next king of South Kepler?"

"No," Nate said.

"Yes," Franklin said.

"Why do you want to abdicate?" Max asked. "Are you sick, too? Like your sister?"

"He's stubborn, not sick," Franklin said.

Max snickered, and Nate hated Franklin a little.

"I'm not the right person for the job," he said. "My brother's a better fit. I'm going to renounce the throne as soon as I get back to South Kepler."

"Over my dead body," Franklin said. "Especially if we go back too soon, since I'm wanted there and you don't have enough power yet to change that."

"But what will you do if you don't become king?" Max asked, as if there weren't a million other career choices.

"Southern Guard." Nate had thought about this a lot. He'd be great in the Guard. Definitely, he'd be a renegade general, and he'd probably die young in some wild offensive launched against the Immortal Empire. He had this fantasy where he died saving Bast's life. Bast would try futilely to heal him, and after he realized it was too late, he'd say, "That was the bravest thing I've ever seen anyone do. I am so proud to be your brother, Nate." Then Nate would say something like—

Max interrupted the fantasy. "I don't get it. You're a magic fire prince, you have a horse you can talk to, and you're the rightful next king of a whole country. You're scary powerful. Why give that up?"

Nate slouched as much as he could with a seatbelt on. "Try a whole *continent*. I can't *rule* that. Bast's the one who knows how to make hard decisions. People do what he tells them to do. And he can freeze someone to death in three seconds."

"You can *fry* someone in two," Max argued.

Nate chewed on the inside of his cheek. "I *could*, but I wouldn't. At least not on purpose."

"Right." Max sounded skeptical. "So, if you don't want to be king, why do you want to go back to South Kepler?"

"You saw the newspaper article. The Immortal Empire is playing up the fact that it only has one Cardinal left to kill. It wouldn't look as bad if there were still two First Degree Cardinals in South Kepler. And Bast isn't expendable. I am. He could send me out to handle the rough stuff."

Franklin glared at him. "You are not *expendable*, Nate."

"If it makes you feel any better, I think you're expendable," Max said.

Max kept up a constant stream of stupid questions for the whole ride from Hypatia to Einsteinian, where Sofie stopped the SUV in front of a tall, bricked townhouse on a downtown main street.

"This is it, gentlemen," she said. "Lizzy Dupree's home-away-from-home. Or one of them. Rumor has it she's been staying here with Raider Agda."

Franklin opened his eyes in alarm, which made Nate feel alarmed.

"You could come in," Myles was saying to Sofie. "Lizzy has probably forgiven you by now."

"Says the only person Lizzy can't hold a grudge against. She's different with you, Myles. You know that, right?"

Myles chuckled. "Only because we're old friends."

"You and I are old friends. You and Lizzy are something else."

They got out of the SUV, and Sofie made a point of pulling Nate aside as everyone else was unloading bags from the trunk. She tugged him into her personal space and pushed her sunglasses into her hair.

Nate hadn't spent a lot of time studying red eyes, but up close, he could see that "red" was a huge oversimplification. It was more like Sofie's eyes were super bloodshot, her pupils were blown out, and her irises were so narrow he couldn't see their true color.

"Reddish-brown," she told him. "Like cinnamon. That's my natural eye color."

"Oh," he said. "They're, uh, pretty."

She smiled charmingly. "Young prince, do you know anything about Mila Hildebrand or Christian Godric?"

He thought that was an obscure question. "Other than they're the power-hungry rulers of an empire hellbent on destroying everything the rest of the planet cares about?"

"I meant more personally."

"No. Do you?"

Sofie put a finger on Nate's cheek and swiped down. "Godric is manic. Constantly fights major depression. When he loses it, he captures Mortals and takes his pain out on them, but he's been madly in love with Hildebrand for all eternity. He'd do anything for her."

Max shuddered audibly from somewhere behind them. "IV-933 Immortals."

Sofie raised a well-manicured eyebrow. "Watch it, newbie. I'm an IV-933 Immortal."

"Sorry," Max said.

Sofie continued her conversation with Nate. "As for Hildebrand, she thinks highly of herself." She tossed her hair. "As she should since she's an actual genius. But several millennia ago, someone treated her like she was nothing but a dumb bombshell babe, and she's been proving to the universe that she shouldn't be underestimated ever since. Bit like your mother, I'm told."

"I don't think anyone has ever underestimated my mother," Nate said.

"But I suppose your brother must be different from either of them, hmm? He's probably capable of empathy. Prioritizes people, not power. Certainly not a black and white thinker or a fundamentalist of any kind."

"Uh …"

"Good," Sofie said. "Because *no one* is more wickedly unhinged than Godric, and no one is more ruthless than Hildebrand when she wants something. And you can't fight fire with fire, can you?"

"No …?" Nate wondered if she was ever going to let him go. If she didn't, that might be okay.

She let him go. "I'm glad you understand. You let me know how that plan to abdicate goes, won't you, Your Highness?"

There was something in her tone that Nate did not like.

"We'll keep you posted," Franklin said. There was something in his tone that Nate *really* did not like.

At the front door, Franklin stuck his hands in his pockets and looked despondently at a welcome mat while Myles slicked back his hair. When Myles knocked, Franklin turned around and began to walk away.

"Franklin!" Nate grabbed his arm. "What are you doing?"

Franklin was sickly pale. "This wasn't a good idea."

"What the hell is going *on* with you?" If this got worse, Nate was going to have to use his secret superpower.

Franklin seemed to brace himself, and a woman with bright, warm hazel eyes and an accompanying smile opened the door. She was wearing a flowery skirt with a white cotton blouse that cut lines that would make a guy want to be affectionate.

"Myles," she said breathlessly, and then she hit Myles with the kind of hug you do *not* get from a woman who isn't into you. For his part, the Guru didn't seem to have any issue hugging back. This was far more intimate than the greeting Sofie had gotten from Myles. Nate averted his eyes because the whole thing seemed personal.

"Hey, Lizzy," Myles said—all soft and, like, cowboy sexy.

Then she backed away, all frowns all at once, and slapped him. "It's been sixty-five *years*, Myles! Where have you been?"

"Mountain, obviously," Myles said gruffly, rubbing his cheek. "I had to go to the last funeral alone."

Which Lizzy responded to by flinging herself at Myles again and including full-on kissing this time in the display. "If you wanted me there, why didn't you *tell* me?" she asked, and when Lizzy addressed the rest of them, she left her arm slipped around Myles.

"Franklin Wellington. You don't have to look so nervous. Agda's not here." Franklin's face fell like he was disappointed, which made no sense, and Lizzy moved on to Nate and Max. "Let's see ... you would be ..." She shifted her gaze between them. "Well, you're Max, aren't you?" she said to the Immortal. "The girls have said things about you."

Max lit up like a holiday tree. "Carina and Miguela *are* alive? Did they say good things?"

"They said *things*." Lizzy came back to Nate. "And you must be Prince Nathanial. I've heard things about you, too."

Whatever Icy had said about him couldn't have been positive, and since they now had confirmation that she was not dead, Nate did not feel guilty saying uncharitable things about her anymore. So, he did what one does when one's reputation is threatened in front of an attractive woman. He attacked the bad-mouther's credibility. "Whatever you've heard is a very biased version of the truth. If Carina had been cooperative, everything would have been fine."

Lizzy smirked. "I wouldn't start with that when you see her next, Prince Nathanial. Actually, maybe start with Miguela. She liked you."

"Oh, the other girl?" Nate said. "She seemed sweet."

"So not fair," Max grumbled.

Lizzy's house opened into a kitchen with the world's largest beverage fridge, where she was stocking beer for an apocalypse. She offered them drinks, and Nate recalled that Novi Dupree Brewery was responsible for a beer he'd tried last summer and craved ever since. He asked Lizzy if she had any, and she gave him such a strange look that he was *sure* he'd committed a major faux pas. Maybe she was out of sassafras?

"My sister loved the tart cherry cider," he said in an attempt to recover. "I'd try any of it. I never get to drink soda beer. Whatever you have is fine."

"Do you have an alcohol problem?" Max asked.

"There's a lot of sugar in soda," Nate explained. "It screws with thermodynamic magicians because it makes our blood sugar spike and drop, which affects our natural energy levels."

"Huh," Max said. "So, you mostly stick with protein?"

"I'm a vegetarian."

Lizzy was now looking at him so intensely that Nate was again tempted to use that superpower.

"Uh, I'm just trying to say you guys make good beer."

Her expression relaxed, and he thought her tone might have brightened up, too. "Thank you, Prince Nathanial." She retrieved a bottle of sassafras from the fridge for him. "This is my favorite, too."

"Oh. You don't have to call me 'prince' anything," he said, grateful that he'd managed to smooth things out and taking the bottle from her. "Most people just call me Nate."

"Alright, Nate. But can I tell the other Sisters that the crown prince of South Kepler likes our beer?"

Nate opened his mouth to tell her Bast was too perfect to drink beer of any kind, but Franklin interrupted. "I'm sure

Nate doesn't care what you tell them. Is there somewhere we can talk? You probably don't want us here all night."

"I told you, Franklin." Lizzy patted his shoulder. "Agda's not here. She's out East. I'll take you to the spare rooms."

She showed them to a room with two beds. Two cats were curled up on one, but Lizzy scooped them up and tossed them to the floor. "Sorry. Raji insisted on bringing them. She says they're Carina's. When the girls came to Novi Dupree, we put Carina and Miguela in the barn for the first night to give us time to clear a room, but Carina liked the barn kittens so much Raji thought it would be better not to move the girls. They slept in the barn with three kittens snuggled up around them that whole first year."

Of course, Icy was a cat person. That explained all *kinds* of things. Cats were selfish, sneaky, narcissistic—

"Wow. That makes me feel so much better. I thought Carina was a rattycat person," Max said. "Those rodents are gross. And why couldn't I have stayed in the barn when I first came to Novi Dupree?"

"Rattycats are extremely clean and clever, given how often they get themselves caught in trees," Nate said, feeling dismayed at his bubble bursting.

"And *you* were not something Agda had time for the day you showed up," Lizzy said to Max. "But you guys can stay here tonight, and Franklin can take the room next to this one."

Myles tossed his stuff down on the second, cat-less bed. "Thanks, Liz. This will be perfect."

Lizzy sauntered to Myles, though, took his arm, and said, "Oh no, you're with me."

And *that* was when Nate's telesthesia gift kicked in. He'd

had it mostly under control all day, but one pretty woman flirting was enough to send a bunch of barely refined men into thinking all kinds of loud, uncontrolled things they didn't want anyone to hear.

Nate knew because *that* was his secret. Telepathy. Frustratingly unlimited telepathy, and not just with animals. With one exception he didn't like to think of, he could read *any* thoughts from *any* sentient living being if he tried hard enough. He mostly tried hard *not* to try, though, because (a) respect for privacy and (b) it was generally disturbing and not especially awesome to read someone else's mind. People thought all kinds of things Nate never wanted to hear.

Unfortunately, when people thought loud, he didn't even have to try—no exceptions to that rule—and Nate was constantly struggling to drown out all those thoughts attacking him. Thankfully, Franklin's mind was unusually quiet. Not surprisingly, Myles also had a quiet mind. Much more surprisingly, *Max's* thoughts were fairly quiet.

But not now.

Now, images of Icy—dressed, thank God—flashed through Max's tiny brain, and Nate *seriously* hoped he could unremember some of the memories Myles had of Lizzy. Franklin's mind was flooded with disparaging thoughts about some woman he'd screwed things up with forever ago.

And *Nate's* head was throbbing in pain.

"Ahh." Myles picked his bag back up. "Guess we can all get cleaned up and meet for dinner in a couple hours?" he said. Then he and Lizzy just left.

"That was disgusting," Max said as soon as they were gone. "Myles could have warned us he was here for his girlfriend."

Franklin picked up his bag without deigning to comment,

though, and then he left, too, thinking no one better bother him until dinner.

"See? Franklin is grossed out, too."

Nate rubbed his temples as his headache ebbed away. He didn't care if Franklin needed space, but where the hell did that leave him? Spending another night with Max?

Thankfully, he spotted a bookcase. Exactly what he needed to shut the world out after that assault. He plucked a history book from a shelf and settled down on the bed where the cats had been. Maybe they'd come back. He was a dog person, but he'd take cuddling with a kitten for comfort in a pinch. Cats were *very* defensive. They hardly ever let out a loud thought.

Max lay down on the other bed and folded his hands over his stomach. "What do you think she *sees* in that guy?"

Nate flipped open his book. "Who cares?"

"She's way out of his league. Think he's, like, a stallion in bed?"

Nate wanted to read, not talk about Myles's sexual prowess. Still. "That was an insult to stallions everywhere. That man is stiff as cardboard."

"More like concrete."

Nate snorted before remembering that he didn't like or trust Max.

"Hey, what's up with Franklin? Do you know why he wanted to talk to Lizzy? Because Myles thinks she has information about some escape pod he's looking for."

"Can you nap while I read? I'm not going to gossip with you like a girl."

Max shut up for a solid minute before he said, "What *is* the difference between how women and men gossip on Kepler?"

"Not doing this, Earthling," Nate said. But then he felt

like schooling the guy. "And South Kepler, at least, is all about gender equality. My mother is much more powerful than my father ever was."

"Are there other demographics that matter? For equality? What about race? Do you recognize race on Kepler? What race are you?"

"Uh, human?" Nate said. Except then he remembered that Max was from Earth hundreds of years ago, and he felt Max might not understand. He launched into a little lesson.

"We recognize race as a historically relevant cultural and social construct that caused massive harm on Earth, but on Kepler, we don't really even have ethnicities since we all descended from a large set of genetically diverse frozen embryos hundreds of years ago. There was a lot of effort taken to avoid artificial distinctions from one human to the next that could be used to create any kind of caste system here, so even our names were randomly generated based on a database of Earth names that was supposed to represent as many Earth cultures and ethnicities as possible. But obviously, magic differentiates us, and different people have different values. The Cardinal families sort of represented those values, so Keplerian culture today is largely based on where you–"

Nate heard a loud snore. He looked over his book. Max was dead asleep with his mouth hanging wide open.

One of the cats jumped back on Nate's bed, and Nate communicated that yes, kitty could claim ownership over his left bicep for a mid-afternoon nap. He went back to reading and wondering if he should try to break into Franklin's mind. He fell asleep a few minutes later with a cat purring in his ear.

CHAPTER TWELVE
GOOD SHOT BUDDY

Despite the warm welcome, Lizzy would barely look at Myles at dinner that night. Still, Myles was chipper, especially after a woman named Lindy introduced herself.

"Lindy's the best cook Novi Dupree ever had," Myles told them. "Try the Kepler blue grain and sweet potato hash. To die for."

"Live it up," Lizzy said tartly. "You'll never get that on Earth."

"Definitely concrete," Max whispered to Nate.

"Not appropriate," Nate hissed back. But he was appreciative of the fact that he now felt perfectly rested and that Lindy was serving a vegetarian meal. Since Franklin seemed despondent, and Lizzy was now in a bad mood, the dinner conversation was stilted, but that just meant blissful mental peace for Nate *and* great food.

When Lindy brought out cheese tarts for dessert, they smelled so good, he couldn't resist magicking one to himself. He took one bite, chewed, swallowed, and decided he needed another bite *now*. The crisp pastry dough practically melted in his mouth, and the cheese filling—savory and sweet at once—was so satisfying that Nate wondered if Lindy was somehow using magic to bake her pastries.

"This is better than anything I've ever eaten in my life," he told the chef before scarfing down the rest of the pastry in two more bites and magicking another from across the table.

Lindy preened with a glow in her eyes that made Nate think the rosy woman would make quite the fierce warrior. "I'll start making another batch right away," she said as she swept back into the kitchen.

Franklin's scar twisted on his face from behind a pint of stout. "Think you just made Lindy's day."

Nate was already eying a third cheese tart. "She just made my *year*." He slid the tray toward Franklin, feeling good about the fact that some excellent cheese tarts had prompted Franklin to speak again. "Try one. I'd flirt shamelessly with anyone for these."

Franklin declined the pastries, though, so Nate magicked it back to himself, and Max snagged a cheese tart for himself as the tray passed by.

"You look like a frat boy," Max said. "You probably flirt shamefully whenever it suits you."

Nate swallowed. "A what? And I changed my mind, Max. I would never flirt with you for anything." He gestured toward Franklin, Myles and Lizzy. "But it looks like you all got to talk. Any decisions get made?"

"Yes," Franklin said. "We have a new destination. If we can find it. But thanks to Lizzy, we at least have a clue about how to do that. And we'll get back on the road first thing tomorrow morning. You'll be happy. We're riding up the Eastern Ridge Trail."

"Are we staying here?" Max asked Myles with his mouth half-full of cheese tart.

"Actually, how fast do you think you can teach Max how to ride a horse, Nate?" Myles said.

"Excuse me?" Nate said while Max started choking.

Myles laughed and extended his arm around Lizzy, who stiffened noticeably. "The famous Sisters of Novi Dupree would never let two men take up residence permanently with them. We're all heading up the Eastern Ridge Trail."

Lizzy took a dainty sip of her beer. "But you don't have to leave immediately, Myles. Don't you want to get in touch with Foster first?"

He squeezed her shoulders merrily. "I'll send word to Gandhi for him, Lizzy. I don't have time to spare."

"You had thousands of years a few weeks ago," Lizzy said. Nate wondered if it would be worth scanning her mind to find out why she seemed so disgruntled with Myles when Myles's eyes were practically twinkling.

"Stella is *alive*, Lizzy. You know what that means to me."

Lizzy glared at her glass. "It means a woman you knew five millennia ago on Earth decided she didn't want to die after all."

Huh. Nate didn't need to take invasive measures, then. Myles was just caught in a little love triangle between Lizzy and some other woman. Anyway, the important thing was what this all meant for Nate. Which was—

Max waved his arms back and forth. "Whoa. What does Doctor Dellucci have to do with *him*—" Max pointed at Nate "—needing to teach *me* how to ride a horse?"

Myles removed his arm from Lizzy's shoulder. "Max, I had no idea until you showed up that Stella Dellucci was still alive. Now, thanks to you, I know she is, and I'm going home.

There happens to be an escape ship stored where Nate and Franklin are going."

"Which is?" Max said.

Myles took a long swig of ale. "Somewhere north of Cerulean."

Nate did not want to continue traveling with Max and Myles, but he and Max hardly had any showdowns after they hit the road again. Possibly this was because riding put Nate in a good mood and watching how much Max hated riding put him in an even better mood.

Also, Max only seemed to have two modes: (1) talk your head off with endlessly annoying questions and (2) stare silently at nothing like the world was coming to an end and no one would care that you were in it. The latter wasn't a problem, and the former at least kept Nate's mind off his real troubles. Despite what seemed to Nate like a very short attention span and poor listening skills, Max had a question about everything.

About Kepler's aboriginal intelligent life: "You mean something is living here that's as smart as us, they're everywhere, and we just can't see them?"

"As smart as me, not as smart as you," Nate said. "And they mostly live on the other side of the planet, but yeah. They're supposedly everywhere."

About magic: "How far can you throw something telekinetically? Can you magic something further than you can see?"

"Can you throw a toggleball further than you can see?" Nate said.

About toggleball: "What's toggleball?"

"Only the best field game in the universe," Nate said,

and that launched a long argument about whether toggleball was superior to football, rugby, lacrosse, soccer, volleyball, and quidditch. They did at least agree that baseball was superior to any other sport played with a ball, but Max had sorely outdated thoughts on what the best team in the universe was.

"Cardinals. Hands down," he said.

"You've never seen the Infernos play," Nate said. "Or you'd know how wrong you are."

One evening, Max asked for a demonstration of Nate's thermodynamic tendency, and Nate was so bored he decided to comply with the request. To Nate's delight, the demonstration completely freaked Max out.

"I do not like humans on Kepler," Max said as Nate tossed flames around their heads. "This is not a good step in human evolution. You are truly terrifying."

Nate reined in the fire and said, "Let me see your gun, and I'll tell you if I'm as terrifying as it." He didn't, of course, expect Max to just hand over the gun, so he magicked it out of Max's holster to himself. The gun Max carried seemed small for such a lethal device, but it was heavier than Nate expected as he turned it around to look at all its parts.

"Apparently, you're terrifying *and* stupid," Max said. "If you don't want to kill yourself, try not to *point* it at yourself. Unless … can you stop bullets like Carina?"

Nate quickly realized his mistake—give a guy a break! guns were prohibited in South Kepler!—and he set down the gun. "I have nothing in common with your icy-as-hell girlfriend. And why are you the only one ever asking questions? Where are you from?"

"St. Louis," Max said.

"What are you here for?" Nate asked.

"Surveillance. I'm reporting back to Earth on the state of human development on Kepler."

"Are we passing?"

"Questionable."

"Were you born Immortal?"

"No."

"You *chose* to be Immortal?"

"I *chose* not to die of brain cancer."

Normally, neither Franklin nor Myles paid any attention to the conversations Nate and Max had, but in this case, Franklin sat up from where he'd been lounging, and Myles set his pen down in his journal.

"Uh, sorry," Nate said. "Guess at least now you don't have to be afraid of dying."

There was a bitter quality to Max's laughter at that. "I can still die anytime. I bet I'm more afraid of dying than you. I have more to lose. Or at least I did."

"Please tell me you don't feel that way because Icy dumped you," Nate said, mindful of the whole brain cancer thing but still thinking that was pathetic. "There are so many ways your life could be worse. Aubrey dumping me was a *blip* compared to all the other ways my life sucks."

"Oh yeah, I feel really bad for you." Max made a fist and twisted it near the corner of his eyes. "Crying on the inside for your poor, doomed life as a Mortal king." He dropped his hand. "Carina dumped me because I lied to her about being Immortal. I have to live with that for eternity."

The thought of being in love with a girl like Icy made Nate want to put on a sweater. "You need a rebound girl," he said. But Max just shook his head and lay down to sleep.

Thankfully, it only took about a week to reach the outskirts of Cerulean, where they made a stop at The Rusty Rail, a dingy, crowded bar situated so close to railroad tracks that all the pictures hanging inside—all of supposedly famous people who'd probably never frequented the bar—were crooked. Inside, Franklin and Myles said hello to a rough-hewn bartender who was missing an eye, told Nate and Max not to get into trouble, then disappeared into a backroom.

By now, Nate was used to being left alone with Max, and he was still a little suspicious of the Earthling's motives, but he no longer viewed Max as a threat. When Max wasn't asking questions about Kepler, he mostly just seemed depressed.

Nate truly didn't understand being depressed over a breakup for more than a couple days. He did, however, understand being depressed over feeling like no one in the universe cared about you. And Nate was starting to realize that Max was even more alone on Kepler than he was. So, Nate refrained from being an ass and tried to cope with the headache he was getting from all the loud, drunken thoughts swimming through that bar. He didn't quite catch it when Max said:

"Want to play darts?"

"What?" Nate said.

Max pointed at a dartboard in a darkish corner of the bar. "Darts," he repeated. "Want to play? Bet you an order of fries, I'll win."

Nate didn't know a lot about darts, but he knew the basic premise. Since he needed a distraction and he was quite sure Max had poor judgment (he'd been dating Ice Witch), he accepted the bet immediately.

"I will own you, Earthling," Nate bragged confidently as they walked over to the dartboard. The confidence, he felt, could only help his game.

Max picked up a set of darts from a table near the board and handed them to Nate. "Let's see what you've got, Pretty Boy."

That was a cheap insult. Bast was a pretty boy. Nate was rugged and manly. He puffed his chest up in a rugged, manly way, stepped to the line, and threw the first dart.

"Ten segment," Max said. "Is that the best you've got?"

Nate was disappointed in his performance. That had not been a good throw. It had felt all wrong. He could do better. He threw his second dart. It landed in the triple ring of the one segment.

"Tough luck. That's three more points," the obnoxious alien said. "You're not doing very well."

That comment bugged Nate, so he concentrated hard before he threw the third dart. It landed just inside the outer part of the bullseye. "Ha!" he shouted. "I ruled that!"

"Good job, Your Highness," Max said mildly. "Thirty-eight points."

Nate sauntered to the side, ignoring Max's taunt, and took a long, celebratory swig of coke while his opponent pulled the darts from the board and stepped back to the line.

Max's first throw was a bullseye in the outer part, just like the last one Nate had thrown. Max frowned, and Nate was about to say, "lucky shot," but Max had already thrown the second dart. It landed in the inner part of the bullseye.

"You owe me a plate of fries, Wellington," Max said as he threw the third dart and it, too, hit the bullseye. Dead center.

Nate's coke tasted bad. "That was ..."

Max grinned at him. "Want to raise the stakes and play best of three?"

There were a lot of things you got that stunk when you were the family screw-up. A misplaced sense of pride was not one of them. "No," Nate said.

Max pulled the darts out of the board. "Want to play again anyway? No bets?"

Nate took the darts back. They played for over an hour.

Kozlov never missed.

Not once. And by "not missed," Nate meant that after that first throw, Max never hit anything but the inner bullseye again, except when he was aiming at the triple ring for the twenty, which he could also hit consistently.

Nate missed the whole board at least once in every ten throws, and he hit the bullseye about the same amount. When he was tired of not improving, he decided it was time for those fries.

"How do you do that without magic?" he asked Max over an enormous, triple serving of fries that they were already halfway through.

Max snagged some fries. "I spent over a thousand years on a spaceship before I got here. The last fifty years, I was all by myself. There are only so many times you can read *Game of Thrones*."

Nate dunked three fries into catchy sauce. "So, you perfected your dart game in your lonely time?"

"Not just darts," Max said, making a face like he was totally grossed out by catchy sauce. He hadn't dipped a single fry in the sauce himself. "I basically have perfect aim with every weapon you can throw or shoot."

"That's ..." Nate struggled for the right words.

"Terrible, I know," Max said. "Because you Mortals here think that anyone who can defend himself with a gun is a monster."

Nate swirled four more fries in catchy. "I was trying for something more like 'frickin' awesome.'"

"Really?" Max asked. "Aren't you supposed to be the only leader left on the planet? Shouldn't you be defending the Mortal Commitments? There must be a Mortal Commitment never to perfect any form of combat."

Nate probably could have come up with five or six of the Mortal Commitments if he had to. He did not have the others memorized. Why would he have bothered? He'd never gone a day when there wasn't someone around who could have recited the whole lot for him.

"Alien, have you not noticed yet that I am a Mortal reject?" Nate held up his glass of coke and looked through it. His glass was far less than half full. "And I support several forms of combat. I would own you in a sword fight."

Max looked skeptically at him.

"What, have you perfected that too?" Nate asked. "Because I gotta tell you, that is one thing I am legitimately good at."

"We need refills," Max said. "And I know how to sword fight, but I haven't done it with anyone in about four-hundred years. It's hard to practice in a simulator because the whole skill depends on anticipating what a live person will do, and live people are irrational."

"Then I would destroy you," Nate said. "Because I am great at anticipating what a live person would do in a sword fight. Gifted even."

Max was still looking at him with doubt.

"What?" Nate said. "I am."

"I think you're going to be the next King of South Kepler."

Nate returned that doubtful look. "I told you. It doesn't matter where I am in line. No one really wants me in South Kepler. I will never be king." He drained the rest of his coke. "I don't even want to be a prince."

Max took the last fry. "But you are one. And I think in a few years you're going to return home, take back your kingdom, and become the next king of South Kepler."

Nate peered into his empty glass. "You need to get to know me better."

Max drained the rest of his coke, too. "Okay. Let's be friends."

"You want to be friends?" Nate said incredulously. "You *shot* me."

Max set his coke down with a clunk. "Well, yeah. I never *miss*. I could easily have killed you. I chose to neutralize you instead."

"Why?" Nate asked. "I thought you were protecting your girlfriend."

"I don't know," Max said. "It didn't feel like I should. So maybe God thinks you need someone to teach you how to play darts."

Nate considered that. He'd never had a male friend his own age. He'd had girlfriends. He'd had Bast. But otherwise …

Max was looking at the empty plate in front of them like he was waiting for rejection. Which is how Nate felt all the time. And he questioned Max's judgment, but he clearly could not question the man's dart-throwing prowess.

Nate picked up the menu. He was still hungry.

"So?" Max asked.

"So maybe God thinks you need someone to teach you how to sword fight. I'm ordering more fries. Want some?"

"Yeah. But do you know what the word for real ketchup is here? Catchy is disgusting."

"What's 'ketchup' made of?"

"Tomatoes and sugar."

"Then, no. There are no tomatoes on Kepler."

Max hung his head. "I'm in hell."

Franklin and Myles returned from their meeting shortly thereafter.

"Great news," Franklin said. "We have a ferry to catch tomorrow. We're almost there."

Nate still thought he shouldn't pry into Franklin's thoughts. "And there is …?"

Franklin chuckled, while Myles snickered, and it was the kind of thing that made Nate feel like there was a serious conspiracy going on.

"All the secrecy isn't that funny," Max said to them, and to Nate, he said, "If you want, we could ditch these guys, take the horses, and head off on our own."

"You hate the horses," Nate said.

"But think about it," Max said. "We could be outlaws. One ex-prince with fire magic. One weird Immortal with a gun. Totally untouchable."

"I am regretting my decision to be friends with you already," Nate told Max, and to Franklin he said, "You better not make me regret following you onto some ferry to nowhere."

"Nate, would I ever take you somewhere I didn't think was safe?" Franklin said, that grin stretching his scar so grotesquely that Nate had to work not to shudder.

"Untouchable," Max said. "Think about it."

Myles showed up at my door last night with Franklin Wellington, as if those were the two men anyone around here wanted to see right now.

It was lucky for Franklin that Agda is out East. She was livid when Raji and I caught up with her. As I recall, her exact words were, "that irresponsible, reckless, foolish, son-of-an-effing-Southerner ran into the girls and let them go. He knew how much danger they were in!"

I pointed out that the warrant for Franklin's arrest might not have made him the safest person to travel with, but she only scoffed at that. Agda doesn't think a measly little warrant is a real threat to Franklin. I forget, sometimes, that Agda and Franklin were wild and unstoppable together, and what ended them happened between them, not to them.

Agda is both furious with Franklin and completely convinced that two girls she cares very much about would have been perfectly safe with him, and this tells me she will never love anyone else.

No matter how much pain that brings her.

In any case, when she and Raji get back from the East, I'll have to explain to her that Franklin is currently busy with another complication. He has in his care the crown prince of South Kepler. That's why he came here. He is convinced that if he returns Prince Nathanial to South Kepler now, the boy will be dead in a few months. Franklin needs a refuge for a future king. He thought we might know how to get there.

I told him what I knew, and I hope it was not a mistake. My thoughts were muddled by the surprise of learning that Myles is going home. Home home. To Earth. Because Stella Dellucci is alive after all. The woman who broke Myles's heart. Now all he can think about are the escape ships we entrusted to the four Cardinal families to hide hundreds of years ago. He thinks he can find one on Aurora Borealis Isle.

Somewhere deep down, I do hope he succeeds. But if he does, that will be my closest friend—the only person on this planet who still knows what hurts my heart the most—gone from me forever.

This is all the newbie's fault. Max Kozlov, who I am suspicious of. He says he is here for "observation." But why is he alone? What is he observing? I have a bad gut feeling about Max's arrival, and once upon a time, someone I loved taught me not to ignore my own intuition.

Intuition, the magic we humans always had, even before we arrived on Kepler. I hope I am wrong.

CHAPTER THIRTEEN
ONE HELL OF A DATE

"*O*ne does not simply *walk* out of Fort Aurora Borealis," is what Eugene told Carina as she waited with Mishe and a team of guards to board a horse-drawn shuttle cart. It would take half an hour to get from the fort to a dock, then the ferry to Cerulean would take three hours, then there would be "special" transportation to the prison itself.

"*Lord of the Rings*," Eugene said. "Have you ever seen it? It's one of Dad's favorites."

"No." Carina wondered why Eugene had decided to hang out with her this morning when he'd been so jealous of this field trip. But she nudged his shoulder. "Hey, is there anything you want me to bring back for you?"

He didn't answer, just stared forward into space at something.

"Eugene?"

He shook his head like he'd been startled, then said, "Did you read that article in the *Times* this morning? Some old lady in Hypatia thinks she rented a room to Prince Nathanial a week or so ago. Said he was with some wanted criminal."

"The prince is dead," Carina said.

"Are you sure? They never found his body."

The shuttle cart pulled up, and she watched Mishe hop up to conduct a security scan (because *maybe* someone had hijacked the cart between the dock and here).

"He wouldn't be the first Cardinal to survive a Miguela meltdown."

Carina frowned at Eugene. "That was an insensitive thing to say."

He frowned back. "What? That they never found a body? But they didn't. That's just factual. And we know it *is* possible for someone who tends hot to create a defensive telekinetic shield. Dad did it injured."

"Dad was an adult and creating a defensive telekinetic shield knocked him out for days," Carina said. "People who tend hot aren't good with defensive telekinetic shields. There is no way Prince Nathanial was powerful enough to do it."

Eugene shrugged. "Maybe people underestimate him."

Mishe emerged from the shuttle. "Cleared!" he announced.

"Maybe not," Carina said, and then she boarded the shuttle cart and the guards filled in all around, avoiding the empty seat next to her. She slouched and looked out the window. At least today, she didn't look like a princess. More like a stuck-up rich girl. She was wearing designer jeans, a Keplerworm silk blouse, a navy blue cashmeresque sweater, and a long gray coat from an expensive New Paris boutique.

She'd added a knitted scarf Sister Elizabeth made her because she needed to feel normal somehow, though, and she'd gotten away without hairspray-helmet head. Instead, the attendants had blown her hair into perfect, soft, bouncy curls.

That had been a win-win. They were pleased that the princess had an actual hairdo request, and Carina felt she would have more power when she talked to Heathrow about Royal Society matters if she was having a great hair day. Miguela, who'd sat in Carina's dressing room while she got ready, questioned this logic, but gushed over Carina's hair, which she said looked "so amazing," and added, "What's important is that you feel confident."

Carina thought everyone had boarded the shuttle, and then, at the very last minute, a girl who looked to be about her age ran up to the cart and boarded with a few bouncy leaps. She was wearing a long coat like Carina's and combat boots. Her auburn hair was pulled into the kind of messy ponytail Carina had worn hers in back when she'd slept too late at Novi Dupree. She had freckled skin like she'd just come from somewhere sunny, and she did something no stranger had done in months as soon as she got on the shuttle. She looked directly at Carina, grinned like she was genuinely excited about something, and plunked right down next to Carina.

"Hey," the girl said breathlessly. "Were you waiting a long time?"

"For … you?" Carina said.

The girl's grin widened. "Obviously."

Mishe smacked his palm against his forehead, then turned from where he was sitting in front of Carina.

"Princess Carina meet Olivette Hutzler. She's your new—"

"Mishe!" Olivette said while the shuttle started moving. "No one calls me Olivette. It's Ollie. And *I* get to be the one to explain it to her." She leaned toward Carina. "But first, tell me about Heathrow Princeton. Is he cute? I've heard he's nerdy. Did you read his book?"

"Parts of it?" Carina said, wondering exactly how a

tornado like this had been allowed into a world that was otherwise being so carefully crafted world around her.

Ollie laughed like Carina was hysterical. "As in, you read the introduction so you could act smart around a certified genius?"

Then, Carina completely forgot the shuttle wasn't well-heated as Ollie began to chat merrily about the profile picture at the end of Heathrow's book ("He's not that pompous in real life, right?"), the board game selection at the lodge ("Do you know any of those games?"), and her combat boots ("Yours are more fashionable, but these are off-road boots.").

By the time they got to the ferry, Mishe looked like he wanted to die, but Ollie boarded the ferry with Carina like she hadn't noticed. The captain of the ship, a salty old seadog with a beard and oddly hypnotic eyes, bowed to them both, and said, "Yer Grace" to Carina. Then Mishe directed Carina and Ollie to a cabin on the upper deck that was reserved for the royal family and their guests while the other guards spread out around the ship.

It was not an inconspicuous rig. They could have driven the shuttle cart right up onto it, and it hardly seemed to be sloshing around in the harsh currents of the Strait of Cerulean at all. Carina watched from the window of the cabin as the magicians who powered the ferry stood on special posts, coordinating their magic like oarsmen and forcing the ferry to plow away from the dock.

"They're *so* showing off for you," Ollie said, earning another annoyed look from Mishe.

"They shouldn't be," Carina said. "I can't do what they're doing."

"You just need the right teacher," Ollie said.

Carina sat down on a plush cushion. "Does that mean

you know about Hess?"

Ollie sat down, too, right next to her again. "Your last teacher? I hear that guy is lucky you didn't kill him."

Mishe snorted from where he was standing in the doorway.

"See?" Ollie said. "Mishe agrees."

"I do," Mishe said, and in a rare show of humanity, *he* made eye contact with Carina, and it looked like maybe he was kind of proud of her.

"Thanks," Carina said.

Mishe nodded. "If Princeton gets inappropriate, you can handle *him* exactly the same way."

"Uh, right," Carina said while Ollie snickered.

"If Princeton gets 'inappropriate,'" she repeated under her breath. "Priceless."

Mishe left Carina and Ollie alone for a few minutes after that to check in with the other guards. As soon as he was gone, Ollie turned her way and said, "I don't know how you've been dealing with him. Have you noticed he's the only guard who always wears the full uniform? Everyone else takes it casual some way."

Carina laughed. She *had* noticed, but there had been no one to gossip with about it before.

Ollie grabbed her gloved hand and squeezed. "I *knew* we'd be friends," she said. "You wouldn't believe the training they made me do first. I had no idea there were so many royal protocols."

"Are you some kind of special guard?" Carina asked.

"I'm your courtier," Ollie explained. "Basically, they give me a room, board, and an allowance to hang out with you."

Carina's heart sank. "You're a paid friend."

Ollie shook her head. "I'm a glorified personal assistant who doesn't do admin. Your second pair of ears, eyes, and hands. Friendship is optional. But we *are* going to be friends. Sister Elizabeth has been telling me stories about you for years."

"You know Sister Elizabeth?"

"I'm her niece. You didn't think the Sisters would leave you alone up here, did you?" Ollie stood—Carina thought maybe she was the kind of person who was always in motion except when she was sleeping—and started opening cabinets under the benches. "Hey, do you think they have snacks on this thing? Maybe they have Novi Dupree beer. I love the apple ale."

"We're definitely going to be friends," Carina said.

Cerulean's skyline was lined with factories that puffed steam into the air and squat apartment buildings sandwiched between. As far as Carina knew, the whole city ran on wave power collected from the steadily churning currents of the strait, and the only other thing Cerulean was known for was chowder. But the docks smelled excessively fishy, and she noticed what seemed like a high level of debris floating in the water as she disembarked from the ferry.

Heathrow was waiting at the dock. He said, "hello, Princess Carina," bowed slightly, then shook Mishe's hand and proceeded to answer question after question about security procedures.

Had Heathrow talked to anyone other than Doctor McIntosh and Doctor Friedman about this trip? No. Had he noticed anything or anyone who seemed suspicious on his way here? No. Did he see anyone following him? No. Did he understand that if he was at any point found to have any intent to harm the princess in any way, he would be charged with and tried for treason, the punishment for which was death?

"Good grief," Ollie muttered to Carina.

"Yeah," Carina muttered back.

But Heathrow took it all with ease, then Mishe, Ollie, Heathrow, and Carina walked to a nearby tram stop, where, somehow, Carina's team had managed to secure a completely empty auto-tram.

Carina stood at one end of the tram near Heathrow while Ollie dragged Mishe to the other end and started peppering Mishe with questions about Carina's security detail. The tram jerked to a start, throwing Carina's balance off and tossing her directly at Heathrow, who steadied her with a hand until she found her balance again. She noticed there was graffiti on the windows of the tram car, then she saw a kid riding a bike near the tracks toss a paper cup at a trash can and miss.

"Polluter," Heathrow said scornfully. "I grew up in New Paris. Still haven't gotten used to Cerulean. They say this place was the perfect, clean, efficient Northern city before the attacks, but the last few years …"

"Oh," Carina said, feeling weirdly guilty about that kid's paper cup. One more problem her family caused by sitting around doing nothing. "That's too bad."

But Heathrow shifted and smiled at her then. "You know, with any other girl, we could have spent the day checking out the docks and getting curry at the best Indian restaurant in town."

"No curry, then?" Carina said woefully, thinking *that* was a damn shame.

"Don't worry. I negotiated to have your guards get it for us while we're at the prison. Our curry will be waiting when we get back to my place." He tugged at the scarf around his neck. "I, uh, hope you don't mind going there. I thought you'd like to see Cerulean Technological Institute, and my dorm is small, but it seemed like as good a place as any to debrief."

She examined his face. Was he telling her he'd set this up so they could go somewhere private after their field trip?

"I would like to see it," she told him.

There was a pleased glint in his eyes. "Really? Because after I saw you last, I thought I might have misinterpreted some things."

"The meeting with Doctor McIntosh didn't exactly go the way I wanted it to," she admitted.

Heathrow winced. "I know. I tried to talk to Friedman about it later. They shouldn't have dismissed all your concerns like that."

Annoyance pecked at her. "I don't need you to speak for me, though," she said, wondering how he would take that. Maybe he thought his genius entitled him to speak whenever.

But to her relief, Heathrow only gave her a small, apologetic shrug. "Chivalry doesn't belong in a Royal Society meeting, does it?"

"I need Friedman and the others to talk to me directly. Not through you." She blushed. "Even when I don't understand what they're talking about."

"Maybe *especially* when you don't understand," he suggested. "We were getting into some obscure details at that meeting. But you do want to see the prison today, right? That wasn't just my idea that you got stuck with?"

It wasn't. Or maybe it was his idea, but she wanted to do this. She needed to understand why her kingdom was keeping Immortals in prison without charging them for anything.

"No," she told him. "I do care about this. I don't understand how it's okay to keep someone locked up just for being Immortal. Feels like something South Kepler would do.

Commitment seven, right? We seek the highest standard of living for all humans, not just Immortals."

Sister Rachel would have been proud of her for that. She'd read the entire commentary on Commitment Seven in advance of this trip.

Heathrow looked out the window, and a shadow hid his eyes. She remembered that he thought this trip might make her more comfortable with the Immortal imprisonment.

"Do you interpret Commitment Seven in some other way?" she asked, wondering if maybe she'd missed something. After all, if anyone might have done more research on this than her, it was Heathrow Princeton.

"I just … hope you're not unhappy with what you see today." The tram came to a stop, and the doors opened. "But I'll let you decide for yourself what you think."

The Immortals were being housed in a building that looked like a rundown warehouse. The warden, a man with saggy jowls and a very red nose, bowed stiffly to Carina, then led her, Heathrow, Ollie, and Mishe down a hallway toward a barred door. Carina was struck by how dimly lit and poorly ventilated the place was.

And cold. Unless that was her.

"Are you warm enough?" she asked Heathrow, remembering that he tended hot.

"No," he said. "It's drafty in here."

Not just her, then.

They turned a few corners before the warden unlocked a door that led to a narrow hallway with several cells. The eleven captive Immortals were housed two to a cell, except for one cell that was hosting three prisoners. Carina didn't think they knew who she was, and the Immortals behind those bars gave no indication one way or another. They simply watched as she walked by, stopping to look in each cell as she went. No one—not Heathrow, Ollie, Mishe, the warden, or anyone in those cells—spoke as she made her observations.

It was unsettling. Carina had, at some point, thought of all Immortals as the enemy. They were monsters. The Red-Eyed Ones. But she'd learned a lot since then, and she no longer thought Immortals were all that special. They had handicaps, like perpetually irritated red eyes and an inability to properly empathize with other humans. They had guns, though that supply, she'd recently learned, was limited. But they couldn't do magic. They didn't have super-human abilities. The difference between her and the humans behind those bars was that they'd caught a bad virus, while she'd been born with the ability to move stuff with her mind.

She was the dangerous one. They were only brain damaged.

Brain damaged and miserable. The prisoners were wearing ragged uniforms that weren't nearly thick enough for the cold of this building. She saw a man who seemed especially haggard put his hands under his thighs, and it made her shiver. The warden's uniform included a jacket and gloves. Carina couldn't even see blankets in those cells.

She asked to see a cell from the inside, so the warden took her to an empty cell at the end of the hall. There were two narrow metal cots with thin, plastic mattresses inside. A single toilet. A metal sink. One tiny window that no more than one person could have looked out of at a time.

"I need to see the rest of the facility," she said to the warden.

"It's not a large facility," he said like he was reluctant to take her anywhere, and she saw Heathrow open his mouth, then glance at her and shut it.

"Then it won't take long to show me the rest," Carina said. She made the warden walk her through a recreation room with nothing but a few tables and some shoddy gym equipment, a filthy cafeteria where a Kepler roach crawled right across the floor in front of them, and a partly flooded bathroom with dirty toilets and showers with stalls but not curtains.

She asked to see the linens, and the warden laughed.

"You want to see the towels?"

"Also, the extra sheets and blankets, please," she said, and she was not impressed with what he showed her. As she stood looking at a sheet that was stained beyond the help of bleach, she imagined Sister Lindy throwing a fit. And Sister Agda …

Actually, Carina thought maybe this would be a good time to channel Sister Agda. She turned to the warden and faced him head-on. "What is the heat set to?"

"Sixty-two."

"Sixty-two? That's not heating. That's … aggressive air-conditioning. Are there extra blankets we can provide the prisoners?" A bad thought occurred to her as she looked again at that disgusting sheet. "Is there hot water here?"

The warden's face was so dull that Carina doubted she'd ever see any emotion on it, but he did have the decency to put the slightest bit of concern into his voice when he answered that question. "This facility houses Immortals, Your Grace," he said. "There's no need to waste further resources on them."

This was all about *resource management?* Where had she heard *that* before?

"Is there anything else you want to see?" Heathrow asked with a tight voice. "If not, I think we should probably go."

She looked his way and realized he'd turned the collar

of his coat up and placed his gloved hands in his pockets. So had Ollie, and Carina could see Mishe's breath in the air. The warden wiped his nose with his sleeve. Carina didn't blame them. She was cold enough that her insides felt shaky and her skin felt stiff.

Oh. This was *her*. She was making it *much* colder than 62 degrees.

But she sucked in a breath and tried to replicate exactly the way Sister Agda would have finished this terrible trip. "Turn the heat up to at least 72," she told the warden. "Make sure the water heater is on. And please plan to send me a full report on the health of the prisoners later in the week. I'll want to know what medical aid they have access to, what their nutrition is like." And what else? There was *so* much wrong here she knew she was missing things. She tried to make herself sound royally confident anyway. "And ... I'll see what I can do about ... reallocating resources here. No researcher meets with these inmates until we fix this situation. Is ... is that clear?"

The warden bobbed his head promptly. "Yes, Your Grace."

Then Carina turned and led her group out of the building, feeling like she needed to exit as quickly as possible. How was this stuff happening in the North? Weren't they supposed to be *better* than the South?

Ollie caught up to her at the exit and grabbed her arm. "Hey, I know that was bad, and I don't mean this as a criticism, but you need to calm down before we leave."

Carina's vision felt gray. Heathrow took her other arm and began rubbing it. "She's right," he said. "You're frosting over the walls. We can't go anywhere like this. It will give away your identity."

A sense of helplessness that Carina couldn't fight down

hit her. She couldn't fix *any* of this. She couldn't even stop herself from making it worse.

Mishe paced back and forth in the hallway, his breath still visible. "We'll have to return you to the ferry, I think, Princess. It's too risky for you to be anywhere else right now."

Carina's heart sank. So much for Indian food and that tour of the Cerulean Institute of Technology. "I'm sorry," she said to Heathrow.

"*I'm* sorry," he said. "I had no idea things were this bad for the prisoners. And I wish I had a stronger thermodynamic tendency. Someone with real power could reverse cold like this."

"Yeah," she said, wishing Miguela were with her. "And I don't think I could eat curry right now anyway."

Heathrow kissed her cheek, and it left a hint of warmth there. "Next time, Princess Carina. But maybe get some hot tea on the ferry. Something to warm you up from the inside."

CHAPTER FOURTEEN
KINGDOM OF THE DEAD

Carina felt her trip to Cerulean had already gone as poorly as possible, so when Mishe suggested that she and Ollie ride out the three-hour ferry back to Aurora Borealis in a secluded cabin on the middle deck, she declined.

"The captain says there are four non-militia passengers on board," he told her. "They're below deck for now, but—"

"Are they threats?" she asked. "I thought everyone who knew about this ferry was supposed to have at least blue level security clearance."

Mishe frowned. "They knew the code words and where to find us. Which means someone we trust told them about Aurora Borealis. And they surrendered their weapons at the dock and submitted to pat-down searches. They say they're seeking asylum and want to speak to the king."

Carina was tired; that's what she later told herself about the mistake she made next.

"Mishe, no one would take a ferry from Cerulean to seek asylum on Aurora Borealis unless they *really* needed help.

They're unarmed, outnumbered, and below deck."

Mishe could wiggle his nose, and apparently, he did it when he was anxious. In this case, he wiggled his nose and said, "They could have magic, Your Grace."

"Mishe, she had a lousy day," Ollie said. "And it's not like she'll be alone. I'll be with her."

Mishe relented and allowed Carina and Ollie to return to the upper deck cabin, and he left to speak to the captain about the passengers. As soon as they were alone, Ollie yawned and said, "That was exhausting. I need a nap," and she promptly lay down on one of the cushioned benches and fell asleep.

Courtier clearly did not equate to bodyguard.

Carina could not have slept if she tried. She was too distraught by the prison tour. She decided she needed fresh air, and it didn't occur to her that it would be a problem to walk out onto the upper deck, where she would only be a few meters away from Ollie. She made her way to the railing, then stood watching the crew shepherding the ferry through the water with their amazing, synchronized, invisible magic.

"I will never be able to do what they're doing," she mused out loud, but, she thought, to herself.

"Oh, you can do much more than that."

She had not expected a response. She turned, and a man was approaching from the stairs to the upper deck. Relief washed over Carina. If this was one of the four passengers Mishe was worried about, then they had nothing to worry about. She knew this man, even if she was surprised to see him here.

"Leo? What are you doing here?"

A gentle smile spread across Leo's face, and he bobbed his head in a slight bow. "Perhaps we could use a more formal introduction, Princess."

He knew who she was. She'd wondered about that before. Now she had a million questions, starting with, "How long have you known who I am?" and ending with "How long have you known Agda Talon?" The first "how" was forming on her lips as someone who shouldn't have been alive came barreling toward them from the stairs.

And *this* was not a friend.

This was a guy who'd tried to separate her from her sister. Who'd threatened to kill her at least once. Who had the most irritating accent on the planet.

"Franklin! Get away from her!" Prince Nathanial said, practically throwing himself in front of Leo at the same time Mishe came running up the stairs after him, holding out a sword Carina hardly ever registered Mishe carrying and followed by two additional guards.

Prince Nathanial jerked his hand through the air, knocking the two guards behind Mishe to the deck with telekinetic magic. Carina's heart pounded in her ears. Leo smacked his forehead and said, "Nate!" while Mishe raised his sword. Then before Carina could think to do anything to protect Mishe, that sword was out of his hands and in Prince Nathanial's hands, and Leo was shouting, "Drop the damned sword, Nate!" while Mishe yelled, "Support!"

Carina was frozen in the middle of the whole nightmare. Prince Nathanial was stronger than her, better at magic, and armed with a sword. She was cornered, and her throat was trying to swallow her heart while the deck iced over below her feet.

Ollie appeared from the cabin. "What's going on?" she said as yet another unwanted threat emerged from the stairs and stopped dead in his tracks as soon as he saw Carina.

"Carina? I didn't think I'd ever see you again!"

What was Carina's Immortal ex-boyfriend doing here? And side note: Max had looked much better with short curly hair. The long mop sprouting from his head did nothing for him as he bolted toward her, then slipped on the ice.

"Max! No! I told you, she's *dangerous!*" Prince Nathanial yelled, and he sent Max scooting magically away from Carina on the ice. The prince's unkempt blond hair seemed even greasier than before.

"Nate!" Leo bellowed. "The princess is *not* our enemy!"

Prince Nathanial's dull, mean eyes got big enough for her to see that they were not just the color of mud. They were more like the color of the debris she'd seen floating around the docks earlier. His irises meeting hers reminded her of wet, muddy, ocean trash.

"Drop the sword, Nate," Leo said through gritted teeth.

The prince shifted those dirty eyes toward Leo, and all at once, the tension in the air seemed to dissipate like a tea kettle taken off a burner. Slowly, slowly, Prince Nathanial turned the sword and handed it back to Mishe with a mumbled, "Sorry about that. I, um—" he glanced at her "—it's hard to explain."

Mishe took the sword and turned to Carina like he wasn't sure what to do next, and she realized she now had to make an awkward call. As much as she hated him, it probably wouldn't look good for the crown princess of North Kepler to greet the crown prince of South Kepler with a "lock him up" order. And was he dangerous with Leo's hand very firmly placed on his shoulder? The prince looked almost contrite.

Carina felt a little out of body when she decided she'd better do the diplomatic thing and said, "Mishe, this is Prince Nathanial. The, uh, crown prince of South Kepler."

"Very sorry," Leo added for Mishe. "I can assure you we

are *not* a threat. But it *is* time for a proper introduction."

He sighed before looking at Carina again, and she thought his eyes seemed fatigued right now. "Princess Carina, my full name is Lord Franklin Leonardo Wellington. For the time being, I am Prince Nathanial's guardian. We're seeking asylum with the North until the prince is old enough to assume the Southern crown."

Max whimpered something that sounded like, "She's a princess," while Prince Nathanial stared at her with an indignant and self-righteous glower that made her feel chagrined about being royal in front of him. So, he needed a place to *hide? Long term?* On Aurora Borealis Isle? That was not going to work for her. She wanted to tell Mishe to turn the ferry around and leave the prince in Cerulean.

Except she couldn't forget Queen Vivian. The queen had never hurt Carina. She'd only asked for help, and Carina had failed to give it. Now Vivian was dead, but her final words still echoed in Carina's mind. *Give him a chance.* One half of a dying girl's final request. Nothing nearly as complicated as, "Tell him I loved him best if he needs to know." Just, "Give him a chance. Because he doesn't need any more enemies."

Okay, then. She had to try. It was the honorable thing to do. Therefore, Carina said the *only* non-hostile thing she could think to say to the prince.

A peace offering of sorts.

"You're supposed to be dead."

His thin lips—clearly evil—twisted into nasty, near-hysterical laughter. "Right back at you, sweetheart," he said.

And Max said, "You're *alive*," and leaped forward at her again.

Nate was not doing this. This was *enemy territory.* He was the crown prince of the Southern Kingdom of Kepler. This place was the secret hideaway of the king of North Kepler. The Northern Royals had every reason to believe that Nate's own family had *hired* the Immortals that *attacked and tried to kill them.* His dad, King Herschel, had always said that wasn't true. But for all Nate knew, his mother actually *had* orchestrated that whole thing. He'd never been brave enough to dig through her mind for evidence, but he wouldn't have put it past her.

There was no *way* Nate and Franklin were welcome here.

"*This* is where we've been trying to get for months?" Nate said to Franklin as they stepped off a grimy shuttle cart into a blast of freezing cold air, then walked into a place that looked more like an Earth-like Scandinavian bungalow than a royal residence. "We are *vulnerable* here. You might as well have walked us onto the Immortal Empire's island."

Franklin rolled his eyes. "I already explained this to you on the ferry. This is not the enemy. The Northern Royals are our closest allies. And they know how to play dead better than any Mortals we know. You need their help."

"I don't need their *help,*" Nate said. He especially didn't need help from the crown princess of the North, who was currently having an indecipherable conversation with a guard.

The only good thing Nate could say about the princess is that at least someone had managed to find her decent clothes. The last time he'd seen her, she'd been wearing ripped jeans and a dirty t-shirt. Today, he was the one in cheap jeans and a worn shirt, while she was wearing a designer coat Bast might have approved of. That long tangly mane of hair still needed work, though, and were her arms perpetually crossed?

So defensive, that one.

"She's alive," Max whispered behind him.

Oh, God. There was another problem. How many times could Nate save his new buddy's ass before Princess Carina decided just to kill Max straight-up? What would her tolerance for her ex be? A day? A week? An hour? What would happen when Nate wasn't available to magic Max out of harm's way?

"The girl of my dreams is alive," Max whispered again, as they both watched Carina, obviously through vastly different lenses. Max didn't seem capable of understanding how lethal the "girl of his dreams" was.

Carina glanced back at them right then, her eyebrows arched evilly while her gaze shifted between Nate and Max. Those icy daggers of death in her abnormally gargantuan brown eyes were for both of them. Nate knew in his heart of hearts that if Ice Princess went berserk, he and Max would be her first targets. But he would at least stand a chance against her. Max would just be toast.

"I'm going to talk to her," Max said, taking a step forward before Myles caught him by the collar and yanked him back.

"Max, I would highly advise that you stay quiet for as much of this as possible," Myles said. Nate agreed and thought Myles mostly had pretty sound advice. Max needed to zip it if he wanted to get back on that ferry in anything other than a body bag.

The guard walked with Carina back toward them, and Nate actually felt embarrassed for Max as he beamed all lovesick-goofy at her. Nate didn't get it. This was his worst nightmare. Well, maybe it was his fourth-to-worst nightmare after Bast killing him, his mother killing Franklin, and Hildebrand and/or Godric killing Bast. He was going to have to be *civil* with the Ice Witch. At least until she tried to kill him. And that was going to happen any second, Nate thought, as Princess Carina opened her mouth and he waited for the scream of a siren. Her mouth was almost as gargantuan as her eyes. That was a *big* mouth. Nate braced for death.

But all that came out were a few words. "My father is on his way." She stood there, then, making everyone uneasy.

Also, it was way too toasty inside for Nate's tastes. The frigid air outside had felt great. Maybe he could go stand there while they waited for the king.

"Would you … like coffee?" she added awkwardly. "Or hot cocoa? While we wait? I could … um … get you some?"

His eyes darted back to her. What was this? Was *she* trying to be civil? But she was looking at the unimpressive floor while she talked, so maybe she wanted this to end as much as he did.

"No, thank you," Franklin said while Max said, "Sure!" enthusiastically, and Myles ignored the question. Nate had noticed that Myles was sort of in that habit. The habit of pretending that conversation wasn't directed at him.

"Mr. Kayes?" Carina asked. "Coffee?"

Myles paused, then answered, "Uh, no, thanks," like he'd needed time to process the whole question.

Carina looked at Nate again. Was that *fear* shining in those buggy orbs? He couldn't probe her mind to confirm—she was the only person he'd ever known who could feel it when he tried to mentally invade—but he knew what fear looked like. Knew because this was a look Bast frequently inspired. She was *afraid* of him. And it wasn't as awesome as he'd have thought.

"Prince Nathanial? Do you want …? "

"Coffee?" he heard himself say with a sneer, because he was getting progressively annoyed at her cowardice now. What kind of useful enemy feared you?

"Yes, *coffee*," she said, thankfully with a little back attitude. Good. He couldn't control this situation if she was going to be wussy about it. He needed her to react to him with exactly the same level of anger and irritation he felt toward her; otherwise, it was going to be hard to sustain. He wasn't Bast, after all.

But he was still capable of being a manipulative, Machiavellian Southern Royal. Then it hit him. He needed her to hate him, not fear him. Hate would give her a reason to convince her family not to let him and Franklin stay here. And he'd made her hate him before, just by playing nice. So maybe …

He switched to a humble smile and ducked his head abashedly for effect. "Sorry. I meant, *thank you*, Your Grace. I never drink coffee in the afternoon. Caffeine and magic. *You* understand." He flicked his fingers to create a quick burst of flames that leaped into the air and disappeared quickly. Nothing scary. Just the tiniest show for the princess.

And her *face*.

Oh. Yes. That was perfect. Max gasped like he was getting ready to have a heart attack. Nate would have to explain the game later. Max probably didn't understand that Princess Carina was now about half a second from throwing their asses telekinetically all the way back into the Asimov Straits. Or that he and Max both needed that ticket off the island.

What to try next? Maybe a question about herself? Something she'd refused to answer the first time they met? That would make it particularly grating.

But the princess was temporarily saved from further torment when a man who looked like he would have been tall if he weren't walking with a cane entered the foyer. He was clean-shaved and had close-cut hair, and he was wearing a sharp black suit with a silver tie that reflected just the faintest blue. He was not wearing a crown, but the parade of guards gave away his identity anyway.

A wispy kid was walking behind him—practically a clone of his father—and another young teenage girl. Nate recognized her immediately. He could never have forgotten that girl. She was the little fireball who'd caused the explosion that had nearly killed him and also basically saved his life. Nate thought she was cute.

Franklin put his hand on Nate's shoulder again, heavily enough for Nate to know that he shouldn't try any games with the actual king.

The guy stopped in front of them, and Nate thought he had surprisingly warm eyes for a man who preferred to conduct his rule from a glorified iceberg.

"Lord Franklin Leonardo Wellington," he said. "Here in flesh and blood. I was wondering when my daughters' hero might show up."

Franklin shook his head at his toes. "Your Highness, if anyone is a hero for your girls, it's Agda Talon."

"Oh, don't be ridiculous, Franklin. There are many heroes in the story of how my daughters were returned to me." The king smiled at Franklin like they were old buds. "Thank you. I am so grateful that someone cared enough to keep them safe." Then he actually went and hugged Franklin. Not shook his hand or patted him on the back or anything. Nope. The king went in for a real hug, and Franklin tolerated it. Nate had never seen Franklin hug *anyone*.

When the king pulled back, he surprised Nate again by saying, "It's good to see you again, Franklin. How's the rest of the family?"

There was a tinge of bitterness in the king's voice with that, though, and Franklin's voice was tight answering. "I can't speak for the rest of the family, Your Highness." He gestured toward Nate. "Only for Prince Nathanial and myself."

"Then Constance is still running the show, huh? Our intelligence units tell me Prince Bastian is expected to take over as king in a few years, under Constance's careful watch, and I hear that you, Franklin, are a dangerous and wanted traitor."

Franklin stood up straight. "You know I'll never be anything but loyal to the South."

The king nodded. "I am well aware of that, Franklin. You will always represent everything that was ever good about the Southern Guard to me. And now—" he shifted his eyes to look at Nate "—you are here with the true crown prince, seeking asylum."

The king didn't have an unkind face. There were laughter lines by his eyes. And while the king scrutinized Nate, Nate took a quick look at the king's foremost thoughts and found at the very top a memory of Herschel that didn't seem to have any ill-will associated with it. Had the king of North Kepler been *friends* with the king of South Kepler at some point? That would change everything Nate knew about the history of their families.

Nate heard the king think, *looks just like Herschel.* Then he said the last thing Nate expected him to say. "I know the rumors, Prince Nathanial. But you should know that your father was a good man. He understood loyalty. He would have protected my family with his own life, and you are welcome here for as long as you need a safe retreat." He held out his hand to Nate. "I'm King Reginald. Welcome to the kingdom of the dead."

CHAPTER FIFTEEN
A QUEEN FROZEN IN TIME

For the most part, Bast believed that his elegant, ageless, brilliant mother was the best thing that had happened to South Kepler in a hundred years. Queen Constance had only one magic ability—telekinesis—but she could inspire dread with words alone. She never dressed in anything short of impeccable, high-end fashion. She wasted no time on people or plans that could not forward her ultimate goal. And that ultimate goal was simple and good:

Destroy the Immortal Empire.

Doing so was the only way to secure Kepler for Mortal humans, and South Kepler was the only kingdom left to handle the fight. Thus, it only made sense for Queen Constance's actions in South Kepler to revolve around her single-minded vendetta. Bast's mother worked tirelessly to make the best and most efficient use of all Mortal Kepler's resources. She was better than anyone Bast knew at removing threats and weaknesses that could prevent the Mortals from ultimately defeating the Immortal Empire.

Bast, of course, *was* the single most important resource they had. He was more than the crown prince. He was the last First Degree Cardinal left on the planet. He had more power than any other living Mortal, and he had an obligation to use it for the greater good. *God* had set this path for him. He had no choice but to walk it.

But his way. Not his mother's.

Because Bast had only been home in Alighieri for a few weeks before it became clear to him that he and his mother had somewhat conflicting views about what Bast's new role in South Kepler needed to be.

From his perspective, Bast should be actively preparing to take an assertive role as the new king of South Kepler the minute he turned eighteen. He had two years or so, but if he worked hard, he would have time to learn the most important affairs of governance, build necessary relationships with church, state, and military personnel, and develop a strategic plan to defeat the Immortal Empire.

But from his mother's perspective, Bast only needed to be protected and stored for later use. That was why she had personally selected twenty royal guards to become his new entourage. It was why she wanted someone at his side every hour of every day. It was why he could no longer go to church without a parade of guards following him and why someone else had to eat a bite of everything on his plate before he could eat.

It was why Queen Constance reminded him every morning that he needed to plan his sister's memorial service. "The sooner we put her to rest, the less time the Empire has to plan another attack," she liked to say to him. "We cannot keep her body in the morgue forever."

Obviously, they couldn't. Which is why Vivian's body

wasn't in the morgue. Bast couldn't stomach the thought of Viv laying frozen in such a cold place. Especially when it was so unnecessary. He tended colder than anyone on the planet. It was a simple thing for Bast to freeze his sister's body solid and surreptitiously move her to her own room in the castle, where she could lie frozen dead on a soft, luxurious bed.

And where Bast could visit her frequently.

And talk to her.

Not that he thought she was in her body anymore. She wasn't. But he was sure her *soul* was always floating somewhere nearby, and he felt better about talking to her if there was a physical body to whom he could direct the conversation.

This morning, he had an especially miserable task to conduct, so he'd come early to her room to chat. He couldn't tell her about the task, so he complained about other things instead.

"I'm essentially prohibited from leaving Alighieri," he told her. "It's absurd. The Immortal Empire is gaining on us, and we're short on magic. Of our twenty highest-ranking generals, only half have any magic whatsoever, and only three have more than one gift. The longer Mom keeps me locked up like this, the more likely it is I'll have to fight Hildebrand and Godric alone and without an *ounce* of backup."

A lock of Vivian's hair was misbehaving. He didn't like touching her, but she wouldn't have liked her hair out of place. He found her hairbrush on her vanity table.

Then he went on. "Mom lies to me. She's a good liar. Which I respect, you know? There are probably plenty of things I've never even realized she's lied to me about because she believes her own lies so much. But she's blatantly lying to me these days. Telling me I'll be able to tour the countryside soon. Hold meetings with the governors. Do you think she doesn't understand how my magic works? Or maybe she thinks my grief is blocking it? She told me at dinner a few nights ago that she selected all those guards herself so she could be sure I was protected by people she trusts. I wish she would just come out there and say she selected guards she knew would be loyal to her, just in case. I would understand that. I know it has nothing to do with whether she trusts and loves me. But *lying* to me about it? That was offensive."

The lock of hair was tucked neatly where it was supposed to be again. He set the hairbrush back down and thought to put away a pair of earrings nearby before he went back to the chair he'd pulled up to Vivian's bedside for himself. It was where he always sat when he came to talk to her.

"She thinks I need to get over you faster," he told his sister. "She doesn't understand. This morning at breakfast, after she told me I had to—well, never mind—but when I tried to postpone it, she gave me that look—you know the one—and said, 'Bastian, I've made you an appointment to see the royal doctor.'"

Vivian was wearing a simple red dress that highlighted all her best features. She would have liked how it showed off the muscle in her arms and calves but still flared out enough to give it a feminine air. He'd chosen the dress himself from her wardrobe, though he'd ordered two of the female attendants to actually dress Vivian. It was only appropriate that way. Then he threatened to freeze them to death if they told his mother about this.

"I don't need to see a doctor. You *died*. I don't need anyone to tell me I'm going through some grief. I need what everyone else needs when they lose someone they love."

Her eyes were always closed, but sometimes the way her lips were frozen in place made it seem as though she wanted to speak to him. Her hands were folded over her stomach, and a few fresh flowers were tucked there. He made sure she had fresh flowers every other day.

"Time. That's all the doctor will say to me. It's all part of the grieving process. In time, this will get better. Eventually, I won't feel like I'm sleepwalking everywhere."

He noticed a wrinkle in her dress and smoothed it away. She didn't react. Nothing. Not a single sign of life.

"I'll arrange your service when I can handle it. And in the meanwhile, this is better than—" he really could barely think about it "—the alternative."

Vivian lay stiff on her bed, and Bast sat waiting for something, but he didn't get what he wanted. He put his hand on hers briefly—to check and make sure she was still properly frozen—then got up to leave. There was an unpleasant task for him to accomplish today.

The Royal Cathedral at Alighieri held over two-hundred years of history within its cool, stone-paved walls. The top of every wooden pew was smoothed with natural oils deposited by thousands of fingertips pressed down during prayers, hymns, and silent grief. The tapestries hanging from the walls told the history of Mortal Kepler interwoven with divine miracles that had moved humanity forward in spite of profane attempts made by Immortals to hold it back.

The high bishops and priests of the Church of South Kepler moved quietly within the cathedral, dressed in simple black robes that would not tell the status of any one person. The woman who passed Bast as he sat in the front pew of the cathedral later that morning was next in line to be admitted to the priesthood, but she wore nothing to give it away. He only knew because of the time he spent at the cathedral himself. The Church of South Kepler was regarded as strict by some, but this was because it held itself to such high ideals. Ideal one: every human was made in the image of God, none to be greater or lesser than the other in heaven.

On Kepler, ranks were established and responsibilities borne by those who had the need to bear them. But Bast, situated at the very top, with the most power and highest duties, expected not that he would be more important to God than anyone else but that he would be judged more critically. He had been given much. He was to give even more back. He knew that.

Why Vivian was something he needed to give back, he did not know. He had been sitting exactly here during her coronation. He'd watched that arrow plunge into her heart from his seat. Watched her fall on the hard, concrete dais. He did not know how his feet had propelled him forward to her. He did not know his brother had followed until he found Nate next to him at Vivian's side. The blood flowering out from her chest onto his hands meant nothing to him. If Immortal assassins were shooting at them, it wasn't bothering him. He knew nothing except her pulse slowing, slowing, slowing, and finally stopping.

For five minutes.

That's how long he'd knelt by his sister after her heart stopped, manipulating every source of power he had, channeling his magic to her brain to keep it cool, Nate's magic through her veins to keep her blood circulating, and her own magic to the wound, forcing the flesh to regrow and heal until her heart was whole again. And it wasn't enough. He'd healed her flesh only to discover another problem.

The Immortality Virus. It took root while he was focused

on her heart, and though he could sense the foreign viral cells in Viv's blood, he couldn't do anything but freeze them temporarily. Slow them down. Turn them into tiny bits of ice that would float in her system until her natural body heat warmed those viral cells back to life.

Futile, though. It had all been futile. His rational brain had known that from the beginning. He'd hoped against hope that he was wrong until he was making terrible, irrational decisions. He'd even let his deep fear of losing Vivian drive him to demand help from a girl whose magic—though incredibly, impossibly, irresistibly strong—could not have done more than his own for his sister.

He'd prayed for a miracle until God let him down. Until he'd given up hope so entirely that his instinct to save his own life overrode his instinct to save Vivian. He only ever let himself feel this in church, but he'd been such a fool. Such a selfish, flawed Mortal.

He bowed his head and prayed for understanding.

"Prince Bastian?"

He raised his eyes to see Father Curro, the high priest himself, standing before him.

"Please, follow me, Your Highness."

Bastian stood and followed the priest beyond the dais, where Vivian's death had started. They walked by the prayer room through which his family had escaped, down a corridor lit only by a few candles—for the Royal Church of South Kepler was as deeply committed to the Mortal Commitments as could be—and down an even darker stairway to a cavern the sun would never reach.

"Watch your step, Your Highness," Father Curro cautioned, though it wasn't necessary. This was not the first time Bast had entered the crypt. After all, he'd seen his grandfather, King Cassio, put to rest here, and then later his father, King Herschel. Though those deaths hadn't meant nearly as much to him as this one. He hadn't been close with Herschel. He'd hardly known Cassio. As Father Curro led him deeper through the crypt, walking him by the dead kings and queens of old until they reached Herschel's stone coffin, Bast hardly felt anything. What was in those tombs but bone and rotting fabric and dust?

They stopped at the stone pedestal next to King Herschel's coffin. There was nothing atop the pedestal yet, and there was only one more empty pedestal after before a wall stopped the deathly progression.

"This is where the queen will be laid to rest." Father Curro gestured back at the line of coffins. "In the memorial hall of the kings and queens of South Kepler."

Bast studied the pedestal, which seemed so cold a place for his sister to rest forever when she had burned such a fiery hot in life. His eyes shifted to the one extra pedestal. *His* ultimate resting place. The cold would be nothing but an extension of his life. Vivian was the only person who had ever been capable of making him feel warm. It seemed both wrong and right that they would one day lie side-by-side in the eternal numb of death.

"We need to know what to inscribe on the plaque," Father Curro said. "There will be room to engrave her name, her dates of birth and death, and a short epithet. No more than fifty characters, including spaces."

Fifty characters, including spaces. Is that what one's life summed up to be?

"What about a verse of scripture?" Bast said, though he heard his voice only as an echo in the crypt.

"We can engrave something on the side of the pedestal,

along the edge."

The vulgar logistics of death.

"Does Queen Constance have anything in mind?"

Bast felt himself ice up at the thought of his mother choosing what would go on Vivian's grave, and all at once, he needed out of the crypt. He turned on his heel toward the exit. "I will let you know what I want engraved," he said as he strode away from Father Curro.

The air outside the Royal Cathedral was fresh and warm. Bast let the winter sun—farther away than the summer sun and more a glowing than blazing heat—seep into his skin. He'd ordered the entourage that typically followed him around to wait for him, and Bast spotted his personal assistant, Gael, at attention just outside the cathedral.

Bast had chosen Gael for himself from a hundred candidates his mother presented upon Bast's return to Alighieri. All the candidates were within a year's age of Bast, who had recently passed his sixteenth birthday. All had extensive royal hospitality training and no known magic abilities. Gael had beaten out the rest by virtue of possessing a combination of traits Bast found appealing. He was bright, obedient, not sullen but also not in the habit of smiling, and capable of taking quick notes. He never showed up less than perfectly groomed and in polished boots.

It had also not slipped Bast's attention that Gael's eyes followed Bast wherever he went.

Gael knew Bast well enough by now to know that he was expecting to be briefed immediately on anything important that had occurred over the last two hours, while Bast had been in the cathedral dealing with death as much as he could handle for the day.

"Another direct attack at the western border, near the wine region, sir," Gael said without needing to be prompted as Bast approached him. "Fifteen wounded, four dead. On our side. No one from their side survived. But reports of sieges in the swamplands are coming in."

Bast stopped in front of Gael and stood there until his assistant made eye contact with him directly. He was pleased with the faint blush that appeared in Gael's cheeks. The sun was at exactly the right angle to hit Bast's best features now, substantially brightening his eyes. That would make him especially attractive, and it made him feel better about life when he felt attractive.

He began walking toward the castle, expecting Gael to follow, which he did. "Thank you, Gael. Are the Northern militias cooperating?"

"Cooperating would be a generous word, sir."

Bast smiled a tight-lipped smile at Gael for that bit of dry humor.

"The Empire issued another statement, threatening another attack on Alighieri. And to kill you, sir."

A growl from the back of Bast's throat made its way nearly to the top of his mouth, but he held back. "They make a lot of statements. If they want me, they'll have to do more than talk."

"Also, Queen Constance wishes to speak to you about prisoner Thurlow's trial."

"She doesn't want to delay it, does she?"

"I believe she wants to push it forward, sir. She said something about this being a good publicity opportunity for you."

Bast had intended to go back to Vivian's room in the castle once he got there, but perhaps he ought to visit

Thurlow again. It was never as easy to think about Vivian being dead when he was thinking about how they could best punish Thurlow for causing that death.

He glanced sideways at Gael. Gael had good posture, and he always stared completely forward when Bast looked at him this way. Normally, Bast had tea with his mother in the afternoon to discuss the business affairs of the kingdom, but today she had some conflicting meetings. So maybe he'd find some reason to need Gael's help with something after he visited Thurlow.

"And one more thing, sir."

"Yes?" Bast liked that when he made his voice a little silkier, Gael's cheeks would flush even more. He liked that power dynamic. He liked that Gael wouldn't break easily if—

"You have a letter."

Well, yes. He received letters all the time. Many from people who wanted to complain about crops or taxes or health care. Those letters were dull and frustrating. But he received even more from ambitious young women who wanted to ensnare him for marriage. Some of those letters were quite fun. He read the best ones to his mother, who usually deemed the writers, "not ambitious enough." ("Because anyone who is worth your time will find a way to charm you in person, Bastian, dear.")

"It's from Jax Channing."

Bast's heart issued a sharp warning at the name. *Thwack.* Right in the middle of its normal beat. *Thwack. Thwack.* Don't touch him. *Thwack.* Don't read the letter.

"I'll take it, please."

Gael fished the letter out from where he'd put it in his jacket and held it out to Bast. He was an excellent personal assistant for knowing this one was important, and it would be best, Bast knew, if he now told Gael that he'd been wrong. This letter was not important. It should please be placed with the rest of the personal letters Bast received, to be read at Bast's convenience. Or never.

But it was from Jax Channing, and Bast had the afternoon to do with as he wished. He took the letter. "Thank you, Gael."

I am messing up this entire mission, and if Myles can figure out how to get one of those escape vessels up and running, I should probably return to Earth with him. That would give me hundreds of years to beg for mercy from the Academy and get reassigned. I could study, get a few more college degrees, maybe go for something like psychology and figure out how I always get it so wrong. It's not like I've done any biological research here anyway. Miguela Garcia had it right when she hugged me and whispered, "Search, rescue, and study the frogs, huh? How's that going for you?"

At least I've reached an understanding with one of the girls. Not how I saw things playing out, but I'm never going to forget Miguela's face when I found her tied up in the back of that bounty hunter's truck outside New America this summer.

She'd heard the gunshots. She should have been so afraid when I pulled down that tailgate and saw her huddled up in a corner. And my eyes were irritated and itchy from heartbroken tears. As red as they could get.

I said, "I'm not going to hurt you."

She said, "Okay."

I said, "I'm Immortal. But I'm not from Kepler."

She said, "I *knew* you were lying about something."

Then she started laughing, and it made me laugh too.

Laughing with Miguela. That's one of the only things I've truly enjoyed doing on Kepler. Even the time I spent with Carina didn't have the same purity.

Now, I'm grateful Miguela and I are friends. It's funny that my best Keplerian friends are Mortals I thought I would never get along with. It was smart not to kill Nate a few months ago. He's my second-favorite Keplerian.

Fairly sure I blew my chance with Carina, though. We had dinner tonight with the king of North Kepler and his family. Carina was across the table from Nate and me. I thought she looked gorgeous when I saw her on the ferry, but she showed up to dinner looking like a crystalline goddess, in a women's suit that was about as far from jeans and hiking boots as it gets.

I spent all of dinner taking that sight in. She wouldn't even look at me. Not once. Nate, on the other hand ... she spent all of dinner trying to freeze him with her eyes. And either he has chosen her as a suicide mission, or he's the most skillful flirt I've ever met. I know he's royalty, but until today I've never seen him act like it. The number of times he threw a "Your Grace" at Carina ...

Don't think he noticed Miguela, though. She was sitting next to Carina, and she looked nearly as pretty—sort of a curvy, mini goddess. But I don't know if Nate heard anything Miguela said to him. He was too busy agitating my ex-girlfriend.

Served him right when King Reginald pushed back his

dessert plate and said, "This is fantastic luck. Carina needs a teacher, and here you are, Franklin, looking for a safe place to train Prince Nathanial. I was never better than when Herschel and I had opportunities to spar. It's perfect timing. Now Princess Carina and Prince Nathanial can train together."

Franklin hadn't warned Nate about anything like that, and Carina must not have expected it either. The temperature in the room fluctuated crazily after. Big chill, then we'd all start sweating, then we'd be shivering even worse than before.

King Reginald only laughed, and Franklin yawned, grinned at Nate, and said, "If we want to start tomorrow morning, I have to call it a night. Seven sharp?"

Glad I don't have to join in *that* fun. Tomorrow, while Franklin is finding out exactly what it's like when Princess Carina and Prince Nathanial are threatening each other with fire and ice in an enclosed space, I'll be with Myles, helping him locate an ancient escape vessel.

Supposedly those escape vessels are fast. They were the first ships to use warp zones. Myles thinks it will be an eight-hundred-year trip back to Earth. Which would be nearly a millennium to lick my wounds and get over the first girl I've fallen for since my last girlfriend ditched me at the planet Saigon.

But I don't want to abandon Nate when the guy obviously needs as many friends as he can get, and I'm not that desperate anyway. No one has ever made it back to Earth in one of those escape vessels, and dozens have tried. They're incredibly risky. Shoddy equipment, impossible to handle.

I regret mentioning Doctor Dellucci's Immortality Virus research to Myles. Now he's hellbent on finding that vessel, which the king only thought was some old legend, and even if Myles finds it, he'll probably die on the way back to Earth.

Why did I *ever* want to be part of this mission?

No, I'd have done it regardless. Because what was left for me on Earth?

Still. Search, retrieve, and fix up a rusty old escape vessel. Not exactly what I was hoping for. But at least I can report that the Kepler Mortals are putting up a fight against the Immortals and attempting to co-exist respectfully alongside the aboriginal intelligent life form. Colonization-correction is an important aspect of the Academy's greater mission. Lots of pressure to "extract or extinguish" humans on planets suffering from humanity. Though if the Immortal Empire *does* gain complete control over Kepler …

But I haven't told anyone here about that. No need.

Yet.

"When were you going to tell me you were planning to negotiate employment with the Northern Royals?"

Franklin and Max were sitting at a table in a scummy little kitchenette off the side of the men's barracks to which Nate and Max were now assigned. Myles had stayed behind after dinner to talk to the king about something "sensitive," but Franklin had agreed to a short debrief with Nate before he left for the fancy officer's quarters in which he and Myles would be sleeping.

Now, Nate was pacing around in front of Franklin and Max, trying not to talk too loud because Northern Militia guys were hanging around. Those soldiers shouldn't be "in" on anything any prince of South Kepler would be saying. But Nate knew he was probably failing to hide his agitation. Between the onslaught of thoughts coming from all those soldiers and Nate's rage over Franklin selling out to the Other Royal Family, it was probably lucky he wasn't turning the whole place into a sauna.

"So?" he said to Franklin. "*When?*"

Franklin was leisurely sipping a mug of hot cocoa, and *he* seemed calm. Relaxed even.

"When it became something you needed to know. If you ever want to return to South Kepler, your skills need improvement. Your mother is going to see you as a threat regardless of how clearly you say you want to abdicate—"

Nate opened his mouth to protest, but Franklin raised his hand and carried on.

"And *yes*, Nate, I realize you think Bast will take your side, but I'm not convinced."

Whenever Franklin said stuff like that, it always felt like a knife being jammed under Nate's sternum. Bast wasn't an easy person to be related to. But he was still the one in Alighieri right now, dealing with the nightmare the Northern Royals had washed their hands of. Also …

"He's my *brother*, Franklin."

Franklin sighed. "Can you just trust me when I say you need to be prepared to face him? Training with Princess Carina is the best thing that could possibly happen to you. She is the only person on the planet who will be able to give you anything like the fight you'll need to win with Prince Bastian."

That was ox beast crap. Princess Carina could not *possibly* have skills anywhere *close* to Bast. And Nate was the only person on the planet able to make that comparison.

"I can't believe she's a princess," Max said. He also had a cup of hot cocoa, but his was sitting untouched on the table, just like most of the food set in front of him at dinner had been left. Nate had never seen Max miss so many opportunities to carb load. "I'm never going to have a chance with the heir to some *throne*. I could have spent the last several weeks preparing for that."

"Um, hello?" Nate waved his arms at Max. "What do you think *I* am?"

Max rubbed his eyes, which were alarmingly pink. "*You* are not someone I care about romantically. I'm canceling our friendship if you keep trying to steal her. And if it comes down to a choice between you and her, I *will* choose her."

That was so funny Nate had to sit down to handle the absolute hysteria. He was going to hurt himself with this kind of laughter. "It will *never* come to a choice like that," he managed to gasp out. "Don't worry, pal. She is all yours. I'm Team Max forever."

"Then what was all that … funny business earlier?" Max demanded.

Ah, yes. "*That* was me showing her I can't be pushed around." Nate had won that battle. Hands down. He was sure of it. Though he still couldn't crack the girl's brain, and she *had* put up a good fight as far as mental warfare went. She hadn't missed a single dig or ever failed to respond with a dig back.

Franklin laughed maniacally. "And I'm sure what you pulled with her is going to make her a *very* forgiving training partner tomorrow, Nate. Should make this fun."

"I can take her," Nate grumbled.

Franklin finished the last of his cocoa and stood up. "Good. Because the king told me in private that she's nearly killed three teachers now, and *I'm* not going to be facing her."

"I don't understand why you hate me so much," Nate said.

"Sleep on it," Franklin said. "Maybe you'll figure something out."

Nate *wasn't* afraid of Ice Witch, but he had nightmares about all the crappy aspects of his life that had led up to this moment. He hadn't always been a screw-up. He'd never been as impressive as Vivian, but the disparity between him and Bast wasn't a gargantuan chasm when they were young.

They were magical complements—that's what their dad used to say—and they'd been buddies as little kids. There was even a brief time when Nate was the leader of their pair. Since Nate tended hot, he had abilities that looked impressive to a toddler Bast. He could fling toys across the courtyard and set stuff on fire. The invisible telekinetic shields Bast produced to prevent himself from getting thwacked by Nate's rogue projectiles didn't look nearly as exciting.

Bast's desire to emulate Nate's telekinetic ability was exactly why the Southern Royals kept opposite tending children together as much as possible. It was why they'd shared a bedroom, a bathroom, and a playroom for years. And the arrangement worked fine for Bast, who learned offensive telekinetic magic so that he and Nate could *both* throw blocks across the courtyard.

Nate's telesthesia ability was what messed everything up. He was six when he first realized he was picking up thoughts from the dogs, and he made the mistake of telling his family about it. They were ruthless about what they saw as a worthless telesthesia ability. *Ha-ha, Nate's the family dog whisperer. There goes Nate, off to the stables to have a heart-to-heart with his best friends.*

Bast's lie detection was wickedly accurate, incredibly useful, and a highly desired telesthesia ability. By comparison, Nate's ability to chat with the pets was nothing to brag about. And it wasn't long before Nate was getting more than canine thoughts. Mice came after dogs. Horses next. Then wild piggies, blue bunnies, rattycats, monk squirrels.

If it had stayed that way, maybe things wouldn't have gotten so bad. But then he heard a human thought. His dad thinking, *you little bastard*. At him. Nate couldn't remember what he'd done to piss his dad off. It didn't really matter. King Herschel wasn't especially patient with either of his sons. And after that, the flood gates opened on human thoughts.

Soon Nate could barely hear himself think because there were so many thoughts coming at him all the time. He had a constant headache. He'd never been very focused, but add the complication of always having to shoo away loud thoughts, and Nate's magic education took a dive. Bast progressed exponentially faster than Nate possibly could. After all, how did you learn anything when you could barely hear your-self think?

He needed help, but he was savvy enough by then to know better than to tell his family the full extent of his telepa-thy. He researched it secretly and learned that telesthesia gifts all fit into three categories. The least common were percep-tion gifts like Vivian's, which allowed the magician to sense relationships in some unusual way. Slightly more common were seer gifts, like Franklin's, that allowed the person to view some slice of the future. Telepathy gifts, like lie detection or the ability to read the thoughts of someone you cared about when they were distressed, were the most common.

Nate's telesthesia definitely fell into the telepathy category, but everything he read told him telepathy gifts were always limited, and Nate's gift didn't seem limited at all. It was what experts called "full telepathy," but only in the hypothetical. Most experts labeled full telepathy "mythical" or "realistically impossible, given the enormous tax such a gift would have on the human brain's ability to otherwise function."

Yeah. He could attest to that.

Only a handful of human Keplerians had ever even claimed to be full telepaths, and none of the claims were substantiated. There was a legend about a couple of First Degree Cardinals from North and South Kepler who ran away from their respective families and took on new identities in the West, but that was such an obviously made-up fairytale that Nate dismissed it entirely.

He was an anomaly, and the only good thing was how easy that made it for Nate to lie about his gift to his family. A little sarcasm, jokes made at his own expense, and a slick ability to tell half-truths, and not even Bast ever suspected. No one guessed he could read human minds, and in the meanwhile, Nate was failing abysmally at controlling the problem.

Then he burned a teacher.

He hadn't meant to hurt her, but that was exactly the problem. The Southern Royals weren't squeamish. If he'd meant to hurt her, he'd have gotten in some light trouble, but he wouldn't have lost respect. Accidentally burning her made him a senseless monster, not a gifted magician.

His family was disgusted. Vivian thought "poor Nate" was never going to catch up. Bast thought this confirmed his prior belief that he was the superiorly gifted son. Queen Constance, his mother, thought Nate was pathetic and unlikely to survive to adulthood.

By far the worst was King Herschel, who was egregiously disappointed with his first-born son. King Herschel had a bad temper, and he'd suffered consequences for his own lack of impulse control. His brilliant-but-unfeeling wife was a consequence of an action that hadn't been very well thought out. More than one rebellion at the border counted as an even worse consequence.

He feared that Nate was too much like him, and this was the last straw. Nate's scorched magic teacher (the *sixth* Herschel had lost trying to find an acceptable teacher for Nate), would have been scarred for life if it hadn't been for Bast.

Nate was hopeless, and King Herschel told Nate so, loudly and furiously, the night it happened, holding back only the worst things he could possibly have thought about his own son. Except Nate heard all that anyway.

He was more than stung by the injustice.

No one understood him. No one loved him. He couldn't trust anyone in his own family. He couldn't *think* with all those people at the castle all the time. He ran away without even bothering to pack a bag, planning never to return.

Of course, as an eleven-year-old, he wasn't as well-equipped for the wilderness as he thought. He was hungry by the end of the first day. It occurred to him to hunt, but how do you kill something when you know you'll hear the animal's terrified cry right before it dies? The monk squirrels were good at finding nuts and berries, but they were insanely selfish, and none of them would share. He was friends with some bunnies who told him where he could find leaves to chew, but that wasn't enough to feed a young boy.

Ultimately, he parked himself in the hollow of a thousand-year suckle tree close enough to the castle that he could still see the towers from the tree, and he vowed to die of starvation rather than return home. He stayed there sulking for four whole nights. Then it started raining, and the coldest Nate ever remembered being was on the fifth evening out, shivering and hungry in the hollow, watching sheets of rain fall through the canopy of trees, thinking about how his family hadn't even cared enough to send the dogs for him.

Nate was contemplating the possibility of locating some wolves and asking them to kill him—quickly, please; a fast neck snap would be good before they ate him—when he heard the sound of wet, sucking human footsteps treading through the mud. A man stopped in front of his suckle tree hollow.

"Prince Nathanial," the man said. Not a question, exactly, but Nate took it as one. There was something about the man—who Nate knew, but only barely—that made him feel he ought to answer.

"General Franklin?" he said uncertainly, though the title wasn't accurate. General Franklin Leonardo Wellington had been stripped of his military rank years before. Nate didn't know why, just that it must have been bad. Franklin was, after all, a Wellington, King Herschel's first cousin, and, technically, a member of the Royal Family. A Second Degree Cardinal, now demoted to a disgraced drunk with an ugly scar.

"Come on out of there, Prince Nathanial," General Franklin said. "I'll take you home."

Those were trigger words. "I don't want to go home," Nate said with the sullen pout of a scorned eleven-year-old. "And don't call me 'prince.'"

Franklin stared at him for a long time. He was wearing an old jacket that was torn at one shoulder, possibly because it wasn't big enough for Franklin's muscular breadth. He had scruff on his face and shaggy hair the color of wet sand. His eyes were hazel like Nate's, but without the tell-tale fragmentation at the pupil that came with tending hot. If Nate had to guess, he'd have said Franklin was at least fifty, though he knew Franklin was only a few years older than his dad, who was thirty-six.

"What do you want me to call you?" Franklin said.

A cold gust of wind blew rain in Nate's face, and he shivered, unable to work up the heat necessary to ward off the chill.

"Just Nate," he said through chattering teeth.

Franklin stared some more, and Nate thought maybe he would leave. No one else in the family would have waited in the rain for some kid to climb out of a suckle tree.

Then Franklin said, "I'm not a general. Just Franklin. Get out of that tree."

And for some reason, Nate did it. Then he followed Franklin on foot all the way back to the castle, where he wasn't even sure he would be let back in.

Nate knew Vivian and Bast often wondered why Herschel decided to hire Franklin as Nate's master that night. "What could Franklin possibly teach you?" Vivian liked to ask. And Bast liked to answer, "Nothing. He has no real magic. All he knows is how to talk himself into a cushy job."

They were both under the impression that Franklin was the one who persuaded Herschel to give him the position. But Nate had been privy to the conversation that occurred between Franklin and Herschel, and Franklin wasn't the one who asked to be Nate's teacher.

Oh no. That's not what happened at all.

It was King Herschel who pleaded with Franklin to stay and take on that miserable role. He said things like, "There is no other choice," and "I'm not asking you to teach him magic," and "Just get him ready to enlist in a few years," and "You're still the best swordsman in South Kepler. If you can teach him enough that he doesn't get killed his first day in the Guard, I'll consider that a success."

Franklin, for his part, responded with things like, "Your son is not my problem," and "I don't need a job," and "What makes you think I'd be good at teaching any kid anything?"

It was in response to that last bit where Herschel finally said the thing that clinched the deal.

"I am the one with the kid who torched his teacher. I am the one he ran away from. I am the one who didn't go after him. I am the one who *never* does anything about his mother. *You* are the one who brought him back. How could you possibly be worse with him than I've been?"

Franklin shut his mouth and looked at Nate, who was sitting at the edge of the fireplace, still too cold and fatigued to make himself warm. There was no emotion in Franklin's face.

"Also, I'm the king, Franklin," Herschel added softly. "And I'd rather this be a request, but I can make it an order if you want. We'll pay you."

Franklin said, "Double whatever you were paying the last teacher, and room and board in one of the guesthouses on the castle grounds."

"Thank you," Herschel said.

Nate never heard his father say anything else that ever indicated he might actually care about his son. Nevertheless, Nate started his lessons with Franklin determined not to lose what he sensed was his last chance at turning things around.

He understood right away that Franklin was different from any teacher he'd ever had. Franklin made his lessons up as they went based on his own experience in the Southern Guard and what he thought Nate might practically need in a fight or any other real-life scenario. When Nate couldn't muster up any magic, Franklin taught him how to sword fight. When Nate mouthed off, Franklin took him on field trips to meet people who he said, "weren't such a privileged pain in my royal ass."

And Nate learned *everything* worth knowing from Franklin. Everything.

So, when he woke up his first morning at Fort Aurora Borealis, he had only one thought in his mind. He was *not* sharing Franklin with Ice Witch. Time to switch tactics. No more antagonistic flirting. Today, he'd show Carina Garcia that he was so much more skilled than she was that she'd never survive a second lesson. By the time this was over, she'd be begging King Reginald to send the Southern Royals away. All he had to do was destroy her.

Yeah. That was a good plan.

CHAPTER SEVENTEEN
HOW TO TRAIN YOUR ROYALS I

Carina trusted Lord Franklin, and she had the gut intuition that he would be a great teacher. But she was apprehensive about her first day of training with him because Prince Nathanial would be there. She didn't trust that guy at all. That act last night had been the most conniving, manipulative ox crap show. Vivian's voice—stuck in Carina's memory and telling her that her hateful brothers were not monsters—was all that got her to the gym that morning, ten minutes early because she didn't want to be anything less than punctual with either Lord Franklin or the prince.

They were already there.

"Look who decided to show up," Nate said as she walked in.

Mishe bristled next to her but said nothing. She checked her watch. Was it behind? No way. It was an atomic watch. She looked at the clock on the wall anyway. Both read ten minutes to seven. "I'm sorry, Lord Franklin. Am I late?" she said. To her new teacher. Not the prince.

Lord Franklin was setting up several buckets of water against one wall of the gym while the arrogant prince stood watching. There was a hefty first aid kit lying nearby and—

"Is that a fire extinguisher?" Mishe whispered, sounding meeker than Carina would have liked her head guard to sound in the face of fire.

"Looks like, Mishe," Carina whispered back.

Lord Franklin placed a final water bucket where he seemed to want it and looked up at her. "Good morning, Princess Carina. You're right on time. Come on over. Your guards are dismissed for the session."

Mishe stiffened, but Franklin looked steadily at Mishe, and said, "Sergeant Lovric, right? I spoke to the king about this, but you can confirm with him before we begin if you'd like. Princess Carina's magic is highly reactive, and she's more likely to perform at her best when she's feeling defensive. Having guards at her call isn't optimal for creating that environment. Please have your team wait outside until our session is up."

The scar. That's what Carina thought accounted for the fact that Mishe took that without any question, despite what had happened with Hess. He merely said, "Good luck today, Princess," and herded the other guards out.

"He's loyal," Lord Franklin said to her. "When you're good enough, we can bring his team back and retrain them. You're going to need them to take orders from you in a fight, not act as your glorified bodyguards."

The idea of ordering someone around in a fight was completely foreign to Carina. "Take *orders* from me?" she said.

Lord Franklin laughed. "I'm sorry, Princess Carina. You haven't been taught to think like a commander yourself, have you?"

She shook her head and stammered out: "Uh, no. And you don't have to call me that. Just Carina is okay. It's … been just Carina for almost seventeen years."

Prince Nathanial rolled his eyes in a circle so big his nose and forehead went with it. "Poor thing," he drawled. "Finding out sixteen years late that she's royalty."

Lord Franklin cuffed the prince on the back of his neck. "You will show respect in this court, Nate." Then he pointed his thumb at his charge. "Nate prefers to go by his first name, too. So, for now, that's what will do. You can call me Franklin."

"Thank you," she said to Franklin, trying to ignore the heat she thought was issuing off Nate as he scowled at a bucket of water. "And, um, thank you for agreeing to work with me. My dad said he told you about some of … well … I've had a hard time with teachers."

Franklin seemed to think that was funny, too. "You will not be the first student I've had who's almost killed a teacher."

"Hey," Nate said, catching her eyes again with an even less friendly scowl. "She didn't need to know that."

She thought maybe she *did* need to know that. He'd had trouble controlling his magic, too? Did that make him more or less likely to hurt her today? Best not to dwell on it, though, so she said, "I thought I would be early today. How long have you been setting up? I can help tomorrow. Should I get here at six-thirty?"

"We've been here since six," Nate said, and Carina instantly felt her chest tighten again.

"But that's because we had prayers to do," Franklin said, not sounding at all put-out. "If you want to help set up tomorrow, get here exactly when you did today."

"Prayers?" Carina was aware of the Royal Church of South Kepler but had not connected that since Nate was the prince of South Kepler, he and Franklin might actually be practicing members of the church. Somehow, Nate didn't seem like the type who would pray.

"Do you know much about the Royal Church of South Kepler, Carina?" Franklin asked.

"Not too much," she said.

"Well, we believe in a Great Creator we call God, and since life comes from God, we believe that all lifeforms can plug into the divine. Part of that is prayer, which we do at dawn and dusk, facing the sun, why Nate?"

The prince looked up at the ceiling and said in a monotone, "Because prayer makes us remember there are greater things in the universe that rise above us and fall after us."

"But why didn't you just pray in the barracks?" Carina asked curiously.

"Nate and I aren't especially evangelical. We prefer privacy," Franklin said.

"He *means* stop asking questions," Nate said. "We don't care if you want to be a heathen. Why do you care if we pray?"

The pinch of guilt in her chest and the nasty expression on his face forced Carina to stuff down a flash desire to cry or run away. She was *not* going to lose it in front of him. She picked up her chin. "I don't care. I just don't want to inconvenience you by not showing up on time."

Franklin looked sternly at Nate. "And Carina is *not* inconveniencing us, is she, Nate? We appreciate *any* effort any Northern Royal makes to understand our culture. It's another reason it's good for you to train together. And today, we're going to jump right into combining your telekinetic and thermodynamic abilities."

"Uh, no. We are not capable of that kind of cooperation," Nate snapped.

"I meant your *individual* abilities to work with more than one of your gifts at a time," Franklin clarified. "My sources tell me you are each at your best in a fight. We're going to take advantage of your current … ah … disregard for each other and use it to motivate you both to naturally excel."

"What are the buckets for?" Nate asked. Which made Carina feel better. She'd thought Franklin would have told Nate all his plans. The fact that he had not at least put them on an even playing field.

But Franklin's scar was certainly something when he was pleased with himself. "I'm glad you asked, Nate. Starting today, we're sparring. But since you both have too much power and not enough control with your thermodynamics, I don't want anyone using heat or cold directly. The rule of today's match is you can only hit each other with the water in these buckets. And no hurling the buckets as weapons."

Carina tried to puzzle that out. He wanted them to …

"This is a *water* fight?" Nate said, like he thought that was a kiddie training exercise.

"I'll be disappointed if you treat this as merely an opportunity to splash each other," Franklin said. "Water is the perfect tool because you can each change it to your advantage. Your goal here is not to soak the other person with liquid H2O."

"Oh," Carina said. "You want him to change the water to steam and me to change it to ice. That seems …"

"Dangerous?" Nate taunted. "Are you afraid?"

The word she'd been going for was "challenging," but Nate's arrogance made her feel like rising to the occasion.

"I have natural healing abilities, and I'm going to be throwing ice picks at you. Why aren't *you* afraid?"

He widened his stance like he could power play her.

"Do you know how fast hot steam can scald you?"

What an egotistical jerk. But she was undaunted. She copied his stance and added some bravado to her tone. "Not as fast as an ice dagger can pierce through you."

Franklin rubbed his hands together and grinned eerily. "Perfect. You can fight it out and see who wins."

They "warmed up" by moving their buckets of water to opposite ends of the training room telekinetically. Then Carina stood at one end of the gymnasium with her buckets of water and faced Prince Nathanial standing at the other side with his.

Franklin stood at the edge near the fire extinguisher. "Alright. You fight to incapacitate, not kill or permanently injure. Fight ends when the water is gone or one person concedes defeat."

"In other words, it ends when you're too afraid to keep going," Nate said to her.

Carina wasn't going to dignify that with a response. She was busy trying to lift water from a bucket and discovering it wasn't easy. With a solid object, she'd gotten better at imagining her own energy affecting the object. She could extend herself telekinetically to grip, push, pull, or throw solid objects as if she had extra-long arms. But water wasn't something she would ever have tried to grip, push, pull, or throw. Not without using some tool. She was struggling to figure out how to get the water to lift at all when she felt something scald her shoulder.

Nate was having no trouble at all with the water.

And he was already sending another blast of steam at her. She shrieked and held up her hands—which was a horrible idea because scalding her hands would not be helpful. But, fortunately, the steam froze like a shield in front of her. *That* she could use. She rotated the shield until it was horizontal, then shot it back at Nate. It spiraled through the air and hit another blast of steam. Little drops of water rained down to the floor.

He had not bothered to wait for her to counter those first blasts of steam, though, so before she could think about what to do next, she was nearly hit by a third blast. She pushed it straight back as a thin disk of ice, but he just let the ice crack against his fist and sent another rush of steam at her.

At least this time she was ready for it. Cold hit the steam somewhere in the middle of the arena. The steam morphed into a cloud of snow, but Nate was relentless, and his next hit went right through that snow, giving her little time to react. She managed to cover her face, but it was a nasty shock when her arms got scalded right before a geyser of boiling water erupted out of one of her buckets, dousing her.

It hurt.

Bad.

She barely heard the guttural yell of pain coming from her throat. But she was *furious* now—how dare he use *her* buckets of water to hurt her?—and that made her more creative. Instead of trying to imagine her hand picking up the water, she just extended her fury to the water. *That* was apparently the kind of energy she needed to turn water into icicles she could shoot like darts through the air. She sent a whole bucket-full at Nate.

He batted the icicles away in a motion that looked sloppy, and she realized that was the trick with him. He was destroying her because he was relying on his strength: the attack. *Her* strength was defense—which is probably why he'd only managed to hit her a couple times so far. As soon as he had to defend himself, he lost focus.

She needed to confuse him. She extended her rage to the water again and succeeded in picking up an entire stream of icy cold water. It flowed slower than the icicles, but he wasn't good at figuring out what to do with a stream of water, either. She had time to direct another bucket of icicles at him immediately after the cold water hit him.

"OW!" he yelled, and she thought she saw blood running down his cheek. She managed to stick him with a few icicles then, but she didn't have time to celebrate because now he was angry, too. While she continued trying to hit him with ice picks from one bucket of water at a time, he moved right to an enormous blast of steam from *two* buckets of water at once.

She felt it coming and lost track of the icicles, prioritizing the blast. She was supposed to have a natural ability to form a defensive telekinetic shield. Still, now that she consciously needed a shield, she couldn't seem to make one. It was all she could do to cover her face again and not collapse as the hot steam hit her, and her body finally told her it was critically injured.

Also, he was a monster, because she was plainly losing, and yet, there was steam swirling around and lashing in at her from all angles. Five minutes from the start, and the fight was out of control. He was going to kill her. Maybe she was already dying. Her skin had to be peeling off. She tore at her shirt to stop the hot water from soaking through and spun, trying to guess where the next lash was going to come from. Then when hot water whipped from her ear down the back of her neck, she began screaming, "Stop!"

There were several minutes after when she had no idea what she was doing at all. She only knew she needed a safe, dark, cool place in which to crouch and hide while she waited for those burns to kill her.

Then the pain began to numb, and as it receded, she realized she was huddled on the ground, covered by a thick, protective bubble of ice. She saw a figure she thought was Franklin runing toward her from the outside, and soon he was tapping on the ice and saying, "Princess Carina? Are you okay?"

Was she? Her skin was healing, but she was shivering hard and terrified of the prince hurting her again. A second figure appeared next to the one she thought was Franklin's, and there had only been three people in the training room before this nightmare, so *that* was the murderous monster she was never training with again.

She cowered, shut her eyes, and waited for something bad to happen, but the ice only began to melt. Soon she found herself dripping wet in a cold huddle with Nate and Franklin watching her.

Franklin crouched down. "Carina? Come on. Let's get you back up again." He reached gently for her wrists—which did not appear to be burned anymore—and she let him help her up. Then she didn't balk as he circled her, asking her to hold up her hair and her arms so he could check for burns.

He tutted over the marks he found. "He got you pretty good, but nearly everything is already healing. Does it still hurt?"

She couldn't tell. She was numb and cold, and she couldn't move her fingers.

Franklin hummed unhappily. "Nate, go get Carina's coat."

Nate was standing with one of his arms twisted so he could examine it. He had a nasty cut on his face. "I'm not getting her *coat*. She's the one who drew blood."

Franklin sighed. "Barely, Nate. And Prince Eugene can probably heal you in a few minutes."

That did not make Carina feel better. *She* was supposed to be a healer. Not that she would have been willing to heal *him*. But if she'd been asked, she would have been forced to say no. She couldn't help someone else when she didn't know exactly how she was healing herself.

Mishe approached—she hadn't seen him enter the gym— and he had her coat. He draped it around her shoulders and started rubbing her arms.

"I need to get the princess to the infirmary," he said to Franklin.

Franklin shook his head. "You can take her back to her own room and set her up in front of a fireplace. She only needs to warm up."

"The king will want her in the infirmary."

Franklin tipped Carina's chin up and looked at her face while Carina held the coat closed tightly around her. Then Franklin let go. "The king gave me the authority to handle her training. She doesn't need the infirmary. She's a First Degree Cardinal with healing abilities. Get her to her room and have her attendants draw her a hot bath."

Mishe did not seem happy with that. "Princess, do you need me to carry you?" he asked.

"No." She wasn't going to let the prince watch *that*. Anyway, her blood was circulating again. She could walk herself out.

"That was a tough match, Carina," Franklin said. "If you need a day off, I understand."

A minute ago, she'd been sure she could never do this again, but that had been a moment of weakness she couldn't afford. She couldn't lose a day of training she clearly needed.

"I can train again tomorrow," she said.

"Alright," Franklin said. "Get some rest this afternoon. You did well."

"I lost," she said.

"You went into thermodynamic panic," he said.

"But, I lost," she repeated.

He nodded. "Yes, you lost. So, let's make it so that you have a better chance at winning, and you can have a rematch, okay?"

Nate wasn't looking at her.

She hated him and wanted him to *suffer*.

"Yeah, that sounds good," she said to Franklin, and she added a mental vow to Nate. *Tomorrow, I will destroy you.*

He finally caught her eye, and she could have sworn she heard him think, *Try it.*

Obviously, he was affecting her sanity, but he wasn't going to keep winning for long. *I will*, she promised, and she left the gym with her head held as high as she could hold it. Screw him. He wanted an enemy? He had one.

CHAPTER EIGHTEEN
THE OTHER GARCIAS

Nate was bleeding through his shirt, his arms were shredded, he had a cut across his left eyebrow that hurt like hell and another below his right eye. He'd won that match, but all Franklin said after Princess Icy left was, "Next time, you stop as *soon* as the girl says stop."

Which made Nate feel prickly shame. He was *angry* at the girl in question. He'd wanted training to be unpleasant for her. He hadn't wanted to *terrify* her. Or make her guards look at him like *that*. Why had she needed to be so delicate?

And he *knew* how to be respectful to girls. In this context, Garcia wasn't a girl. She was his opponent. No Immortal was going to be nice because she was a girl. Bast would have been pissed about gender being considered at all. What, were they supposed to be acting like sexist, pig-headed Westerners here?

Nate walked to the infirmary injured and with his tail between his legs anyway. He'd never been hurt this bad without Bast around to heal him. Now one of the Northern Royals—some kid he'd barely met—would be tasked with that job.

He opened the door to the infirmary telekinetically to avoid getting blood on anything and stepped into a waiting room with several shiny, green couches. A computerist sat behind a desk, glaring at one of those super-expensive Robust Renewable Energy screens. In South Kepler, computerists mostly only worked in academia, publishing, and church. Everyone else used old-fashioned pen and paper. It only made sense from a sustainability standpoint. It took far more energy to manufacture and power a computer than to make, use, and recycle paper.

When Nate walked up to the desk, the computerist pushed down his glasses, sneered, and handed him a clipboard. He said, "Fill it all in back and front. Return it here."

Nate took a look at the questions. Name, date of birth, address, emergency contact, phone number. "Who has a *phone number* here?" he muttered. He flipped to a medical history survey. Any history of heart disease? Diabetes? High cholesterol? He was a magic seventeen-year-old Keplerian. Were caffeine and sugar sensitivities on this list? Tendency to set shit on fire? He tried to hand the clipboard back. "I don't think any of this applies to me."

The computerist refused to take it. "Fill in as much as you can."

"I'm bleeding everywhere here," Nate said.

"Can't check you in until you finish the forms."

Nate reluctantly sat on a couch that squawked awkwardly and started checking "no" to everything. He'd smeared blood on five pages when eleven-year-old Prince Eugene emerged from a door near the check-in desk. He scanned the room quickly and seemed to instantly understand Nate's problem.

"Why haven't you sent Prince Nathanial back already?"

he said to the computerist.

"New patient, Prince Eugene," the guy said. "He's filling in the registration forms."

Prince Eugene shared a lot of Ice Witch's features—arched eyebrows, skinny physique, spider hands—but none of it made the kid look nefarious. On Eugene, those features just made him look like an uncannily astute pre-teen.

Eugene took three long steps to Nate and held out his hand. "I'll take that."

Nate side-eyed the peeved computerist. "I'm not done."

"That form wouldn't give me the right details to treat you anyway," Eugene said. "It's not right for someone with magic like we have."

We. Nate was going to have to think about that. So far, his contact with the Northern Royals had been mostly limited to Carina, who Nate was incapable of thinking about in terms like "we." But Eugene? Nate wasn't sure about him yet. He handed his clipboard over, and Eugene directed a curt instruction that could have come from Bast's mouth to the computerist:

"Put a note on this patient's records. This is Prince Nathanial. He is to be sent back to me immediately when he comes in. No one else treats him unless I am completely indisposed."

The computerist huffed loudly, but Nate followed Eugene to an office where Eugene's name was engraved on a placard on the door. "You have your own office?" Nate asked.

"I'm the only magical healer around. None of the civilian doctors can do what I do, so ..." Eugene held his arms out wide as they entered the room. "Private office." He pointed to the examination table. "Shirt off, lie down, don't make it weird."

"Uh, yes, sir." Nate sat on the edge of the table and dutifully stripped off his shirt while the kid washed his hands in a sink. "I guess this probably is weird for a lot of people, isn't it?"

"Oh, you don't think it will be for you?" Eugene said sarcastically, coming over from the sink. "I said, lie down."

Nate obeyed. "My brother's been healing me for years. I know what this is like."

"Don't be so sure. Every magic healer does things a little differently." Eugene wiped the blood off Nate with alcohol swabs, then put his hands over a spot with an especially deep gouge. "This is going to be cold."

Nate studied the ceiling and braced himself while Eugene set his ice-cold hands down on a wound. With Bast, cold healing always felt worse before it got better, like someone aggressively yanking flesh back into place. With Eugene, it felt more like skin being zipped together under cold metal.

Since talking made it less strange, Nate craned his head up to watch and asked, "When did you start doing this?"

"Here? Officially? Last year. But I've been healing things for years, obviously. Close your eyes, I'm going to do that gash on your forehead, and I don't want to freeze your eyeballs shut."

Nate closed his eyes tight. "Do you get a lot of practice?"

"Enough. Geez. She really got you."

Nate opened his eyes. Eugene was smiling grimly.

"She thinks she's bad at magic. She's too powerful. Dad can't find anyone good enough to work with her, and Miguela's got the same problem except she's afraid of magic. Carina's only afraid of being *bad* at it. Who won this fight?"

Nate recalled the pain *Carina* had inflicted on him. That first ice dagger struck him directly over his heart, vampire slayer style, and it hurt so bad he thought it had gone right through. He also remembered how she'd cowered as he corralled swirls of steam around her, and that he kept it up even after he saw her start to panic.

"You did, huh? But don't act like she's magically disabled or something," Eugene said. "She would hate you forever for that. Better if—" He stopped mid-sentence to stare at Nate, or *through* Nate, for so long that Nate thought maybe this was the signal for "we're done."

"Uh, thanks?" Nate said. "Should I … can I leave?"

Eugene startled and blinked rapidly again. "Sorry." He walked over to the sink and started washing his hands. "How long have you been sword fighting?"

"Since I was about your age. How'd you know?" Nate sat up and found his shirt, which was covered in blood. Eugene frowned at it.

"Don't wear that."

"Little cold for walking around shirtless outside, Gene," Nate said, deciding this was not his last encounter with Doctor Eugene and that they should, therefore, be on friendly, first-name terms.

"Maybe for me, *Nate*. Bet it would feel good for you. But we'll get you a robe."

"Thanks," Nate said. "This was better than what Bast does."

"Told you, I'm good at what I do."

Nate hopped off the exam table. "So is he."

Max had spent the morning following Myles around on a solar-powered jet ski.

"You basically played in the snow for hours," Nate said

while they got trays for lunch at the fort's mess hall.

Max sniffed and wiped his nose with the back of his sleeve. Somehow, he'd managed to find a flannel shirt this morning, and Nate had also seen Max layering up with insulating, full-body underwear. Now he had a wool scarf draped around his neck, too. He looked like a puffy lumberjack.

"What I did was nearly *freeze* to death in the arctic while Myles tried to find the equivalent of a four-thousand-year-old emergency lifeboat."

After his infirmary fun, Nate had changed into an undershirt and a thin sweater. "Any luck?" he asked while they moved through the food line.

"No." Max flicked scoops of unidentifiable meat hash onto his plate. "And instead of spending the afternoon getting back on Carina's good side—" flick, another scoop "—I have to go out with Myles again. Did she mention me to you at all?"

"The girl you like tends *cold*, Max." Nate enunciated "cold" carefully and tried not to think about the meat hash. "Being with her would be like freezing to death *all the time*. And no. She did not confess her latent feelings for you during the *brawl* Franklin made us participate in."

They found a vacant table, and Max began to dig into his lunch while Nate tried not to get sick. That hash had once been an animal. Someone with thoughts, feelings, and a desire to live.

"Did you mention me to her?" Max asked.

"No, because *I* have a desire to live." He would have expounded on that if Icy's little sister hadn't approached them then, carrying a tray of her own.

"Hey, Miguela. Want to sit with us?" Max said. He angled his head toward Nate. "You remember the prince of South

Kepler, right?"

"So not necessary," Nate said, annoyed at Max for playing up his title to a girl who seemed shyer than a rattycat. He smiled as warmly at Miguela Garcia as he could. It wasn't *her* fault that her sister was a witch. Nate knew better than anyone what it felt like to be associated with difficult family members. "But sit down, Princess Miguela."

Miguela's ears pinked up, and she stammered something so quiet Nate couldn't hear.

"Come on, Miguela. You have to tell us how it feels to be a fire princess now." Max grinned and giraffed his neck toward her conspiratorially. "Have you set anything awesome on fire yet?"

Sweet little Miguela Garcia shrank, and Nate wanted to smack Max. "Ignore him," Nate said to Miguela. "You don't have to answer his questions."

Rosy spots glowed on her cheeks, but she sat down. "Thanks."

Nate forked a barely cooked carrot and used his fingers to produce a tiny fire under the carrot. He roasted it while he kept talking. "People like us have to stick together, Princess. Commoners like Max don't understand what it's like to be able to burn down a whole castle." He took a bite of perfectly cooked carrot. "Not that I ever burned down a castle. Only this one wing where Bast was practicing magic without me."

The corners of Miguela's mouth turned up, and Nate decided he and she were good.

"So has Carina said anything about me being here to you, Miguela?" Max said. Sort of. Because somewhere in space, he'd clearly forgotten how to chew meat hash with his mouth closed.

Miguela wrinkled her nose. "I wouldn't count on it, Max."

She looked down at the bowl of soup on her tray. "I don't think she's happy with either of you being here."

"Carina and Nate got off to a bad start," Max said.

"Say *that* again," Nate said.

"But she and I had something *real* together."

Miguela's lower lip trembled briefly before a tiny giggle escaped.

"What?" Max said. "We did!"

Nate caught Miguela's eye. Her eyes weren't as abnormally large as Princess Icey's eyes, and the hint of a violet starburst in her otherwise chocolate brown irises twinkled as she thought, loudly, *Carina is never going to fall for Max again.* Nate couldn't hold back his own laughter at that, even when he tried to hide it behind a sip of water, and that made Miguela laugh out loud.

"Oh, so this is how it's going to be, huh?" Max grumbled. "I'm not giving up *that* easy."

"She's going to kill you," Nate said.

"*And* she has a boyfriend," Miguela added.

Max dropped his knife and fork right out of his hands. "What? *Who?*"

"Heathrow Princeton," Miguela told them. "He's this incredibly smart guy—"

"*I* am incredibly smart!" Max yelped.

"—and he tends hot—"

Max scowled at Nate. "She doesn't *like* guys who tend hot!"

"And he's the darling of the Royal Society of North Kepler."

"What is *that?* Is it a *cult?*"

Nate put his hand on Max's shoulder. "It means he's out of your league. The Royal Society in the North is like the

Royal Church in the South. It's the North's most powerful institute. And North Keplerians think marriage is a useless religious construct, but historically, the Northern Royals are more likely to meet their life partners in the Royal Society than anywhere else."

"You know a lot about North Kepler," Miguela said, sounding impressed while Max pushed his tray forward and threw his head down on the cafeteria table.

Nate shrugged. "I like history. I read a lot."

"End my misery, Nate," Max mumbled.

But Miguela smiled again at Nate. "When you're done ending Max, do you want me to show you around the rest of the fort?"

Nate perked up at the thought of a real tour. "Can we visit the stables later?"

"Sure," she said without the slightest hint of coldness or hostility.

"*So* not fair," Max moaned into his arms.

Miguela walked Nate around the entire fort, pointing out the assembly building where the Royal Society met, the officer's cabins, housing for guests and staff, and the commissary. Then she took him to the Northern Royal's "summer house," which was a big manor house with tall windows, long lines, sharp points, right angles, and washed-out color. No moats or throne rooms or even a courtyard.

"It's calming," Nate said as Miguela was walking him through the house.

"You mean boring," she said. "Nothing like the Royal Castle at Alighieri. It must have been amazing to grow up there, right?"

"Amazing in the lots-of-expensive-things-to-break way," Nate said.

They passed Queen Lucia, drinking a cup of tea alone in a small sitting room. Nate hadn't wanted to gawk during dinner last night, but Miguela's mom was supposed to be about the same age as his own, and he'd noticed last night that she was either pregnant or unfortunately pot-bellied for an otherwise petite woman.

Miguela stopped when Queen Lucia called out hello, and Nate thought the queen seemed really nice. A whole hell of a lot nicer than his own mom, anyway. Queen Lucia told them her little one tended cold and had been giving her a hard time about it, very much like Prince Eugene had when he was a baby.

"Not like Carina, though," Queen Lucia said. "With her, I was never sick once, and not a thing in the world would have bothered me the whole time I was carrying her. Her natural disposition is just as calm as can be." She patted her belly and eyed Nate mischievously. "Though I hear *you* had her riled up this morning."

"*Mom*," Miguela said. "He doesn't want to talk about that." Then she whisked him away and took him to the lodge instead, which was an enormous and yet somehow cozy cabin that seemed to serve as a recreation center for the fort.

"We can't have an official ball or anything," Miguela said while they looked over bookshelves stocked with cheap romance novels and sci-fi sagas. "But this place isn't bad."

"Balls are over-rated," Nate said. "And I bet you had plenty when the Northern Royals were still living at the Winter Blue House. I've seen pictures of that decorated during the Festival of Lights. Must be something to see in person."

"I wouldn't know," Miguela said. "It's boarded up. No

one's lived there since before Carina was born. Does the South still celebrate the Feast of Plenty? I always imagine it as this huge holiday party where you just eat rich chocolate desserts and wear your fanciest clothes and stay up dancing all night for two weeks."

Nate ran his finger over the spines of a few books. "You are absolutely right. It's two weeks of drunken debauchery, and the Royal Church approves of it."

She smiled, and he had the thought that there was some-thing truly bright and beautiful fueling her from the inside. Nate had some experience with pretty girls. It was easy to attract them when you were the royally broken prince. Miguela, though. She was special. He wanted to—he wasn't sure—kiss her forehead or something. He only smiled back at her. "But you know a lot about South Kepler, Princess Miguela. I'm impressed."

She blushed. "I like history. I read a lot. Speaking of which, I'll show you my dad's library. It has real books."

After Queen Lucia's comment, Nate was nervous about running into the king, and King Reginald was in his library when they got there, working at an expansive, white oakory wood desk. He greeted them with bemusement Nate couldn't quite interpret.

"Ahh, I see my fire princess is giving you the tour, Prince Nathanial. I suppose Franklin decided to postpone any more training until tomorrow?"

Nate winced and ignored Miguela's sideways glance. "Yes, sir."

"I saw the video," the king continued, making Nate's stomach drop into the ground. Franklin could have told him they'd been *recording* that. "I hope you made friends with Prince Eugene today, too. I hear my *ice* princess is perturbed."

Nate tried to figure out if he should apologize, but the king's mind was quiet and his face neutral.

"I could lighten up next time. If you want, sir," he offered. Not for Icy's sake. Only out of respect to the king.

King Reginald pushed a book on his desk toward him. "Have you read this one?" It was titled *Defense for the Naturally Offensive*, by … Herschel Wellington?

"Your dad?" Miguela said.

Nate picked it up and touched the cover gingerly. "I … didn't know my dad ever wrote a book."

"He did this one on, well, I guess you could call it a dare," King Reginald said. "Small batch print run. But I suggest you take a look. It would be wiser to work on your defense than to lighten up on Carina." King Reginald winked at him, then nodded at Miguela. "Miguela, did you know Nate can talk telepathically with animals? I bet he'd like to visit his horse."

Miguela's eyes popped out at Nate. "No way. You can talk to animals?" she said, and she pulled him eagerly away from the king's library to take him to the stables. But he did not miss a big, juicy thought from the king as they left: *He'll be lucky if Carina doesn't try to kill him tomorrow.*

"I'm glad you're here," Miguela said as they walked.

He couldn't bring himself to agree with the sentiment. The Northern Royals were great. Except for the one who wanted him dead. And no matter how you sliced it, Nate still just wanted to go home.

CHAPTER NINETEEN
GHOSTS OF THE PAST

"A guest is coming to see me," Bast said as he sat by Vivian's deathbed. That's how he'd come to think of it. Though sometimes, Bast caught himself imagining she *was* only sleeping. Or frozen in time. Perhaps she could be reawakened if he—

But no. She was not living. She was dead. It was, therefore, not her bed that he kept pulling her favorite reading chair up toward. It was her deathbed. There was a difference.

Nevertheless, he took her hand as he always did and tried not to flinch at the cold. Tending cold did not mean *liking* the cold. There was also a difference there.

"He could be here sometime this afternoon."

Bast felt he was being coy speaking like that. Viv would have caught on. He watched for her face to pinch up. If it did, he might have to tell her everything about his guest. But her face remained frozen, so he brought up another subject. Brandon Thurlow. A subject that now felt much safer.

"We're giving Thurlow one more opportunity to confess

before his trial," Bast told Vivian. "I know. You still think he cared about you. But I'm going to find out what he did. He'll pay for it."

Ahh, yes. That was better. Threatening Thurlow was an enormous stress relief. And today, it was keeping his mind off Jax Channing. Beautiful Jax. Who wrote beautiful letters that destroyed Bast's soul. Whose most recent letter had words that seemed to burn Bast's fingertips as he read them, over and over, trying to decipher what they meant. Why did Jax think *now* was the time for a visit? Didn't he know better? Couldn't he have stayed away?

And why on Kepler couldn't Bast talk to Vivian about this? She'd have understood. She'd have kept his secret. But still, there was something raw and fragile about this. If Bast shared it, it might break. He left Vivian earlier than normal to walk down the tower stairs slowly, trying to figure it all out before Jax showed up.

Jax had come into Bast's life one summer while Vivian was away, traveling with the king. He arrived like a prayer Bast hadn't known he needed answered, on an Evening of Communion, at the children's service. It was a shortened version of the adult mass that Nate, a year older than Bast, now had to attend. There was playtime in the children's version, and Bast normally spent that time reading, away from the others. But that evening, a new boy sat by him, as though completely undaunted by the cold prince of South Kepler.

No, not just undaunted. Jax was *unimpressed*. Bast was reading *The Chronicles of Narnia*, and Jax didn't speak to him right away. At first, the boy only sat in the foam bag next to Bast, reading his own book quietly. But after ten minutes or so, he set down his book, and said, "I expected the prince to be beyond *Narnia*."

Bast knew an insult when he heard one, but when he looked over, he was surprised to find a boy with skin paler than his own, hair lighter, and eyes an even clearer blue. It was like looking at a ghost of himself. And because of that familiarity, rather than try to scare the other boy away with a chill, Bast replied: "I like C.S. Lewis."

Jax nodded, then surprised Bast again with the kind of overly intellectual response you get from a grown elder of the church, not a ten-year-old.

"Yes, as far as capacity to imagine the mysteries of the divine and depict them in ways children can understand, Lewis is one of my favorites. I only thought you would have Lewis's work memorized by now and be moving on to the *Greater Theological Collection*, like me." He held up the book he was reading. "I read the entire Christian-Judeo Bible last year, and now I'm on the Vedas. This is a Keplerian translation, but I also have a copy in classical Sanskrit. Don't you think Sanskrit is the most wonderful form of writing?"

Bast said, "Who *are* you?"

"Jax," the boy said. "Jax Channing. My parents are vicars, and we're in Alighieri so they can attend the Royal Church's continuing education summer program. Also, I like your bookmark." He pointed to a gold-plated bookmark Bast's mother had given him for his birthday. "Should we be friends?"

And so, they were. As simple as that. For one glorious summer, Bast had a friend. Not a family member forced to associate with him. Not a servant, attendant, or personal guard. Not one of the children sometimes brought to the castle to socialize Bast and his siblings.

A friend. A boy his own age, as smart as he was, mostly interested in the same things, though admittedly, Bast's curiosity about religion didn't take off until Jax came around.

Jax knew so much more about the subject. They spent hours together in a quiet corner of the Royal Library, Jax telling Bast everything he thought about the Royal Church and asking and answering questions that seemed deeply important, like, "Why was the advent of a messiah so important to early religious communities but not to us?" and "Do you think it's more important to be kind to the poor or to honestly believe in God?"

Bast could have spent forever listening to Jax. And it was in the library, in the religion section on the fourth floor, where Bast learned he preferred kissing boys.

They had spent that particular day searching for a book that could explain the origin of a phrase inscribed on a gold plate below the Altar of the Warrior Saint in the Old Church Cathedral. It said, "He who conquers his desires is braver than he who conquers his enemies, for victory over self is divine." Bast said he thought the statement probably had an Eastern Asian origin, maybe a Chinese philosopher. Jax believed it was Earth Western in origin.

"Here!" Jax said, holding open a book for Bast after many hours of searching. "I found it. And I was right! It *is* from an ancient Greek philosopher. Aristotle wrote it thousands and thousands of years ago."

The library was, like most buildings in Alighieri, lit by natural light, and the philosophy section felt dim except for where the sun pierced through curtained windows. A beam of light struck Jax as he held the book up triumphantly, and Bast was struck by the thought that dust was beautiful when floating through the sunlight around Jax.

Jax set the book down on a shelf and met Bast's eyes with a familiar smile. It was the sort of smile you give someone you've known and loved for ages. "Though you're probably right, too, you Ecclesiastic," he said, "Even the oldest stories have been told before. I bet if we look long enough, we can find this same phrase in the *Tao de Ching*. We could find anything together. Especially in ancient literature."

Bast, who was charmed by Jax's optimism, particularly concerning their capability to accomplish difficult tasks together, said, "I bet you're right." Then, for reasons he could not later explain to himself other than that he felt an irresistible pull, he put his hands on Jax's face and kissed him.

Probably Bast would have regretted it if Jax hadn't immediately said: "I was wondering when one of us would try that. I guess you're the brave one."

"I don't think that's what Aristotle meant," Bast said.

"I think it's *exactly* what he meant," Jax said. Then he proved that he could be brave, too, by kissing Bast, who decided then that he would *far* rather be kissed by a brave boy who *meant* it than some silly girl who didn't know what she wanted.

For two more weeks, Bast had everything good in the world. Then disaster struck, and Jax became the one secret Bast would keep from everyone forever. Even Viv. Even now, when talking to Vivian only meant talking to her frozen corpse.

And why was that? Over the last few weeks, Bast had obsessed over the question.

It had nothing to do with sexuality or gender. Bast did not believe in a binary world. Why should he? A central tenet of the Royal Church was that God's power extended across the full spectrum of infinite possibilities. Sure, Bast mostly thought of himself anatomically as a man, but he had no trouble expressing femininity when he so desired, and he assumed God meant him to be that way.

As for who he was attracted to? He'd never thought of

making a declaration, but he never had any romantic interest in a girl. He sometimes *noticed* feminine beauty. After all, he had great respect for the beauty of *all* God's creations. A few of the girls Nate had gotten involved with were pretty. The girl with the cold magic, Carina, had been very pretty. Vivian was beautiful. That didn't mean he cared for any of those girls romantically or sexually.

Furthermore, Bast knew no one in his family—or even his kingdom—would be bothered by his preferences. The Royal Church was open to any expression of love or identity that didn't trump your respect for the Great Creator. If someone mistook his intentions because he didn't go around acting like some beast marking whatever he later wanted to hump, that wasn't his problem. He didn't owe anyone an explanation, and no one would have asked for one.

But more relevantly, Bast's lack of willingness to make sweeping statements about his gender or sexuality was *not* why he'd kept his feelings about Jax under wraps for so long. *That* was a far more serious problem. It was about loyalty to the Crown. Bast had to keep Jax at a distance—had to keep him a secret—not because Jax was a boy but because he was *disgraced*. Tainted by the sins of his parents, traitors to the Crown.

That's why Jax was torn away from him after their perfect summer. The Channings had used their connection to the Royal Church to cover that they were members of a known terrorist group, GAP, the Gandhi Allegiance of Peace. GAP claimed to seek "peaceful" means of re-uniting all Mortal Kepler under a new democratic government, but the brutal truth was anything but peaceful.

GAP was known for orchestrating the deaths of high-ranking government officials, members of the clergy, and even influential businesspersons who were friends of the Royal Kingdom of South Kepler. Brandon Thurlow could be a member of GAP. That was the kind of person the group employed. The kind you didn't expect to be terrorists.

The Channings were arrested at a GAP meeting. Though they first claimed the meeting was purely a "thought discussion," they later confessed they were planning a double assassination. Of the two young princes of South Kepler, who were vulnerable while the king was away.

Jax's parents were executed a day later, while Jax himself was taken into custody, even though he swore he had no idea what his parents were planning. Bast *knew* Jax was telling the truth, but his desperate pleas only prevented Jax from being imprisoned for treason for life. Jax was still sent to live in an orphanage. Far away from Bast.

"Because we can't take any chances, dear," is what his mother said.

What she meant was that Bast's testimony couldn't be trusted. Constance was a smart woman. She knew her ten-year-old son was still young and innocent enough that he might have covered for someone he cared for.

Bast said goodbye to his grief-stricken friend, alone and confused in the dungeons below the castle, and Jax was removed from Bast's life.

"So, don't be an idiot, Jax," Bast thought as he descended below the castle. He'd written back to Jax that a visit was a terrible idea. Not that Jax was a threat, but Bast knew he shouldn't ever have real contact with him again. Not in person. At least not until Bast was the king. Maybe even then.

The correspondence they'd managed, under various

pseudonyms, was risky enough. Gael could already identify Jax's handwriting, and he'd easily guessed who those letters were from. (Gael was an exceptionally good assistant.) So, a visit? Not smart. Loving another boy was fine. Loving a suspected traitor to the Crown could mean execution for Bast and Jax both.

Maybe Bast needed to remind Thurlow of that today, actually; the Royal Family was not exempt from scrutiny. If anything, they were held to higher standards. Bast was on his way to the dungeons now. Where Thurlow would be waiting in a small, miserable room, under a bright light, by a table with various tools Bast could use at his discretion to make Thurlow talk. An electric shock device. A strobe light that could temporarily blind its subjects. Syringes of various substances that could cause disorientation, hallucinations, excruciating pain.

Nate had referred to this as their torture chamber, and he always said it with the kind of naïve repugnance that made it lucky Nate had not survived the Mountain of Peril. Bast, who was better suited to be royal, much preferred to think of it as an interrogation room.

When he arrived, Thurlow was already chained to an uncomfortable metal chair bolted to the floor. Bast had never understood what his sister saw in Thurlow from a physical standpoint, but months in the dungeons hadn't done Thurlow any favors. He looked hideously bedraggled now. His hair and beard were shaggy and dirty. His face thin and drawn. His body was winnowed to bone, sinew, and what muscle Thurlow had left. The guards said Thurlow exercised in the morning. Did push-ups and crunches for hours before breakfast. But he didn't have much to show for the effort.

"God, Thurlow, imagine what you'd look like if you

weren't working out," Bast said as he stepped toward the table of interrogation devices. He picked up the shocker and turned it on. A quiet buzz issued from the device. He held it in front of his face. Odd that this little thing was supposed to make someone reticent talk.

"It won't drag anything out of me," Thurlow said. He sounded haggard and raspy. Maybe he had a cold. Poor, pathetic Brandon Thurlow.

Bast held the shocker to his own skin, just to see what he was dealing with, then switched it off with a disappointed sigh. "You're right," he said to Thurlow. "This device wouldn't get anything out of a sociopath like you." Then he turned from the table. "I can do *much* better without any of that garbage."

"Nothing will get you what you want," Thurlow said, but Bast could see him shivering beneath his ragged clothes at just the touch of a chill in the air.

"Because you'll protect whomever you conspired with to your final breath?" Bast asked. "You know, we have multiple methods of execution. But if you cooperate, I can do it myself. Make it painless. Quick."

Thurlow's lips were blue, but he kept his head up. "Because I didn't do anything wrong. Ask me anything. You know I've never lied to you."

That *did* still trouble Bast. Even when Bast asked Thurlow questions he assumed would be humiliating, Thurlow didn't lie. Bast was dealing with a mastermind.

"That's why we're here today, Thurlow," Bast told him. "Obviously, I haven't been able to sweet talk you into telling me what really happened. So—" He directed a blast of cold to Thurlow's left arm, freezing it solidly from elbow to fingertips and ignoring Thurlow's howl of pain. "—Let's see what a different technique can get us."

Thurlow passed out four times before Bast gave up. By then, Bast himself was feeling sick. How ineffective was his magic that he couldn't get a low-level like Thurlow to talk? He stormed up from the dungeons in an awful mood, planning to retreat to the courtyard. Torture was cold business. Bast needed to warm himself in the sun.

Gael was waiting for him along with a butler holding a platter with a hot lunch. Bast didn't think he was hungry, but he could have been wrong. Probably he *was* wrong. Gael was the only reason Bast ever managed to eat anything these days. His assistant had an excellent sense of when a hearty stew might serve Bast well. Had it been only Gael and the butler standing there, Bast might have recovered from his encounter with Thurlow easily.

Instead, Bast's insides threatened to out themselves. Because a third man was standing there with them. Lithe limbs, hair so blonde it was nearly white, skin like it was never touched by a UV ray, and when the man turned toward Bast, his eyes were diamonds cut to slice open old wounds.

Early. He was early.

"Jax," Bast heard himself say.

"Are you feeling alright, Prince Bastian?" the man said. "It's Vaughn Johnson."

Right. Fake names. Bast tried to pull it together.

"I told Mr. Johnson you might prefer to meet with him later, sir," Gael said, sounding rightfully anxious. "He said he was an old acquaintance."

Jax smiled at Bast, and it seemed like a falsehood. "Can we talk privately somewhere, Prince Bastian?"

No. That was what Bast wanted to say. That was what he

should say. But what he did say was, "Gael, you are dismissed for the day. The meal can be returned to the kitchen."

"Yes, sir," Gael said, and he and the butler disappeared, leaving Bast along with Jax, who dropped the smile as soon as they were gone.

"You aren't doing well," Jax said then.

"My sister just died," Bast said.

"Your sister died half a year ago."

Bast wanted more than *anything* for Jax, who suddenly looked as hard as granite, to embrace him. To be there for him. To be the person who took away his pain. Instead, something in Jax's tone made Bast snap back: "What makes you think grief should have a time limit?"

Jax hardened further. "I know *grief*, Bast," he said in a low, smooth tone that was so much more intoxicating than Jax's voice had sounded when they were children. "And what I *think* is that grief doesn't suit you. You look terrible."

Those statements hit hard and low, but Jax had made a mistake. Had forgotten something important about Bast. "You're lying," Bast whispered.

Jax stared at Bast.

Bast stared back.

Then in a flash so fast it felt unreal, Jax's mouth was against Bast's, and it was not at all like it had been when they were children. This was beyond that. This was Jax saying Bast wasn't the only one who had been waiting half a lifetime for a reunion. Even if it *was* bad for them both.

There was a pause, and with his forehead leaned into Bast's neck, Jax said, "Is there somewhere we can go to be alone? I think we have private business to attend to."

Bast said, "I think we do."

CHAPTER TWENTY:
HOW TO TRAIN YOUR ROYALS II

Franklin stuck to individual skill drills for the rest of the week but restarted the water wars the following Monday. As a result, Carina went into thermodynamic panic three days in a row. Thursday, she managed to stave off the panic long enough to see what it looked like when her skin was scalded all over. Eugene was called in, but it wasn't for her. She'd hurt Prince Nathanial so bad he couldn't drag his butt to the infirmary.

Franklin said, "That was good," to Carina, briefly, while he rushed to Nate's side. Then she passed out from the pain. When she came to, she was in her bed, and Ollie was sitting in a chair at her bedside.

"Warm bubble bath?" Ollie asked. "Franklin said you'd be healed but cold when you woke up. Glory-Jane is pacing around the front room, fretting about what kind of essential oils to put in the water."

"Is the prince alive?" Carina asked weakly.

Ollie pulled her knees up to her chest. "Do you want him

dead? He's sort of cute."

Carina pulled her blankets to her nose. "He lived."

"Consolation prize—he was throwing blood up every-where when Mishe and I came in. You have the day off tomorrow. Franklin said he's planning a new training proto-col this weekend." Ollie's eyes lit up. "Which *might* mean—"

Carina felt woozy. She pushed herself up and leaned away from her pillow as drool puddled in the back of her throat. She was going to vomit on the sheets and then have to sleep on them because she wouldn't be able to move for the sheets to be changed. She felt her shoulders heave and saw a bucket appear below her chin.

"Here." Ollie held Carina's hair back and rubbed her shoulders while Carina threw up into the bucket. The last person who'd done that for her was Sister Elizabeth, the year everyone but Elizabeth got food poisoning from something Sister Raji brought back to Novi Dupree from a market that Sister Lindy *so* did not approve of.

If someone had to hold her hair back while she threw up here, Carina wished it could have been her mom or sister. But Mom couldn't be here, and Miguela was proba-bly hanging around Max and Nate. Because for whatever sick reason, Carina's little sister *liked* both the guys now. Miguela had started getting up in the mornings, bathing, and eating outside her own room because of them. She was supposed to be a feminist. *How was this okay?*

Tears rushed Carina—clearly a result of her frustration and disappointment over basically everything that related to either Max or Nate—and Ollie stroked her hair. "Hey, it's okay."

Carina looked into Ollie's big eyes. "I miss the Sisters," she said. "I wish I were back at the sanctuary."

Ollie continued to pet Carina, but her face got long. "They didn't tell you? They keep *so* many secrets."

Carina looked at her vomit in the bucket. At least it wasn't blood. She rested her cheek on the edge. "What didn't they tell me?"

Ollie winced. "The Immortals who were coming after you and Miguela caused so much destruction at Novi Dupree that no one can live there right now. Most of the Sisters moved out."

Carina pushed the bucket away. "*What?* The sanctuary was *destroyed?* What about the brewery?"

"*That's* still intact," Ollie said, setting the bucket aside and handing Carina a cloth to wipe her mouth with. "Raji would have died otherwise. And they're rebuilding, but—"

The door to Carina's room creaked open to reveal Glory-Jane's nose. "Princess? The king is here to see you."

"We can talk more later if you want," Ollie said. "Do you need me to get anything for you?"

Carina felt miserable. "Trashy romance novel?" she said. "Because—"

Ollie laughed. "Because that's what Aunt Elizabeth would have done."

"Exactly," Carina said.

King Reggie entered the room after Ollie left. He was leaning heavily on his cane, and Carina thought he looked anxious and *old*.

She sat up in bed. "It's not as bad as it looks."

He pointed at the chair near the bed. "Franklin showed me the tapes of this morning's training session. Can I sit down?"

Carina was stressed enough about these training sessions,

and she hadn't realized they were being recorded. But she was too exhausted to feel betrayed. She stared down at the fringe of her thickest blanket.

"I should have told you," her dad said. "After Hess, we felt we needed to record the sessions as a precaution. Not that we don't trust Franklin, but—"

"You don't trust the prince?" Carina asked.

Her dad smiled wryly. "We *do* trust Prince Nathanial. But we've had poor judgment before. And if you feel this isn't working out, we can find another teacher—"

"I didn't ask for that," she said quickly.

He raised his voice gently. "I know. And you're already performing at a much higher level than either Franklin or I thought you were currently capable of. It's going *well*, Carina."

She curled her shoulders in. "Not well enough. He burns me every time. This time—"

"*This* time you mortally wounded your opponent," the king said. "He'll live. But only because Eugene was right there to fix it. It was a good fight. You won."

He said that like he was proud of her, and Carina couldn't help but feel gratified.

"Franklin tells me Nate is also performing at a higher level than before. So that wasn't a softball fight, and I'm glad you don't want to quit. This is how you get better." Her dad slouched and let his legs stretch out long while he folded his hands over his stomach. "Want to cheat? Nate fights like his dad used to."

"I cannot believe you were *friends* with King Herschel," Carina mused.

King Reginald chuckled. "Herschel and I attended a boarding school in Gandhi together for a few years. It's not easy for a First Degree Cardinal to find a master, and the best fire master of our time was teaching there. That's how I know Franklin. He grew up in Gandhi, and Herschel looked up to him back then, before … well, that's Franklin's story. I don't think he likes to talk about it."

"But why didn't you stay friends with King Herschel?" Carina asked.

Her dad slouched further and looked sideways. "Immortal Empire took a turn for the worse, your grandmother was killed, and King Cassius wanted to fight back using our land. We lost a lot of territory to the South."

Carina had read about Immortal siege of the Winter Blue House. Queen Ezmeralda was killed protecting her fifteen-year-old daughter during the siege. The surviving members of the family, including the twenty-one-year-old crown prince, the eighteen-year-old "middle" princess, and their father, William Wright, moved to some small town in the North.

Crown Prince Reginald Garcia assumed the throne, but the family tragedy continued when Reginald's youngest sister and father both drowned in a freak boating accident. Reginald's remaining sister became estranged from the family. The young king married a few years later and had children of his own, but he and his entire family were killed in yet another Immortal attack when the children were still young.

That was her family, but Carina still could not associate her life with that story. It was all so foreign to her. The only part she could wrap her head around was that her family had some work to do if they ever wanted their status as the Royal Family of North Kepler to count for anything.

"What are we doing to get our territory back?" she asked her dad.

"To reclaim it?" King Reggie laughed. "We spent the last few years just *recovering* from the attack six years ago. The

Immortals ransacked the homes of several of our most important council members and military leaders. Many of our best were killed. We lost you and Miguela. I still haven't recovered."

Carina thought of all the things that had happened to her between Novi Dupree and here. "But things are *bad* out there. The Southern Guard is terrible. People in the border towns hate Queen Constance. And no one should have to fear being kidnapped by an Immortal bounty hunter. The Northerners need our *help*."

He gave her a *look*. "And yet, you want me to declare that we can no longer arrest someone just for being Immortal."

Her cheeks warmed. With all the training, she'd barely had the energy to think about those prisoners in Cerulean. The warden had sent the report she wanted. She'd read it, then she'd written a formal request to her dad for better resources, but that's all she'd had time for.

"I approved your request, by the way," he said. "I didn't know conditions were that bad. But there's no way for us to know which Immortals are working for the Empire. We can't afford innocent until proven guilty with them."

"That doesn't seem like a good excuse," Carina said.

"And you have your mother's bleeding heart. But as king, I have to choose my battles." He patted his leg. "And I can't change anything myself weakened like this."

As far as Carina could tell, her dad hadn't chosen *any* battles in *ages*. "But you're a First Degree Cardinal. Even with a limp, you have magic. You don't need training."

He sighed. "You think that, but I'm not as powerful as I was. I'm not as powerful as *you* will be. If you want us back out there, you need to do exactly what you're doing. Learn how to get along with the Royal Society. Train with someone who challenges you. Help your sister so we can get her training, too. Until we're strong enough as a *family* to handle a real fight, we can't be what the kingdom needs us to be."

Carina wanted to get better faster, but since training was canceled Friday, she had three full days to worry and attempt to avoid Prince Nathanial, something she was largely unsuccessful with. He showed up everywhere she went. At the gym to run when she ran, despite the prayers he supposedly did every morning at dawn. In the cafeteria for breakfast, always getting peanut butter right when she needed it. In the stables, bothering the dogs she wanted to play with.

She had some time to catch up with Heathrow, but only over the phone. He'd been concerned that she didn't want to see him anymore after her field trip to Cerulean.

"It's not that," she said. "My training is just harder now."

"Because you're working with the prince of South Kepler," Heathrow said. "I heard."

He sounded mildly jealous, so Carina said, "The prince is a terrible person. He doesn't care at all if he hurts me."

"Never occurred to *him* to be chivalrous, huh?" Heathrow said, and that made Carina want to switch the subject.

Monday morning, Carina skipped breakfast and her workout because she didn't want to accidentally run into Prince Nathanial any earlier than necessary before their training session. Then he showed up to training right when she did.

One minute before seven.

Franklin was sitting in the middle of the gym like he'd

been meditating. He opened his eyes. "Ahh, Nate, Carina, I hope you both had a restful weekend. Today I have a real challenge for you."

"Let me guess," Nate said as they walked toward Franklin. "You're going to make us use buckets of hot oil this week."

"That would give you an unfair advantage," Carina said dryly while she tried to avoid being in step with Nate. But she thought he was probably right, and the grotesque twinkle in Franklin's eye did not make her feel better.

"You will not be fighting each other today." Franklin stood up. "I spent the weekend prepping training partners for you. I expect them to be right on cue."

The door to the training facility opened, and in walked Max and Ollie, both dressed in combat boots, helmets, and training gear and armed with *guns*. Big, dangerous, highly illegal, and definitely prohibited guns. Max looked grim. Olivette was grinning like a loon.

"Um, Franklin?" Prince Nathanial said.

"Try not to get shot," Franklin said as he walked toward the door. "I'll be watching from out here. Oh, and I told Max and Ollie that their job today was to take you both out as quickly as possible. We'll discuss how you did after."

Carina felt a little dumb as Max, who she'd avoided since his arrival at Aurora Borealis, pointed his gun at her. "Sorry, Carina," he said, and she didn't even have time to yell before he'd fired and something green splattered against the defensive telekinetic shield she managed to produce instinctively at the sound of a gunshot.

She heard another blast, and Prince Nathanial howled in pain. Apparently, he *didn't* produce defensive telekinetic shields instinctively. Now a thick, blue substance was spurting from the middle of his chest.

Carina couldn't work out how she felt about Max killing Nate today, though, because her courtier was far more talented than she'd realized. While Max stood stationary, firing at her and Prince Nathanial, Ollie flipped through the air like a crazed gymnast. She landed on an elevated platform none of Carina's trainers had used for anything yet, gave out a "whoop!" and started shooting at Carina from that elevated position.

This was when Carina learned something critical. Defensive telekinetic shields were not easy to move. As soon as Carina tried to shift her energy to shield herself from Ollie, Max managed a shot that felt like a blunt impact to Carina's lower back. She screamed and tried to touch the wound. Could she heal this? Would this kill her? Franklin wouldn't have allowed a deadly exercise, would he?

Her fingers came away from the wound sticky and yellow while another bullet struck her thigh and made her stumble forward. Why were her fingers yellow? Why was there green blood coming from a wound on her thigh?

"Garcia! Don't be *stupid!* Magic always trumps *guns* if you have time to think about it!" Prince Nathanial yelled. Which is also something she didn't understand. Why wasn't he dead on the floor? Why was Max's gun airborne?

Another shot struck her back from Ollie's direction, and Carina thought she wasn't going to breathe again. But the prince was bleeding weirdly colored blood from several places, and yet, *he* was standing there, holding Max's gun like he'd just magicked it away from Max.

She took a second to think about.

Those guns couldn't be loaded with real bullets.

Ollie jumped down from the raised platform and began circling Carina like a hawk. "That's right, Princess," she said.

"The other guy with the gun is down, I'm the only one left, and it's my job to kill you. I'm Immortal. I'm rash. What are you going to do?"

She fired at Carina, but this time Carina was more in control of where her energy was focused, and the fake bullet splattered blue against a telekinetic shield she produced on purpose while she began moving.

"Good, don't be a sitting duck." Ollie fired the gun again, and it splattered purple against the shield.

"What are you shooting with?" Carina asked.

"Paintball gun," Ollie answered, splattering the shield with green this time. "But the prince is right. Magic trumps guns. Focus on disarming me, not just defending yourself."

Nate and Max were brawling on the floor like baboons. But Prince Nathanial seemed to get the upper hand for a milli-second, and Max went flying into the air and landed against a padded wall with a thud. In no time, Max was surrounded by a ring of fire, and Prince Nathanial looked satisfied that he'd won. He turned toward Carina and crossed his arms. "That's how the professionals do it, Garcia!" he called out, right before Max lunged *through* the fire, knocking Prince Nathanial to the ground.

"Ignore them," Ollie said. "Max and I watched all the tapes. Prince Nathanial acts fast but doesn't think things through like he should. You think too much. Take away my gun."

Carina refocused on Ollie. She had magic. She could do this. She extended her energy toward the gun, got a grip, then pulled back. Ollie held tight to the gun.

"Gotta work harder than that," Ollie said as she broke Carina's hold. But Carina thought maybe harder wasn't the answer.

"Maybe I just need to work faster," she said, jabbing her

telekinetic energy toward the gun again and yanking back as soon as she could. The gun flew out of Ollie's hands, and Carina realized she needed to do something to make it impossible for Ollie to retrieve the gun. She lifted it into the air and let it land on a ceiling beam too high for a human—Mortal or Immortal—to reach.

"Very nice!" Ollie said, taking that opening to pounce toward Carina. "But are you trained in hand-to-hand combat yet?"

Carina squirmed under Ollie's grip, panic seizing her when Ollie produced a *dagger* from who-knew-where. She felt her body go cold.

"Ouch!" Ollie sprang back, giving Carina a chance to begin circling her apparently-very-badass courtier.

"I never needed hand-to-hand combat before. But I take it you *are* trained in it?"

"It's my specialty." Ollie leaped forward again, knocking Carina to the ground but rolling away fast. "Aerial and mixed martial arts."

"HA!" Carina heard Max yell from across the gym, and she looked to see that Max had the gun Nate had previously disarmed him of. He was now holding it to Nate's head, execution-style. "I win. In real life, you're dead, bro."

She shouldn't have looked. The next thing she knew, Ollie was behind her, holding that dagger hard to her throat with one hand while she restrained Carina's arms with another.

"And I win, too, Princess Carina," she said before Carina could react by pushing all her telekinetic energy away from herself in one rush and sending Ollie flying back.

"Oh, that was smart," Ollie said from where she landed on the floor. "You'd have been dead before you could do that, but still."

Ollie began shivering noticeably while Carina felt herself getting really cold. "Don't come any closer," Carina warned. "I don't want to accidentally hurt you."

Ollie nodded and looked past Carina. Franklin was standing with a stopwatch by the door. "How was that, Franklin?" Ollie called.

Franklin's scar stretched down. "Twelve minutes, Ollie."

"Is that good?"

"For you and Max," he said. "Pathetic for two First Degree Cardinals against two barely armed kids with no magic."

That made Carina feel disheartened. Her heart was beating hard, she was sore from all those paintball hits, and she had been working hard there. *Nate*, however, was storming toward Franklin with his hands on fire. "What the hell was *that*?" he yelled. "That was dirty!"

Franklin was downright serene in his response. "This wasn't nearly as dirty as what you and Princess Carina did to each other all last week. It's more like the fights you're likely to face in the real world. And Max and Ollie both happen to be highly trained combatants familiar with Immortal weaponry. Until you can best them, this is how we work. For now, everyone take a break. We'll start again in fifteen minutes."

Carina touched her hand to her cheek to see if it was still cold. It seemed like now that the threat was gone, she wasn't feeling cold anymore.

"I don't understand," Carina said, reaching for Ollie's hand to give her what was probably an unnecessary lift from the ground. "Why are you familiar with Immortal weaponry? You're not Immortal, are you?"

Ollie laughed. "Like Max? No. But, you know, I'm a Dupree. My family *is* unusual."

"You said you were Sister Elizabeth's niece," Carina said.

"Yeah. Her great-great-niece. Anna Dupree was my great grandmother."

Things were clicking in Carina's head. "As in … Anna Dupree of Novi Dupree? Is Sister Elizabeth related to Elizabeth Dupree? The other founder?"

Ollie's mouth opened into an enormous "o." "Oooh, I'm sorry. I thought you knew. Them and their stupid *secrets*! Aunt Elizabeth isn't *related* to the Elizabeth Dupree who co-founded Novi Dupree. She *is* Elizabeth Dupree. She's an Immortal, Carina."

CHAPTER TWENTY-ONE
TOGGLEBALL AND MALAMUTES

Nate hated Franklin. Hated Max. Hated Princess Icepick.

"Don't take it so hard," Max said as their Friday training session wrapped up. "It took all morning for me to beat you this time."

"But it's not fair," Nate complained. "You can use weapons. All I have is telekinesis. If I could use fire, you'd be toast every time."

"As in, *actual* toast," Max said. "And Franklin said you could use fire indirectly. If you want to be direct, you just have to be controlled enough not to accidentally kill me."

Control. Right.

This new training setup was terrible. Nate had actually been improving when he was only fighting Ice Witch. Now he was training with Max, Ollie, and the random Northern Militia soldiers Franklin brought in sometimes, and he had the same problem he'd always had when he trained in Alighieri. There were too damn many loud thoughts in that gym all the time, and he could barely hear himself think because of it. No way could he use "controlled" fire during their training sessions.

At least he wasn't getting Icy's thoughts, though he wanted to know why. Trying to get into that girl's head was like hitting his own head against a brick wall. She mostly only thought loud enough for him to hear when she was terrified to the point of panic, and he didn't care to hear her thinking that he was going to kill her.

He. Didn't. Kill. People.

Not even annoying people like her. It would never have gotten that far. Although he had, admittedly, come close to killing her in that last water fight. In self-defense. And only after she sliced him up so badly he reactively defended himself with a wall of flames. The fire was very much out-of-control, as well as dangerous and against the rules. But apparently, Franklin thought it was justified because he didn't even say anything about it while he knelt by Nate and Nate's vision blurred. He just said, "Stay with me, Nate. Eugene is going to be here any second."

Eugene managed to heal those wounds, but Nate still spent the rest of that day vomiting, and later Max, Franklin, *and* Myles all saw him lying on his bunk, looking like a dead man.

"She won that match," Nate had said to them.

"*And* would have killed you if the healer kid hadn't been around," Myles said. "We watched the video *several* times."

This did not comfort Nate. "Why were you involved?"

"Myles is coming to Cerulean with me for the weekend," Franklin explained. "I asked for his help on a new training solution."

"Find me a way home," Nate begged Franklin. "That's the solution. I can train with Bast when he needs downtime from whatever you do when you're preparing to be the next king of something."

"You are doing what you do when you are preparing to be the next king of something," said Franklin, and then he left and returned with frickin' paintball guns.

Nate *hated* Franklin.

Thank God, the weekend came, the weather on Aurora Borealis Isle turned almost warm, and a bunch of the militia guys set up a game of toggleball in a muddy field outside the lodge. Nate dragged Max out to watch the game.

Vivian and Bast had considered toggleball a "game of the commoners." They'd both missed out, though, because there was real finesse to toggleball. There were three types of toggleball—yellow goal balls, blue multiplier balls, and red penalty balls—and the players had to be sharp to keep track. Nate had watched every game he ever had the opportunity to watch. He explained the rules to Max from the sidelines.

"See, the yellow goal balls are the most important," he said, pointing to three tenders standing around a yellow ball at one end of the field. "Each team has one, and the whole point of the game is to run your yellow ball across the field from your home zone into the other team's home zone."

"It's football," Max said.

"No, it's way more complicated than football," Nate said. "Because while the tenders are trying to run the yellow balls, the defenders have red penalty balls in play—each team starts with two of those—and you can only catch, throw, kick, or headbutt those. If you get hit by one, you're out until the next run begins."

"It's wannabe quidditch."

"No. They only play quidditch in the East."

"They *actually* play quidditch here? What about those balls in the middle of the field?" Max pointed to three blue toggleballs.

"Those are multiplier balls," Nate said. Then he launched into a detailed explanation of penalty strategies, interceptions, tag-team plays, and the difference between how a team with good defense would play versus a team with good offense. He was about to get into famous tactics used by the best teams on Kepler when Max started rubbing his temples.

"I need diagrams for this," Max said. "And why didn't that guy just catch the red ball? He saw it coming."

"Yeah, but his team *wanted* that guy out. And I can draw you several … oooh, that did *not* look good." Nate winced as one of the tenders with a yellow ball went down under a tackle play. "That's gonna put that guy out for a while."

"Lucky they have a magic healer," Max said as everyone huddled around the injured player.

"Oh, Gene won't be asked to heal that," Nate said. "If he had to heal everything, that kid would never do anything but heal. They only triage important stuff to him."

The player was carried to the side of the field.

"Why don't they wear helmets?" Max said. "Nothing on Earth gets played without helmets. We should find something else to do." His face lit up. "Want to find Carina and Ollie?"

Nate was appalled. "Isn't it bad enough that we have to spend most of the week with them?"

"You like Ollie."

That was not the problem. "What's not to like about Ollie?" Nate said. "She's cute and enthusiastic."

"I know," Max said. "So is Carina. Let's hang out with them."

That was the problem. "Carina is not *cute*."

Max frowned. "No, you're right. She's *beautiful*."

Nate opened his mouth to explain that Princess Icy was only beautiful in the way monsters willing to rain ice down on their foes were beautiful. But then he saw Miguela Garcia walking toward them. She said hello, then said, "Are you explaining the rules of toggleball to Max, Nate?"

"More like he's reading me a toggleball treatise." Max pointed his thumb at Nate. "This guy thinks this game is interesting."

"I'm trying to help you understand the finer parts of Mortal Keplerian culture," Nate said, and he added, "Hey Miguela," but instantly felt weird about it. He tapped her shoulder. "What do other people call you?"

She seemed confused. "Uh, Miguela?"

"No, I mean, what do your *friends* call you?"

"Miguela," she repeated.

"Not everyone has a nickname, Nate," Max said.

"On Kepler, they do," Nate said seriously. "It's another fine part of our culture."

Max rolled his eyes. "Stop making shit up, Prince Nathanial. People call Miguela Miguela."

"That can't be right." Nate stared at Miguela. The name Miguela was just so *formal*. "Your friends don't call you *any*thing else?"

"I … don't really have other friends," she stammered.

Nate wasn't sure why, but Miguela Garcia just had a way of making him want to hug her. And protect her from all the bad stuff in the universe. He thought Max felt the same way because Max punched the girl's shoulder lightly. "So that makes three of us. And Nate's right. If *we're* friends, we all need nicknames. There's no way I'm letting you guys call me

Maximo. Doesn't Care call you Guela or something?"

"*Guela?*" Nate rolled that over in his mouth. "Ugh. No. That's not a good nickname at all."

"And it's something I only let her and Eugene call me," Miguela said with a very skeptical look on her face.

"We have to come up with something else," Nate said. "So … how about … Miguel?"

"That's the male version of Miguela," Max said.

"Ella?" Nate suggested. "That's pretty."

Miguela pursed her lips. "But it's kind of precious, don't you think?"

It was *totally* precious. Apparently, she didn't like that, though, so he moved on. "Fine, how about Migs?"

"Migs," she said, repeating the name.

"Migs … Migs," Max said, trying it out for himself. He put his arm around her shoulders. "So Migs, how do you like the food here?"

"Uh, it's not as good as Sister Lindy's," she said, squirming under what was probably a very heavy arm. "Can you get off me?"

"Maybe," Max said. "But first, hey Migs, can you explain toggleball to me like a normal person? Nate's about to start drawing diagrams in the mud."

"Maybe if you remove yourself from my personal space," Migs said, still squirming.

Max let her go and addressed Nate. "Nickname's perfect. We shall call her Migs."

"I am not your rattycat," Migs said.

"Of course not," Nate said. "You're our Migs."

She had a seriously precious blush.

Max decided to spend the afternoon stalking his ex-girlfriend, but Migs was still up for hanging out, so Nate took her to the stables.

Pepper was quite happy in the fort's stables. At first, the horse hadn't liked the hay much—he thought it had a mineral flavor—but he adjusted thanks to the ridiculous number of treats available. Sugar cubes, carrots, green apples … it was a horse paradise.

And Nate had more time here to take care of Pepper. Almost every afternoon last week, he'd come to brush Pepper's coat, say hello, and enjoy a midday ride. He wasn't exactly making plans, but he knew it would only take about thirty minutes to get from the fort to the ferry dock on horseback. If Franklin found some worse way to torture him, there might be an escape route.

Thanks to his time spent in the stables, Nate was also now acquainted with the Garcia's dogs. They were purebred Kepler malamutes, so they were a little pretentious, but Nate knew all the dogs by name and had figured out which lived to play, which were all about pets, and which were best with commands.

He even ingratiated himself enough to play with a new batch of puppies currently residing in a cozy kennel in the corner of the stables. The new mommy was proud and protective of her pups. Still, Nate thought he could probably talk momma malamute into letting Migs play with them.

"Wait a minute, okay?" he told Miguela when they got to the stables. "You're going to love the puppies."

He went to the kennel to say hello to momma and talk to her about his friend. He communicated that the girl was gentle and sweet. Momma wasn't sure she trusted the new human—after all, *that* human wasn't chatting with her—but

Nate reminded the dog that she couldn't shelter her puppies forever, and it was good to socialize them when they were young. Five minutes later, Nate had five puppies scampering around him and Migs with their little tongues hanging out, playing the game where they each try to get the humans to pick them up and scratch behind their ears.

"Oh, they're so cute!" Migs said.

Nate knelt down, rolled one over on the ground, gave it a belly rub, and told it what a great boy it was. Then he introduced it to Migs. The puppy liked her right away. He even tried to pee on her shoe. "Oh good, he wants to be friends." Nate handed the puppy to Migs.

She took it like the puppy was the Best Gift Ever. "Are you sure I should be holding it? I haven't even seen Carina pick up any of the puppies, and she's really good with animals."

"I am an *actual* dog whisperer," Nate said. "It's fine. I have their mom's permission." The puppy squirmed nearly out of her grip. "Oops ... but that one's a bit wiggly. You might have to use telekinesis to keep her there."

Her eyes got big and panicked. "I don't use telekinesis. I don't like magic."

Ahh. Well. She tended hot. Also, he'd seen her blow up a house. He could guess why she didn't love magic. "You can't control your thermodynamics yet, huh?" he said.

She nodded.

He picked up another puppy. "You're in good company. There is no way you've blown up more stuff than I have. I have blown up spectacular things."

"And made it seem like everyone in the explosion died?" she said, more morosely than someone being licked by a puppy should ever sound.

"And give people serious burns that can only be handled

by my genius healer brother."

She seemed pensive. "So why aren't you afraid of fire?"

"I don't know. It never occurred to me to be afraid. It's not like we can just bottle up that energy and pretend it doesn't exist, right? No sense in being afraid of something I can't get rid of." The puppy Migs was holding wriggled in her arms. "Oh, that one wants down."

"Is that what he's saying?"

"He's so young that he's mostly just communicating incoherent pictures and smells and stuff. Right now, he's curious about the hay on the ground that the others are messing around in." Nate held his puppy up. "This one is too. We should set them down and let them get lost in there." He plunked his malamute into a pile of hay, and it hopped around like a little blue bunny.

Miguela did the same, and her puppy wiggled its tail and bounded into the hay. Soon, there was a whole pile of puppies tumbling over that haystack.

"Gosh, they're so cute!" Miguela said as the puppies scampered around. Then one got brave and took a flying leap from the top of the hay to a bucket of water nearby. It plopped into the water, and Nate had to scoop it up.

Miguela giggled when the puppy shook and got him all wet. Then it started shivering.

"Oh no, it's cold!" she said.

He handed it to her. "So, keep it warm."

"What, with magic?"

"Sure. What better purpose?"

Then all the fun came to an end as a cruel voice snapped, "*What* is going on here?"

Nate flinched and turned around. Ice Witch had found her way to the stables and was now blasting ice picks at him through her eyes.

"We're playing with the puppies, Carina, isn't that neat?" Miguela said innocently.

Carina huffed. "The puppies are way too young to play with. There's no way their mom would let them do this."

Nate took the puppy from Miguela, who was obviously not going to be able to warm it up herself.

"They were having fun," he said while he held the puppy to his chest and gradually transferred heat to it. "And I have their mom's express permission."

The temperature in the stables dropped. "You have *what?*" Ice Witch said.

"Nate can talk to animals," Miguela explained. "The dogs love him."

A vicious scowl took over Ice Witch's face. "*You* were the one who sent those wolves after me?"

"The wolves were yours?" Miguela said, with curiosity, *not* hostility. Ice Witch could have tried it.

Still, Nate didn't want Miguela to think poorly of him. "They weren't *mine*," he said. "They were working for me temporarily in exchange for food."

Carina put her fist on her hip. "See, you can't trust him, Miguela. He was trying to kill us with those wolves."

"I was *not*," he said. "They were running surveillance for me. And they never came back after the last time I sent them for you." A terrible thought occurred to him. "If you hurt them—"

"She didn't," Miguela said quickly. "Animals *like* Carina. And she likes them, too. She used magic to shield them when Max tried to shoot them. Then she told them to go away."

Nate felt *extremely* threatened by that, so he did the only thing that made sense. He taunted her. "Ahh. So, if Carina is *so good* with animals, does she *ride?*"

"We didn't have horses at Novi Dupree, but when we were kids, the horses loved her. You guys should go out together sometime," Miguela said, all innocently again. She clearly did not understand what was going on here.

But Princess Carina did.

"In my nightmares," she scoffed. "*You* go out with him."

Miguela got a look on her face that seemed like trepidation, and since she didn't guard her thoughts like her evil sister did, Nate could skim the surface to see what was wrong. He discovered fast that she was only afraid of riding on her own.

"You should," he said to Migs, walking over to Pepper with the warmed-up puppy now curled asleep in his arms. He gave Pepper a pat on the nose. "If you want, you can ride with me. Pepper won't mind. He knows all the best places to trot to."

Ice Witch began to turn the stables into a freezer.

"Really?" Migs said. "Because it's just … I've been on a horse before, but I always feel like I'm going to fall off, and I couldn't keep up with you."

"Then you won't need to worry about anything because I can fix both those problems," he assured her. "If you ride with me, you'll be sitting in front, I'll keep my arms around you the whole time, and I'll tell Pepper to be extra good. There's no way you'll fall off. And when you want to learn how to ride on your own, I can teach you."

Migs beamed at him so bright it made him think of sunshine. Nate usually didn't let anyone ride with him, but Migs was a worthy exception. Pepper neighed his approval and expressed to Nate that this one was a special human. Nate concurred. He and Pepper both hoped Princess Miguela would want to be friends with them for a long time.

Then Pepper added that he should also take Princess Carina out, because for some sick reason, Pepper *liked* her. Apparently, she came to the stables sometimes, too, and when she did, she always brought sugar cubes and never neglected Pepper.

What. The. Hell.

"What are you *doing*, Wellington?" Ice Witch growled.

Nate shoved down the urge to actually growl back and addressed her sister, who was looking peeved at Icy. "Let's go out riding tomorrow," he suggested to Miguela. "And if you want, we can go somewhere another time to practice thermo-dynamic magic together."

"Because you're so good, you think you can teach her?" Carina said sarcastically.

He had never met someone he disliked more. "People that tend hot don't react to fire the same way everyone else does, so Miguela won't have to worry about hurting me while she tries stuff. Anyway, teaching is a good way to learn."

"You really don't mind?" Miguela said.

"Not at all," Nate said, smiling at her and subtly warming up the stables while Ice Witch began to turn a sick shade of blue.

"Too bad your brother isn't here," Miguela said. "I bet he could have helped Carina."

That was a horrible idea. And he got a loud thought from Ice Witch over it, too. Which went like this: *Oh, no. I am never letting Prince Bastian help me with magic. Team Nate any day of the week if it comes down to that.*

Nate took the sleepy puppy back to his momma's kennel. "Guess there's at least one thing we agree on," he muttered to Ice Witch as he passed her.

She grunted an affirmative.

CHAPTER TWENTY-TWO
MELTS LIKE CHOCOLATE

A few mornings later, Ice Witch showed up to the gym the same time Nate did. This happened frequently, but normally they ran on treadmills as far apart from each other as possible.

Not today. Today, she chose the treadmill right next to him and then started to run. Fast. Now Nate was sweating profusely. Because he ran faster than her, damn it, but every time he tapped the "up" arrow on the dash of his treadmill, she hit the "up" arrow on hers, too.

Nate was at least six inches taller than Princess B. What was wrong with her that she couldn't run at a respectably slower speed than him? He was getting along well with everyone else here. Saturday, the princess's head guard, Mishe, had invited him to play toggleball with the militia guys to replace their injured player. Sunday, he'd taken Miguela out on Pepper. Nate was getting to know Gene, too, who liked asking questions about the South, and sometimes, when Princess Carina was busy after a training session, Ollie had lunch with Nate and Max. Ollie was hot *and* hilarious, and she stuck her mouth in it almost as often as Max.

The only problem was Ice Witch, and if the girl could ever show any humanity, maybe he could like her, too. But it was not human to run with a perfectly even stride and perfect posture. And human girls had sweat glands. She should *at least* have a dewy sheen on her skin.

She caught his eye in the reflection of the glass window in front of them. "Struggling, Wellington?"

God, she didn't even sound tired. He had to perform epic breath control to make it sound like he could run all day answering, "Hardly."

In response, she tapped the up arrow on her treadmill twice. *Why?* Also, why had he told Max that Garcia was showing up at the gym the same time as him in the mornings? Nate could see Max behind them in the glass. He'd positioned himself on a bench near the treadmills with some weights, but Nate would have bet his horse the princess hadn't noticed Max doing bicep curls shirtless to impress her.

Nate tapped his "up" arrow three times. He had longer legs and more muscle. He was *supposed* to run faster. She tapped the arrow on her treadmill again and spoke to him. "I hear you're taking my sister out again this afternoon."

Why did she think he wanted to *chat* while they ran at crazy speeds? Ollie was on a stationary bike at the far side of the fitness center. Carina could have hopped on the stationary bike next to Ollie and chatted with her if that's how she liked to get in her cardio.

"Are you jealous?" he retorted.

"No," she snapped. "But I do want to know what game you're playing with her."

He was dripping sweat everywhere. He wiped his

forehead, slowed the treadmill down, and said, "I don't know what you're talking about, Garcia. I'm not doing anything but being nice to your sister."

Carina slowed her treadmill down, too. "You are almost four years older than her," she said sternly.

Nate didn't get it. Who cared how old the girl was? "Is there an age limit on who you can be friends with? Because Max is four-hundred years older than me."

Carina groaned loudly. "She has a *crush* on you, Prince Oblivious. Can't you tell?" Then she sped her treadmill up to a run again. He sped up, too, and watched Max angle bar lifts so that if Carina bothered looking, she'd get an especially good look at his chest. Poor Max. The princess was way too busy being furious at Nate for that.

As for Miguela having a crush on him … Nate had the uneasy feeling that Carina Garcia had figured something out he probably should have figured out. Miguela had a crush on him. That explained why she was always popping up to see him, why she laughed at his worst jokes, why she pinked up whenever he complimented her.

How had he missed that?

Still, he didn't see the problem. A crush was hardly the worst threat Nate was facing. Sheesh. A little more love between the North and South was probably a good thing, no matter how small. Anyway, Miguela was a sweetheart, and if she liked him that way, it only made him feel more protective of her.

Princess B cleared her throat.

"Okay. She has a crush on me," Nate said. "And the problem is …? "

"You don't care about her feelings at all, do you?" Carina demanded. "She's going to figure it out, and you'll hurt her, and that is *not* something my sister needs right now!"

He had no idea how she was running so fast and yelling at him, but he was forced to slow to a jog. "I'm not going to *hurt* her," he said. "And I do care about her."

His opponent's abnormally large eyes narrowed suspiciously. "Not the way she cares about you."

"Well, no," he admitted, "because she's a little young for me right now and I'm not a creep. But if Miguela has a crush on me, it's no big deal. It'll fade eventually. I'm not going to make an issue of it."

Carina only glared harder. "It's an issue whether you make it one or not. And you better not do anything to encourage her."

"This is ridiculous," Nate said. "What do you think I'm going to do? Ask her out on a midnight stroll? Snuggle with her in the lodge?"

"How about take her for a romantic ride on your horse," Carina said wryly. Then she punched that stupid treadmill up to a dead sprint while a few more things clicked in Nate's head. It made him feel mortified. And mildly ashamed. Two things he never wanted to feel in front of Ice Witch.

He sped up to an even faster sprint to work that off, and finally, he got some revenge when she didn't speed up with him. He sneaked a look and was extremely pleased to see a gratifying drop of sweat was running down her temple. Ha. Maybe he'd missed Miguela's crush, but he *could* run faster than Carina.

Now if she would only slow the hell down.

She jammed that arrow up to match his pace.

Oh, no. He was *not* slowing down.

She ran.

He ran.

Pain shot through his legs. He stopped thinking. He watched Max try to bench press a barbell that was too heavy for him. He saw Ollie get off her bike and walk toward Max. And probably he'd have run until he died except that Ollie yelped out, and that gave Nate just enough time to notice Max about to drop that barbell on his neck.

Nate stopped short to provide some telekinetic spotting assistance and save Max's sorry ass. The barbell rocketed up much faster than Nate had anticipated, slamming into the ceiling lights, which shattered and rained over Max and Ollie while Garcia's guards came running.

The barbell stayed levitated in the air as Nate tried to pull it down. "What the—"

"Let go, you idiot!"

Carina was breathing heavily now, there *was* sweat on her neck, and she had her hand in the air like she was trying to pull the barbell down. So, he hadn't been the only one who'd noticed Max nearly meeting his demise, and now they'd caused major property damage.

"You let go!" Nate shouted back.

He should have known better than to say something like that.

"If you hurt my sister, I *will* seek vengeance on you, Nate Wellington," she said savagely. Then she dropped the barbell. He only barely prevented the thing from conking Max on the head as Garcia stomped away from the treadmills toward the showers.

"Oh, so are we done, then?" Ollie said, trotting cheerfully after Carina.

Nate grabbed a towel and began wiping buckets of sweat away as he walked toward Max, his shoes crunching on broken glass.

"What the hell were you thinking? You nearly killed your-self!" he said to Max.

But Max just sat on the bench, looking dreamily after Carina. "She *saved* me."

Nate was *surrounded* by insanity.

Unfortunately, Nate couldn't get his conversation with Ice Witch out of his head. When Migs met him later at the stables, he was confronted immediately with a problem he'd never had before:

Where was she supposed to ride?

Yesterday, Nate hadn't thought twice of putting Miguela up on Pepper in front of him. It was a safety precaution, not some smooth move. But it was all different now. He couldn't put his arm around her shoulder. Or hug her. Though how was he going to avoid that? Miguela was the kind of girl who became a hugger after she warmed up, and she had warmed up to him. As soon as she saw him in the stable, she skipped over to him like a happy little fairy. It felt like he *should* hug her. Thankfully, she didn't seem to notice how awkward it was, and he thought fast about the horse.

"Hey, why don't we get you on your own horse today? Since this is a day of overcoming fears. You ride Pepper, and I'll take one of the other horses."

"Are you sure?" She eyed Pepper, who made a pleas-ant neighing nose that Nate interpreted as *I promise to be safe with her.*

"He promises to be safe with you," he told Migs.

"Okay," she said. "I suppose if you don't mind helping me up."

Gah. So much for eliminating the romantic-with-a-horse

issue. He gingerly helped her, being exceedingly careful about where he put his hands, and then he took it easy the whole ride. You did not show off on a horse around a girl who had a thing for you that you didn't reciprocate.

He took her to a cave he'd seen while they were riding yesterday and used a palm-sized flame to light up the back while he felt around with his mind for animals. There were four mice and two Kepler polar lizards in the cave. A Kepler polar lizard was the size of a small dog, but they weren't active during the day. Nate asked the mice to keep watch on the sleeping lizards for him and told Miguela the coast was clear.

"I guess this is basically a fireproof room," Miguela said as she walked in. "I wouldn't want to hurt any of the animals, though."

"You don't want to hurt *anyone*. I get it. But today, you're not going to have to think about that." He took a bar of chocolate out of his bag and unwrapped it.

"I don't understand," she said.

He broke a piece of chocolate off. "Hold out your hand."

She held out her hand. "I don't think chocolate is going to help me learn how not to cause explosions, Nate."

He grinned. "Don't you like chocolate?"

A half-smile appeared on her face. "I love chocolate."

"Then, this is perfect, because you can't eat that chocolate for another ten minutes."

"Is this a diet exercise?" she said suspiciously.

"No, but look at the chocolate." He pointed to her palm. "See how it's already melting at the edges? It's cold in here. That chocolate wouldn't be melting on a normal person."

"Oh," she said glumly. "And I'm not normal."

He was worried about her crush, but he wasn't going to let her talk like that about herself. "No. You're *exceptional*. But your job is to lower your own body temperature enough that you can still eat the chocolate in ten minutes."

"I could eat the chocolate melted."

"Sure, but you'd have to lick it off your palm." He winked at her, then remembered he wasn't supposed to be doing stuff like that and supplemented with a pretentious and correctional, "*Princesses* do not lick chocolate off their hands."

"Carina wouldn't have a problem licking chocolate off her hand," Miguela told him.

"Carina's an exception to *all* the rules." He broke a piece of chocolate off and put it in his own palm. "I'll do this with you, okay? And at first, we won't talk, because I want you to focus. But if things seem to be going well …"

"You're going to make it harder for me by talking?"

"I'm going to make it harder by talking about things that might piss you off."

She shook her head and laughed. "Alright. I'm focusing now."

He thought the chocolate exercise was a stroke of brilliance on his part. Franklin had done this with him with ice cubes long ago, but Miguela deserved positive reinforcement. And the exercise *was* right for her. Five minutes in, the chocolate had completely melted, and she was distraught.

"Now, what am I going to do?"

"Lick it off," he told her. "We'll start again."

Miguela frowned.

"Turn around if you don't want to do it in front of me," he teased, then mentally face-planted again, because *really?*

She daintily licked the chocolate away, then held out her other hand. "So how did you do it? Is there a trick?"

He handed her a new piece of chocolate. "The more adrenaline and cortisol in your system, the hotter you are.

And people like you and me are especially hot—"

She was grinning at him again, and he was incapable of not messing this up.

"You *know* what I mean. But if we proactively de-stress, that changes our physiology enough to keep us cool."

"I thought Southerners believed magic was all about some god," Miguela said.

Nate considered that. "Just because we believe in God doesn't mean we reject all science. We know humans got to Kepler on spaceships. We have universities and research facilities. We just don't accept that the origin of magic—or anything—is random chance."

"No, you choose to believe that some mythological being handed magic to us," Miguela said. "It's completely irrational."

"Says a princess of North Kepler."

"Your chocolate is melting." Miguela held her hand toward him. "And mine's not. I think that says something about *you*."

The chocolate in his hand *was* melting. It made him feel disgruntled. "Yeah. It says I don't like to argue with my friends about religion."

"But I'm not mad at you for disagreeing with me," Miguela said calmly. "I think it's interesting to see how different people think."

He licked up the melted chocolate. "But it's easy to get in a fight over something like this."

"Why?" Her chocolate was still solid. "I like and respect you. You like and respect me. All we have to do to avoid a fight is listen to each other. We don't have to agree."

"I don't have a lot of friends like you." He pointed at that still-not-melted chocolate in her hand. "And I think we just figured out what you have to do to get your adrenaline and cortisol down."

She beamed. "Get in a fight about religion and science?"

"More like talk objectively and rationally about something. Maybe that's your de-stressor." He gestured toward the chocolate. "You can eat that if you want."

She bit off a piece of chocolate and chewed thoughtfully. "Do you think maybe if I can be like that while I'm trying to make something hot, I'll be able to control it better?"

"It would help prevent explosions." He thought about how the hot tendency worked for him. "But if you want to work with fire, you need to allow some of the energy you're bottling up run through you. If you try to stabilize and control that energy too much, it won't flow."

She seemed to think that was helpful. "Maybe first I need a better sense of what it feels like when I'm calm as opposed to what it feels like when I'm energized."

He licked the rest of the chocolate off his hand. "Maybe we both do."

Nate felt his afternoon with Miguela had been largely successful despite a few awkward blips. When they got back, Miguela said, "Thanks for your help, Nate," without any blushing. That was great. If he acted like they were just friends, maybe she would catch on and start feeling that way, too.

Princess B, however, confronted him by the dessert buffet at dinner that night.

"I *thought* we'd reached an understanding," she said.

"Princess, we will never reach an understanding," he said. "And you're blocking me from cupcakes."

She did not move. "I *told* you to stay away from my sister."

He looked around to see if Miguela was nearby. She was

at a table with Eugene, and they were chatting about something that seemed to be keeping them too busy to notice him
over here with Carina.

He lowered his voice just in case. "And *I* told you I wasn't
going to stop being her friend."

"But you thought it was appropriate to take her out alone
again today?"

Nate thought maybe Carina should find the equivalent to
the chocolate lesson. She was constantly making him shiver,
and if she could do that to him …

"Relax, C." He moved around her to pick up a key lime
cupcake. "It was benign. We rode our own horses, ate chocolate, talked about fire, and argued about God."

"So, you staged the perfect date for my sister."

Nate picked up a chocolate cupcake, too. "How would
that be *anyone's* idea of a perfect date. A good date needs to be
more—" he contemplated the cupcake "—active."

She made a repulsed noise and took a vanilla cupcake,
then a strawberry one. It made him feel like he should pick
up a third cupcake, just to beat her on who could eat more
cupcakes. He grabbed a red velvet.

"Look, all I care is how you're treating my sister." She
grabbed a cupcake with sprinkles and turned away from the
buffet table. "So, get your act together before I have to take
matters into my own hands."

He thought the cupcake with sprinkles looked good, and
there were no more of those left. He swiped the cupcake
with sprinkles from her plate, took a bite, and then set it back
down there. The cupcake lifted telekinetically from the plate
like she was thinking of smashing it into his face. Then Max
popped up behind Carina. "Hey Carina, hey Nate," he said.

The cupcake swirled around and hit Max in the face.

Max wiped frosting from his nose and held up a newspaper. "Um, I just wondered if you guys had seen this?"

It was a copy of *The Cerulean Times*, and there was a huge picture of the Royal Castle at Alighieri with a hole blown through the south wing and a turret burning. The headline read, "Crown Prince Bastian Fends Off Attack."

Nate handed his plate of cupcakes to Max and took the newspaper from him. "Here. The princess wanted me to bring these to you."

Max's eyes lit up while Carina scowled like he and Max were twin devils. But Nate didn't care. He had bigger problems to deal with tonight. What was going on in Alighieri?

STAFF EDITORIAL IN *THE CERULEAN TIMES* DATED TUESDAY, MARCH 29, 882 AAH

With regard to the recent attacks on the castle at Alighieri and other South Keplerian regions:

The editorial board of this news publication is by no means in favor of Southern rule in North Kepler or any encroachment by South Kepler into the governance of North Keplerian territory. Nevertheless, it cannot be denied that North Kepler's current lack of central leadership directly affects the ability of any North Keplerian city, village, or region to protect its interests.

Furthermore, it is clear that the Immortal Empire is intent on destroying what remains of the Cardinal Families of Kepler. The assassinations of Queen Vivian and Prince Nathanial came on the heels of the death of King Herschel, suspected to be the result of Immortality Virus poisoning, and also not long after the brutal attack on King Reginald and our own Cardinal Family of the North. Now, the last remaining Cardinal is a sixteen-year-old prince who, by all reliable accounts, is whithering away in Alighieri as the young prince's grief for his lost family consumes him. Queen Constance, ruling as consort until Prince Bastian comes of age and can be installed as the King of South Kepler, is the only monarch left taking an active leadership role anywhere on the mainland Kepler continent.

The leadership vacuum has gone on long enough. It is therefore the strong opinion of our entire editorial staff that North Kepler has only two choices and must make one expediently. One option is for the North to officially join with South Kepler, such that our regional governors and local militias may serve to aid Mortal Kepler as a whole in its fight against the Immortal Empire. As it is, South Kepler is stretched too thin and cannot continue to fight a war against the Immortal Empire without the full cooperation of its North Keplerian allies.

If, however, the bad blood between North and South Kepler makes this option unpalatable, then it is imperative that North Kepler find a leader to fill the hole left by King Reginald. The time of rule by the Cardinal Families may thus come to an end. We believe, however, that there may be a few remaining Cardinals left to guide us. We call on these persons—however distantly they may be related to King Reginald—to step forward and assume their leadership roles. If this does not happen soon, we can be sure that Empress Hildebrand will step in where she sees an opportunity, and soon we may all be citizens of the Immortal Empire.

CHAPTER TWENTY-THREE
BALM FOR THE SOUL

Bast prayed in his own private prayer nook every morning at sunrise and every evening at sunset. And tonight, he especially needed to pray. The kingdom of South Kepler had never been in such a hairy predicament. Every day, news came of a new attack. Sometimes it was a small skirmish—a few soldiers gunned down at a border post. Sometimes it was something more serious—an Immortal raid on a formerly Northern village.

But last night it had been something truly threatening. An attack on the Royal Castle itself. Very fortunately, Bast had been with Jax at the time, revisiting a corner of the Royal Library after hours, or he could have been injured. The attacks were clearly targeted at the next king. If he'd been home, the terrorists might have realized they were targeting the wrong place. Nate's rooms were destroyed. Bast's were fine.

Still, Bast felt he should devote extra prayer to the kingdom because of this. He'd been stewing over their troubles all day. The North barely had a military to speak of.

Mostly, it's military had only ever been a loose collaboration of scattered, disorganized, regional and local militias. It was time for South Kepler to start drafting those militias into the Southern Guard and retraining them to think like real soldiers capable of functioning in the farthest corners of Kepler.

Bast's mother was also pushing to begin Thurlow's official trial and conduct the memorial service for Queen Vivian and Prince Nathanial. Constance felt they needed to wrap up their investigation of the assassination sooner rather than later, and Bast had recently learned that she was leaving him *out* of key military and political meetings.

Then there was the matter of Vivian, and Bast never quite knew how to pray about that. He wasn't sure what God's plan had been with Vivian. It made perfect sense that God wanted him as the next king, but it made no sense that God hadn't wanted Vivian as the next queen. What should he say to God about this? A simple request for peace of mind was all he could ever manage.

Gael was waiting for him when he was finished, just outside the prayer nook. "Sir, the queen would like to know if you will be dining with her tonight," he said as Bast emerged.

Bast's assistant had an agreeable, narrow face, and he was excellent at keeping his emotions wiped clean from that face. You would need to be extremely observant to notice the tiny difference in the way Gael's lips thinned, tensed, or lifted at one side or the other depending on his mood.

Bast was extremely observant.

Because of that, he knew that since Jax had arrived in Alighieri, Gael had developed a touch of attitude. Now, for example, the left side of Gael's lower lip was sucked in. That,

Bast knew, was "Gael" for "I know you're planning to dine with that guy again, but I'm trying to pretend I don't know and don't care."

"Alone," Bast answered. Which, of course, was "Bast" for "I will be joining Jax Channing for a late supper outside the castle grounds after my mother retires to her chambers."

The slight pause before Gael said, "And would you like me to put an order in for a snack before your private supper?" was another indication of Gael's feelings on this matter. He *wanted* to advise Bast not to spend as much time with Jax, but instead, he was saying he would have discretion.

"My appetite is poor," Bast said. "A light tray of fruit will be acceptable."

Gael jotted a note down. He didn't *need* a note. There was no way he would forget that order. He simply didn't want to look Bast in the eye as he said, "Yes, sir. I'd be happy to retrieve that for you."

After all, they both knew he was lying.

Bast watched Gael leave the room. Jealousy was a pleasing trait in an assistant. Useful. Something Bast could manipulate. But now that he was alone, there was a stack of letters he needed to read before he could safely leave the castle to meet Jax.

He settled down at his desk to manage that correspondence and soon found himself so immersed that he barely noticed when someone other than Gael entered the room. Then a familiar hand and wrist appeared in Bast's peripheral vision with that tray of fruit. Nearly translucent skin, purple veins, and perfectly manicured fingernails.

Bast looked up at the bringer of fruit.

"I intercepted Gael," Jax said with a soft smile. "I don't think he likes me much."

Bast sat back and watched as Jax leaned against the window near his desk. He could read Jax so easily that every lean was a word, every blink a sentence. Jax was silent now, but Bast could read, "I hope you don't need much more time for your correspondence," and "your secret tunnels could use better light," and "I couldn't wait another three hours."

If he had to be honest with himself—and Bast usually did—he felt very much the same about those three hours. He considered the possibility of getting up to greet Jax, but he didn't relish the idea of looking too eager. He purveyed the fruit tray instead. Pearberries, green apple slices, and bright blue Kepler grapes, plus several slices of fresh cheddar and a bowl of olives. He picked up a bunch of pearberries, plucked one from the stem, and positioned the juicy fruit at his lips.

"You shouldn't be here," he said to Jax before popping the berry in his mouth. His appetite was always better when Jax was around. The fruit was perfectly tart.

Jax watched with stony eyes. "I'm tired of sneaking around to see you. We should be dining together tonight. With your mother."

Bast plucked off another berry. "And risk your execution? You aren't supposed to be within a hundred miles of Alighieri. Exposing you to my mother would be suicide."

Jax took three green apple slices and ate them one after another with aggression. "You are going to be the king of South Kepler in less than three years, and she knows I was only a child when my parents committed their hideous crimes. She would be insane to think you'd invite anyone into your bedroom who would ever have been involved in a plot to assassinate you. Surely you *gut* the truth from all your lovers before they get anywhere near you."

Bast picked an olive up, ate around the pit, and then

chewed on the pit while he thought about that.

"Unless you *don't* believe me anymore," Jax said. "Perhaps you think I was in on that treachery. As a ten-year-old."

Bast took the pit out of his mouth and set it down on a napkin. "Don't be dramatic." He picked up an apple slice. "I'd just like to know who told you I've ever allowed *anyone* into my bedroom other than the cleaning staff."

Jax came closer, leaned his hip against Bast's desk, and picked up a bunch of pearberries. "Then *Gael* hasn't shared your company?"

"Yet," Bast said. But he watched intently while Jax ate those pearberries. One berry at a time, held between two fingers, then placed—so carefully—against perfect, pale lips, which Jax opened only wide enough for one berry at a time. Bast imagined the juice bursting inside Jax's mouth, seeping over his tongue before Jax chewed the flesh of the fruit, slowly and deliberately.

When Jax opened his mouth for another berry, Bast could see his tongue was now tinted blue.

Bast took two more slices of green apple for himself, then wiped his fingers on the napkin. "Gael *would* be good company," he said. "But I've rather been thinking of someone else I might *invite* in."

There were five berries left on the bunch Jax had in his hands. Jax ate each one methodically, his eyes locked on Bast's until Bast felt such a strong desire to know what blue grapes tasted like on Jax's lips that the tension was unbearable.

He stood up from his desk at approximately the same time Jax moved to set the barren stem back on the tray, putting the two of them directly in each other's personal space. But no one backed away.

"I would like," Jax said—slowly sliding his arms around

Bast's neck as Bast's hands settled on Jax's waist and they leaned in at the same time "—to be—" Bast thought the tartness of the pearberries on Jax's lips was just right "—invited."

It seemed appropriate after that to allow all the air between them to disappear, and Bast thought at a breath that Jax's eyes were so clear there wasn't a single petal of color he had not previously seen in those irises. Only a reflective pale pool of gray, though this was disappearing as Jax's pupils dilated.

"Would I be the first?" Jax said in a whisper.

"There was never any other way," Bast answered.

Bast was in an excellent mood the next day as he met his mother for breakfast after the morning prayers. When they dined together in the evenings, it was nearly always in the private dining room reserved for the royal family alone. Classical music would play while Queen Constance sat at one end of their long, elegant Gandhiwood table and Bast sat at the other. Sometimes they spoke briefly about affairs of the kingdom, but usually not. Without the three members of the family who would have chattered away, dinner was solemn and quiet.

Breakfast, on the other hand, always occurred in their sunny conservatory. They ate casually at a much smaller table with wrought-iron legs and a glass tabletop, surrounded by sample specimens of all South Kepler's most interesting plants.

The greenery thrived in the conservatory—meticulously maintained by the staff gardeners. If Bast and his mother arrived for breakfast at the same time and conversation was sparse, Bast could take his breakfast to the davenport, stretch out his feet casually, and read the news. Or he could pick up his coffee and sip it while strolling by the cascading herb wall.

This morning, Bast sat directly across from his mother at the table. Gael had ensured that a glass of fresh-squeezed juice would be waiting for him, along with a fluffy egg white omelet and another lush bunch of pearberries. He plucked off a pearberry first, and the splash of juice in his mouth made his mind flash back to the pleasant evening he'd spent with Jax.

"Another village was raided early this morning," his mother said. "Near the swamplands."

"Former Northern village?" Bast asked.

"Yes, I'm afraid so," she said without any regret whatsoever in her voice. "Supposedly, the village had a militia, but they never stood a chance against Hildebrand's army."

Bast began eating his omelet. It was appetizing. He would ask Gael to have this breakfast prepared for him tomorrow as well.

"And was it a slaughter, or were children taken?"

"Thirty-six dead, fifty-four injured, and twenty-nine children taken." Constance was sipping hot tea, but the toast on her plate was untouched. "That's twice as bad as the last raid on a Southern village. The Northerners simply aren't equipped to handle this."

Omelets were such a satisfying breakfast food. Bast took another bite, chewed, and swallowed before responding.

"Then send Southern Guard soldiers to nearby villages temporarily and bring anyone claiming to be part of the militia back to the capital to retrain with the Guard," he said. "Northerners or not, those people are under our rule."

His mother smiled. "And redirect forces away from Alighieri immediately after an attack on our home? Bastian, is your mind idling?"

Normally, Bast agreed with his mother on strategies necessary to further the kingdom's primary cause, but in this case, he thought there might be a conflict.

"That attack was merely a gamble on the part of the Immortal Empire," Bast said. "A few renegades with some weak explosives? They're only provoking us. They want us to feel threatened, so our attention will be too focused on our own safety to protect the bigger prize. I say we shift resources from Alighieri and send them to the borderlands."

Constance chose to pick up her toast and eat an entire corner before *she* spoke again. "I would concur with you, dear, except for the fact that the Immortal Empire has already succeeded in killing both your brother and sister. Hildebrand has reason to believe she doesn't need more than a few grenades to destroy you."

"They cannot possibly think I am that vulnerable," Bast said. If they did, they were quite wrong. Bast was feeling nearly invincible today.

"Perhaps their sense of your vulnerability has something to do with the fact that we still have not yet scheduled the memorial service for your siblings. An invulnerable prince would have grieved his sister's death by now."

That was a low blow, and since Bast now felt this conversation would not have a satisfactory resolution, he returned to his omelet in the hopes that at least something about breakfast could remain enjoyable.

"I have decided we cannot wait any longer. I contacted the bishops this morning. The memorial service will take place three weeks from Sunday."

Bast set down his fork. "But we still don't have a confession from Thurlow."

"Unrelated," Constance said. "We have plenty of evidence to convict the man."

"All we have is circumstantial evidence," Bast argued. "We need him to give us details about how he orchestrated the attack. He could have been in contact with Lord Franklin."

Constance took another sip of hot tea. "We don't need Thurlow to get to Franklin. We can execute the captain whenever we want. And I fail to understand how this relates to when we schedule the memorial service."

"Obviously, the execution needs to be over before the memorial service," Bast said. "Otherwise, we're essentially telling the kingdom that we're closing our files on Vivian's death before properly determining who was at fault."

Constance tossed her readers on the table carelessly with a huff. "Then execute him tomorrow. You've tortured him plenty. Thurlow is never going to talk."

Bast's omelet was now far too cold to be enjoyed. "There is no *need* to rush the memorial."

His mother stood up abruptly. "Bastian, I am only going to say this once. The kingdom cannot sustain your grief any longer. You need to move on."

Bast's mouth snapped shut. The statement seared through his heart. He didn't care if he was inconveniencing the kingdom with his grief. He wasn't done yet. He wasn't ready for the memorial. He wasn't ready to see Vivian entombed. And it was important for the kingdom to let their future king go through his grief as *he* needed it to happen.

His mother dealt one more blow. "If you disagree, perhaps you should ask the gentleman who left the castle this morning before dawn for *his* opinion on the matter? I'm sure your friend can think of better ways to use your unresolved feelings than to delay a simple memorial service while your sister's body rots in the morgue."

A layer of ice crystallized over the glass tabletop.

Queen Constance looked at the ice with disdain. "A king cuts his losses," she said. Then she sailed out of the conservatory, leaving Bast alone in the cold.

Bast needed to talk to Vivian, so he told Gael to delay all his morning appointments and he marched up the stairs of Vivian's tower. It had been almost a week since he'd last checked on her, but the cold magic he'd put into freezing her hadn't failed within that time. She was as cold as he'd left her.

So, he sat down in her chair, picked up her hand, and began to talk. First about Jax.

"I should have told you about him. He's smart. He doesn't make mistakes. I think he's in love with me."

Vivian betrayed none of her feelings about that.

"He doesn't like me torturing Thurlow to get information out of him, either. He thinks it takes too much warmth from me. And Mom says we should just kill Thurlow and get it done with, but I can't do that. Thurlow has dangerous secrets locked up in that mind." He squeezed Vivian's hand. "It wasn't your fault you fell for him. He is, by far, one of the most manipulative people I've ever met."

Vivian's face was lifeless, though Bast could imagine some hint of something passing over her lips. Was that a slight wrinkle in her forehead?

It was surely him seeing things. But sometimes, when he wanted more than anything to talk to her, he let himself try to sense the virus inside her. It was still there, frozen in her blood. And maybe if he could destroy all the viral cells—if he could eradicate them one-by-one, then allow her to thaw and attempt just a little healing …

Couldn't a heart be restarted several hours after death? Maybe he could restart hers. She'd only been dead a day when he'd found her. Was that too long?

A noise seemed to issue from her mouth—a small hiss, probably only air naturally escaping—and it jerked him out of that line of thinking. You couldn't bring back the dead. You couldn't fix that kind of problem. Only God could work those miracles. Though it *had* crossed Bast's mind that God had gifted *him personally* with phenomenal healing abilities.

"There's only this one other thing," he said to her. "I haven't told Jax yet that you're here. I'm not sure he would understand."

Though that could have been wrong. Jax did know grief. He was here right now for Bast because he knew grief. And Jax knew Bast in ways no one else ever could. If there was *anyone* Bast could trust, it was him.

Vivian's hair looked dull. He reached out to comb his fingers through it and realized it had become dusty. That wouldn't do. He brushed some of the dust out of her hair, then swiped more dust from her sleeves. How had he missed this? And how to prevent it again? But a solution came to him. A blanket. He could cover her with a blanket. There was a throw blanket draped over the back of his chair. He unfolded it and tucked it over her face and body.

There. No more dust.

"I'm going to tell him," he told Vivian. "He'll understand. I'm sure of it."

Then Prince Bastian descended the tower and went to the dungeons, because he was now stressed and a very haggard Brandon Thurlow was due for another talk.

It satisfied Bast that Thurlow looked especially bad when

Bast arrived in the dungeons.

"Thurlow," he said as he approached. "Are you sad that the bombs missed you?"

"You son of a bitch." Thurlow snarled. "When are you going to understand that I never did anything to hurt your sister?"

Bast cracked his knuckles. "Try telling me that after I've frozen your tongue in place," he said. "Then tell me why I should believe you. And come up with something good, because I've had a shitty morning and there's only one thing that can cure it."

"What's that?" Thurlow said through gritted teeth.

Bast answered with great pleasure. "The thought of your execution."

CHAPTER TWENTY-FOUR
BITTERSWEET VICTORIES

Carina was so pissed off at Prince-I-Talk-To-Puppies-And-Make-Your-Sister-Swoon after the whole cupcake debacle that she had shoved her perfectly good cupcakes at Max, too. Then she stormed off toward the exit opposite from the one the prince had stormed to, and Mishe got up to follow her.

Ollie, who had been eating dinner with Carina before that disaster, bounced out of her seat. "It's cool, Mishe," she called, waving her hand at him. "I'm hanging out with the princess tonight."

That was at least a good development. King Reginald had decided Carina was now lethal enough not to need a million guards. They could follow at a respectable distance, and they weren't needed at all if Ollie was with her. (Or Max or Nate, though Carina would *never* have trusted her life to those guys, and she didn't understand why her dad thought Miguela was safe with them either.)

"What happened?" Ollie said as they left the mess hall.

"Did you get in a fight with Nate again? Or Max?"

"When am I *not* fighting with both of them?" Carina answered.

Ollie skipped ahead of her and walked backward through a mucky path from the mess hall to the summer house. "Should we talk about rules with them? Because Aunt Elizabeth says—"

"Sister Elizabeth is Immortal," Carina said. "I don't care what she says."

Ollie didn't seem to get it. "But she's the kind of Immortal Max is. And so what if she's been around for a while? She has lots of useful wisdom."

Carina did not think being Immortal automatically qualified you as wise. She had now received three letters from Elizabeth—because Ollie had gone and told Sister Elizabeth that she'd given away her dirty secret—and Carina hadn't opened any of them.

Ollie shrugged. "Okay, so let's pretend I *didn't* hear this from Aunt Elizabeth then. Some *other* wise person told me that if you want to be friends with someone, it's important not to get in the way of their relationships, and it seems like there's some tension there between you and our adorable playmates, so ..."

That made Carina cold enough to put her gloves on while they walked. "They are *not* our playmates. And they are *not* adorable."

"Of *course*, they're our playmates. All we do with them is play fight. Hence, playmates." Ollie turned and looped her arm around Carina's like she hadn't noticed the freeze. "And I know you think Max is attractive, or you wouldn't have dated him before. Those deep blue eyes? Staring into your soul like 'let me tell you what I've learned over the last five-hundred years?'"

Carina was scandalized. "Let him tell *you* what he's learned. His blue eyes turn red."

"Nate's eyes don't. They're just that earthy-greenish color—"

"The color of mud."

"And have you noticed his hair? Don't you want to touch it? It *floats* when he fights."

Carina had her own thoughts about Nate's hair, which never seemed clean and was nearly always matted down with sweat by the end of a training session. "I've noticed he doesn't bother to shower often enough."

Ollie grinned. "I kind of like a guy who doesn't mind getting dirty."

Carina was *appalled*. "I kind of like a guy who *bathes*."

They reached the house, and Ollie followed Carina up the stairs to the second floor. "Okay, fine. But we should be friends with them anyway. Bet we could talk your dad into letting the four of us go to Cerulean together. Where we can find someone better for you to date. A college guy or something."

"I *am* dating a college guy," Carina said. But Heathrow hadn't called for two weeks, and she wasn't sure why. If it had anything to do with Nate and Max, then she was angry at all three guys.

They walked into Carina's suite, and Ollie plopped down on the sofa while Carina tugged off her jacket and noticed a new installation. Her own beverage station. She was going to have perfect hot cocoa her whole life. She made some for her and Ollie, happily assuming that Ollie's silence meant they were done talking about boys.

Then Ollie said, "Carina, do you think maybe you should

try to get along with Nate anyway? Since you'll probably have to work with him your whole life?"

Carina watched a generous handful of marshmallows melt in her freshly made cocoa.

"Hey, want me to paint your toenails tonight?" Ollie asked.

"What color?" Carina said, thinking they had finally gotten off the subject of annoying boys.

"Ice blue, obviously," Ollie said. "To symbolize your undying commitment to the Kingdom of North Kepler. And provide a morale boost when I make you sit next to the future king of South Kepler at lunch tomorrow."

"You do want to be friends with *me*, right?" Carina said.

Ollie smirked. "Socks off, Princess, and if you let me use glitter, I won't make you sit across from Max, too."

But for whatever reason, Ollie did not show up the next morning to work out with Carina. No one did. This did not bode well for Ollie's lunch diplomacy plans, and Carina ran completely alone on a treadmill for the first time she could ever remember. No guards. No prince. No Max. Just her.

Then she arrived at the gym for training before anyone else and sat on a bench alone, listening to the lights buzz and watching the clock tick past seven, then seven-fifteen, then seven-thirty.

Max walked in at seven forty-five.

Only Max.

Carina had suffered through a nasty dream the night before about ways she and Prince Nathanial could accidentally cause an all-out war between North and South Kepler, starting with one of them smashing a cupcake in the other's face. Prince Nathanial was kind of a known evil, though. He was an arrogant jackass, but his disregard for her was completely genuine. What you saw was what you got with Nate.

Max was a totally different story. Carina still didn't know his motives for being on Kepler or dating her or befriending Nate. He'd lied to her repeatedly. She didn't find him attractive anymore at all. His nose was enormous. He had zits on his forehead. He smelled even worse than Nate after a training session.

Miguela said he'd saved her life this summer, but Carina preferred to conveniently ignore that, exactly like she preferred to ignore Max himself. He'd probably created some problem for everyone else this morning so that he could get some alone time with her at training.

She was not interested.

"Franklin said we should start without him and Nate today," Max said awkwardly. "And Ollie might not make it. I saw her with Mishe and a bunch of the guards earlier. They're having some security meeting about you."

Great. Then he hadn't orchestrated this. "Where's Franklin?" Carina asked. "Is this about the attack on the royal castle at Alighieri? Is Nate going home?"

Max shook his head. "He wants to. But Franklin's sure Nate is dead if he goes back. They had a fight about it last night."

That was confusing. "And Franklin let Nate off the hook from training this morning?"

Max dragged the toe of his boot against the floor. "Nate told Franklin he wasn't training with you anymore. Franklin told Nate that if he wasn't training with *you*, he wasn't training with *him*. It all got nasty from there. So, uh, should I get a paintball gun?"

Carina nodded silently. Nate was boycotting, then? Did

that mean the prince would never scald, scorch, or singe her again? Why didn't that make her feel happy?

Max returned from a supply closet with a paintball gun. He hesitated, then walked her way and held out the gun. "Since no one else is here, do you want to try the gun yourself?"

She did not take the gun. "I don't shoot guns."

Max laughed grimly. "Not even at your *Immortal ex-boyfriend?* Because I bet that would feel pretty good for you."

It was literally the first thing he'd said to her in months that made her not absolutely hate him. She wondered what mood he was in that he would say something like that, and she took the gun.

"Do you need me to show you how to shoot it?" he asked.

"Did you offer this so you could give me a physical demonstration?" she said suspiciously. "Because I almost killed the last guy who did that."

Max put his hands in the air and backed away. "No. I'll just tell you how to do it. It's not that hard, except—" he started laughing a little while she began examining the gun "—does *any* royal Mortal know how to hold a gun? Nate did the same thing. Don't point it at yourself. Point it at me."

Carina reddened, and she changed how she was holding the gun. "Like this?"

"Hold it against your shoulder," Max said, then he pulled down the visor on the helmet he always wore to training sessions. "Now, it's just point and shoot. All you have to do is look down the barrel, aim, and pull the trigger."

She felt clumsy with the gun, and it made her think of Vivian Wellington yelling at her the day Max shot Nate. *We're Mortals! We don't carry guns! And we certainly don't shoot other Mortals with them!*

She magicked the gun back to Max. "I don't want

to do this. Let's just get to the sparring session. Nothing hand-to-hand."

He didn't fight her. He only took the gun, said "Yeah, okay," then waited for her to say "start" before he began shooting at her.

Max normally practiced with Nate, so Carina wasn't used to working with him like she was now used to working with Ollie. She realized fast that Max wasn't as mobile in a fight as Ollie. This made it easy for her to create a defensive telekinetic shield that would prevent bullets from hitting her. She couldn't do anything *else* while she was holding a shield like that, though, so she decided she needed better cover. She spotted a stack of mats she might be able to hide behind, then she waited for a chance to drop the shield and run for the mats. Ollie usually couldn't hit her with a gun if she was moving fast enough.

But a paintball splattered across Carina's back as soon as she turned to run. She was dismayed. "You already won," she said to Max.

He lowered the gun. "You're kind of predictable. And you focus more on defense than Nate does."

"I'm the crown princess of the North, and I tend cold," she said. Defensively. "It's in my blood to do that. But let's try again."

They set up. It took him less than a minute to shoot her that time. So, she asked him to do it again. Then she attempted the exercise a fourth time. A fifth. And again. On a seventh or eighth try, he hit her with a gut shot, and she paused to hold her stomach protectively while the ache ebbed away.

Max immediately pulled up his visor. "Damn. I'm sorry. I didn't even think because I never have to with Nate. But you probably don't have abs like he has."

She was offended. "I have *abs*." She *did*. She'd been doing all kinds of weight training up here. But that shot to her stomach had still been unpleasant.

"We can take a break if you want," Max offered.

Carina shook her head. "No. I don't get better if I take breaks."

Max said, "One more time, then," and he pulled his visor down while Carina prepared for another paintball to hit her. Except this time, if it was going to happen, she decided it wasn't going to be because she couldn't defend herself well enough against him. It was time to see if she could just pull the gun from him before he shot her. No shields.

She said, "Start now," and Max lifted the gun to fire at her. But it turned out that she *could* get a telekinetic grip on that gun faster than he could aim and fire. His first shot went wild, and he fought her physically for the gun, rapidly switching to a two-handed grip while she attempted to wrench it away from him with magic. He was stronger than Ollie. Still, after a minute or so, the gun flew out of his hands, and he stumbled back while it sailed toward Carina.

Max pulled his helmet off. "Nice! You did it!"

She almost felt goodwill toward him. "Thanks," she said. And she meant it.

Then he sort of shuffled his feet side-to-side and said, "So, do you think you might ever let me apologize for not telling you I'm Immortal?"

The goodwill instantly vanished, but Eugene popped into the room then, looking anxious. "Have either of you seen Miguela this morning?" he said. "I can't find her anywhere."

There wasn't *anyone* Carina cared about more in the world than Miguela, and Max had said Nate was missing, too.

"She's probably with stupid Nate Wellington," Carina

said irritably. "He went off somewhere this morning on his horse."

"No, Nate wouldn't have taken Miguela with him for that," Max said. "He's protective of her. If he decided to go blow off steam, there's no way Migs is with him."

The statement was a reminder for Carina. Max was Nate's friend, not hers. Not anymore.

"I'm worried," Eugene said. "She's been experimenting with magic, and she's not exactly good with thermodynamics. All the guards are in some meeting, and I can't … um …"

Carina could feel a freeze surrounding her. She was *sure* Max was wrong. So sure that she was freezing over the gym because it made her that angry that Max was trying to cover for Nate. She left the gym to try to find Miguela, hopefully in the stables, and the whole way there, she spewed venom to Eugene about Prince Reckless and what she would do to him if Miguela was hurt.

"But if Miguela did go riding with him, can you ride well enough to find them?" Eugene asked.

Riding. That was something *else* Nate had ruined for her. She'd been able to ride as a kid and having horses around was one of the few things she'd truly liked about Fort Aurora Borealis. She had been planning to spend time this spring learning again. Then *he* arrived and took all the fun out of it by being able to *talk* to horses.

Well, that wasn't going to stop her from actually getting on a horse today if she had to.

"I'll figure it out," she told Eugene.

"What are we going to do if she's *not* with him?" Eugene asked. "I think Max is right. Nate wouldn't let Miguela do something risky with magic, but she's still dangerous. I know he's been trying to help her—"

"Nate is *not* a substitute for a real teacher," she said.

"I know," he said hastily. "I don't understand why Dad isn't working with her. You'd think he could teach her how to do some things."

That made Carina uneasy, but they had reached the stables, and as soon as they walked in, Carina could hear Miguela talking to someone. Carina gritted her teeth. If she found *Nate* doing *anything* inappropriate with her sister—

But Miguela was only sitting alone on a bale of hay, chatting softly to a malamute puppy curled up in her arms. She looked up at Carina and Eugene with innocent surprise.

"Look!" she said happily, tilting the cozy puppy toward them. Carina felt a surge of peace and contentedness that was quite the opposite of what she'd been feeling an instant before.

She knelt down toward her sister while Eugene sighed out a huge breath. "What are you doing out here, Miguela?" Carina asked. "We've been worried about you."

Miguela frowned. "I thought everyone was worried about Nate. I saw him at breakfast, and I came out here in case he wanted to talk." She pointed to the stall Nate's horse was usually in. "He was already gone, but the puppies remembered me, and when I picked this one up, it seemed cold." Her frown flipped back to a triumphant smile. "I'm warming it up."

"You're *warming it up*?" Eugene said like that concept was as foreign to him as it sounded to Carina.

Miguela laughed. "With *magic*!"

"Oh." Carina sat back in the hay and let another malamute puppy climb into her lap. She patted its head. "That's … that's …"

"That's *great*," Eugene supplied. "You're actually using your magic. And you're not afraid of it."

Miguela beamed at them. "I *know*. Nate showed me how to do it. I've been practicing keeping chocolate from melting in my hand for control and heating up cups of cocoa, and I can't make fire, but I can do *this!* And look at how *happy* this little guy is."

"That's amazing, Guela," Eugene said, sounding genuinely pleased for her.

Miguela looked at Carina.

"It … really is," she said, not quite feeling able to muster the same genuine enthusiasm.

Eugene tapped Carina's shoulder. "So maybe now you and Miguela can both spend time with Mom, and no one has to worry about Mom getting too cold."

Miguela's brow knit together. "What are you talking about?"

"Nothing," Carina said, cutting off Eugene with a look she hoped clearly said, *we are not telling her this when she is is finally feeling better.*

He blinked at her a few times. "Did you just—"

"*Lie* to me?" Miguela finished for him. "What are you lying *about?* Why are we worried about Mom?"

"We're not," Carina started again, but Eugene apparently wasn't interested in playing along.

He ignored the dirty look Carina was giving him. "Because the baby tends cold," he said, "and when Carina is with Mom, the balance is so off-kilter that Mom gets hypothermic."

"Wait, what? Does that happen with you, too, Eugene?" Miguela asked.

"No," he told her. "I can't spend too much time with Mom these days, but it's okay for a little while or when Dad's there because my magic isn't as powerful as Carina's yet."

"Shouldn't *Dad* be able to counterbalance Carina?"

"Yes," Eugene said adamantly. "He *should*. But either he won't, or he can't, and if you two would ever just talk to me *together*, maybe we could work out what the hell is going on with him."

Now Carina was ticked off, though. "We have been a *little* more concerned about not putting extra pressure on Miguela than about *me* not being able to hang out with Mom," she said, raising her voice higher than she ever remembered doing with her little brother.

A circle of frost spread out at his feet exactly the same way it often did for her when she was enraged. "*Maybe* the problems are related!" he yelped. "And even if they aren't, Dad is *hiding* something, I've been trying to figure it out myself for ages, and I could use some help from my *sisters*."

Now there were overlapping circles of frost at their feet. But Miguela stepped between Carina and Eugene, and as soon as she did, the ice started to melt. Then Miguela faced Carina directly, like she was ticked off, too.

"Does this mean you haven't been talking to Mom *at all* since we got here?" Miguela asked with her arms now crossed tightly over her chest.

"It means she can't even *hug* mom," Eugene said with his arms crossed exactly like Miguela's

And this wasn't fair at all. Carina hadn't committed some major betrayal. She'd only been trying to protect Miguela. "I was trying to help *you*," she said.

"By *lying* to me? I thought we weren't going to do that to each other again."

Then, Prince-I-Have-Terrible-Timing-Nate rode back into the barn on Pepper. He stopped the horse at the door. "Uh, thanks for the welcome," he said. "But what are you guys doing here?"

Miguela glowered at Carina. "Learning that one of us is a *liar.*"

"That is *not* true," Carina said, but Miguela stomped out of the barn after that with Eugene behind her, and that left Carina with nothing to do but follow.

Nate saluted them all on their way out. "Hey Northern Royals, be happy you're all still together and alive," she heard him say as she passed him.

She spun back. "We are *nothing* like your family."

He cocked his head at her. "When did I say you *were?*"

She had no one else to take her fury out on, so she responded with a spiteful, "I *hate* you."

Hatred flashed back at her in his eyes. "Same."

CHAPTER TWENTY-FIVE
THE THERMODYNAMICS OF IT ALL

Mishe intercepted Carina on her way back from the stables before she could make up with Miguela and Eugene. He said she was needed at the assembly building.

"By whom?" she asked.

"The Royal Society, Your Grace," Mishe said, and then he escorted her to the atrium where the Royal Society met. The group gathered was smaller than it would have been for a full Society meeting, but Carina saw Doctor Friedman and Doctor McIntosh there, as well as Heathrow, who came right over as soon as he saw her.

"Hey, sorry," he said. "No one wanted to disrupt your training, but your dad isn't here yet, so—"

Carina was confused by that. Where *was* the king?

Friedman sauntered toward her, his voice booming louder than necessary for the size of the group. "The princess has arrived!" he announced. "We can start the meeting now."

"We can?" she said.

Heathrow nudged her toward Friedman. "We have to,"

he whispered. "New Paris was attacked last night. Governor's mansion was ransacked by Empire Immortals. Decisions need to be made."

She wanted to say, *By her?* What she said was, "What? Is the governor okay?"

Friedman caught her arm as she got close to him—which seemed so much chummier than she thought she was with him—and she had the feeling she was being taken *way* out of her comfort zone as he tugged her into the center of the group. An older woman with steel gray eyes, weathered skin, and lines that drew down the corner of her lips held her hand out toward Carina.

"Your Grace," she said. "It's good to finally meet you, despite the circumstances."

"Princess Carina, this is Elvinia Borgis, the Governor of New Paris," Friedman explained. "She arrived this morning with her partner and their two children."

"We were lucky," Governor Borgis told Carina. "Nora is gifted with dream visions. She woke from one just in time for us to evacuate. We didn't have time to call in the New Paris Urban Militia."

"I'm glad you're safe, Governor," Carina said. "I didn't know there had been an attack."

The corners of Governor Borgis's face stretched further toward her chin. "They've been threatening us for months, and none of the local militias have the resources to fight the Immortal Empire for more than a few weeks without reinforcements. Not even New Paris. We need the family to call for those at once, Princess Carina. Or New Paris will fall."

Friedman maneuvered himself physically between Carina and the Governor as if she needed to be protected from Borgis. "I said you could *speak* with her, Governor," he said.

"But the princess is not in a position to call for reinforcements. If you would like to detail your plan to evacuate the rest of the city with her—"

"Over five-hundred thousand citizens are living in New Paris, Friedman. We are *not* evacuating." Governor Borgis's tone was brittle, and Carina noticed she could see her own breath in the air, but she didn't think it was *her* making it cold. Did Governor Borgis tend cold?

"Where would the citizens evacuate to?" Carina asked her.

Borgis shoved around Friedman to speak directly to Carina. "*Exactly.* There is *nowhere* for most of them to go. If we call for an evacuation, only fifteen percent will get out, at *most*, and it will be the fifteen percent who have the means to leave."

"Who are also the citizens who have the most magic in New Paris," Heathrow said.

Boris nodded. "A disparity *we are working on*, Doctor Princeton, but yes, that is also a concern. An evacuation will leave our most vulnerable citizens even more vulnerable *and* magically vacant."

"Nevertheless, sending reinforcements will leave other areas of North Kepler vulnerable to attack," Friedman said. "It cannot be done."

A hint of frost hit Friedman's nose as Borgis responded. "Would you rather New Paris become a city of *Immortals?*"

Friedman rubbed his frosted nose. "I sometimes forget that you're a Second Degree Cardinal, Governor."

Borgis scowled, but reached for Carina's hands and held them, and Carina was surprised that the shared cold didn't bother her, though she was very uncomfortable being at the center of this conversation.

"Princess, you understand where I'm coming from, don't

you? We can't let our people suffer. We *need* to use the family's power to our advantage. Your return is—"

"Elvinia, couldn't you have started with how cute you thought she was as a baby?"

Carina felt a rush of relief as her dad appeared at her side and put a hand on her shoulder. "Princess, I see you've already met your Great Aunt Elvinia."

"I see *you* haven't thought of introducing your kids to the rest of the family yourself, Reggie," Elvinia said sharply. "I spoke to Bryna last week. You could call your own sister once in a while."

"Are you still in touch with her?" Carina said to her dad, now feeling extremely out of the loop. "I thought she was entirely estranged from the family. The only other First Degree Cardinals anyone talks about being left are Prince Nathanial and Prince Bastian."

Elvinia huffed angrily. "Oh, he knows how to get in touch with her. Bryna Garcia isn't estranged as much as she's a conscientious objector. She tends hot, she has crack tele-kinetic skills, and she has telempathy that lets her sense fear in other people. She would be an asset to the North except that she refuses to use magic unless she absolutely has to in self-defense." Elvinia caught Carina's eye. "Our whole family has nasty magical constipation."

"It isn't even noon yet," King Reginald said. "How about we sit down for lunch, *then* you can insult us all."

"*I* need a commitment for reinforcements, Reginald," Elvinia said, her voice now sounding shrill. "Unless *you* want New Paris to become the regional HQ for the Immortals in *our* kingdom."

The king sighed. "Then we can work on a strategic plan to bolster New Paris without making the rest of the kingdom weak. *After* lunch."

"It is *time* for the family to stop hiding," Elvinia practically spat, clearly not satisfied with his answer.

And at that, Carina saw her dad do something she had never seen him do. He swept his cane out and up, and a whole arc of fire moved with it in a frightening whoosh. The chill that had pervaded the room instantly vanished.

"*Enough*," he said. "Elvinia, I will speak with you *alone* and *after lunch*." He glared evenly at everyone. "For now, this meeting is dismissed. We'll reconvene later today."

Carina had never seen another woman look so furious.

Heathrow asked if Carina wanted to have lunch with him, and she did, but she didn't want to do it in a public space or with the Royal Society. She suggested they eat in her suite instead, and she was surprised when Mishe facilitated the privacy by telling her he would post a guard outside the room.

It was someone she didn't know.

"I'm sorry, princess," he said. "I would stand guard myself or send Olivette, but your primary staff is meeting today for some additional training, and I need to be there for as much of that as I can."

"Additional training to protect me?" she said.

"I think the idea is more to prepare us to start taking orders from you, Your Grace," Mishe said. "Lord Franklin is leading it. Came up in response to the attack on the Royal Castle in Alighieri and now the attack on New Paris."

"What does *that* mean?" she asked.

"Probably that they need to deploy you sooner than they wanted," Heathrow said grimly.

Mishe nodded. "Most likely."

After Mishe left, Carina used her com to order lunch while Heathrow paced the room. When she was finished ordering, she sat down on her sofa and watched him walking around.

"Sorry," he said. "I have all this extra energy to burn off. I can't believe the governor's mansion in New Paris was attacked. I guess I just thought the Immortal Empire was so far away."

"I can't believe I have so much family I've never met," Carina said, but she immediately took that thought back. "Although I guess *that's* stupid on my part. There are plenty of more relevant things my dad fails to tell me about."

"Have you ever seen your dad mad like that?" Heathrow asked. "Sometimes I forget he tends hot at all. I've never seen him produce fire. He must be furious at Governor Borgis."

"No, I haven't." Carina tucked her feet up under her. She was still in training clothes, and there were bits of hay on her legs from being in the stables this morning. She started plucking them off one by one. "I didn't know there was anyone else who thought we shouldn't be hiding anymore, either."

Heathrow smirked as he paced around. "Oh, there are *lots* of Northerners who think that. It's only the Royal Society that wants to keep you hidden. Everyone else thinks it's because they have more power when your family has less, and you have *far* less power if no one is supposed to know you're alive."

"So, what do you think of all this?" she said curiously.

"I think I got a call from my mother this morning. I grew up in an affluent neighborhood of New Paris. Almost everyone there had some magic gift or another. And she says most of our neighbors have already left. They're evacuating to their fancy lake homes or to stay with rich family. It's going to mean a lot of militia members drained from New Paris real fast."

"How will it work if reinforcements are called in?" Carina asked. "What's the leadership structure?"

"*That's* why Borgis is pissed at your dad," Heathrow explained, finally slowing his pacing a little. "The Northern Militia is a loose network of local militias. Leadership is local, *except* when the king calls for collaboration."

"Oh. But the king is dead. So right now, the only way to get reinforcements would be, what, for New Paris to beg a neighbor for help?"

"Pretty much." Heathrow threw himself down next to her on the couch, then their conversation was paused while someone brought in sandwiches and coffee, and after that, Carina wasn't sure she wanted to talk more about how bad things were in the North. Sometimes it was just too much to ruminate on disasters you didn't have the power to fix yet.

Anyway, there was something else to talk about. "You haven't called in a while," she said.

He cringed. "I know. I'm sorry. I should have."

She chewed on a portabella panini. "Why haven't you?"

Heathrow didn't answer initially, and she didn't push the issue. She thought maybe they both needed a minute to relax. Then he finished his sandwich and pivoted toward her.

"Do you know just sitting next to you makes me feel calmer?" he said. "I usually have all this pent-up energy, and I pour it into my research and studies. But with you ... I've read about thermodynamic reactions, but I've never experienced it."

Carina finished her panini and wiped her fingers on a napkin. "Are you sure it's thermodynamic? I don't feel calmer."

"You wouldn't. If you were reacting thermodynamically to me, you'd maybe feel more agitated. Or angry or energetic. Like you would suddenly have the energy to be a sprinter when normally you're only a jogger. But you wouldn't react to me because it would take someone as powerful as you to make you feel that way."

Like Miguela, Carina thought, recalling their fight from earlier in the day.

Heathrow picked up her mug of hot cocoa, and she watched as steam began to rise from the mug. Then he handed it back to her. "*That* is the extent of what I can do with my thermodynamic magic," he said. "If I get *really* mad, I can make someone not want to touch me. That's all. I've never seen *anyone* produce fire in person like your dad did today."

"It was intense," she said.

"Yeah, but it didn't scare *you*. I could tell from your face. You didn't expect it, but the fire wasn't anything you haven't seen before."

"My sister has blown up a building twice with both of us in it," she said dryly.

"But that's different. Your sister wasn't in control when she caused those explosions. Your dad *purposely* created a huge arc of fire because he wanted to shut Elvinia Borgis up, and you didn't even flinch."

"Because that was stage magic compared to an explosion." She thought of the more dangerous shows of fire she'd seen recently. "And I'm training with Prince Nathanial right now, and—"

Heathrow interrupted. "*Exactly*. Your dad sent Friedman a tape of the last sparring session you had with the prince. We watched it together. I don't think Friedman is going to treat you like he did before at the next patronage meeting. Did you notice how he was different with you today? We saw you *obliterate* the prince with cold *water* in that video. The guy was so critically injured, he hit back with an entire wall of fire."

That was *not* how Carina had thought that fight went.

Heathrow leaned his head back against the sofa. "Carina, I can heat up a hot beverage. The future king of South Kepler can *engulf* you with fire, and you are so good at defending yourself, you walk away with just a couple of burns you can heal before dinner. I bet you could freeze me to death in a heartbeat."

"I don't think I'm *that* strong," she said.

He laughed. "You're right. You're probably stronger. I bet you could freeze a few *dozen* men to death all at once."

A conversation she'd had with Max that felt terribly similar came to mind. "So, are you *intimidated* by me?" she asked. "You're an actual genius. It doesn't seem like you should be intimated by much."

"I'm not *afraid* of you if that's what you mean," he said. "But North Kepler is in trouble, and those problems are going to start falling on you because you represent the Crown, and the Royal Society wants us together."

"For dating. Not marriage or something," she pointed out quickly.

He grinned wryly at her. "You know your parents aren't married, right?"

"I *know* that," she said, thankful to have at least one critical piece of information about her own family. "But that's the point, isn't it? So what if the Royal Society wants their favorite son dating the princess? No one is expecting a commitment right now, and if this works for us later, great. That's a win for everyone."

He stared at her for a while. "You know, it would be hard for any straight guy not to be attracted to you. You're incredibly pretty."

She felt a smile on her face. "Also, very prone to flattery."

He scooted toward her, reached for the edge of her jaw, and leaned toward her.

"Is it okay if I kiss you?" he said.

She liked the fragmentation in his eyes, and she thought she might really enjoy being kissed by Heathrow Princeton.

"I think I'd like that," she said.

So, he kissed her. And she did like it. It was easy. No awkward clanking of teeth. No unnecessary slobber. His lips were warm but not too warm. His hands were gentle but not too gentle. It inspired good feelings to buzz inside her, and she wanted to keep kissing him. Since he seemed to want that, too, they continued. For a while.

Then some time had passed, and it seemed like the right time either to separate or make a conscious decision to move forward, so Carina thought it was a good sign that Heathrow seemed to pull back around the same time she did. They were on the same page. Except, the kissing had been quite pleasant for her, and *he* didn't seem happy at all.

"Did you … not enjoy that?" she asked. "Because we don't have to—"

He stroked down her cheek again with his thumb. "How could I *not* enjoy that? But Carina, I don't want to be the jerk who makes you think I'm in this for the long-term. I don't think I want the kind of responsibility you're going to have. Math is *much* easier than politics."

She thought that if she could only date guys like Heathrow for the rest of her life and never date another Max, that would be simply fine. As far as she was concerned, he was making this easy for her telling her something like that.

"Then let's just be honest with each other about what we want in the short term, and no one will get hurt," she said.

"Just like that?"

"I'm a Northern Royal. Isn't rational decision-making supposed to be our thing?"

Heathrow's eyes flashed as he grinned at her again. "Yes, I think that's exactly how you are supposed to be."

Many minutes later, Carina had also decided that if you were having a lousy morning, it was useful—and fun—to have a friend you trusted to kiss all the bad feelings away.

The rest of her day was far more complex. It was hard not to feel concerned by the perturbed look of betrayal on Elvinia Borgis's face when everyone reconvened for another meeting.

Carina's dad opened that meeting with, "Governor Borgis has decided to return to New Paris immediately and call on the Orchid Lake Regional militia to send as many volunteers as possible to bolster New Paris's militia. This will send a sign to the Immortal Empire that we were not intimidated by their attack."

"This is *not* a satisfactory response," Governor Borgis said. But she looked directly at Carina and said, "However, when *you* want to step into the light, I will be there."

And what exactly was Carina supposed to do with that? All she could think to do was smile awkwardly at Governor Borgis.

Then later, Carina had another awkward moment when she found Miguela waiting in her rooms for her. Did this mean they were in for another fight? It didn't, though. Miguela was there to apologize herself.

"I know you were just trying not to put more pressure on me," Miguela said. "Sometimes I get so frustrated, and I don't know why. I didn't mean to take it out on you."

Carina hugged her sister gratefully and thought of everything Heathrow had said about hot and cold magic. "We're just getting used to things. Eugene's right. Our thermodynamics are all out of whack.

Miguela smirked slyly at her. "Speaking of which. Did you and *Heathrow* spend some time together today? Kind of seems like you have chemistry with him."

Carina considered lying but decided Miguela was a better judge of her dating life than she was. She told Miguela everything, and Miguela said, "I like this. It's a good step for you."

"You approve of me and Heathrow dating?" Carina said.

"I approve of you doing fun, consensual, physical things with a nice, respectful guy that you like and can trust," Miguela said.

Ollie, however, felt differently when Carina told her about it. "You just decided to keep seeing him on a *casual and non-exclusive* basis?"

"Why not?" Carina said. "He likes me, not my crown, you know?"

"Yeah. And if someone liked me for me and not because I'm your courtier, that would be fine. But you *are* the crown," Ollie said. "What if you get attached?"

Carina was unconcerned, though. Because the thing is, Heathrow *was* fun, but she'd known after that first kiss that Heathrow wasn't capable of shattering her world. She liked him the same way she liked, say, drinking hot cocoa. He was good—deliciously good, even—but she had the gut feeling that he wasn't *special* for her. He wasn't sassafras beer.

"Well, I guess it's better for you not to have relationship drama when you have the Immortal Empire breathing down your neck," Ollie said. "Franklin is prepping your whole team to be a special force you command. Your life is going to be all about war soon enough. But you should talk to Aunt Elizabeth about dating Heathrow in the meanwhile. She has experience with casual relationships."

"When would I do *that?*" Carina said.

"Tomorrow," Ollie said. "You're officially free from your guards, and your mom told your dad that if you're going to be actively battling the Immortal Empire soon, you need to be independent first. So, we're going to Cerulean to have lunch with the Sisters. Then if you want, we can meet up with Heathrow or shop or whatever. There's only one condition."

"What's that?" Carina asked suspiciously.

Ollie hedged. "I'll ... tell you tomorrow. It's not as bad as you think."

It wasn't as bad as she thought.

It was worse.

CHAPTER TWENTY-SIX
A FIELD TRIP GOES SOUTH

Nate threw this morning's newspaper down next to his toast. "Franklin's wrong," he said to Max. "My brother needs help. He needed help *yesterday*."

Max picked up the paper and began reading out loud:

South Kepler Responds to Immortal Empire. Empress Hildebrand issued another empty threat last week in a letter sent directly to the Royal Family. The letter, which was full of meaningless hyperbole, promised 'an end to the age of Mortals on Kepler' and a 'full-scale attack on the last standing so-called Cardinal family.'

Though Queen Constance was unavailable to comment, Prince Bastian, who continues to prepare for the beginning of his reign as king, provided us with this: 'As always, the Immortal Empire is reduced to relying on empty threats and scare tactics to compensate for their utter failure in battle. There is no need for alarm. The citizens of South Kepler can rest assured that the crown is in complete control of this situation.'

"So, everything is fine," Max finished.

Nate pointed to the picture of Bast on the front page. "He's *exhausted*. And this language does not imply 'fine.' We only say, 'there is no need for alarm' when there is *every* need for alarm."

"What do you do when there isn't any need for alarm?"

"Throw a party at the castle."

"Because nothing says 'worry-free' like a royal soiree," Max said, waving his hands around jazz-like while he said that.

Nate did not appreciate Max's cavalier attitude, though. "The *point* is that my brother needs help."

Max dropped the humor. "That's not what Franklin says."

"Franklin isn't even *here* right now," Nate said. He'd left the isle last night on some kind of errand with Myles. Hadn't even bothered to tell Nate. Only left a note. *Busy tomorrow. Don't do anything stupid.*

Max probably would have argued, but Ollie showed up with a half-eaten bagel in her mouth then. She put one knee down on the bench and leaned over the table next to Nate.

"I need you guys to come to Cerulean with Carina and me today."

Max lit up. "Like a field trip?"

Ollie bobbed her head. "Like a field trip *without guards*. The king thinks the four of us are capable enough on our own, and any extra security would just make us look more suspicious."

"And Franklin's okay with this?" Nate said.

"Franklin approved it before he left. I think he's hoping

some social time will improve diplomatic relations between the North and South.”

Max stood up, practically glowing. “This is going to be awesome.”

“Cool,” Ollie said. “We’ll meet you at the shuttle in an hour.”

Nate did not think it would be awesome, but he was opportunistic. He packed a duffel bag, hoped Pepper would understand, and told Max he was bringing a few extra things “in case the ferry is cold.”

Which Max bought because he was so busy gushing over getting to spend time with Carina today. That girl was going to destroy Max somewhere in the near future. Nate had repeatedly tried to warn him. Max didn’t think it was possible, though. “Because we’re in love,” he’d said just a few days ago, and that made Nate feel so bad for Max that he just said, “okay, buddy,” and let it slide.

Nate only had to tolerate the ferry ride with the girl, though, then he’d be rid of her for a long, long time. So, he ignored the princess and her conniving eyes as he and Max showed up for the shuttle, and he took the bench farthest to the back. Then Max went and sat on the bench directly in front of Nate and looked up hopefully as Ollie shoved the princess their way. There weren’t any other open seats, but Carina looked at Max as she approached, looked back at Nate, then *passed* Max and sat down next to *him*.

Nate could barely hide a snicker. Apparently, he wasn’t the worst of two evils. Or maybe she preferred an argument with him to an awkward shuttle ride with Max. But Nate’s amusement died down as he felt her very cold shoulder near his.

"Remind me never to break up with you if we date, Princess," he said. "And don't think I'm going to talk with you the whole way to the ferry."

"Good," she retorted, slouching and shutting her eyes. "And we will never date."

Nate did the same. He hadn't wanted to spend more time with C today than necessary, but he felt edgy about his spontaneous plans. Franklin was going to be pissed later. Then again, Franklin wasn't the one having bad dreams about his dead sister and super-needy-perfectionist-control-freak brother. Nate had to return to Alighieri. There was no choice.

It did not, therefore, entirely suck that the princess was sitting next to him. Nate would have sold his left arm before he admitted it—and that was his sword arm—but she might have been making him a little calmer now than he otherwise would have been. It wasn't *personal*, obviously. But if a basic thermodynamic reaction could take the edge off, Nate didn't mind. He'd have bet his horse he did something to her, too. Probably made her feel agitated or nervous.

"So, what's your plan in Cerulean?"

He opened his eyes. She had her arms crossed and her eyes fixed on him like *she* was the one trying to read *his* mind.

"Are we talking now?" he asked. "And why?"

"*No*," she said. "But I want to know what you're planning."

Why did she have to be so weird? She was already making this trek a drain on his energy levels. He yawned and talked through it. "Again, *why* are we talking? And what makes you think I'm planning *any*thing?"

She pointed to the duffel bag he'd carried onto the shuttle and now had under his feet. "*I'm* not tired enough to nap. And I'm not stupid. You're up to something. Are you going to need to hide a body anywhere when you're done, Your

Highness?"

He should have expected that his effect on her would be to make her more annoying. Max twisted around in his seat in front of them, and Ollie turned with him.

"What are you guys talking about?" Max said suspiciously.

Princess C puckered her lips before she said: "You don't know what he's up to either, do you? What's the duffel for?"

Max looked chagrined but attempted a fast recovery. "It's not good to cage a guy like Nate with expectations. Also, he said he was bringing an extra sweater or something for the ferry."

"The prince of hellfire is bringing an extra sweater?" Carina said.

Nate resisted a snicker again and employed a handy skill for telling half-truths. "Save it, Princess. I'm not revealing anything about my amazing plans for our expedition to Cerulean."

"Well, *my* plan in Cerulean is to find Carina a college guy to flirt with," Ollie said, through an early morning yawn of her own but wagging her eyebrows at the princess anyway.

Max coughed like he'd swallowed a mouse. "Why would you do that?"

Nate saw the militia soldiers in front of Ollie and Max start to shiver. "Turn back around, you idiots," he said as he put some energy into correcting the cold. "You can piss off the princess when we get off the shuttle."

The princess made an annoyed tutting sound, but the environment didn't get any colder. Ollie and Max turned back around.

"Take it you're not up for flirting?" he muttered to Carina.

"Take it you're not telling us what you're doing in Cerulean," she muttered back.

Nate sighed and considered telling her. He suspected that she was going to badger him until he did. And she couldn't possibly want him staying in the North.

Also, the girl had uncanny intuition. "If you're running away from Fort Aurora Borealis, I am the last person who will try to stop you," she said.

"Keep it quiet!" Nate hissed as Max turned back around.

"What are you talking about *now*?" Max whispered.

"Damn it, Garcia." Nate slunk down as far as he could in the bench seat.

"Are you *going* somewhere?" Max said to Nate in a hushed, but forceful voice. "When were you going to tell *me*?"

"Never," Nate said.

"But you left your horse! And Franklin!"

"I'll come back for them after I finish abdicating to Bast!"

Max rubbed his eyes while sweat formed on his neck. So much for Nate benefiting from Ice Witch's presence.

"You're not running off to Alighieri alone like some—" Max began, before needing to wipe his brow. "Damn it, Nate! Stop trying to *toast* us back here for caring about you!"

The princess waved both hands in front of her. "*I* don't care about you. But how do I … you know …?" She scowled deeply before letting her hands fall back in her lap. "This is so *frustrating. You* make it look like magic when *I*—"

The shuttle wagon hit a bump going around a corner, and Icy lurched his way. For a second or so, her arm was in contact with his, and he could hear her cussing in her head. She had a colorful vocabulary. It amused him enough that the heat on the shuttle began to dissipate.

Then he remembered who she was.

"Watch it, Icy." He shoved her away. "And what I do to warm things up *is* magic. But it's probably not the same as what you have to do to cool things down. I just let some of my inner energy flow into the air."

"Oh, and I'm sure *that* voodoo advice will help her," Max, who still had sweat dripping down his temples, said. He glanced down at Ollie, who had not turned around through any of that. "I think she fell asleep. How do you *sleep* through this? And can we get back to the part where you decide to leave by yourself?"

Nate could not comprehend Max's ire. "Why are you so mad at me?"

Icy held her hands in the air again and made a motion like she was trying to mime pulling something heavy back to herself. The air around them actually began to cool.

"I *can* do it!" she said with a sudden smile. Which is not something Nate had ever seen on her. He caught her eye, and things were less hostile than normal until she wiped that smile off her face. Then they both looked back at Max to discover that *his* eyes were bright red.

"Um …" Princess Carina said.

"Uh," Nate said. "Look, Max, I'm sorry. This is just something—"

"You are *not* running back to Alighieri to face your deadly brother *by yourself*," Max seethed. "You are my best *friend* in the whole universe. I can't *believe* you were going to cut me out. I'm coming with you."

"Oh," Princess Carina said softly while an emotion Nate had never felt before washed over him.

"You're … what? But it's not going to be a very safe trip," he practically stuttered. "I don't even have a real plan."

"I am trained in almost *every form of combat*," Max said. "I can shoot *any weapon* and never miss. And I am *five-hundred years* wiser than you. I know how to take a calculated risk, and right now, I calculate that *you* will be much safer with me, especially if you have no plan."

Was the feeling relief? Some kind of manly affection?

"Okay?" Max said.

"I … guess. Okay," Nate said. "Thanks."

"I *told* you we should be friends," Max said. Then he sat back with enough gusto to punctuate the decision. But at least Nate didn't have to talk to the princess for the rest of the shuttle ride. She was stunned as silent as he was.

Something unexpected had happened to Carina, and as she, Ollie, Max, and Nate got off the shuttle wagon and boarded the ferry for their three-hour ride to Cerulean, she couldn't put her finger on it. She attempted to analyze it while the four of them sat together in the first-class cabin reserved for the royal family and guests.

Was that it? That her suspicion of Prince Nathanial had dissolved so much that it hadn't occurred to her until they were all in the cabin that maybe she should make Max and Nate sit elsewhere? It almost looked like the four of them *were* friends from how they were arranged in the cabin.

Ollie was asleep again. She'd apologized as they boarded the ferry. "Sorry. I was too excited to sleep last night, and I get motion sleepiness," she'd said. Then she curled up on a bench and zonked out as soon as the ferry started moving.

The prince had yawned, *taken off his shoes*, and stretched out across an entire length of cabin bench himself. Now he was sleeping, too. Carina *never* would have slept in front of that guy. Sleep made you vulnerable.

"She snores a little," Max, who was sitting on the third bench seat in the cabin, noted. He was pointing to Ollie but keeping his eyes on Nate. "It's cute."

It *was* cute. Carina was sitting next to Ollie's head, and she had the urge to stroke Ollie's hair like she would have Miguela's. She did, and Ollie made a contented little noise that made Carina feel relaxed despite everything.

"But *he* doesn't normally sleep like this at all," Max said, nodding at Nate. "Not unless he's gone into thermodynamic overdrive or whatever. And I don't think what happened on the shuttle counts."

Carina watched Max watching Nate. Max's eyes were back to their normal blue, and he seemed older than she remembered. Had his face been that angular previously? Had he always had that darkish scruff? And why was she choosing *now* to notice the way his shirt rested loosely over his flat stomach? Why was she suddenly worried about Max traipsing off with a prince who was probably going to get them both killed?

"It's not a good idea," she said. "I'm not going to try to stop him, but you should."

Ollie stirred in her sleep, and Nate mumbled something that sounded distressed.

Max said, "He probably needs the rest. Do you want to take a walk? We can talk outside the cabin."

They walked into the gusty air, and stopped by the railing, and it occurred to Carina that maybe for the first time ever, Max wasn't doing *anything* to try to impress her. He wasn't even thinking about her. He was busy worrying about Nate, and because of that, Carina was worried about *him*.

"Look, I know this isn't a great idea, but he's been trying to go home forever," Max told her as they watched the magicians driving the ferry. "I'm not going to be able to stop him."

"Franklin brought Nate to the North for asylum, Max,"

Carina reminded him. "He doesn't think Nate's welcome in the South. And if Prince Bastian views his brother as a threat … Well, I know what Prince Bastian is like. He could try to hurt Nate."

Max's face was set. "But Nate doesn't believe that. And I don't think you understand. He's going no matter what I say, and I can't let him go alone."

An urgent flash of concern popped up in Carina's heart, and it made her do something she hadn't wanted to do in months. She grabbed Max's arm, lifted herself onto her toes, and kissed his cheek.

"He's lucky he has such a good friend," she said. "But if you care about him that much, you should still find a way to stop him."

Max looked at her like this was the last conversation they might ever have. Then he leaned in, cupped her face with his hands, and kissed her lips. "Sometimes caring about someone means being there for them when they need you, even if they're being a dumbass."

He kissed her again, and it felt like goodbye, and she realized *far* too late that she didn't *want* him going. She hadn't even thought she still cared about Max. At all. Evidently, she'd been wrong. There was far more passion in this than what she'd felt while she kissed Heathrow earlier in the week.

She stopped thinking and let herself get lost in the feel of Max drinking her in like he'd been thirsty for so long he could barely keep himself from swallowing her whole. She played with the hair curling at the nape of his neck, and she felt fear-longing-anxiety for Max.

After all, maybe Max had lied about some things, but he had good qualities, too. Loyalty. Persistence. She didn't want him going off on some foolish, crazy trip with reckless Nate

Wellington. He was better than that. She wanted him safe with her. Even if that meant Nate had to stick around, too.

Max stopped kissing and stood with his forehead against hers, breathing in the same brisk air she was breathing. "I would like … very much … to kiss you forever. But I care about him as much as I care about you. It's different. Not less, though. And he needs a friend." He made the last kiss a hard, desperate kiss. "So please don't be angry."

She wanted to tell him he shouldn't go. She wanted to tell him it wasn't safe. She wanted to tell him that she wasn't sure why she wanted him to keep kissing her, but if it was a reason to stay, then they should keep kissing.

"Also, Carina, you should look away before I open my eyes."

She opened her eyes. "I saw earlier. I don't mind."

His eyes were closed tight. "It's not because I'm stressed. It's because—"

"Then, I especially want to see."

He opened his eyes. They glistened red, but not for too long. As she stared into them, they turned indigo blue again. The same color as the deep icy waters of the Asimov Straits.

"So, does this mean anything?" he asked. "Other than you're afraid for me?"

She had no idea. So she said, "It means be careful and come back alive. Because if you don't, we'll never find out."

He laughed. "Okay. I'll do what I can to get us back alive."

She frowned. "You could leave Nate in South Kepler. You're the one I'm worried about."

He grinned and kissed her again. It was amazing how fast a kiss like that could erase terrible memories. "Right, well, if Ollie finds some college guy for you to flirt with, don't enjoy kissing him more than you enjoy kissing me while I'm gone."

"I'll enjoy kissing whoever I *want* to kiss until someone

persuades me to stop kissing anyone else entirely," she said cheekily.

"I did *not* see that coming," someone with a grating accent said from behind them. The prince himself was standing there with his hands in his pockets and a look of disgust on his face.

"Is Ollie awake, too?" Max said.

"No," Nate said. "That girl could sleep through the apocalypse. I'm never taking her riding. Dead girl on a horse is so not sexy."

"She'd never do something like that with you," Carina said, hoping it would come off as a warning that would stick.

He gave her a cocky but grim smile. "Never say never, Princess. But could you maybe not tell her Max and I are about to split? She's technically a guard herself. She might feel obligated to try to stop me."

"You know this is stupid, right?" Carina said.

"Would *you* have abandoned your sister to the Immortal Empire?" he demanded.

She wouldn't have. Ever.

"Fine," Carina told him. "I'll take Ollie to the bathrooms at the ferry station, and you can ditch us then. I'll tell her after you're gone."

For the briefest moment, Carina thought she saw something like gratitude on the prince's face.

"I can't believe you're actually helping me," he said.

She shrugged. "Don't come back, and we can both pretend it never happened."

M. KAYES MISSION LOG #219971

The purpose of sending a small group of IV-1052 Immortals from Earth to Kepler was to safely transport a cryogenically frozen bank of all the best Earth had to offer to a planet that was soon going to have to deal with all the worst. That was our mission. Beat the rash, vicious, soulless IV-933 Immortals here. Raise the first bunch of mortal humans on Kepler to be better than any of us. Correct a mistake none of *us* made.

So, we journeyed here. A hundred of us IV-1052 Immortals with thousands and thousands of cryogenically frozen embryos. Then we set about raising those embryos in batches. We were a tiny cluster of Immortal humans with more Mortal children than we could handle. Then we became the elderly Immortals in a village of children ruled by young adults. Then those adult Mortals began having children of their own, and they raised their children alongside the fresh batches of Mortal babies we continued to grow like crops in those artificial wombs we had onboard our ship.

As our fledgling human project grew, we taught our Mortal progeny to be idealistic. We educated them about the mistakes of humans past. Once upon a time, we told them, humans lived on a planet they called "Earth." They thought they were at the center of the universe, and they believed their planet was flat. They fought constantly for resources, even when those resources were abundant. They enslaved each other for progress. Sacrificed each other to deities they called "gods." Crafted weapons of mass destruction so they could rule absolutely over each other. Invented technology with intelligence much greater than that of the human mind. Used skin color to categorize each other into a gross and systemically flawed hierarchy that did massive damage to billions of people and was still relevant when humans finally left Earth to come to Kepler.

It took little over a hundred years before our project overcame us and the Mortals began to see *us* as a problem. We should have expected it. Humans always find a way to evilize the "other," and we, the Immortals, were the natural "others" to our Mortals.

Oh, *we* were not the ones who made up that lie about "android nannies" raising the first Mortal human Keplerians, nor were we the ones who started the fight that led to the All Saints Massacre, where the majority of my Immortal colleagues died. We were simply the ones who lost the fight, and it doesn't matter where you are in time or space. History always belongs to the winners.

What is ironic is that the Immortals on this planet—even the IV-933 Immortals—are far less prone to prejudice than the Mortals. Supposedly, the Empress hates unjust prejudice more than anything else.

I must confess, there have been times when I've considered

joining the Immortal Empire exactly for this reason.

Sofie and I had a conversation about it once. She said, "Myles, darling, just because the Empress prefers fair play doesn't mean you want to be a part of her empire. Make no mistake. Mila Hildebrand is after ultimate power, and the only reason she doesn't have it yet is that she's too smart to kill off everyone who opposes her. She knows if she does that, she'll have no one to rule. Do you want your life controlled by a power-hungry Immortal?"

I don't. But for many millennia, I haven't wanted much of anything. I've had nothing to fight for or against. I simply expected to live the rest of my Immortal life out alone, with the hope that one day, some accident or unknown illness would befall me, and I would finally turn to dust, as all humans are eventually meant to do.

I no longer wish to turn to dust. Not now. My whole world is all lit up again. Because Stella Rose is alive, she is an Immortal, and there is some chance that she might still love me. I *must* return to her. It has been an extreme frustration to me that I finally located one of the four escape vessels we hid on Kepler only to learn that it is inoperable.

Or rather, only to discover that I cannot operate it on my own. I was able to power it up, and then a rude interface informed me that to launch, I needed *six* personal escape imprints. I'd entirely forgotten about that failsafe, and this is my only practical way back to Earth. This is my only way back to Stella. The Keplerian Mortals have no interest in space exploration. They refuse even to put satellites into orbit. No GPS. No real cell phones. No new spaceships.

That means, if I want to leave, I will need to talk five of my original Immortal colleagues into helping me launch, and how will I do that? Only a handful of us is even still alive.

There's Lizzy, of course, and Foster Hinks at the Gandhi Medical Centre. The others scattered here and there could be impossible to find. I am desperately worried that I will not be able to accomplish this.

Long ago, I knew how to pray. I am trying to learn again. Because there's a woman out there who I still love. I'd have given her my eternity if she'd allowed it. Now all I want is for my eternity to stretch long enough for me to see her again.

Stella is alive.

I will do anything necessary to find her.

Anything.

CHAPTER TWENTY-SEVEN
UNFORGIVABLE ROMANCE

Ollie was irritated with Nate and Max. "They didn't want us to go *with* them? They'll be *toast!*" she exclaimed. But she agreed that Carina should tell Franklin everything, even though she was sure this would make them all prisoners on the isle for the rest of their lives. "Carina, you'll never date *anyone* your dad doesn't know," she lamented. "And it'll all be for nothing because the guys will probably bite the dust in some stupid, macho fight with a gang of bounty hunters before they ever make it to South Kepler."

"Speaking of prisons, I want to check up on the Immortal prisoners before we meet the Sisters for lunch," Carina told Ollie.

"Do you *remember* what that place was like?" Ollie said.

"Clearly," Carina said. "And I need to see if anything's changed."

It had. The Immortal prisoners now looked healthy and mean rather than cold and miserable. They jeered as Carina walked by their cells. "Think a few extra blankets make up for experimenting on us, Princess?" "You Mortals think you're so good with your Mortal Commitments, but you're just as hateful as the rest of us. And *you* don't have an excuse."

Carina hadn't expected gratitude, but respect would have been appreciated, and she'd have taken indifference in a pinch. She tried not to be annoyed when one of the female prisoners shivered, pulled her hands into her sleeves, and said, "I wouldn't want *that* problem."

Carina stopped, and at first, all she could see in the woman's face was her red eyes. But didn't the Immortals here have a point? How much worse was this than what Queen Vivian and her brothers had done to her?

"I wouldn't want to be Immortal," she said to the woman. "And I don't have much control over what happens to you here. But I can try to make sure the conditions here are humane. Is there anything you need?"

The woman spat at Carina, and the spittle landed on Carina's boot. Lovely. Carina returned to the exit, but as she walked, another woman spoke up without any hostility.

"Books," she said. She had short-cropped hair and a mark under her left eye that looked like a burn scar. "Fiction."

Carina nodded at the woman. "Fiction it is."

Outside the prison, Ollie said, "Well, *that* was depressing. But you at least stopped yourself from freezing everyone. What did you do?"

What she'd done was only to stop focusing on the negativity and attempt to see things from a new perspective. "I think I just changed my mind about how I felt," she said. "Had it gotten that cold at first?"

"Not nearly as bad as the first time," Ollie said. "Franklin's a good teacher. He probably knows you can't learn stuff like that from anything he can throw at you as well as you can from real-life experience. That's why he approved this trip."

Carina felt the same, and she was not looking forward to telling Franklin about Nate. "Think the prince thought to leave a note?" she asked Ollie, but that seemed implausible. Prince I'm-Running-To-My-Doom-Nathanial probably never thought of that kind of courtesy. Nor did she think Max would manage to talk Nate out of this on the way there. The prince was stubborn as hell. No one was talking him out of anything. They'd just all have to hope he made it back anyway.

Even her. Because given a choice between attempting to negotiate with a future King Nathanial and future King Bastian? Well, as Nate had said once, only one of those guys would worry about where to hide a body.

Sister Agda, Sister Raji, and Sister Elizabeth met Carina and Ollie at a sunny greenhouse café in Cerulean's Little California for lunch. Carina thought the place looked cheery but that it couldn't possibly be safe to meet up here. The whole front of the café was glass windows anyone could see through. She told Ollie she was concerned.

"Don't be," Ollie told her. "Aunt Elizabeth says this place makes the best tuftberry shortcake you'll ever have in your life. Everyone will be cleared out except us and a couple vetted staff members. And anyway, the Sisters are more dangerous than they look. Did you know Raji was in the Northern Militia when she was younger? And Agda—"

Sister Agda opened the door to the café just then to greet them. She was wearing jeans—something Carina was *never* going to get used to—along with a pretty black blouse and a stylish green swing sweater.

So, What. The. Hell.

"Are you going to stand there like targets?" Agda said.

That was the Sister Agda Carina knew. A woman with a voice that cut like an ax and zero tolerance for foolishness. Except things had changed between Carina and Sister Agda, and Carina could not resist saying, "I *still* can't believe you have an orange pickup truck, and I like your sweater."

Agda snorted and pulled Carina into the café with a bony hug that contrasted perfectly with the hug she then got from Sister Raji, whose beer gut smashed into Carina like a force of its own.

"Where's the smile I'm used to seeing on your beautiful face?" Raji asked as soon as she'd let go. But Carina couldn't answer because she'd caught sight of Sister Elizabeth, standing hesitantly at a table set for five.

Ollie tapped Carina's shoulder. "She asks about you all the time. She misses you."

The truth was, Carina missed Elizabeth, too, but in some ways, that made this betrayal hurt more. Sister Elizabeth was sunshine and snark, romance novels and paleberry ale, green polka-dotted dresses and f-bombs. Carina had looked up to her, and she'd hoped to be like Elizabeth when she was older, too. But that was when she thought "older" meant twenty-six or twenty-seven. Sister Elizabeth was closer to five-thousand.

She felt Sister Agda's hand on the back of her arm. "It's not easy to reveal something like that, and you were so young."

Did she seem significantly older now? She was still only sixteen. But maybe she'd changed more than she thought, because her feet were already moving her forward and her arms were reaching out, and once it was happening, hugging Sister Elizabeth didn't *feel* any different than it had before.

"I'm so sorry, Carina," Elizabeth said with her nose stuck in Carina's hair. "I love you, no matter what. I never meant to hurt you.”

The last of Carina's bitterness seeped away. It wasn't so hard to forgive Sister Elizabeth. She'd forgiven Max, after all, and she could think of reasons why you might lie to protect someone. So, she only said what mattered to Sister Elizabeth:

"I love you, too, and I'm so sorry about what happened to Novi Dupree."

Elizabeth said, "Novi Dupree has been through much worse." Then she hugged Ollie and asked, "Are you two getting along as well as we expected?"

"No!" Ollie said. "The princess hardly ever gets us in trouble!"

Agda said, "Oh, there's plenty of time for that."

Raji said, "We tried to order a round of sassafras beer, but they were out, so we ordered an entire round of paleberry ale instead."

And it felt like a family reunion was supposed to feel, and Carina's heart became lighter than it had been since before she'd left Novi Dupree Sanctuary.

Over lunch, Sister Elizabeth told them wild stories about the trip from Earth to Kepler, a best friend she'd lost along the way, how her sister had disappeared from Novi Dupree for decades to fall in love and start a family, and how she'd had the *worst* crush on Myles-the-Guru for so long.

"So embarrassing," Elizabeth said. "He never felt the same way. And the guy I *should* have been paying attention to—"

Raji chortled into her beer.

"He *didn't*, Raj! Myles never got over that girl he was in love with on Earth. He *still* hasn't. That's why he's trying to get back to Earth."

"Not what Lindy said," Raji told her beer.

Elizabeth huffed. "Several thousand years of close friendship ought to come with a *few* benefits."

Carina couldn't understand how anyone could be attracted to creepy Mr. Kayes. Still, Ollie jostled her and said, "*See*, if *anyone* can give you advice about Heathrow, it's Aunt Elizabeth."

Which prompted a conversation with much teasing that made Carina want to crawl under the café table's red checkered tablecloth, especially when Agda gave her some sage, practical advice about where a young woman could procure an ample stash of syns. Syns were biodegradable condoms, and Agda said they were, "the only safe, effective way to avoid STDs and unplanned pregnancies." She also warned the girls "not to trust that Kepler berry herbal tea *some* women rely on."

Carina was officially traumatized.

But the conversation came to an end when Agda stood up abruptly, glaring at the door.

Raji picked up two empty bottles of beer and flipped them in the air like she planned to use them as weapons. "What's wrong, Agda?" she said. "If someone's coming after the princess, they'll have to take a piece out of *me* first."

However, when the door opened, Agda was the one who flung her lager at the intruder telekinetically. Except, the intruder wasn't a threat. It was only Franklin, with Myles Kayes and some guy with crazy curly hair behind him. The beer sloshed over Franklin as he held his arms up to block it. "Was that *necessary*?" he demanded, wiping lager from his face.

Agda did not seem remorseful. "With you, it's *always* necessary. What are you doing here? How did you find me?"

Franklin's scar was a bright purple line across his face. "How do you *think* I found you?"

Agda and Franklin glared at each other, but Myles and the other man with Franklin pushed around him. They greeted Sister Elizabeth with more affection than Carina thought she'd *ever* let either Heathrow or Max pull in front of a crowd, and Elizabeth said to Myles, "So you found it, huh?"

"Yep," Myles said. "But I can't *use* it unless I have six security imprints."

"Which is why you retrieved Foster from Gandhi." Elizabeth put her arm around the other man's back. "What did he promise you in exchange for this, Fost?"

"Immortality Virus research," Foster said. "He tells me the Northern Royals have another unique sample."

"Something we can discuss later," Franklin said to everyone. "No time now. Turns out the Empress doesn't think the Northern Royals are dead, and she's taking any tip she can about where the lost princesses might be. There's a small group of armed Empire Immortals on their way here now." He smiled grimly at Carina. "How do you feel about making this a real practicum?"

Sister Agda shoved Franklin telekinetically, and he fell hard into a table. "*What* do you think you're doing?" she screeched. "If armed Empire Immortals are coming, then Carina is *leaving*!"

Franklin rubbed his backside tiredly and got back up. "Ag, I *know* you're trying to protect her, but the Empress isn't messing around. This won't be hired bounty hunters with fancy crossbows. This will be a military operation. I'm expecting them to have five assault rifles."

"Not paint guns," Carina said, mostly to herself. She wondered if she had the skill to deal with something like that.

"Not paint guns," Franklin affirmed. "But that doesn't mean you can't handle this."

Ollie stepped in front of Carina protectively. "No, Sister Agda is right. We need to get Carina out of here."

Myles spoke up. "We're only talking about five guns," he scoffed. "The Princess of North Kepler ought to be better at defending herself than *that*."

"Aw, she's a kid, Kayes," the guy Elizabeth had called Foster said.

"A kid with more defensive magic than anyone else on Kepler right now," Myles said. Which didn't make Carina feel better, considering what had occurred the last time that guy had told her she wasn't defenseless.

"How do you know they have five guns?" she asked Franklin.

Agda pointed to the back door. "The numbers don't matter, Carina. You and Ollie need to get out of here now. Raji and Elizabeth will go with you."

Ollie began pulling on Carina's arm, but Carina didn't feel good about fleeing. Five guns. *Was* that more than she could handle? It's not like she'd be alone dealing with it if she stayed. "Without *you*? Or Franklin?" she said to Sister Agda.

"Doesn't matter. You don't have time to leave," Franklin said. "I came as fast as I could, and I'm expecting two vans right about—"

Carina saw two black vans pull up in front of the café, and it seemed like everything started moving in double time as a soldier in an Immortal Empire uniform jumped out of the first van with a rifle.

Sister Agda cursed.

"Told you," Franklin said, a little self-righteously.

Raji kicked a table over and dragged Carina and Ollie behind it. Sister Elizabeth, Myles, and Foster did the same with another table, and Myles pulled out a handgun.

Franklin didn't bother hiding, though. He did draw a sword, while Agda picked up a whole café table telekinetically and chucked it at the guy with the rifle just as he entered.

Agda put *force* behind the throw. That Immortal was not going to harm anyone today. But then Carina thought it was strange that Franklin and Agda couldn't seem to decide where they should stand in relation to each other. They conducted an awkward little dance, both attempting to get closer to the door than the other as more Immortals climbed out of the vans.

"What's up with them?" Carina whispered to Raji.

"True love," Raji whispered back.

Carina would need to think about that later. For now, the Empress's armed soldiers were pouring into the café with rifles and purpose. One aimed directly at Agda, who howled, "No!" as Franklin yanked her behind him roughly with a grip on her arm that looked painful. The soldier fired at them, but the soldier's shot went wild because Max had been a hell of a lot faster, and Carina had *plenty* of time to yank that rifle up and out of the Immortal's hands, protecting two of her best mentors in the process.

She stood, ignoring Ollie, Raji, and Elizabeth all shouting at her to get down. "But magic *always* trumps guns if you have time to think about it," she said, feeling fairly calm. She magicked that rifle toward Sister Elizabeth, who took it like it was second nature for her to handle a rifle, despite the bewilderment on her face.

After that, the chaos that broke out made Carina wonder what else she didn't know about the Sisters of Novi Dupree. She would not be shocked if she later learned that the Sisters only recruited women trained in adventurous forms of combat.

Raji leaped from behind the table and started chucking beer bottles at Immortals. Ollie pounced at a woman with a dagger. Elizabeth picked off a soldier aiming another rifle at Ollie, which gave Carina another gun to magic out of anyone's reach. Then she saw Agda wrestling a fourth gun from another Immortal, so Carina magicked water from a pitcher into an ice pick and shot it at Agda's attacker. That Immortal looked surprised as blood spurted from his neck and Agda plucked his weapon away.

"Nice," Franklin called to Carina. He was fighting off two soldiers at once, but neither seemed to have guns. She winced as he sliced clean through one of the soldier's collarbones to somewhere deep in the guy's chest with his sword. Then she shuddered when Agda flung the other man away from Franklin so hard they heard the man's bones snap as he landed.

It all made the last soldier who barreled in with a gun seem almost pathetic. It dawned on Carina that Empress Hildebrand must be inspiring and terrifying. Otherwise, why wouldn't this soldier just retreat? But it was also a moment of clarity for Carina. The Immortal Empire was hellbent on killing all the remaining First Degree Cardinals, but Carina was the *crown princess of North Kepler*. They were going to have to try *much* harder to kill her.

Additionally, someone should tell the next batch of Empire Immortals coming after her not to threaten her friends first. Because that made it *much* easier for Carina to laser focus on exactly how much she wanted to eradicate this evil. Every cold, angry feeling she'd been carrying around for the last six months or so hardened into one single point of chilling fury. She held her hand out, and before that last soldier could pull the trigger on his rifle, Carina allowed her fury to flow from her to her would-be killer, who froze solid in an instant and tipped to the ground.

There. No more Immortals with guns. Carina felt safe again. Then her perception of reality returned to normal as she realized she'd just frozen a human to death. Killed him. Just like that. And she felt *good* about that victory, even if everyone was looking at her like they'd never quite known her before. Everyone except Franklin, who was busy wiping blood from his sword onto the shirt of a dead Immortal slumped nearby.

"It's time we bring Mishe and his team back into your training sessions, eh?" he said to her. "Until we know if Nate's coming back."

Carina's sense of victory vanished. "You know he's gone."

Franklin wiped the sword off several more times. "It's my gift. I see things that will happen in the future to people I genuinely care about. I knew Nate was going home someday. I delayed it as long as I could."

"Because his brother's going to try to kill him," she said.

He sighed. "Yes. And I've never seen if Nate survives that."

There was Immortal carnage all over that cute little café. Any staff in the back were probably terrified, but no one else was hurt.

Not *once* had Carina felt afraid during that scuffle, either. Because the Sisters were far more dangerous than they looked and Ollie was skilled in hand-to-hand combat. Because Max was a perfect shot and Nate never treated Carina like anything less than an opponent worthy of a hard fight.

All of that led back to Franklin.

Sister Agda had taken Carina in because of Franklin. Ollie, Max, and Nate all trained with Carina because of Franklin. Franklin always knew what lesson his students needed most, and Carina was mostly just an incidental player in Franklin's world. Prince Nathanial was the one Franklin truly watched out for.

Franklin's sword was going to be extremely clean. Sister Agda approached him, though, and said, "For once, try putting your faith in someone you love."

Then Carina got busy with the others righting tables and cleaning up the mess they'd made because it didn't seem respectful to watch her best teacher cling to her fiercest guardian. But later, she didn't understand why Agda and Franklin both left the café looking furious at each other anyway.

"They were inseparable forever," Sister Elizabeth told Carina. "Then Franklin misinterpreted a vision, and Agda couldn't forgive him for it. I don't know the full story, but she might tell you if you ask."

"Why would she tell *me*?" Carina said.

Elizabeth hugged Carina. "It's funny how relationships can surprise us, isn't it? Agda sees herself in you. And by the way, Lindy and your cats all liked the prince."

"Traitors," Carina said darkly. But for the second time that day, she found herself hoping Prince Nathanial would make it back to the North soon. Though this time, it was because she had the feeling Franklin would never be the same otherwise.

CHAPTER TWENTY-EIGHT
HOW TO CROSS THE DESERT IN STYLE

Nate was not the poster boy for the Royal Church of South Kepler. He didn't question the existence of God but didn't think much about God either. He believed in angels but suspected they were all as self-righteous as Bast. He assumed he'd end up in heaven someday but only because he didn't think he had any mortal flaws God couldn't get over.

And he didn't think it was critical to pray. A few "thank Gods" and an occasional "God, if you can hear me, this would be a good time to step in" were mostly all Nate thought the Almighty needed.

He'd never asked God to prevent Bast from smiting him down for some sin. He'd never requested special protection from his cruel, manipulative mother. To be honest, Nate was going to be very unimpressed with God if it turned out He (or She, as Bast would have reminded him) didn't know how screwed Nate usually was.

The only thing Nate ever specifically prayed for was that God would watch out for Bast. That was all he could think of that God might not expect him to want. The rest, he was willing to leave to faith.

So right now, Nate didn't need to pray that he wasn't hitchhiking his way to demise as he and Max picked up a ride from Cerulean to Kochu Azhi in the East. Their driver was a sickly thin Immortal who said anyone willing to pedal on the uphill could have a seat on his quadrokart, and Nate didn't need to ask God to prevent the Immortal from getting suspicious of him and Max. He only had to tell the guy he and Max were looking for girls and booze on the Kochu Azhi Strip. Totally believable without divine intervention.

"Transportation on Kepler is insane," Max observed as they got onto the quadrokart and started peddling. "And tell me you're thinking up a plan?"

Nate was winging this whole thing. He and Max had a duffel with a single change of clothes between them and a toothbrush Nate was not sharing, but plans were like prayers. Mostly unnecessary. Anyway, there were plenty of ways Nate could think of getting from Kochu Azhi to Alighieri.

Some were safe.

Max had doubts. "What *is* this place?" he said as soon as they made it to Kochu Azhi and the Immortal let them off on the strip. "Vegas meets the wild wild west meets a motorcycle gang convention?"

It was evening on the strip by then, and Kochu Azhi was a rough-and-tumble sort of place. The strip was lit up and lined with body art parlors, cowboy saloons, mixed yoga studios, smoothie bars, game arcades, marijuana clubs, and questionable lounges. The place was active, too. Franklin would not have approved. Nate and Max immediately started running into people—both Mortal and Immortal—with crazy piercings, deep scars, bulked up muscles, and full-body tattoos.

There were all *kinds* of people Nate could have gotten in a bar fight with. The chaos was perfect cover.

"No, we're in eastern territory now," Nate told Max. "And Kochu Azhi isn't like the legends of Vegas on Earth because casinos are the only thing the Cardinal Family of the East ever forbade. Easterners love a good wager, but people were, like, betting away their firstborn children. So, no gambling here. Just mad hippy paradise."

Two hang gliders outlined with glowing neon lights swooped down over them, and Max covered his head as one of the rider's feet dipped and nearly hit him.

"What the hell was that!?" Max cried. "There's no breeze! How are they *flying*?"

Nate watched the gliders with fascination. "Aerodynamic magic. I've never seen it before, either. Easterners are hardly ever born with a hot or cold tendency, but every now and then, they're born with a limited ability to control air currents."

"Humans on Kepler can fly," Max said flatly.

"*With* the right machinery," Nate said. "Though I don't think many airplanes are being manufactured anymore. It was a big thing before the Western Republic fell. Used to be that the First Degree Cardinals in the East and West were all jet pilots. But Kepler magic likes balance, so now the West is just a dump for the Westerners who survived after the Immortality Virus decimated the Republic, and since hardly any Westerners have elemental gifts, the Easterners lost most of their magic, too."

The hang gliders reversed course and flew back toward them, riders whooping with glee as they dipped toward the strip.

"That's a huge shame," Max said. "Fire is cool, but flying is better."

"I know," Nate said. "And this is where I would have come for asylum. Which, by the way, is another reason I should abdicate. I do not tow the party line. The king of South Kepler does not *approve* of Eastern indulgence."

"Maybe that's why you *should* be the next king," Max said, which left Nate feeling grumpy and realizing he was also hungry. He spotted a community buffet down the street and suggested they stop for a meal.

"But can we pay?" Max asked. A fair question since neither Nate nor Max had income and Nate had not been willing to steal from anyone at Fort Aurora Borealis.

"Yet another reason we're traveling through the East," Nate told Max as they walked into the buffet and got their first look at the smorgasbord Eastern community buffets were rumored to be. "The Easterners all do a month of service each year herding, hunting, farming, or working in these buffets. In exchange, everyone eats for free."

Max was eying the food like he'd never eaten before. "But we haven't done any service," he said reluctantly.

Nate picked up a plate at the start of the buffet line and handed one to Max. "Nope, but hospitality is highly valued in the East. No guest would be refused food. Don't worry, though. If we were staying long-term, they'd assign us a rotation."

Max was enthusiastic about Eastern culture after the free dinner buffet. He was less enthusiastic after a night in a hostile and a morning spent procuring new transportation: two wild hairyhump ponies.

Hairyhumps were native to Kepler, and the ponies were more like small, hairy omnivorous dinosaurs than horses. But they were easy to locate outside the strip, and Nate could talk to the hairyhumps almost as well as he could talk to actual ponies. The two he found agreed to an overnight trip to the Eastern Desert Oasis Airport in exchange for some apples Nate had snagged at the dinner buffet the night before.

Max clung to his hairyhump's neck for dear life as they galloped away from Kochu Azhi. "How long are we going to be on these things?" he asked, his teeth clanking between words.

Nate patted his hairyhump—Arnie, he'd decided—and told it to go faster if he wanted. "Couple hours this morning?"

The hairyhump Max was riding—Arnie's buddy Percy—was the docile one of the two. Arnie took every opportunity to leap rocks and divots on the road, while Percy trotted evenly along.

"I'm not going to be able to walk after this," Max complained anyway.

"It won't hurt so much if you don't slouch," Nate told him. "And the hairyhumps will go slower once the sun goes down. Then you can just sleep while they bask in a moonlight jog."

Max jerked his head up. "We just had breakfast! You said a couple *hours*."

"This morning. Then we let them break for apples. But we'll get to the airport by tomorrow afternoon and say goodbye to Arnie and Percy there."

Max shut his eyes like he was in major pain. "Please tell me what comes after this is a ride on a luxury yacht."

"Close?" Nate bluffed.

"I see no yachts here," Max said the next day when they arrived at the Eastern Desert Oasis Airport. He was walking like his legs would never function right again. "Why do they call this an airport when it looks more like a rental car place with dinky hover jets? Also, Carina and Miguela are better at cross-country journeys than you. The three of us always found a bus, a van, or something less painful and labor intense."

Nate ignored that as they approached the airport, which wasn't nearly as busy as the Kochi Azhi strip. Only one woman was hanging around, and she was polishing a hover jet. Nate noticed she had a sword strapped to her side, she was wearing a jacket that might have been made from hairyhump hide, she was chewing something—probably gum brush—and she had a claw piercing her left ear.

Talon clan, then. Interesting.

The Talons were the Cardinal Family of the East, and they supposedly had no magic anymore, but the clan was still badass. Also, if the Garcias were lax about decentralized government in the North, the Talons were absolutely blasé. They didn't give a damn how the other Eastern clans handled leadership these days.

"Keep your mouth zipped for a minute," Nate whispered to Max. "The Eastern clans are anarchists. And that woman is probably extremely dangerous."

"More dangerous than *you*?" Max said.

"Maybe," Nate said. "But those dinky hover jets are the fastest moving land vehicles on Kepler, and no Easterner worth their salt backs down from a good wager. So ..."

The woman sauntered up to them with her sword swinging from her hip. "You two looking for a pilot?"

Nate wondered if the woman might have a little aerodynamic magic. It wasn't impossible. Or maybe some weak telekinesis? He let himself skim the surface of her mind. She thought there was no way two kids who'd ridden hairyhumps here had enough money for a hover jet ride. But maybe she could challenge one of them to a duel and take whatever money they had left anyway. And the bulky one with the dark hair would be hilarious to humiliate.

Excellent. Nate puffed out his chest for a show of what would hopefully come across as bravado and said, "Yeah, what'll it cost us?"

"We don't have money," Max muttered.

"Shut up," Nate muttered back.

The woman threw back her head and laughed. "You boys can't afford me." She touched the claw piercing her ear, though, and her eyes glinted at them. "How about a little bet for a ride instead? Either of you want to duel a master? I got a second sword in the hut. I'll go easy on you in exchange for those jackets if I win. Those'll sell nicely on the black market."

"I'm up for it," Nate said, throwing lots of arrogance into his voice. "But if *I* win, you give us a ride anywhere we want to go in that jet."

The woman cocked a thick dark eyebrow at Nate and spat some of the gum brush into the sand. "For that, I'll need you to put more than those jackets on the line."

"Uh, no," Max said.

"Fine," Nate said. "Boots, too."

"Are you insane?" Max hissed.

The woman jutted her chin at the hairyhumps. "And the ponies."

Nate cringed. Arnie and Percy were not up for grabs, but he was fairly confident he could take this woman. "Done," he said, and the woman's face lit up like she was absolutely delighted.

"Wait there," she said enthusiastically. "I'll be back."

She jogged away to the hut, while Max freaked out. "You're gambling for a ride? With a stupid *sword fight*? This is the worst idea you've ever had!"

Nate, however, felt pretty good about this bet. "I told you. Sword fighting is one thing I am damn good at," he said. "This is perfect. We don't have money, we need a fast ride, and that lady's hover jet will get us to Alighieri in three days, tops. No more hairyhump rides."

Max made a guttural noise of pain. "*Or* we'll lose our shirts! Why did I decide to come with you on this asinine adventure?"

Nate snorted. "No idea. I was going to leave you out."

The woman walked back out of the hut with a second sword in hand. She'd taken off her leather jacket, so they could now see that her biceps were at least as big as Max's.

Nate took his jacket off, too, and threw it at Max. The woman handed him the second sword. "Good," she said. "Don't want to get blood on that pretty thing."

"I'm going to start praying now," Max said nervously.

But this was the time for focus, not prayer. A sword fight was the only thing Nate could do to put all his gifts to use exactly the right way. His hot tendency gave him plenty of force and energy, his telekinesis made some fancy pants tricks possible, and he could usually listen well enough for his opponent's thoughts to anticipate their every move.

The woman began circling him. "Not your first rodeo, huh, kid?"

People tended to think in images when they engaged in something like a sword fight. The woman imagined a first strike at Nate's right shoulder. She swung the sword, and he easily countered it, using his sword to swing hers left and around, then go for a center blow.

She dodged, slashed down, and caught his sword coming up. But she was imagining he would push back, so he did the opposite, letting his sword drop, then lunging. He sliced into her upper arm, and her eyes widened like she couldn't believe he'd drawn blood.

He smiled at her charmingly. "Might be my third or fourth rodeo."

She growled in response, and he saw her thinking of a fierce swing at his torso. He met her at a lower angle, hooked her sword out to the side, used the momentum to round up, then brought his sword down to her neck in a quick and dirty trounce.

An easy victory. Her eyes popped, and she threw her sword to the ground to signify surrender. "Who *are* you?"

He removed his blade from her neck. "Someone who needs a ride?" he said. "To, uh, Alighieri."

She angled her head at him, then she began to laugh like the joke was on her. "I'll be damned. I'd heard a rumor, but I didn't expect to meet it in person." She took the sword back from him and pointed at the hut. "Why don't you boys get washed while I fire up the jet?"

Nate strolled to that hut feeling better than he'd felt in ages about life as a whole.

"I guess you *are* good," Max said.

"Told you," Nate said.

For the next couple days, Nate thoroughly enjoyed riding in the hover jet and even felt content in the evenings, when the woman—whose name was Cedar Talon—would stop wherever in the desert, toss him and Max blankets, and warn them to listen for the Kepler coyotes.

But she was on to them. The third night it was cold, and she just looked at Nate and said, "Need me to spell this out, kid? Or can you just start a magic fire?" He did, and then Cedar slept in her jet while he and Max lay down on their blankets near the fire and watched the stars, which seemed especially close with so much open space around.

"Do you at least have a plan for when we arrive?" Max asked.

One of Nate's fingernails was jagged. He chewed it anxiously until he'd torn the top of the nail off, then he watched the skin start to bleed.

"That's disgusting," Max said.

"Says a five-hundred-fifty-year-old Immortal who's crushing on a sixteen-year-old Mortal witch," Nate replied. Though mostly he'd been blissfully free from thinking about the princess since they'd left Cerulean. Almost a week to erase the memory of Max with his face attached to hers.

"Why do you have to be such an ass about her?" Max asked. "I'm friends with you, I'm in love with her. Can't you try to get along?"

Nate wasn't interested in *getting along* with C, but more importantly, he still felt like he needed to protect Max from her.

"Look, Max, even if I liked her, she's a Mortal and you are an Immortal. She's more likely to get together with *Bast*, and that's saying something because it is politically impossible for the king of South Kepler to marry the crown princess of North Kepler *and* Bast was a complete dick to her."

"But she never liked your brother," Max said, staring dopily at the stars. "She did like me."

Nate was defeated. This was hopeless. "Want to start asking questions about birth control on Kepler, then? Because she'll break your heart, and that could go especially badly if she gets pregnant or something, and—"

"I wish *you* would come to your senses," Max said, sitting up.

Nate sat up, too. "What, with the princess? That's—"

"With your *kingdom*. You just said it. Your brother's a dick, and you think *he* should be the next king of South Kepler?"

Nate picked up a random rock and chucked it into the dark as far as he could. "You don't understand."

"*What* don't I understand?" Max said. "That you think you're not good enough to be king? You're afraid you're not smart enough? Don't have enough magic? What am I missing? Because I'm looking at this from a neutral position, and all I see is you're the only member of your family fit to be a king of any kind. You empathize with normal people. You're powerful but still anti-violence. You don't think like a fundamentalist. You don't automatically dismiss cultures different from your own—"

"Who cares?" Nate interrupted. "No one wants me to be king."

"Bullshit," Max said. "Franklin does. So do the Northern Royals, and—"

"No one in the *South*," Nate clarified. "My kingdom wants *Bast*."

"But what if your kingdom *needs* you?"

Nate saw Cedar sit up in her jet and look over at them. He didn't want to talk to her about this, too. "They don't," he said firmly. Then he decided this conversation was over and he was sleeping now. He would arrive home tomorrow. He'd abdicate the throne to Bast. He'd clear Franklin's name. He'd help his family prevent the Immortal Empire from taking over all of Kepler.

The end.

CHAPTER TWENTY-NINE
THE WOUNDS YOU CAN SEE

Things at Aurora Borealis took on a somber tone with Nate and Max's absence. Miguela was distraught, Franklin seemed barely to be sleeping. Even Mishe seemed down, and no one was playing toggleball, though the weather was warm enough.

Additionally, King Reginald decided Miguela, not Carina, should train with Franklin until the prince returned.

"What happens if he doesn't return?" Carina said to her dad while he informed her and Eugene of the switch, together, but without Miguela, in his library. Dad stood in front of an expansive hearth while Carina and her brother sat side-by-side on his couch. She watched the fire in the hearth ebb and flow with the conversation.

"He will return," Eugene said like it wasn't even a question. Fire died down.

"Franklin sees the future, and he isn't sure," Carina said. Fire heated back up.

"But he's only there to abdicate, right? And—"

The fire flared, and King Reggie thwacked his cane against the hearth. "He *can't* abdicate. Franklin says Bastian takes after Constance. If that's true … I've met Queen Constance. She is the most conniving, manipulative, heartless person I have ever known. Herschel *never* loved that woman."

"They had three kids together," Eugene said. "They must have had *some* kind of relationship."

Dad leaned on his cane. "Yes. It's called *marriage*. It's what happens to First Degree Cardinals in the South when they get drunk at parties and do stupid things."

"Sounds like Herschel was a real winner," Carina said dryly.

"Sounds like hell," Eugene said, equally dryly.

King Reginald laughed even more dryly. "Spoken by two First Degree Cardinals of the North who tend so cold even *I* need a fire to have a conversation with them. Now, look, we're going to assume Prince Nathanial lives through this because if he doesn't, a few years from now there will be four Cardinals on the planet who tend cold and one who tends hot and is afraid to use magic, and that is a *serious* imbalance that won't help defeat the Immortal Empire."

"What about *you?*" Eugene muttered.

"Who cares?" Carina muttered. "It's not like anyone in our family is fighting that war."

Dad frowned. "Being strategic about how we use our resources is not negligence. And this is exactly why Miguela needs Franklin's help. Franklin has a knack for teaching Cardinals, and anyway, that poor man needs something to keep his mind off everything. Until Nate returns, Miguela works with Franklin. In the meanwhile—" he pointed his cane between her and Eugene "—I need *you* two to focus on cold magic and Carina's healing skills."

Carina did not want to build ice castles with her brother when New Paris was being attacked and Prince Nathanial was being an idiot. She didn't want to think about her healing skills compared to Eugene's at all.

"I don't think—" Eugene said.

"I *know*, Eugene," Dad said. "But you are the most skilled healer we've had in the family in decades, and it doesn't make any sense for the crown princess to have natural healing abilities and not know how to use them. You will teach Carina everything you can."

The fire died out entirely, and Carina had no idea if that was her or Eugene taking all the heat out of the room.

"You have to be kidding me," Eugene said.

But the king was uninterested in complaints. "I am not. Get started this afternoon."

Carina had been to the infirmary once since she'd arrived at Aurora Borealis, during Glory-Jane's tour. But Eugene walked in like he was more at home here than anywhere else on the isle. He greeted a receptionist with, "Send any injuries that come in today directly to me." Then he opened a door, and Carina followed him into the back.

Eugene gave quick, blasé notes as they walked. That's the storage room for medical supplies. This temperature-controlled cabinet is for antibiotics. Lab's over there, say "hi" to Alek—he's one of our phlebotomists. Nurse's station here, but they mostly only help the "real" doctors (he made finger quotes). I'll show you how to chart later, put on this extra lab coat—

"How many doctors do we have?" Carina asked as she slipped on a lab coat that fit worse than anything she'd worn up here in months. Eugene's coat fit perfectly and had his name embroidered on it.

"Three," he told her. "And me. But they refuse to call me "doctor" because I don't have an M.D. Eugene gets all the emergencies, but we wouldn't want him to think too much of himself." He hung a stethoscope over his neck. "Not like any of those classes would change how I heal people. But people don't like what they don't understand."

True, Carina thought. She didn't understand anything about magical healing abilities, and she did not like Eugene being "the best healer the family has had in decades." Then they got to his office, and extra sparks of jealousy crackled below her skin. His name was on the outside of the door, and he had a complete set up with a desk, cabinets, an examination table, and even a sink. He sat down on a rolling stool near the desk and said, "You can sit in the chair if you want."

She didn't want, but she sat anyway and looked at the posters hanging on the walls. Facts about the Immortality Vaccination. Common Cold Prevention—Wash Your Hands! And then, on the back of the door, there was a vintage poster of two kids flying kites on a rocky coast by a sign that read "Patton's Beachhead." Patton's Beachhead had been a well-known vacation spot for the Cardinal Family of the West. Before they were all dead. Did Eugene have a secret desire to be part of some other family? Sometimes Carina did.

Eugene stretched his legs out, crossed his arms over his stomach, and said, "So what do you know about healing?"

"Nothing," she said.

He stared sullenly at her. "Nothing at *all*? But you're further along in your pre-med studies than me. You must know *something*. Have you ever healed anyone other than yourself?"

The answer to that was "probably no." She shook her head silently.

He slouched. "Okay, look. I don't want to do this anymore than you, and this *cannot* be a one-way street."

"It *has* to be," she told him. "I have no idea how I heal myself. You, on the other hand, are supposedly an amazing healer. So, *you* go first. What do you do when you heal someone?"

There was frost spreading across the floor of Eugene's office. They both tried to pretend not to see it until it began to climb the walls. Then Eugene toed a line through the frost with his shoe. It wasn't close enough for her to do that. Did that mean …?

"Yeah, *I'm* causing it," he said. "You're probably helping, but it's mostly me. Because you probably won't believe this, but I feel even more supremely awkward about this than you. This is the stupidest thing Dad has pulled since you and Miguela got here, and he hired Terrance Hess."

The note of hostility in his voice was so cold that Carina was reminded of Prince Bastian. She softened her own tone. "*Do* you know what you do when you heal someone? Or is it more complicated than that?"

His face was stormy, but he answered without sarcasm. "Option B. The reason mostly only First Degree Cardinals who tend cold can heal is because it's a combo effect from all our magic gifts. It's slowing down bleeding and inflammation with cold thermodynamic energy, moving tissue around with telekinetic energy, and using whatever telesthesia gift we have to guide the whole thing."

"I don't think I have a telesthesia gift," she said.

He rolled his eyes. "Then add that to the list of stupid shit Dad does to try to make you and Miguela feel better about being left behind. Every First Degree Cardinal has a telesthesia gift. Our family just prefers 'self-discovery' to whatever they do to kids in the South to start honing their gifts when they're toddlers. It's ox beast crap. Dad says it's important not to 'limit' our abilities by trying to self-identify too early, but really, it's just one more way we're slower than Nate's family."

"I probably have a telesthesia gift, then, but I have no idea what it is, and you don't have any easy way to teach me how to be a magical healer?" she said.

"Precisely. The only way to learn is to try and fail until you succeed." He sighed heavily and stood up. "But I don't feel like sitting here and turning into an ice cube because we communicate poorly, so how about I take you to the lab, set you up with a microscope and some blood samples or something, and you can experiment while we wait for something interesting to come in."

"Experiment with what?" she asked.

He rubbed frost off his stethoscope. "See if you can freeze virus cells in healthy blood samples. Or look at some of the cultures we have of the Immortality Virus if you want. I don't care. Just stay out of my office."

Carina spent the rest of the afternoon examining blood samples in a chilly laboratory. Two hours later, when not a single injured person had shown up to the infirmary, Eugene came to the lab and told her he was going back to the house for a few minutes.

"Why?" she asked him.

"To get a warmer sweater," he told her crossly.

So, of course, a patient showed up right after he left.

"Eugene's not here," she told the receptionist who called back for her. "Can't one of the doctors see the patient?"

"The patient specifically asked for you, Princess Carina," the receptionist said.

This seemed like a trick, but Franklin turned out to be the patient standing in the lobby. She wouldn't have known from his facial expression that he was in pain, but he held up his palms, and she could see puffy blisters forming all over.

"Your sister," he said without Carina needing to ask. "I sent her to the stables to play with the puppies as a reward for a good session right after it happened, and I think I hid it well enough that she doesn't know I was hurt. Can you heal it?"

"Eugene would be better," she said apologetically. "He'll be back in a minute."

Franklin said, "I need someone with discretion, Carina."

So she said, "I guess I can try."

They went back to Eugene's office, and Franklin sat on the examination table.

"I don't think it's as bad as it looks," he said while Carina washed her hands in the sink and tried to figure out how to approach this. "They're maybe third-degree burns? It was my fault. I was testing her current skill level. Asked her to heat up a dumbbell because I wanted to see if she could conduct heat through metal, and I've never seen something get so hot so fast. The bar started buckling, I reached for the weights, and—" He held up his hands. "I've never seen *Nate* do that. Your sister is something else."

Carina appreciated Franklin's assessment of Miguela. "I've seen her do some things."

Franklin chuckled like he wasn't in immense pain. "I know you have. She can't know she burned me, though, because she's got a Northern guilt problem Nate never had, either, and I don't want her to be afraid of working with me tomorrow."

Carina understood. She nodded and took one of his hands as gently as she could, holding it up and trying not to actually touch any of the burns yet. A pocket of pus was bubbling near the top of his palm, there were several smaller pockets on his fingers, and what had probably been a blister on the heel of his palm was split open.

"I've never done this before," she told him anxiously.

"Oh?" he said like that was funny. "My favorite student never scalded you? Give it a try."

She touched a small blister on his thumb, then immediately pulled back when he hissed in pain.

"No, ignore that," Franklin said with his face still twisted up. "*Anything* that touches that burn will hurt right now. It's probably good for you to get used to seeing someone wince."

"I do not like this," she said, but she tried again, touching that little blister and this time ignoring his grimace.

Eugene had said healing was some combination of telekinesis, thermodynamics, and whatever your telesthesia gift was. She had no idea what her telesthesia gift was, but anyone with any empathy would have known Franklin was still in pain, and she could sense heat in the blister. She imagined transferring cool calmness like it was a liquid that could flow from her to him, and to her relief—and probably his, too—the blister actually seemed to recede.

Franklin breathed out a sigh. "*Knew* you were the right healer for this."

She considered the blood samples she'd been studying most of the afternoon. She thought maybe she could sense platelets in Franklin's blood and gather them, and as soon as it occurred to her to try, it seemed like some magic she hadn't known she had was manipulating his blood.

"Have you ever studied intuition?" Franklin asked. "Some people have natural instincts with particular skills. I bet you have it with healing. You don't have to know exactly what you're doing. You just have to talk yourself into believing you can do it."

The blister on his thumb was completely gone.

"Maybe you're right. That one's done, a dozen to go," she said. But now that she felt more confident, it did seem easier to heal the next blister. "Maybe if I get in some practice, I'll have a better sense of how I'm doing this," she added as she went on.

Franklin closed his eyes. "I'm sure you will, Princess." It was a good moment to see his face almost relaxed. He had strawberry-blond scruff around his chin and mouth, and there were laughter lines on his face, but there were also dark circles beneath his eyes and age spots. She had half a mind to try to heal that scar. Or maybe he wouldn't want that.

He opened his eyes and caught her looking.

"Sorry," she said, hastily moving on to one of the unhealed blisters.

He didn't seem bothered, though. "Scar's crazy, right? I got it in a fight with one of my own men, back when I was in the Southern Guard. We'd just spent a week trying to rid a village of Empire Immortals, then one of my soldiers found some Immortal teenagers hiding in a wine cellar. Scared kids. Probably they'd been Mortals snatched from the village at some point, and somehow, they'd made it home. Soldier was going to kill them."

Carina decided she could do the split blister on the heel of his hand while he was talking. "That's horrible."

Franklin nodded grimly. "He thought he was doing right.

We had fresh orders from Cassius at the time. 'The only good Immortal is a dead Immortal.' But Immortality isn't an anti-humanity switch. The brain damage Immortals get doesn't set in for hundreds of years. I fought my own guy defending those kids. Got this scar for it and kicked out of the Southern Guard." He lifted his shoulders sheepishly. "I had a temper back then."

"I don't believe it," Carina told him lightly while she continued her work. "And I wouldn't want to know what shape the other guy was in after that fight."

"I will take that as an incredible compliment from a princess who tends cold," Franklin said, squeezing his now healed hand in and out in a loose fist. "Good as new. Exactly as I expected."

She thought she was even more pleased than he was, though. "Did you know I could do it?" she asked. "Had you already seen me do it?"

"I *hoped* you could do it," he said, and he held out his other hand, which was much worse than the first. Several of the blisters on this hand were broken and oozing.

She began fixing it but decided that chatter between her and her patient was useful for this. "Maybe sometimes it's not as hard as you think to heal wounds that look bad."

He hummed. "If you're talking metaphorically about me and Agda, *that* wound is much worse than it looks. I made an unforgivable mistake, and Agda is skilled at holding a grudge."

Carina wouldn't have expected Franklin to talk about Sister Agda at all, but since he was, she thought of some grudges she'd held recently. She'd been furious at Max, misunderstood by her own family, hurt by Sister Elizabeth.

What kind of betrayal would be unforgivable?

"Did you kill someone she loved?" she asked while she

cooled over another broken blister.

Franklin had a self-deprecating smile. "Not that unforgivable. But still complicated."

Carina did not say what she was thinking, but however complicated things were, Sister Agda clearly wasn't over him. Maybe it wasn't as uncorrectable as he thought.

Franklin was silent while she finished the rest of his hand. When she was done, he flexed both hands and said, "I know the Northern Royals don't over-focus on telesthesia, but some telesthesia gifts are empathy-related. Maybe you should look into that, too." He tilted his ear up. "Do you hear sirens?"

Carina listened, and yes, somewhere, a siren had started going off. Eugene barged into the examination room before they had time to investigate, though.

"Dad wants us in the bunker in twenty minutes," he told her. "We might have to stay for a few days, so you should throw some things into a bag to take down there."

Franklin was gone in a flash while Carina digested that news. "The bunker? Where is *that*? And why would we stay there a few *days*?"

"Underground, *obviously*," Eugene said. "And because Cerulean is under attack."

CHAPTER THIRTY
VISION OF THE FUTURE

The bunker was under the summer house, and it was small for a place that was supposed to keep the whole royal family safe during an attack. There was a bathroom with a rudimentary shower and a rusted out toilet, a small conference room from which the king or queen could take private calls, and a living space with a kitchenette, two futons, three narrow bunks stacked up above each futon, and about a dozen folding tray tables leaning against a wall. There were two lighting options—dim and dark—and a steam heater that wasn't working well.

Or maybe that was Carina and Eugene. They were sitting on the floor against the door, as far away from Mom as possible. Mom and Dad were sitting on one of the futons, Mom with her legs tucked sideways and a blanket wrapped around her shoulders and Dad with his feet square on the ground, his elbows pressed into his thighs, his head bowed toward the concrete floor.

Miguela paced back and forth between the futons,

wringing her hands. "How long until the sirens stop and we know we're safe?" she asked for the third time.

"Miguela, we're already safe," Dad said. "You can sit down. This is only a precaution. No one's going to reach the isle."

She did not sit down. "But the sirens won't keep going the whole time, will they? They'll stop sooner or later?"

"Preferably sooner," Eugene muttered.

Carina hoped sooner, too. They'd only been down here for thirty minutes or so, but the sirens were driving her crazy.

"Probably in the next few minutes," Mom told them, then she shifted positions on the futon so that her legs were tucked the other way. She'd shifted every time Miguela asked when the sirens would stop.

"And then what?" Miguela said. "After they stop, what does that mean? How do we know what's going on up there? What happens if they do get to the isle? What if someone attacks the house?"

"No one will," Dad said.

"But what if they *do*? And what about the staff? Are *they* safe?"

Carina wondered that, too, and she was also concerned about the guards. Where was Mishe? Ollie? Was Heathrow okay in Cerulean?

Dad listed all the reasons Miguela didn't need to be worrying. "The ferry was on this side of the isle when the attack began, it's a limited attack, and we don't have any reason to think the Immortal Empire knows we're even here. The Royal Society prefers for us to hunker down whenever there's even the *slightest* possible threat. Everyone else at the fort is getting on with what they usually do. Think of this as a drill. It's more that than a real alarm."

Carina felt a wave of heat hit them.

"But what if there's a security breach?" Miguela asked. "What if Empire Immortals *do* attack? What if they take out our guards? What happens *then*?"

Dad looked toward Carina, and she could practically hear him thinking, *Can you please calm your sister down?* But she couldn't do that because *she* didn't think it was right for them to be down here either. Especially if this was a "drill."

"I agree with Miguela," she said. "That siren has been blaring for an hour, and we're the ones with all the magic on this island. Why are we hiding?"

She did not say that she was also concerned about the heat in the air, but she knew what happened when Miguela felt her family was threatened. Things *exploded*. And it was getting very hot in here.

Dad's cane was resting next to him. He reached for it and began bouncing it on the ground. Then he seemed to realize what he was doing, and he threw it aside, leaned back hard, and let his head hit the wall behind the futon with a small thud.

Miguela continued to pace, now alternately wringing her hands and wiping tears from below her eyes with her knuckles.

"Miguela, honey, why don't you sit between Eugene and Carina?" Mom suggested. "We're going to be here for a while. You should try to relax."

Eugene side-eyed Carina, and they both scooted to make room. But Miguela wouldn't sit. "Am I making it too hot?" she asked. "I am, aren't I? Because I'm scared, and I can't control this. I can't even *remember* what happened after the last two times I felt this scared, and both times I blew something up and people *died,* and magic *isn't* a gift, it's a stupid *curse*."

"You're agitated," Dad said, sounding calm despite the

obvious clench in his jaw. "It is completely normal for a First Degree Cardinal who tends hot in a situation like this. I was the same at your age. People who tend hot don't like to be contained. It makes us edgy. But magic is *not* a curse, and this is not the same as what happened when you were a little girl or on the Mountain of Peril last summer."

"And Mom's right, Guela," Eugene said. He patted the floor and looked hopefully at her. "You have two siblings who tend cold. Come on and grab a slice of nice, hard cold concrete. I bet that'll take the edge right off."

Miguela took a step toward them, then hesitated, so Carina patted the floor exactly like Eugene had. "It's okay," she said. "Just come sit down."

Miguela frowned. "*You* don't believe that. You're looking at me like I'm a bomb that might go off."

Carina winced. She probably *did* look like that.

But Eugene groaned. "We're *looking* at you like our sister who is making the bunker so hot *we're* toasty. That does not mean you're dangerous. It means we feel *bad* for you, and we wish you weren't so upset. You're not going to blow anything up today, and no Immortals are showing up on Aurora Borealis Isle."

"How do you *know*?" Miguela asked.

"Eugene," Dad said from the futon like he was issuing a warning of some kind.

Eugene pulled his knees into his chest. "This isn't helping them."

"*What's* not helping us?" Carina said.

Eugene gave Dad a *look*, and Dad hoisted himself up with his cane. "Eugene, do we need to speak privately?"

But Eugene scrambled to his feet. "No! We do not need to speak *privately*. All we *ever* do around here is keep secrets that make everything worse for *everyone.*"

"No one is keeping it a secret that Miguela has been trau-matized by magic," Dad said. "And we are following advice from the Royal Society's *best* psychologists to help her. Just like we're doing everything we can to make up for the holes in Carina's training so that—"

"The *holes.*" A fine layer of frost spiraled out at Eugene's feet. Carina shivered, and Miguela backed toward Mom and the futons.

"Sit back down, Eugene," Dad said, and when Eugene didn't, Mom said, "Eugene, your father told you to sit down," in a voice Carina would not have dared to disobey.

Eugene only clenched his fists while snow started swirl-ing around his ankles. "He *also* said Carina's training had *holes* and the best way to help Miguela with her *real and serious fear of blowing things up and killing people she cares about* is to listen to some psychologists from the Royal Society that she's *never met.* And in the meanwhile, North Kepler is under attack, and instead of going out and fighting the Immortal Empire like we should, *we're* hiding in an underground bunker and fight-ing each other." He pointed at Dad's cane. "And don't even *try* to tell us you're not keeping other secrets. *Why* won't you let me try to fix that limp? What are *you* hiding to protect us?"

Carina thought maybe Miguela was right about the "magic is a curse" thing as she watched snow start falling around Eugene's tightly clenched fists and sparks start flying near Dad's equally tightened fists.

"I am *more* than aware of the challenges North Kepler is facing, Eugene. But my *children* do not need to know every-thing. We are already pushing you all as hard as we can to make up for—"

That snow flurried out around Eugene. "To make up

for *what?*!" he shouted. "Carina and Miguela weren't missing anything at Novi Dupree except *us*. They were safe and educated. They had clean clothes and healthy food and people who cared about them. They weren't *here*, and they weren't learning magic, but they were *fine*. And if you *really* want to make up for what they *were* missing, you could start by not using the problems they've both had with magic to make them feel like inadequate *strangers!*"

That actually made Mom stand up, which made it impossible not to look at her burgeoning belly. She was due in a month or so. Stress like this could not be good for the baby.

"That is *enough*, Eugene," Mom said in a clear, *I may not have magic, but I am still a force to be reckoned with* voice. "There is no guidebook on how to reunite two halves of a family. Everyone here is doing the best they can with a difficult situation."

"But it's *not* enough!" Eugene cried. "We're all tiptoeing around each other because our family never faces things head-on. We need to talk about the things that are hurting us!" He pointed at Mom's belly. "Like, did it ever occur to you to ask Miguela how she feels about you having a *replacement* baby?" Then he pointed at Carina. "Or did you ever think to ask how *she* feels about being the crown princess of North Kepler? Our closest ally is trying to give up his throne right now. She could be thinking of doing the same. Because maybe she doesn't *want* to inherit a royal mess."

The sirens stopped, and for a moment, all the noise that could be heard in the room was a buzz from the dim lights and Miguela sniffing up tears. Carina suspected that her own face was as blank as the looks on her parents' faces, and then Eugene spun toward her.

"By the way, *you* could *ask* me how I feel about not being the crown prince anymore. Instead of just *assuming* things." His mouth twisted into a distorted smile. "Mom and Dad don't want you to know, because they think it'll make you nervous about being more behind, but I *do* know my telesthesia gift. I *can* see the future, and I've seen myself as a doctor several times, but I've never seen myself as the king. And I don't know who ends up being the king of South Kepler yet, but a few weeks ago, I saw *you* as the queen of North Kepler."

Dad made a noise like someone had punched him hard in the gut, and Mom sank back down onto the futon, holding her belly while Eugene crossed the bunker to Miguela and grabbed her hands.

"And Guela, I *promise* you don't need to worry about blowing something up today, because right when the sirens started, I saw us leaving the bunker later and you telling me we should go play with the puppies."

Miguela's tears stopped. "Are you sure?"

"I've never been wrong yet," he said.

His statement made Carina feel like there was a knife she'd only just realized was there being turned in her gut. "Never?" she asked.

Eugene and Miguela both looked at her like they'd just realized what she was realizing.

"You were older in the vision," Eugene said.

"How *much* older?" Carina asked while Dad grimaced.

"Well, not ancient, but … at least a few years?"

A voice came over a speaker. "Your Highness, you're clear to come out. The attack in Cerulean was an isolated event. Just a prison break."

Mom stood up and put her hands on Miguela and Eugene's shoulders. "Come on, you two. Let's go. Carina needs to talk with Dad."

"If there's something he's not telling *us*—" Eugene started.

"*Later*, Eugene," Mom said. "This affects Carina more than anyone else." Then she ushered Miguela and Eugene out of the bunker while Carina stood frozen in place.

The current king, who was apparently not going to retain his position for nearly as long as Carina expected, sighed heavily and leaned back again while he watched her.

"You're much better at controlling your magic than you were a month ago," he said with what seemed like an incredibly exhausted smile. "Given what you just learned, you're keeping it together fine. No frost."

Carina came over to the futon and sat quietly by him while she tried to process what Eugene had just revealed. It was bad enough to be a princess. But a young queen? She knew someone who'd gone through *that*. That girl was currently dead.

Still, there were a lot of reasons someone could become the queen of a country that didn't involve the previous king dying, right? Like abdication. But why would her dad abdicate? Were there other, non-tragic ways to become a queen?

"Eugene doesn't know exactly when it happens, Carina," Dad said. "Or how. I didn't think you needed to have that extra burden yet or I would have told you. It never occurred to me to ask how you felt about being the crown princess because no one sane would *ever* want to be the next king or queen of North Kepler. There's nothing we can do but try to prepare you the best we can. And we're *not* letting the kingdom just rot. We have people spreading rumors among the magical elite that the Northern Royals are alive. The District Reps know, and the Royal Society, plus all the top-ranking militia, the governors of every major region—"

"So only the people who really need us are still in the

dark," Carina said.

It made her dad look even more uncomfortable. "I know. But that's not because we're trying to delay. It's because we need to make sure you're strong enough to handle it when the Immortal Empire does come after you, and Miguela and Eugene, too, because they will, and you'll need back up."

She didn't want to ask, but she felt like she needed to know. "Is there something else you're not telling us? Why won't you let Eugene try to fix your limp? It's a real limp, right?"

He rubbed his hip. "It's real. The truth is, I should have been strong enough that day years ago to destroy those Immortals that came to our house. At my strongest, I could have diverted Miguela's energy and created a defensive teleki-netic shield that would have protected all of us. As it was, all I could do was direct the energy from Miguela around us and use some telekinesis to make sure the barn didn't kill Eugene and your mother as it came down around them. I got buried in the fallout and badly injured."

"So, you didn't create a shield for yourself?" Carina said. "But I thought—"

He laughed. "You must think it's pathetic, huh? Since Prince Nathanial managed a defensive telekinetic shield on the Mountain of Peril, and I should have been much more skilled than he was then? But there were other factors at play. Eugene is right. I could let him heal the limp any time. It's just helpful to have something to cover the real problem."

"Which is …?" Carina prompted.

He cringed but did not refuse to answer this time. "Which is that my magic is dwindling. Has been for a long time."

That caused a little frost to nip at Carina's fingertips. "Dwindling *how*?"

"Dwindling like I couldn't shield myself back then

and like it takes a tremendous amount of energy for me to produce fire," he admitted. "My telesthesia gift is unreliable, and I can't teach you telekinesis myself because you're already ten times stronger than me."

Carina didn't really want him to explain why—she had her suspicions now—but he didn't make her ask.

"It's the Immortality Virus," he told her. "I'm infected."

Images of Queen Vivian's death flooded her mind.

He went on. "It's a slow-moving strain, and very few people know. The higher-ups in the Royal Society are aware. Doctor McIntosh's research is especially important to me. People like us can't become Immortal. If we can't find a cure, the virus will eventually kill me. The Immortality Virus research McIntosh is dong is critical to my survival."

"But I don't understand," Carina said. "How did you ever get infected?"

He laughed bitterly. "Probably the same way Herschel did, doing something extremely stupid and reckless years ago. Neither of us knew we were infected for some time. Your mother is immune, and Constance must have been, too. We also think this strain might have been targeted specifically at people with powerful magic."

"I thought King Herschel died years ago, though," she said.

"It wasn't *that* long ago. And Herschel didn't have the benefit of treatments developed at New Paris Medical School. I might have years left thanks to that and Doctor McIntosh. But even if I do, my magic isn't coming back. If the Immortal Empire becomes more aggressive, North Kepler will need a Cardinal Family with real power. It might make sense for me to hand over the throne early."

"Which at least means I might end up queen without you dying," she said.

"Maybe," he said. "But I hope you understand why I'm pushing you so hard and why I didn't want to tell you. Also why we're a little loose on our ethical standards with the blood we obtained from Queen Vivian."

"We should have been cooperating with South Kepler on that anyway, though," she said. "They're at risk, too. Two of them have died of the Immortality Virus already."

He laughed. "Can you think of any way to 'cooperate' with the Southern Royals without us announcing ourselves to Prince Bastian and Queen Constance? Because Constance saw our downfall as a win, and she's almost as power-hungry as the Immortal Empire."

Carina knew that, but there *was* one representative of the royal family of South Kepler that she might be able to negotiate with. Assuming he came back.

"Maybe," she said. "And I'll work harder on my magic."

"You're doing your best already," her dad said. "And I guess I better go tell Eugene and Miguela. Maybe give you some space to take this all in."

He got up, and she did, too, and then she reached out to hug him. Dwindling magic or not, he was still warm and still her dad, and she understood a lot better now why things had been so difficult up here for her and Miguela.

"It'll be fine," she said. "We'll figure everything out."

"It's in your nature to keep calm in the face of bad news. He kissed the hair near her temple. "But we can talk again if it hits you later, and thank you for not being angry at me. That's my telesthesia gift, by the way. I sense negative emotions."

She felt a bit of guilt over that. She'd had a lot of negative emotions recently, and many had been directed at him. But there were positive things, too, so she said, "I love you."

He said, "I love you, too."

CHAPTER THIRTY-ONE
A QUESTION OF LOYALTY

Cedar Talon dropped Nate and Max off outside the walls of Alighieri, where anyone who wanted to enter had to pass a guarded checkpoint.

"What's our story?" Max whispered as they got in line. "We need to keep our lies straight. How about you're a knight, I'm your loyal liege, and we got stranded on an island in the North, but now—"

"Say it louder," Nate hissed. "I sincerely hope the lies you were telling Icy were better than that."

Max let his shoulders droop. "Probably not. Since Migs never believed any of them."

"Then let's keep this simple," Nate said. "We're coming from the North, I'm here to visit family, you're here with me."

"As your liege?" Max asked.

"There are no knights in South Kepler," Nate said. Then he busied himself checking out the people in line ahead of them at the checkpoint. There were about twenty, and no one thought loudly at a checkpoint unless they weren't who they were supposed to be. Nate could only hear one person in that position. It was a girl maybe two or three years older than him, thinking, *What if someone from my hometown reported me for being telekinetic? What if they have my whole family on some list? But my sister was charged with treason. What normal girl wouldn't show up before her sister's execution? That's not suspicious, is it? And I know she didn't have anything to do with the assassination.*

Nate had been sure the investigation into Vivian's assassination would be over by now, so that seemed odd. He dug a little further and found nothing indicating that this girl or her sister had any involvement with the Immortal Empire. He shook himself out of the girl's mind, though. Her problem was one more thing he could fix after he abdicated. First, though, he had to get to the Royal Castle.

He tried to locate the thoughts of the checkpoint guards. Nate didn't recognize four of the guards, and he quickly confirmed that those guards had only seen stuffy, formal, outdated pictures of him. They probably wouldn't recognize him now. The fifth guard had briefly worked at the Royal Castle, but that woman looked right at Nate and didn't have any thoughts of recognition.

The sixth was a potential problem. Nate knew that guy by name. Cecil Mierels. He'd been one of King Herschel's personal guards, and Nate had always liked him. Good guy. Smart, loyal, solid sense of humor. On several occasions, Cecil had "not seen" Nate stealing midnight snacks, sneaking rattycats into the castle, and accidentally-on-purpose setting something on fire because he was throwing a tantrum over a new injustice.

But checkpoint guard wasn't a high-honor position. If Cecil was here, it was because Constance had kicked him out of the Royal Guard. So, where would his loyalties lie now?

There was nothing Nate could read in Cecil's mind that would say one way or another, but he decided to take a chance. He purposely held Max back and let two people in line behind them go first so he and Max would end up at Cecil's checkpoint station.

"Names?" Cecil said as they stepped up, apparently not making the connection, though he was also mostly looking down at some papers he probably had to fill in about everyone he checked into Alighieri.

"Uh, hey Cecil," Nate said nervously, keeping his voice down.

As soon as Cecil looked up, Nate could hear him thinking, *Holy shit, is that Prince Nathanial?*

Cecil stood from the stool he'd been perched on, announced, "Random screening," then gestured for Nate and Max to follow him inside the checkpoint station. He led them to a private screening room where he flipped down all the shades fast.

So much for trying not to get caught, Max thought loudly.

Nate was worried, too. His gut intuition was that Cecil was a friend, but he knew he could be wrong about that.

As soon as all the screens were closed, Cecil turned to Nate and said, "Prince Nathanial? How is this possible? They told us you were dead."

"Not dead," Nate said. "I've been recovering somewhere safe for a while. My family doesn't know."

Cecil's eyes looked tired, but Nate was surprised at the hope that lit up in his face at that one statement. "Oh, my *God*. Then *you're* the rightful king, not Prince Bastian. This changes *everything*."

Nate immediately began to refute that false belief. "No, no. I'm not. It doesn't. I'm returning to abdicate to my brother. But then I can—"

Cecil seemed stricken. "You can't *abdicate*. Your mother is ruthless, and they say your brother is worse. They're on a witch hunt for anyone they can blame for Queen Vivian's death. They're planning to execute the captain of the guard that accompanied you three out of Alighieri after the coronation."

The hair on Nate's neck rose. "Brandon Thurlow? *Why?*"

"Conspiracy to kill the queen, Your Highness. But I know Thurlow. Saw him coming up in the guard from when he entered as a kid. He would *never* have betrayed the crown."

Nate knew *that*. "Is the execution scheduled?"

"I believe they're planning it for next week, sir," Cecil said.

Max had a very "I told you so" look on his face, but it *didn't matter*. Bast wasn't himself right now, and if Nate abdicated, he could counterbalance that. Make sure Bast didn't freeze into a heartless tyrant. He could. Couldn't he?

"I can talk my family out of it," Nate told Cecil. "But I have to abdicate first. Otherwise—" Well, *maybe* his family wouldn't be so terrible. *Maybe* they wouldn't sacrifice him to keep Bast's path to the throne clear.

"Otherwise, they'll kill you," Cecil said like there was no question there. "Don't go back, Your Highness. Or go back to free Thurlow, then get out of there. Find Lord Franklin. He's at the top of Constance's hit list, and you know the higher a traitor is on *that* list, the more likely it is they're one of the good guys. We can gather resisters. People will rally if they know there's a better option than Prince Bastian."

"I am not a better option," Nate said.

Cecil seemed to be assessing the truth of Nate's words for a moment, but then he said, "You need to see what's happening yourself," and he followed that by *bowing*. "When you are ready for it, you have my allegiance and the allegiance of many others, and we will help you."

Nate had no idea how to respond.

"He'll take that under advisement," Max said.

Nate led Max quietly through Alighieri, assuming they were safe from recognition for the most part until they got to the castle. Alighieri was a vibrant city, even under the Immortal Empire's constant threats, and this time of year brought breezy, blue skies that made people eat lazy lunches outside at wrought iron café tables. The people sipped white wine from squat glasses and watched cyclists zip down the red recycled rubberized bike paths.

It made Nate miss his hometown, but he couldn't drown out the disturbing thoughts coming in at him from all those people, despite the relaxed afternoon ambiance. It was hard to ignore, *How am I going to afford groceries when they just raised taxes again? What will happen to my teenage son if I don't register him for the Southern Guard? Are we safe when the Immortals are raiding farms just outside our walls?*

"Maybe we should sneak in through the tunnels and scope things out," Nate told Max. "Then we'll find Bast. It'll be easier to talk to him first than my mother."

"Your mother must be some piece of work, huh?"

"She's exceptionally beautiful and remarkably terrifying," Nate said truthfully. "The perfect Southern Royal. The ends always justify the means for her."

"She's a bitch," Max said.

"Absolutely," Nate said. Also truthfully.

He would have liked to visit the stables and make his way into the castle from the tunnel entrance there, but the castle grounds were sure to be heavily guarded. Unfortunately, he could only think of one other way in. The Royal Cathedral. It would be quiet right now and not guarded. Nate hadn't spent any more time there than necessary, so most of the clergy wouldn't recognize him. If Bast happened to be there, great. It would be harder for Bast to smite Nate down right in front of God.

Still, they got to the cathedral, and Nate stood across the street in its shadow, not wanting to go in. The Royal Cathedral was by far the most beautiful building in Alighieri. Probably in all South Kepler. Also, the most terrifying. Spires and pikes everywhere, stained glass depictions of grotesque demons and warrior angels, doors twice as tall as the tallest humans.

"What religion is your church based on?" Max asked.

Nate would not normally have prattled on about his religion, but in this case, talking about church was easier than going inside.

"Mostly the major Abrahamic religions in terms of sacraments and traditions and in that it's a monotheistic religion. But we treat the old holy texts as human-written attempts to understand God, and we don't worship any savior." Nate didn't care about any of this, but he couldn't make himself move any closer to that cathedral yet, so he kept talking. "Lots of feminist influence, too. The Royal Church is gender neutral. Children should be raised by married partners, but no one cares who those partners are. God takes whatever form you need He, She, or It to take. Anyone willing to devote themselves to the church can study to become clergy regardless of sex, gender, ethnicity, magic."

"Solid," Max said.

"Except for when they're trying to control everything."

"Are we going in?"

Yeah. They had to. Nate forced himself to cross the street. So what if the last time he'd walked through those front doors, it had been for Viv's coronation? She hadn't died here. He climbed the steps and pushed the doors open. It was light inside like it always was during the day thanks to the dome skylights. Clergy were milling around, but no Bast, so Nate went for a bench and tucked his head down like he was praying, and Max followed.

Nate's worst memory was of an arrow piercing through Viv's chest like she was target practice for some Immortal, and she'd been right here when it happened. But he let that go and focused on the prayer chapel, searching for thoughts that might be coming from there. He couldn't sense any, but clergy members often had quiet minds. He needed to create a distraction just in case.

What should he use? There were tapestries to light on fire, but those were valuable. Communion bowl on the altar? Probably even more valuable. Row of urns containing the ashes of the church's most esteemed leaders? Sacred *and* valuable.

Stack of bronze offering plates a good distance away from the prayer chapel? Perfect. He kept his head down and magicked the stack into the air before letting them drop. At the clamoring, several clergy rushed over, but none emerged from the prayer chapel.

"Come on," he said to Max, and they slipped into the prayer chapel. Then Nate went right to the tapestry covering the secret door through which he, Bast, and Viv had last exited the cathedral together.

"This is medieval," Max said as Nate lit the tunnels up with a small flame and looked for the light switch. He flicked the switch, and the tunnel's emergency lights all flashed on.

"And now it's less medieval," Max said. "So this tunnel will lead us to the castle?"

"Yes," Nate told him. "But first, we hit the dungeons."

They never ran into any Royal Guards, which Nate thought was odd. Maybe not even the Royal Guards wanted to hang out down here. Or something was going on, and the castle wasn't as well-guarded as usual. In any case, he and Max made it to the dungeons without any trouble, and there was only one guard there, sitting in the chair and holding a set of keys.

"Prince Nathanial?" the guard said.

Nate didn't want to hurt the guy, so he did something he normally only did with animals. He went into the guard's head and spoke to him, so it would seem like Nate was talking without moving his lips.

I am Prince Nathanial, he said.

The guard clutched the edge of his seat. "Are you … ghosts?"

Nate thought hard of the grim reaper and tried to project that image into the guard's head like he might have projected an image of a delicious carrot to Pepper.

The guard began to sweat. "What do you want? I don't want to die."

Give me your keys, Nate thought to the man.

The guard got up, held the keys out with a shaking hand, and then dropped them right into Nate's palm.

Now go, and don't tell anyone what you saw, Nate thought.

The man took off running, and Max snagged his elbow. "What the hell did you just do?"

Nate brushed off the question—not a good time for this

conversation—and unlocked a door to a tunnel of cells that smelled like feces, mold, and body odor. There was a man in the first cell, sleeping restlessly on a hard bunk, and a woman in the next, sitting on the floor. There was blood caked below her nose, and she called out, "water," hoarsely.

"This isn't ethical," Max said. "Can we get her water?"

"Once we get into the castle," Nate said reluctantly, feeling terrible that he could not help the woman right now. "And I know it isn't ethical. It's worse than not ethical. Probably none of these prisoners deserve to be here."

He stopped at a cell where a man was standing with his hands clasped around the bars. He held a bony hand toward Nate. "Prince Nathanial? Are you a ghost?"

"No, that's the real deal," a thin man in the cell across from this one said.

The man had a scruffy beard and long brown hair. His eyes were hollow, but Nate recognized him. "Captain Thurlow?"

The captain bowed, then seemed to attempt to smile. "Your Highness. I *knew* you weren't dead. Vivian wouldn't have let that happen."

Nate immediately began searching for the key to Brandon's cell in the keyring he'd taken from the guard. "I thought you would have returned to the castle with Bast. Why is my mother holding you here? What do they have you on? Some kind of petty crime?"

He found the key and unlocked the door to the cell, but he was unprepared for Brandon to immediately embrace him like they were brothers. When Brandon backed away, Nate realized the guy was in terrible shape. There were deep cuts on his face and bruises on his arms. His fingernails were bleeding.

"Who did this to you?" Nate asked.

"Prince Bastian," Brandon said. "He blames me for Vivian's death. They have me here on treason charges." He gestured to the others in the cells. "They scheduled some big, public execution next week. Everyone here supposedly conspired to kill the queen."

That wasn't possible. Nate knew it wasn't. But he didn't want to think of Bast being that cruel to anyone without a reason, so he listened for any thought in Brandon's mind that might betray the captain. Nothing on the surface, so Nate dove deeper into Brandon's mind. Still nothing to indicate he'd been involved in Vivian's death, but there were plenty of images of Bast torturing him.

Nate's stomach turned over. "But Bast is a lie detector," he said. "He *knows* you're innocent."

Brandon nodded. "Everyone in here is innocent. We were all loyal to the crown. Prince Bastian can't understand that. He's looking for anyone he can pin the blame on for Viv's death. If *you're* here, though ... None of us could be loyal to Prince Bastian, but we'll be loyal to *you*, sir. You're the *true* crown."

Nate's voice felt weak as he said, "I'm not here to claim the throne."

Brandon grabbed Nate's arm. "*Sir*. Prince Bastian *cannot* be king. He's become cruel. An extremist. He only sees what he wants to see. It has to be *you*, sir, not him."

It was the last part that got Nate as he realized Brandon *hadn't* been saying "sir." He was saying, "sire."

"Brandon, you can call me Nate," he tried saying.

"*No*, sire. I will not disrespect the king."

Nate's own hands were shaking now, and he could have sworn he felt cold sweat down his neck. "Trust me, Brandon. I'm no king. It's better for it to be Bast."

"Sire." Brandon sounded like he was begging with the word. "*Nate*, he'll kill me." He gestured at the other prisoners. "He'll kill *all* of us. Then more after us. The kingdom is in trouble. It won't *survive* without—"

A cold, harsh voice interrupted them. "Without a ghost as it's king? Pity the kingdom if that happens."

Nate felt the temperature in the dungeons drop. He turned slowly from Brandon to see Bast sauntering toward them. Nate wasn't sure what he'd expected his first encounter with Bast to be like, but this wasn't it. Brandon tensed up, and Max put his hand on that gun he still kept tucked under his jacket. Bad idea. A gun with Bast was a bad idea.

"If you were returning to haunt us, you needn't have come through the dungeons, Nate," Bast said. "The front door was passable."

Nate stepped in front of Brandon as Max pulled that gun out and pointed it at Bast. *Terrible* idea. Why hadn't Nate mentioned to Max that pulling a gun on Bast would be an incredibly stupid thing to do? It would only give Bast an excuse to kill Max. And Nate didn't think Bast would hesitate. The freeze in Bast's eyes …

"These people are innocent," Nate said to Bast. "You need to let them go."

Bast laughed a shrill laugh. "Is that what you're here for? To free traitors responsible for killing our sister? You *must* be a ghost and not my brother. My brother loved Vivian. He'd have protected her with his life." Bast laughed again, and the sound gave Nate real chills. "Or he'd have died trying."

This was *not* Bast the way he'd been before. Nate searched Bast's thoughts and could only hear, *You're dead* and *I can't trust anyone.*

Nate handed the keys he'd been holding over to his

brother. "I'm not dead," he said carefully. "You can trust me. And I'm only here to talk. But you have to let these prisoners go."

Bast's eyes scanned Max, still standing with his gun drawn. "*You're* the dirty Immortal who betrayed those girls. Figures you'd be here."

This was why Nate had wanted to do this alone. So that no one else would get hurt. He braced for the possibility that Bast would try to freeze Max to death or that Max would try to shoot Bast, but Bast simply plucked the gun away from Max telekinetically like it was a toy.

Max said, "Hey!" as Bast magicked the gun to a rafter out of anyone's reach and looked at Nate again.

It struck Nate that Bast's eyes were sharp and mean. Like the eyes of someone who wasn't keeping a body count.

"Keeping some rough company these days, huh?" Bast said to Nate. "Consider me surprised. I didn't think *you'd* ever be a traitor to the crown."

"*No one* down here is a traitor," Nate said.

Except maybe Prince Bastian, he heard Brandon think.

Bast waited for a pause more, then suddenly lashed out, icing over the ground beneath Nate and sliding him out of Brandon's cell and into the bars of cell across from Brandon's. Nate probably would have fallen if it hadn't been for all his recent training. Instead, he caught his balance, and the ice melted under his feet.

Bast seemed slightly confused. Probably he'd never seen Nate recover so fast from something like that. But then Max and Brandon both stepped forward as though they were going to try to help Nate, and Bast swished his hand, sweeping them both back into Brandon's cell and closing the lock telekinetically.

"I think we'll deal with all of *you* later," Bast said to them. "It seems that my *brother* and I have some things to talk about."

Bast waved Nate toward the dungeon exit, and Nate could hear Max thinking loudly that they were screwed, but he still felt there was hope. He just had to avoid losing it with Bast. That couldn't happen here, where a fight between them could easily hurt innocent people Nate cared about.

He followed Bast out of the dungeons, trying to look like the submissive screw-up brother Bast expected him to be. But as Nate passed each locked prison cells, he quietly broke each lock telekinetically. Bast didn't seem to notice.

Bast had always underestimated Nate.

CHAPTER THIRTY-TWO
SOMEONE WILL BE KING

As a kid, Nate had gotten lost several times trying to find his own bedroom in the Royal Castle. Both the north and south wings hosted living quarters, and it was easy to take a wrong turn and end up in a guest suite in the north wing rather than the royal family's quarters in the south wing. Just one more reason for Bast to think he was stupid. The royal quarters were positioned such that the family could always rise facing the sun. Bast didn't understand why Nate's sense of direction wasn't intuitively God-based.

Official royal business occurred in the galleries connecting the two wings. There was a proper throne room, executive management offices, a state dining room, various thematic parlors, and a conservatory that opened to the courtyard. The kitchen, laundry facilities, and servant quarters were all located toward the rear of the castle, along with the door to the dungeons.

Bast led Nate up the stairs from the dungeons, making idle small talk. "I'm assuming you aren't expecting to see

Mom immediately. She's probably too busy for you anyway. You know how she is. Always dealing with some matter of state affairs. We'll go to your room if you'd like. It's a mess, of course."

"You're lecturing me about how clean my room is?" Nate said, wondering if he could even remember how he'd left it the morning of Vivian's coronation.

"You didn't know? The explosions hit your quarters. Divine intervention, obviously. I'm the one they meant to kill."

Nate shoved down his guilt about that. "I know, Bast. I'd have come back sooner, but—"

Bast turned and walked backward while they talked. "But you weren't ready to face me with your new Immortal friend?" He lowered his voice. "Does he have you drugged or something, Nate? Is he threatening someone you're dating?"

"I'm not *dating* anyone," Nate said.

"Did he capture you with those girls, then? Bet that guy's associates are holding *Carina* and her poor little sister somewhere, and you had to bring him here or they'd killed the girls. Can't resist being a *hero*, huh?"

Nate had forgotten how good Bast was at grating down all his nerves. "Just take me to my room," he said.

"As you wish," Bast said, but when they got there, Nate sort of wished they hadn't bothered. It was one thing to be walking through the halls, feeling like a stranger sneaking through someone else's castle. It was another to look at his room with holes blown out of the walls.

Nate had been grateful when Herschel finally decided the boys needed separate living spacing. His room had been one of his only sanctuaries in the castle. It was not a functioning sanctuary anymore. His four-poster bed with the cushy duvet was burned and broken, as was his nightstand, his bookshelf, and the two wingback chairs by the windows, which were now boarded up. He'd had diagrams of sword fighting techniques and historic timelines hanging on the walls, but those were all ruined. So were most of his books and the collection of toggleball cards he'd accumulated. Some of those cards had been valuable.

He picked up a framed picture of him, Viv, and Bast that he'd kept on his desk. They looked almost happy together in the photo, but now the glass was busted and the edges of the frame were singed. He took the picture out of the frame, folded it, and stuck it in his jacket pocket.

"Aww …" Bast cooed from where he was leaning against the door frame. "Sweet of you to care."

"Shut up, Bast," Nate said. "What happened to my sword?"

Bast shrugged. "Don't know. Where were you keeping it?"

Nate lifted a corner of his bed telekinetically and spotted the hilt of his sword. Thank God. That sword had been made for his great great great great grandfather. It was about the only family heirloom Nate cared about. He was so happy to see it, he kissed it.

"Wow, I've never seen true romance before," Bast said smarmily.

Nate didn't bother scowling. He went to the wardrobe— the only undamaged furniture in the room—and found a leather jacket he'd forgotten about. It was nicer than what he was currently wearing, so he tried to put it on, but it wouldn't fit. The sleeves were too short, and even if they hadn't been, his shoulders were too broad for this thing now. He put the jacket he'd come in with back on, then found a baldric, adjusted it to fit, and slipped the sword into it.

"Now that you're dressed for battle, shall we go somewhere more appropriate to talk?" Bast asked.

"What, to *your* room?" Nate said.

"I was thinking somewhere more neutral."

Sunlight shone in between the boards over the windows, giving Nate just enough light to get a good look at Bast standing there. Nate knew *he* looked different from the last time they'd seen each other. He'd been training hard these last weeks, working out, riding, eating hearty Northern food, and sleeping relatively well. The last time he'd seen Bast, they'd both been drained, but Nate was far healthier now. He was probably even healthier than when he'd last been home.

Bast did not look healthier. He may have grown a little taller, but his skin was pale and paper-thin. There were shadows where his cheeks were sunk in. If he had visible abs under that shirt, it was because he was that skinny. And those eyes … they made Bast look frozen to the core.

"Bast," he heard himself say softly, and he began walking toward his brother, reaching automatically for his shoulder. Instinct of some kind, Nate supposed. He'd never been able to stand seeing Bast hurt, even when Bast was being an ass.

But Bast jerked his shoulder away from Nate and walked out of the room. "I suppose you've come to claim the throne, then?" he asked, drawing out every word lazily as Nate followed.

Nate had planned to start this whole conversation by telling Bast he *didn't* want the throne. And yet, the words that slid out in response to that were, "What are you planning to do with Thurlow?"

"The traitor who killed Vivian?"

"Has he *confessed* to being involved?"

Bast didn't answer, so Nate skimmed his mind. But Bast was protective of his thoughts, and Nate didn't want to waste energy trying to crack that nut. "When you interrogated him, did he ever lie to you?" Nate asked as they turned a corner.

Bast answered coolly. "He evaded. Which does not mean he wasn't involved. He was in the best position to hurt Vivian and take her away from me."

Nate did not call Bast out on his use of the word "me," but it made him wonder if maybe Bast was just weirdly jealous of Brandon. Presumably not in a creepy way. Because Nate didn't *think* Bast was like that. Still …

"You do know she loved him in a very different way from how she loved you, right?" he said to Bast. "But if you execute him, you'll definitely lose her to him."

At that, Bast actually went for Nate's throat. With his hand. He spun and pinned Nate to the wall, gouging his elbow into Nate's gut and holding his neck with an ice grip that made the veins around Nate's neck feel too solid for circulation.

"Say. That. Again," Bast hissed.

"You'll lose," Nate choked out. "Because if you kill Brandon, *he'll* be the one with Vivian." He struggled to get Bast's hand off his neck without accidentally burning him. "And *she'll* know the truth."

Bast's hand dropped away, and he seemed to compose himself. "I'm sorry. You're grieving, too. It's natural for grief to make us less rational than usual."

Nate massaged his throat. "We both miss her."

Bast nodded. "Then I'm terribly sorry you won't make it to the memorial service. I'm thinking open casket for Vivian, but we'll keep your casket closed since your body was so mangled it was unrecoverable. That's what we told the press anyway. We're putting up a professional photo of you instead. The bishop will talk about what a hero you were." He snickered. "Though you didn't manage to save anyone, did you?"

A shiver that had nothing to do with cold ran from the base of Nate's neck to his spine. Were they going to exhume Viv's body from Memorial Hall to lay it out in an open casket? *Now?* That was grotesque.

Unless …

"Bast, she's already entombed, isn't she?" he asked.

Bast flipped his hand to the side. "Proper funeral preparations take time."

"She died in August."

"And your point is?"

"It's *April.*"

Bast stopped walking and looked squarely at Nate. Those winter-gray irises gave them an eerie quality that made Nate miss the perfect clarity of Bast's blue eyes when he was well.

"Where is her body now, Bast?" Nate asked steadily.

"In her bedroom, Nate," Bast said, replicating Nate's tone. "Don't worry. It's all sanitary. I froze her. I'm not ready to bury her yet. And you can see her. We're almost to her tower."

Nate had been too preoccupied with Bast to watch where they were going, but apparently, he was following Bast to the princess tower. That was the only place in the castle where any Southern Royal ever slept besides the south wing. Viv had loved her room, and Nate understood why. As he recalled, it had been airy with a quaint bay window, a great view, and lots of built-in shelves and cozy furniture.

But she was *dead* now.

"She looks exactly like she looked the day she died," Bast said as they reached the tower and started climbing the stairs. "You would know how she looked that day, wouldn't you? You probably saw her before you *left* her there." He stopped abruptly in the middle of the spiral staircase, turned on Nate, and leaned in close. "Did you make *friends* with Carina and the

Immortal? Did they *save* you?"

Nate had to remind himself that Bast could not read minds. Still, his brother had uncanny perception. Bast went on with a dangerous edge to his voice.

"Perhaps Carina and her sister weren't rebels after all? Maybe they were just Northerners. Or maybe those girls were more than *just* Northerners. *Maybe* they were the lost princesses. Is that why *Carina* had so much magic? Did that whole seduction thing backfire? You put so much effort into hating her. Is she your *girlfriend* now?"

That trap was a disaster waiting to happen, but Nate wasn't going to fall for it. Bast was the highest-ranking person in a South Kepler regime controlled by Constance of Galileo, who still thought of North Kepler as the enemy.

There were things South and North Kepler would never agree about, but Nate knew the Northern Royals weren't the enemy. Not generally anyway. They were more like a brother you didn't get along with. You didn't *annihilate* your own brother for having some opinions you didn't like and not doing everything your way. Nate wasn't going to betray the Garcias.

"What are you talking about?" he said. "If Icy is alive, I still hate her. Did she live through that? It's not like I stuck around to look for her body."

Half-truths. That was the only way to handle Bast, who continued to look critically at Nate for many long seconds before he seemed to let it go.

"Then that traitor Franklin found you? Can't imagine the ideas *that* jackwagon's been feeding you."

They reached the top of the stairs, and Nate followed Bast into Vivian's room. There was a body lying on the bed with a blanket draped over it. A few thin cobwebs gathered near the bedposts. Nate tried to look away but couldn't as Bast pulled down the blanket.

Vivian's body. It was frozen. Not entombed.

Nate took a step closer that he didn't want to take, and Bast pushed a chair toward the bed. "I talk to her sometimes," he said. "I can give you some privacy if you want."

But Nate didn't even want to *look* at this. It gave him the worst feeling that Bast's inability to bury their dead sister was keeping her soul from resting in peace anywhere.

"I know it's hard," Bast said. "I wanted Viv to be the queen. But here we are. We have to deal with this, someone has to be king, and we both know *you* can't do it. I mean, you could try, but then we'd probably have a *body* to bury with your picture at the memorial."

Nate had *not wanted* to be the king of South Kepler.

"I really don't know if I could take that," Bast said. "Two siblings in one year? And the Immortal Empire constantly threatening me, too? It is my strong preference to know you're safe somewhere. Why don't we find you a nice ranch somewhere in the country? Set you up with a staff and a salary. You don't have to be exiled to be dead."

Vivian's face, colorless as it was now, seemed younger than Nate recalled. She had only been eighteen when she died. A year older than what Nate was now. Bast was only sixteen. That was incredibly young for someone who was supposed to hold the responsibility of a whole kingdom, and Bast was trying to do it without letting go of his grief for Viv first. Nate didn't envy Bast. He *still* did not want to be king.

"Though I suppose if you *insist* on returning, we could work up paperwork to officially recognize your abdication. Your choice."

Nate *had* planned to abdicate. He wasn't equipped to be

king. He wasn't cut out for the sticky manipulation of politics. He'd thought his kingdom would be better off with Bast.

…

His kingdom.

Nate couldn't imagine he was a good choice to be anyone's king, but that ice clouding Bast's eyes just kept getting thicker, his voice more malicious.

And Viv …

She deserved to be put to rest.

"Things were fine with you gone, Nate," Bast said. "Stay dead, and everything stays fine."

Oh, screw it. Bast had been keeping their dead sister frozen in a tower for over half a year. No one was safer in Bast's hands.

"I'm *not* dead, though," Nate said. "*I am* the crown prince of South Kepler, and—" A scowl on Bast's face forced Nate to buck up some courage. "—And this is *my* kingdom, Bast, and I am *not* giving up the throne."

A blast of icy air hurtled toward him, and for the first time, Nate thought Bast might actually try to kill him. But he wasn't caught off guard. He countered easily with a quick burst of heat, then ran for the tower stairs, trying not to slip and fall to his death as Bast iced over the stairs.

"You *are* dead!" Bast yelled as they ran. "And *I'm* the next king!"

Nate was now concerned that he was not going to live to prove Bast wrong. Franklin had been right about everything. Including his decision to force Nate to train with Princess Carina.

Nate reached the bottom of the stairs and skidded into a hall decorated with flower arrangements while Bast pulled the water from the vases and shot it at Nate in ice pick form.

Had Franklin seen that coming? Nate transformed the ice into steam and blasted it back at Bast, who yelled like he'd been scalded.

But this was not the time for Nate to start congratulating himself on any win, even a minor one. Also, he could do better. He didn't need to slip on sheets of ice. He could leave a trail of fire blazing behind himself instead. He started to do that, and Bast shouted, "You idiot! This castle is four-hundred years old! You do not set the castle on *fire!*"

"Oh, sure," Nate shouted back. "But it's completely appropriate to attack your brother."

"My brother is *dead!*" Bast screamed.

"Your *sister* is dead," Nate yelled.

And at that, Bast shrieked, "She is *sleeping!* I can still save her."

It gave Nate the sick realization that his family *wasn't* the last Cardinal family left standing. If that's what the Immortal Empire thought, they had that all wrong. Nate's family was not standing. Not at all. That was the Northern Royals. Nate's family had crumbled.

Ice hit Nate's left shoulder and numbed his arm. He created a wall of fire between himself and his brother, then ripped down several paintings and hurled them back through the flames. That bought him a slight lead, but where to go now? Back to the tunnels? Out the front door?

He let his feet choose until he realized he'd run right to his own room again. Shit. What now? His room was on a second story. He ran to the windows and when his arm didn't want to work right, he tore the boards off telekinetically. He could see the stables in the distance and a group of people on horses gathered like they were waiting for something.

Was that *Brandon and Max* and those escaped prisoners?

Hadn't there only been ten prisoners?

A rush of ice up Nate's neck told him Bast had caught up, and Nate realized he had to jump. No problem. He'd jumped from a second-story window before. Except, the castle had much higher ceilings than that old woman's house in Hypatia. This was going to be more like a four-story fall.

He glanced back at Bast, who looked like the prince of a frozen-over hell. He was thinking loud thoughts. *He doesn't deserve the throne. He can't have the throne. Vivian saved me. I'll kill him first.*

Hopefully not today.

Nate took off his sword and chucked it telekinetically out the window so he wouldn't risk landing on it and impaling himself.

"I'm coming back," he told Bast, as he climbed onto the window ledge. "In a few years. I don't want to hurt you, but I'll fight you for the throne then if I have to."

"You can have your fight right *now*," Bast said, hitting the back of Nate's legs with another chilly freeze. But Nate didn't want that fight right now. He thought hastily to ask God for a soft landing, and then he jumped, using telekinetic magic as best as he could to slow the fall.

He landed clumsily on his ankle, which made a nasty cracking noise and sent spikes of pain up Nate's leg. But Brandon had reached him on a horse, so he only had to listen to Bast's angry howl for a few seconds before Brandon was pulling him up onto that horse.

Nate spotted his sword in the grass and magicked it to himself. "Thanks," he told Brandon. "We need to get out of Alighieri fast. There are about to be a couple dozen royal guards on our tail."

Brandon looked ten times better already now that he was

out of the dungeons. He shook his head. "Five or six tops. Turns out the vast majority of the guards at the castle are loyal to the crown, not to your mom or brother. And word has been spreading all day that Prince Nathanial has returned. There's a call going out through the city that anyone who wants to join the true king should saddle up and head to the northern gates." Brandon smiled wryly at him. "So *please* tell me you didn't abdicate."

"I didn't," Nate said, while the numb in his shoulder seemed to spread to all the rest of him, too. "But I can't be the king yet. Not right now. I'm not … good enough. I have to go North again. I need more training. And I don't have the resources to support a whole army."

Brandon grinned. "Nope. But you have an army to support you, Your Highness. So, let's get the hell out of Alighieri and get you where you need to be."

CHAPTER THIRTY-THREE
A FROZEN HEART

Bast was frozen like a block of ice at the window Nate had leaped from, ignoring several painful burns that weren't healing as fast as they should have been, and looking into the distance as someone who should have been a ghost fled the castle grounds with a known traitor, an Immortal, a bunch of high-profile prisoners and several members of the Royal Guard who were apparently all treasonous dirtbags.

Nate—Bast's own brother—had returned as if from the brink of hell only to release several murderous fiends, steal a dozen guards, place judgment on Bast's treatment of their dead sister, and challenge Bast's right to the throne of South Kepler.

His kingdom.

Nate had called it that. As if it were not *also* Bast's kingdom. As if *Bast* should not be the king. As if Nate would stoop to *fighting his own brother* for a throne they both knew Nate couldn't handle.

What a ridiculous notion. How could Nate possibly be

king? Nate didn't have *nearly* the power Bast had. Or the intelligence. Nate didn't know what was right for South Kepler. Nate was the kind of person who would set aside his own welfare and run headfirst into a collapsing house to save someone who *did not want* to be saved. Bast was clever, strategic, deadly, and cunning. Nate was stupid, reckless, and heroic in the way that got people killed.

Or at least that's how it was *supposed* to be.

It was hard for Bast to feel as comfortable about his assessment of Nate now that he could see his own guards deserting him for his stupid brother. That could not possibly have been Nate's doing. Nate had to be someone's pawn.

Bast felt relieved as soon as that thought occurred to him. Of course, that's what was going on here. Nate didn't have it in him to stage this kind of attack. This was an organized attempt to thwart the good plans Bast and his mother had for the kingdom. Probably it was all being led by Franklin Wellington. A traitor to the kingdom, the crown, and his own family.

Maybe they'd even gone and hooked up with the Northern Royals. Who were alive. Bast was sure about that now. Nate was a *far* better liar than Bast had ever given him credit for, but he'd fumbled on Bast's questions about Carina. *What are you talking about? Did she live through that? It's not like I stuck around to look for her body.* No lies there. Very nice, Nate. But you *still hate her?*

Nope. So now, Bast was sure *Carina* had been the one who'd produced the defensive telekinetic shield that had preserved Vivian's body and kept Nate alive. Not something you did without a Cardinal lineage.

Nate's new posse wouldn't win, though, and if Nate wanted a new mortal enemy, Bast would happily take on that role and be happy to kill Princess Carina in the crossfire if she was part of it. Because that girl had *played* them. She had all kinds of power. She *could* have saved Vivian. She'd chosen not to.

The world was a terrible place.

"Bast! Bast?"

Oh, well, maybe the world wasn't *such* a terrible place. At least there was one person he could count on. He turned stiffly to see Jax running toward him, feeling just the slightest thaw before Jax stopped abruptly and pulled back the arms he'd been reaching out.

"You're … cold …" Jax said from at least two meters away. It was, by far, the dullest thing Jax had ever said to Bast. And what did it mean? Was Jax suddenly *afraid* of him? If so, he wasn't safe where he stood now. Two meters? Pfft. Bast could easily freeze someone solid from that distance. He *should* have done it to Nate a few minutes ago.

Jax's attempt to use a little space for protection—if that's what he was going for—was laughable. In fact, Bast did laugh, and the hysteria he heard in his own laughter only made him laugh louder.

"Are you only learning how cold I am *now*?" he asked Jax between peals of laughter.

Jax's left eye twitched. Distress. That's what that was. Bast knew because he knew *everything* about Jax.

"You don't have to be like this with me," Jax said. Reproachfully. Like Bast was doing something *wrong*.

"Be like *what*, Jax?" he said, replicating that nauseating tone.

"Like you don't care about anything." Jax took a cautious step forward. "Bast, you're *actually* hurt. Did *he* do that to you? Your brother? Your assistant Gael said word was going around that Prince Nathanial was back. Gael got in a fight with a couple of the other Royal Guards over it. He's banged up, but nothing like this. Those are bad burns. Do you need a doctor? Why aren't you healing?"

Bast's teeth chattered through his laughter. He *was* healing. Only very very slowly due to the frozen state his body was currently in. Really, anyone else going through this kind of pain would have passed out by now. Nate could do serious harm when he wanted to. It was a testament to how strong Bast was that he was still conscious.

"It will heal as I thaw," he said, no longer laughing, but still very out of touch. Very out of touch with Jax, who hadn't moved close enough to be within arm's reach, even when he noticed that Bast was wounded. *Why* wouldn't Jax get closer? If he knew Nate had shown up, if he knew what had just happened, why wouldn't Jax try to fix this? If Jax would only embrace him, things would get better. Jax could make this whole nightmare disappear. Jax and his perfect perfection.

"I looked for you in your sister's room," Jax said, and a gnawing pain in Bast's stomach added itself to the list of other things that were hurting him. "Gael thought you might be there."

So, he'd gone to Vivian's room? So what?

Jax lowered his voice. "I saw the body, Bast. I had assumed it was frozen in the *morgue*. I can't believe Gael was covering that for you."

Then, Bast had been right not to reveal any of that to Jax before because clearly, Jax didn't understand. He thought Vivian should be lying in a morgue. He probably thought it was psychotic to let her lie in a bed instead.

It *wasn't*. Bast had done research on this, just to ensure that he was, in fact, sane. There was *nothing wrong* with laying a loved one to rest on a bed after they died. The human distaste for dead bodies hadn't always existed. There had been a time, thousands of years ago on Earth, when humans *hadn't* shuttled their dead off into freezers the moment their last breath of life left their body. Dead humans had rested in parlors, or even on their own beds, exactly like Vivian was doing now, while the people who'd truly cared about them grieved.

But Jax thought Bast was doing something wrong.

Jax would betray Bast. Just like Nate had.

"She didn't *belong* in the morgue," Bast tried to explain anyway, though his whole chest shook while he spoke. Why did he have this sense of dread now? Why this feeling of doom?

"She's *dead*, Prince Bastian."

Formal names now? And not a single step closer—not *one single step* to indicate that Jax wanted to comfort Bast. Not even as tears began to run down Bast's face. He hadn't cried up until now. Not in so many months. He didn't want to. Tears were a sign of weakness. He froze the traitorous tears on his face, then pulled back in the rest of his emotions. No one was going to break him. Especially not *Jax*.

"She's *my* sister, and until we put her to rest, *I* will decide where she belongs," he said to Jax, so very, very coldly.

"You *do* know she's dead, though, don't you?" Jax said. "You aren't … trying to bring her back? You know you can't do that, right?"

He knew. But what was the harm in attempting to kill the remnants of the Immortality Virus in her body? He'd destroyed several of those cells. If he could kill them all, allow her to thaw, perhaps Viv's soul would float back into her body. Without the Immortality Virus there, it was a perfectly serviceable body. Maybe she *was* only suspended in time right now. Merely sleeping. Waiting for the right moment to return so she could be queen. It wasn't *so* unreasonable for Bast to hope for a miracle not just for himself but for the entire kingdom.

"Why didn't you tell me?" Jax said softly.

"Tell you *what?*" Bast said.

"That you were struggling so much with your sister's death. If you'd told me, I could have helped you. You could have *trusted* me."

Bast had never before noticed, but Jax's left eye—the one twitching now—was slightly smaller than his right eye. A tiny hint of imperfection. Not Jax's most attractive quality. Nor was this suddenly patronizing, pitying demeanor.

"You didn't need to know," Bast said.

"*You* needed me to know," Jax said.

Bast scoffed at that. "*Why?*"

Jax finally took that one step closer. "Because I care about you, Bast. Because I'm *concerned* about you."

"What, because *you* need for there to be a time limit on my grief?" Bast demanded. "Or because you can't handle the idea of Vivian lying in her own bed instead of in some refrigerated *box.*"

"That thing you have lying in your sister's bed *isn't Vivian,*" Jax said. "*That* is a dead corpse that you are keeping frozen like a psychopath. Vivian isn't contained by that body anymore. She's *not there*, Bast. She's somewhere you can't go yet."

That cut Bast hard. "If you think I'm a psychopath, then I hardly think you should be sleeping in my bed at night."

"You're right," Jax said seriously. "I shouldn't. And you need professional help."

Bast's cold tendency took on a more kinetic nature with those words. He moved forward like he was gliding toward Jax, who took a quick step back.

"Are you afraid of me?" Bast asked as he continued to move closer.

Jax didn't answer. Well, he couldn't now, could he? Because he knew Bast would know if he was lying.

"So that's a yes, then," Bast said as Jax's face paled. "Which I understand. Because if you honestly think the prince of South Kepler is a *psychopath*, then you have every reason to think the kingdom should never be placed in his hands."

"I didn't say that," Jax said, though his voice was shaking now and Bast could see goose pimples on his porcelain skin. "I am concerned about you. I care about you. I—"

"You don't care enough to let me grieve the way I need to grieve," Bast noted as he finally backed Jax into a corner parapet. "Or enough not to question the way I'm handling my sister's death."

"I love you, Bast," Jax whispered.

Bast laughed. "If you loved me, you would understand."

Both Jax's eyes were twitching now, and he'd drawn his arms up around himself. "Are you going to kill me?" he said. "Because if so, you should do it now. If you don't, I'm going to do *everything I have to do* to help you."

"Starting with what?" Bast seethed.

Jax winced. "Starting by telling your mother about the body."

"You wouldn't," Bast said.

But at that, the snappy click of heels surrounded by a softer patter of footsteps alerted Bast to another presence.

Queen Constance had found them.

"He already did," Queen Constance said.

Bast felt panic he'd never felt before. The floor of the hallway and the walls and ceilings iced over. Jax began shivering wildly. Bast's throat tightened, and he found he couldn't take a deep breath. He *was* able to point a stiff arm at Jax and choke out to his mother, "Whoever he told you he was, he's not who he says he is."

Jax sucked in a gasp.

Queen Constance merely appeared bored. "Oh, he's not? Then who is this man who has so enthralled you?"

"Bast," Jax said. A plea. But not one Bast felt like responding to.

"Jax Channing," Bast said. "His parents were terrorists. He's been seducing me. He can't be trusted."

Jax's eyes turned to pure fear, and the gnawing in Bast's stomach morphed into devouring, searing pain.

"I thought you cared about me," Jax said.

Bast hardened his heart and his eyes and ignored the cowardly man standing before him. "We should throw him in the dungeons," Bast told his mother. "I think there might be a vacancy down there."

"What are the charges?" Queen Constance asked, her teeth looking sharp and white as a wolf's.

Bast thought of how Jax had hurt him. Betrayed him. Manipulated him. It was worse than trying to kill him. He'd tried to drive the crown prince of South Kepler mad.

There was just this one thing. A voice that nagged in his head even though he tried to ignore it. Whose was it? Not his voice for sure. Maybe some demon impersonating Vivian. Because Vivian herself wouldn't be saying the things he was hearing someone say in her voice.

Let him go, Bast.

Let him go, and let Nate go, and let Brandon go.

Let me go.

Bast turned his back on Jax. "Disorderly conduct," he said. "No trial is necessary. A night in the dungeons should be warning enough."

"Very well," Queen Constance said. "A night in the dungeons, then he will be returned home. And it would be wise if Mr. Channing never returned to Alighieri again. Or I might remember why his name sounds so familiar."

It was hours later that Bast's mother found him sitting in Vivian's room again. Vivian's body was gone, and her bed was empty. A hair from her head was lying on her pillowcase. He kept wanting to brush it off the pillow, but then he couldn't.

"I had the body moved to the morgue below the church," Queen Constance said. "I'm sure you know what it will look like if you go there asking for it."

Bast thought of Vivian's body in a metal tray in a cold freezer, close to where she would ultimately be confined to a coffin, perhaps lying now with a tag on her toe. "She was fine up here."

"It is unsanitary to keep a body in the castle."

"She was frozen."

"She is *dead*."

Bast didn't respond. There was simply no way for him to come to grips with Vivian's death. Vivian couldn't be dead. Because if she was dead, that meant he was here and alone, and no one was ever going to care about him like she had. Jax certainly wouldn't. His mother couldn't. His brother downright hated him.

"Additionally, I have set a date for the memorial service," Queen Constance informed him. "Two weeks from today. If you want to choose the words engraved on her tomb, you will let me know by the end of the day tomorrow. Otherwise, I will choose for you."

"Prayer of Colors," Bast muttered. It was the prettiest prayer they had, a prayer of praise for the miracle of color in the world. He'd thought of it months ago. He simply hadn't wanted to commit to any step that would move them closer to putting Vivian to rest. "And I want to choose what she'll be wearing and how her hair is arranged. Gael can supervise."

"Gael has been fired," Queen Constance said. "*I* will supervise."

She didn't have the right to do that. And Gael had remained loyal. Maybe Gael was even in love with him. Bast only thought of Gael as a servant, but it was good for your servants to love you. Bast needed more Gaels in the world.

"Do not attempt to rehire him," his mother warned. "He is aware that if he is ever seen in your presence again, he will be locked up, tried for treason, and executed. It is too dangerous for a future king to have attendants around who won't speak up when he is ill."

"I'm not ill," Bast said.

"There is another matter we need to discuss," his mother said. "Your brother. He was here today, and he took several members of the guard and some of the staff with him."

"He was here to claim the throne," Bast said stonily.

"*That* cannot happen. Do you believe he'll be back?"

Bast felt tired. "I believe he's working with Lord Franklin. And possibly the crown princess of North Kepler."

"Then you think the rumors about the princess being alive are true?"

Bast did not feel a shred of sympathy for the princess. "I believe she was the girl we met on our way to the Mountain of Peril."

"And that your brother is now in league with her as well?"

Bast nodded again.

"Then the longer we allow your brother to remain alive, the more likely it is that he will return with fortified backup. We must do what we can to eliminate that threat. I will put out the word that the impostor of Prince Nathanial is to be killed on sight. Do you agree with my decision?"

Bast felt something in his chest yank hard, as if his heart wanted out or maybe at least wanted to expel something unwanted. *He* had wanted to kill Nate today. He probably *would* kill Nate at some point. But it didn't feel the same, somehow, to think of someone else doing it.

Still, Nate had betrayed him. Jax had betrayed him. Vivian was dead. Even Gael was gone. Bast had felt so alone his whole life, but now he was truly alone. A prince without a single friend. No one would ever come to his aid. He was the only person he could trust. And in the face of that kind of aloneness, you could not afford the luxury of emotional sensitivity.

He stood up and plucked the stray hair away from the pillow on Viv's old bed. "The cleaning staff should strip those linens," he said. "And tell the bishops to engrave the standard prayer for the dead on Nate's tomb."

"Nothing special?" Constance asked tonelessly.

"No. But make sure the picture on the kill poster is accurate. Have the artist age him up. He's not as scrawny as he was a year ago." Bast paused briefly in the doorway and wondered if he would ever want to come into this room again. Probably not if he could help it. "Actually, let's ask the cleaning staff to clear this place out entirely. Turn it into a library or something."

"There is no need for unnecessarily draining reminders of the ones we've lost," Constance said.

"Exactly," Bast said.

Though young women on Kepler enjoy significantly greater equality with young men than was ever the case on Earth prior to the departure of humans to alien planets, certain biases continue to pervade our society.

Take, for example, the expectations of perfection placed on a young woman. Although study after study proves that propensity and willingness to accept failure are critical elements to success in the vast majority of human endeavors, women continue to be held to such high standards of perfection that these standards become a barrier to success for them.

In our qualitative research on the matter, ninety percent of women report that they have, at least once in their lives, missed an opportunity because they were too afraid to try something they thought they might not succeed at the first time. Comparatively, only twenty percent of men report the same. Targeted research on girls and the practice of magic in North Kepler shows that while girls and boys appear willing to attempt to use their magic with equal effort at age five, by age ten, girls are three times more likely to refuse to try using magic to perform a task they have not previously performed than boys. When asked why they do not want to attempt the task, common responses are, "It's too hard," "I can't," and "I'm afraid I'll do it wrong."

We believe this is a reflection on the vitriol with which society continues to treat *any* young woman who has the nerve to make a mistake. As the admirable research performed at CTI as part of the Five Hundred Years Project shows, women who exhibit traits of confidence and are willing to fail are still perceived as stubborn, bratty, bossy, arrogant, and not relatable. Men exhibiting the same traits are perceived as persistent, bold, ambitious, courageous, and admirable.

Despite the light years between Kepler and Earth, we Mortals continue to live in a world where women are told to aspire to perfection and then *penalized* for not having the confidence to make mistakes. Meanwhile, men are allowed, and even encouraged, to overestimate their own abilities at every turn. They apply for jobs they are not qualified for, accept praise for accomplishments that are not theirs, boast about their biggest failures, and never take "no" as a final answer. They get ahead by *not* being afraid of screwing up.

Disturbingly, these hypocritical standards are not present amongst Kepler's Immortals. Though less research is available to us on the matter, what research we do have indicates that Immortal women are at least as likely, if not more, than Immortal men to be willing to attempt tasks they are likely to fail at. While some suggest this is due to the nature of immortality, the Immortals we interviewed for this book attribute the difference to Empress Mila Hildebrand's direct guidance and leadership on issues of gender equality.

CHAPTER THIRTY-FOUR
HERE ON KEPLER

Carina saw Heathrow Princeton three times after Nate and Max left Fort Aurora Borealis. They talked about the attack on Cerulean. There'd been a prison break, and those eleven Immortals were free now. Carina worried they would reveal her existence to the Immortal Empire.

"No, you want news spreading," Heathrow said. "The Immortal Empire probably already knew, and rumors will make it easier for people to believe it's true when the official announcement comes out."

They talked about her father's illness. Carina felt she had been naïvely protective about Queen Vivian's blood, but Heathrow didn't think so. "You've had more contact with both the princes of South Kepler than anyone in the Royal Society," he said. "You know better than anyone how they might take our experiments."

"It would be easier to talk to Prince Nathanial about it than Prince Bastian," she said.

"Another reason for everyone to hope Prince Nathanial

doesn't abdicate," Heathrow said, and then he reheated her hot cocoa.

Finally, they talked about Max. Which was more comfortable than she'd have expected, especially given that the conversation happened in a somewhat intimate context.

"Do you think you're in love with him?" Heathrow asked. "Or just attracted to him?"

"I don't know," she said. "I was worried about him when they first left, and I felt like I *had* to kiss him. Not that he was forcing it. I just had the feeling I would never forgive myself for not doing it if something happened. But the longer they're away …"

"You don't exactly miss him?" Heathrow said.

She kissed one side of Heathrow's very symmetrical face. "It's complicated." She kissed the other. "You're much easier, but I don't know if he could handle something like this."

"Meaning you don't think he could take a fun, safe, physical, compassionate, consensual relationship with a friend he's attracted to?" Heathrow asked. "Isn't the guy Immortal? What other relationship does he think he can *have* with a Mortal? He knows you age, right? And does this mean we're on a break if he comes back alive? Because there's this girl I met last week. She's taking a class I'm teaching at CTI—"

"Oh, salacious," Carina teased.

He laughed and nuzzled her neck. "A little. She's our age. But the class will be over in a couple weeks, and I think maybe there's something more than fun there. Any thoughts from a good friend about how I should handle that?"

Carina told him the most important thing she could think of: "Don't take her to prison on your first date."

In Prince Nathanial's absence, Carina started going out to the stables and playing with the malamutes. Guards weren't trailing her everywhere anymore, and Ollie was in some kind of training with Mishe, so she even got to try riding the horses on her own. She loved it and decided that if Nate Wellington ever came back, he wasn't going to have a monopoly on the animals. He could learn to share.

Miguela came with her one afternoon, on Nate's horse.

"Are you sure he'd be okay with that?" Carina asked. She was riding a gorgeous alabaster horse named Ice Dancer, who she liked because he was comfortable galloping across icy fields. But she had the weirdest feeling there was some tension between Ice Dancer and Pepper.

"I think Nate would be deeply hurt if I neglected Pepper in his absence," Miguela said.

Carina tried not to roll her eyes too hard.

"I don't understand why you hate the idea of Nate and me so much," Miguela said. "He's so nice to me. And I've been supportive of you and Heathrow."

"You weren't of Max and me," Carina said.

Miguela made a face. "Oh, weird. Are you and Max a thing again?"

It *was* weird, but Miguela was over secrets, so Carina told her everything that had recently happened between her and Max and then said, "So? What do you think?"

They rode around while Miguela pondered it all. Then eventually, Miguela said, "Well, I like Max a lot. He's awkward, but he's a genuinely good guy, and I understand why it made you see him in a positive light again when he decided not to abandon Nate."

"But—?" Carina prompted.

Miguela looked uneasy. "I don't know, Care. It's good for

you to date lots of guys, but make sure you're honest with Max about how you feel. He's in love with you, and it would be easy for you to hurt him."

"I can't believe you're more worried about him than me now," Carina said.

Miguela's face finally relaxed. "But I'm *proud* of you for it. You're not some silly, breakable little girl anymore. You don't need bodyguards, and no guy's going to crush or manipulate you, and that's going to make you a much stronger queen someday. Also, want to have lunch with Mom after this?"

That was a new development. "You're not mad at her anymore?" Carina asked.

"I think we have bigger things to be bothered by than a new baby, don't you?" Miguela said.

Carina was proud of her sister, too.

The tension in Carina's family had faded considerably since their bunker non-blow-up, probably because of exactly what Miguela said. The stakes seemed too high to waste energy on family tension. Carina decided she needed to make up for several months of resentment she'd harbored against Eugene, and one afternoon, she dressed in her heaviest outerwear and went to his door. She heard him call "come in, Carina," before she managed to knock, so she stepped inside and found him lying on his leather couch with a book in his lap.

"Miguela isn't here," he said grouchily.

Carina perched on a chair near the end of the couch. "I'm here for you, actually. But shouldn't you already know that because of your telesthesia?"

"I only get visions of inevitable futures, so I only saw

408

you showing up at the door. Nothing after." He tossed his book down on his coffee table and tilted his neck to make eye contact with her. "So, what *are* you here for?"

"Well, there's this witchy thing I've been doing ever since I showed up here," she started.

He folded his arms behind his head silently.

"It has to do with me assuming you were ticked off at me for taking the crown away from you. I should have talked to you about it."

She paused for a reaction and he only gave her a look like, *go on.* So she did.

"Uh, *do* you feel like you've lost privileges or something now that you're not the crown prince anymore?"

He laughed at that. "As if there are any real *privileges* to being the crown prince or princess of anything. I feel bad for you, though. Honestly, it was a huge relief to give that up. Do you know how many guards they had hovering around *me* all the time before you got here?"

"How many?" she asked.

"At least twenty-five." He gestured around his room. "There aren't many other kids up here. These chairs aren't for my imaginary friends. You got off the hook *fast.*"

Something else they had in common, she thought. Kind of. She and Miguela hadn't had contact with any other kids while they'd been at Novi Dupree. Max was the first real friend Carina had ever made. But now she had Ollie and Heathrow, and she'd always had Miguela around to keep her company. Eugene had been entirely alone.

"What *was* it like for you when we showed back up from the dead?" she asked.

He finally smiled at her. "Like the impossible thing I'd always secretly wished for had come true. You're not supposed to get people you loved back from the dead. But I did."

"Me, too," she said.

"It's lucky and unlucky at the same time, right? But I was never angry, and I only wanted to spend as much time with you both as I could. Especially with you. Because you're like me, and no one is like me, and it's hard to explain accidentally freezing something because you got peeved."

She gestured at her heavy coat and boots. "Do you think maybe you'd want to mess around with cold magic a little, then? Build an ice castle? See if we can make it snow?"

"Seriously?" he said.

Carina felt encouraged. "Miguela said she'd sit around with us later when we're both too cold to move and make sure we have a steady supply of hot cocoa."

He actually grinned. "Show off. But she'll be way overworked when the baby gets old enough for us to start teaching *him* tricks."

Carina scooted forward on her seat. "Wait, is it a boy?"

That grin got even bigger, and Carina thought it was cute that Eugene could smile so big that it almost seemed as if the corners of his mouth were reaching to his ears.

"Don't tell anyone. They're going to name him Jaime. And we have to be a united front because he'll be Miguela's favorite sibling."

"*So* not cool to choose a baby over your pre-existing siblings," Carina said with a serious tone that didn't match the huge grin on her face.

"*So* not," Eugene agreed.

Max and Nate finally showed back up late one afternoon. Carina was playing a game of chess with Ollie in the lodge when they came in, and they watched Prince Nathanial slink directly toward the king's library, limping and looking like a defeated gladiator waiting for a death sentence.

Carina *almost* felt bad for him.

Max looked like he'd been to hell and back and like he'd had to cart the prince of hell with him the whole way. He came over to her and Ollie and said, "We are alive. I am going to bed. For three days."

Carina didn't think he would mind a tiny bit of company first, though. She sneaked away to the barracks as soon as she could. The one Max stayed in had thirty beds lined up against the walls, with a trunk at the end of each and a locker and chair between all the beds. Every bed was made with the covers pulled tight over the mattresses. It looked like everyone had fairly thick bedding, and there were rugs between all the beds and photos, posters, and other personal stuff hanging all over the walls. With one exception. Nothing hung on the wall above the bed Max was sitting on or the one next to his.

Max was looking at his boots like he couldn't remember how to remove them. He sighed as she approached. "If you're here because you want the whole story, I don't think I have the energy to tell it right now."

She *did* want to know the story—who wouldn't have?—but she was here because she wanted to know what was going on with her and Max. "I wanted to make sure you were alright," she said.

He started to untie his boots. "Is it possible you wanted to kiss me again, too?" he asked, his voice an even tone.

She didn't know exactly how to answer that. None of this made sense to her anyway. But she had cared about Max, and she thought maybe she owed it to herself to explore that.

He patted a spot on his bed. "You can sit by me. I'd

suggest you sit across from me, but that's Nate's bed."

She appreciated that, so she walked over and sat next to Max, leaving a solid elbow's length between them, just in case.

"So, are you okay?" she asked.

He kicked off his boots, scooted around her, and stretched out on his back. "I'm *exhausted*. Nate comes up with more ways to get himself killed. He never has a plan. He instigates fights he doesn't know he can win. He hardly gives anyone enough time to help him with anything. But yeah. I'm okay. And it's good to see you. Even if you don't want to kiss me again."

She lay down next to him and curled gingerly toward his side. "I was worried about you." He held his arm out, and she took that as a sign that it was okay if she rested her head on it. "Maybe I should have come with you."

He laughed. "To protect me?"

"I'm more skilled than when you first met me."

"No kidding. You were always crazily talented. Now, you're talented and trained." He leaned in to kiss her forehead and immediately drew back. "I'm sorry. I shouldn't have done that. But is it okay if I fall asleep like this?"

She leaned up on her elbow and looked down at him. There were dark circles under his eyes, which were blood-shot, but not red. "Can I kiss you once, first? For real?"

His lips curled up, and he reached to toy with a lock of hair hanging down around her face. "I would *never* be able to turn down a request like that."

She bent down for that kiss, and there wasn't anything sloppy or overly passionate about it. It felt more like relieved-grateful-restrained. She waited with her lips a breath away from his, not wanting to push him, but he didn't need encouragement for a second kiss, which felt relieved-grateful-even-more-restrained.

Then he reached for the back of her head, the kissing transitioned from relieved-grateful-restrained to needy-wanting, and it felt good as it progressed. Good enough that if Max hadn't pulled back several minutes later, sucking in air as he hovered above her and staring at her with bright red eyes, she'd have suggested finding more privacy elsewhere.

Instead, he put his arm over his face and collapsed down onto his back. "I'm sorry …" he gasped. "I'm not thinking straight anymore. I have to stop or …"

"Or what?" she asked curiously, wondering if there was some Immortal thing she didn't know that related to intimacy.

"Or I'll try to get you to cross lines with me that you don't want me to cross." He uncovered his face briefly, and his red eyes roaming up and down her body made her want to forget *lines*. "And you look like you've just been thoroughly kissed, so I think I could be persuasive right now."

"Oh," she said, but what she was thinking was that maybe he had this all backward, because *he* was the one with the red eyes, and she thought *she* could be quite persuasive right now. What did he want that she didn't? And why did she feel annoyed with him now? If he wanted to stop, he wanted to stop. That wasn't a problem.

To Carina's dismay, the mood was ruined further when the door to the barracks opened and Prince Nathanial walked in. He stalked to his bunk, flopped down, and said, "No, please, don't let me stop you from what you were doing." He grunted. "Or whatever you were *going* to be doing."

Carina sat up. This escapade was clearly over. "We were going to be doing nothing," she grumbled.

"Not what it looked like to me," Prince Nathanial said snarkily.

"Me neither," she said under her breath.

"Oh, come *on*," Max complained. "I'm trying to be a gentleman! I didn't think you'd *want* to be doing more."

Carina did not like the way Nate's eyes sauntered lazily from her to Max and back again to her.

"Oh, I see what's going on here." He nodded at Max. "Buddy, here on Kepler, the keywords are 'mutual consent.' Means you decide what *you* want to do, she decides what *she* wants to do, and if you want to do the same thing, you do it. You don't decide for both of you."

"I wasn't deciding *anything* for her!" Max exclaimed.

"Except for what I *didn't* want to do," Carina noted, trying not to dwell on how much she hated Nate Wellington. She'd been feeling kind of bad for him, but he was at his most annoying when he was right about something, and he was right about this. He'd nailed the problem, in fact. She was disappointed that Max didn't want to continue, but if he wanted to stop, she didn't mind giving him space. Her frustration stemmed from the fact that he *didn't* seem to want to stop. He'd just assumed *she* wanted to without actually bothering to talk to her about it.

"Carina, that's not—"

She pointed at Nate. "Can we not talk about this in front of him anymore? I'm going."

"Always good to see you, too, Garcia," Nate said, waving with mock cheer. "And good news. You are not the coldest person I know. My brother is officially worse."

"Shut up, Nate," Max said. "Don't take your trauma out on Carina."

"Hey, all I'm trying to do here is help you both out," Nate said.

Carina felt a surge of hatred blast through her again. Max shivered, and Nate pulled his covers up over him.

"Bye, Garcia," Nate said.

"Let's talk later, Carina," Max said.

That, she supposed, is what she got for trying to be civil with two guys she didn't want in her peer group. But at least they were both alive. She would not have to figure out how to negotiate with a King Bastian, and she could figure out how to kiss Immortal Max later.

That was a pseudo-win.

CHAPTER THIRTY-FIVE
THE PRODIGAL PRINCE

Nate had wanted to talk to Franklin before he talked to anyone else on Aurora Borealis Isle, but Franklin wasn't anywhere to be found. Nate found King Reggie in the king's library first, told him everything instead, and then the king called around, but none of his guards knew where Franklin had gone either.

King Reggie got up with his cane and said, "I'm going to try to find him myself. Wait here, okay? Try to relax."

"Franklin is *never* going to forgive me," Nate said.

"Why don't you let him decide that?" King Reggie said.

Nate said thanks, but he felt miserable as he waited in the library while the king went out to try to find his mentor. Nate had acquired nearly fifty soldiers as he left Alighieri. Then, after a private meeting with only Brandon, Cecil, and Max, the four of them decided Max and Nate needed to return to Fort Aurora Borealis alone while Brandon and Cecil went with the soldiers to rally a rebel army.

"You need solid magic skills to defeat your brother,"

Brandon said. "And we need allies. Your job right now is to go North and train your ass off."

"And in the meanwhile, we'll go town-by-town, gathering a resistance army," Cecil said. "So next time we all go back to Alighieri, we'll be prepared to storm the castle."

Nate reluctantly agreed to the plan, but it meant that a group of Southern Guard rebels was making its way through South Kepler to build him an army that he was not in any way equipped to lead. In the meanwhile, he'd gone and betrayed his best teacher, who clearly wanted nothing to do with him anymore.

Nate was nearly done waiting in the library when Miguela came in and sat down in a chair across from him. He didn't feel like talking—even to Miguela—so he said, "Hey, Migs," and then went back to a book he'd picked up and was not reading.

She didn't say anything at first, but soon she said, "I get it."

He thought about pretending he hadn't heard, but this was Migs, and he didn't have it in him to be a jerk to her. "I really appreciate your concern, Miguela, but I'm not in a good place right now," he said, hopefully without any animosity.

"Yeah. Okay. You don't have to talk then." She paused. "And I can leave if you want, but I thought you should know that I get it. I love Carina more than anyone, and I always love her, even when she's being self-absorbed and making terrible decisions. We're nasty to each other sometimes. We shout and say things that should be hard to forgive. She hates it when I give her the silent treatment, so I use that tactic when I'm especially peeved."

Nate thought he knew where this was going, and he considered asking her to stop. He was tired of thinking about Bast.

"You're a good person, Nate," she said. "You care about

your brother. Because he's your brother and you were always there for each other even when you weren't. And Franklin's probably going to chew you out, but he gets it, too. You wouldn't be you if you were the kind of person that would have given up on Bastian. You had to go."

Nate knew he should say thanks or something, and he didn't want to hurt her feelings, but no one could make this feel better. He doubted anyone could possibly understand the screwed-up relationship he had with Bast.

Then Miguela said, "But—" she picked at a hole in her jeans "—I didn't really come here for that."

Nate had not anticipated a "but." "What did you come here for?" he asked curiously.

"It's embarrassing. And silly." She held her elbows with her hands and averted her eyes. "I was thinking … and I hope you're not annoyed … but it seemed like you might need a hug."

Nate could never have been annoyed with Miguela for something like that. He appreciated hugs, and there weren't a lot of people offering them to him these days. "It's not *that* embarrassing, is it?" he said. "Because you're probably right. You're a good friend, Miguela."

Perhaps there was something on the carpet, though, because she didn't look up. "Well, I wasn't sure if you thought of me as a friend or more like, a little sister or something, and I didn't want to do something weird. Sometimes I'm worried you only like me because I remind you of Vivian."

He almost laughed. "Vivian was about the coldest hot person that ever walked the planet, Migs. You do not remind me of her."

She finally looked back up at him. "So, you don't think of me as a sister?"

That was when he knew he was trapped. He tried not to wince visibly. He couldn't tell her that yes, actually, he *had* started to think of her kind of like a little sister. If she had a crush on him, that would crush her, and he hated the idea of crushing her. After all, he completely adored Miguela … in a protective, doting, older-brotherly way.

When he tried to think of her as a girl he could date, though, his brain flashed big red warning signs. He could not imagine kissing her. He could not imagine her less than fully clothed. He couldn't even imagine cuddling with her. Miguela was less likely to appear in his sex dreams than Ice Witch (and no, he was not interested in analyzing *that*).

As much as he hated to admit it, Carina Garcia had been right about this one. If he cared about Miguela at all, he could not make her think he had feelings for her. At the same time, he suspected that Miguela's thing for him was only a crush. One day, it would fade and ideally leave them with just a really solid friendship. But that would only happen if he could avoid hurting her with the realization that he wasn't into her first.

She was giving him the cutest hopeful look ever.

"No," he said nonchalantly.

Her face fell a million miles.

He set his book down. He'd screwed up big time with that one "no," though he didn't know how. Had she *wanted* him to say he thought of her as a sister? He scanned her thoughts, but her mind was heavily guarded.

"Miguela …" He got up, went over to her, and crouched down next to her. He considered hugging her but didn't think that would send the right message. He put his hand on her wrist. "Migs, I'm sorry. Whatever I messed up there … I really do care about you."

She sniffed. "But that was the first time you've ever

lied to me."

Nate felt his heart sink. He wasn't sure why he hadn't seen it before. It all made perfect, tragically good sense now that he knew what had just happened.

She was a lie detector.

She puffed air out of her nose in a short, bitter laugh. "Did you just figure it out?"

He'd made a mistake underestimating her. How could *he* have done that? But if she could detect lies, there was no use trying to hide the truth.

"That you're a lie detector?" he asked. She looked steadily at him without answering. "Or that you wanted me to like you as something more than a friend?"

Her shoulders drooped. "I only realized it was my telesthesia gift recently. And I guess if you're going to lie to me, it's nice that you at least do it to protect me from a truth you thought would hurt me."

"But you need the truth anyway, don't you?" Nate said, thinking of how Bast had described it to him once upon a time when they could still be civil to each other. "It hurts you worse to be lied to."

She nodded.

He wished she hadn't chosen today for this, but he wasn't going to make this harder for her. "Then the truth is that you're my favorite person here," he began. "I'm glad we're friends, because I've had a bad year, and sometimes you're the only thing in my day that doesn't suck."

There were tears in her eyes. "Really?"

"Yeah. You're an incredibly special person, Migs. You're smart and funny, and you have an enormous heart. I think it's so awesome how you want to rid the world of injustice and have no fear of arguing with your friends about politics or religion." He thumbed a tear off her cheek gently, no longer afraid she'd misinterpret. "You're also very pretty, and what guy doesn't want to hang out with a pretty girl?"

She looked thoughtful. "Then, are you sure …? "

"I don't know," he said honestly. "I'm flattered that you like me enough that you'd want me to be attracted to you that way. But …"

"But you have started thinking of me like a little sister, haven't you?"

"I wish you *were* my little sister, Migs," he confessed. "I'd much rather have you in my family than Bast."

She was quiet for a minute before a smile crept over her face.

"What?" he asked.

She scrunched her nose playfully. "I was just thinking it would be funny if you ended up with *my* sister. Then I *would* be your little sister. But you're not attracted to her at all, are you?"

"To your icy, cold-hearted sister who hates me?" Nate said, feeling quite scandalized. "*No.* I am not that messed up."

She paused for half a beat longer than he was comfortable with, then she said, "Bast is lucky that he is your little brother, though."

Nate hadn't thought of Bast as his "little brother" in forever. It was strange to hear it put in that context, and stranger that the wording sort of took the edge off some of the things Bast had said and done back in Alighieri a few days ago.

"Do you want that hug now?" Miguela asked.

"Do you still want to hug me?" he asked in return, but she launched herself at him, and hugging Miguela felt a lot like hugging Vivian had always felt. She squeezed tight, and she was warm, and there was nothing romantic about it, but he could have held on for a long time anyway.

"Let me know when you want to talk about Bast, okay?" she said. "And thanks for being kind to me about my crush."

"Well, if you ever need someone to threaten some guy that's bothering you …" he offered, and she laughed, then let him go and left the room.

Franklin never did show up that night. King Reggie came back, though, and said, "Franklin says he'll talk to you tomorrow morning and asked you to meet him in the stables then. He doesn't want to have a difficult conversation with you when you're both tired."

Nate didn't think he would be any less tired tomorrow. He wasn't tired the way you get from a hard run or when you've been up too late for several nights in a row. He wasn't even tired the way you are after you've done your best to help your sister survive the Immortality Virus by letting your brother leech magic off you for weeks or tired the way you feel when she dies anyway.

He was the kind of tired you get when a major responsibility—like the fate of the Mortal world—gets dropped on your shoulders, and you have to fight your crazy genius brother for a crown, possibly imprison your own mother, persuade your kingdom that you're the true king, persuade the neighboring kingdom that you want to be friends, and, ultimately, wage war against and defeat the Immortal Empire.

And he didn't feel better when he met Franklin in the stables the next morning just after dawn. Franklin was *furious*. Nate could tell by the way Franklin's jaw was set, the way he refused to make eye contact, the stiffness in his shoulders, the dead quiet of his mind.

Franklin acknowledged Nate silently. They saddled up the horses and rode across the isle silently. When they'd reached the cliffs at the south side of Aurora Borealis Isle, Franklin got off his horse and walked to the very edge.

Nate got off Pepper and went to stand next to Franklin, and they looked out over the water—wine-dark and treacherous, like Homer's waters of the *Odyssey*—and Nate knew only three things.

One, he *was* exhausted.

Two, Franklin had never been angrier.

Three, they were looking South to Nate's godforsaken kingdom.

"I wanted to hope you didn't make it back alive," Franklin said eventually. "My life would be easier without you."

Nate swallowed. "It was irresponsible—

"Very," Franklin snapped. "Did you even *get* to Alighieri? Or are you back because you got there and learned that even if you abdicated, your family would still want you dead?"

It was harsh but not wrong, and it hurt. Maybe mostly because somewhere deep down, Nate was still holding out hope for Bast. Somewhere even deeper, he was still making excuses for his mother. They weren't fundamentally bad people. They just couldn't handle all they were up against— who could?—and when *they* felt the world on their shoulders, what bent was love.

Franklin was so much stronger. Yet, Franklin seemed to slouch under the weight of what he was feeling now, and he spoke softly to the ground. "I see Bastian do terrible things before he's even old enough for a coronation. He's cruel. You would never have been." Franklin laughed harshly. "Except to me, I guess."

Nate tried to apologize. "I never meant to hurt you, Franklin. You were right about everything, and I'm sorry I disappointed you. I understand if you don't want to be my teacher anymore."

Franklin kicked a rock off the cliff. "Don't be stupid. I'll still teach you. Things are going to be much worse now than before. Did you see they put out a wanted poster for you? Kill the impostor on the spot."

Nate choked down his feelings. He hadn't known that, but what mattered was that however immeasurably difficult things would be now, Franklin wasn't going to desert him. He smeared tears from the corners of his eyes. Then he had to do it again. Then Franklin turned all at once and hugged him roughly, and this wasn't exactly normal, so Nate couldn't pull himself together or say anything useful or even figure out what to do with his arms.

He just stood there feeling completely broken until Franklin said, "Nate, I know you think I'm furious, and I am. I wanted better for you. But I also know you went back because there are no conditions on how much you love your brother. It was reckless, but don't think I don't care about you because you did it. *You're* the person I'd go back for no matter what."

Which was so immeasurably beyond anything Nate felt he deserved that he was now basically sobbing and thank God Franklin had dragged them all the way out to the cliffs for this. Nate was going to do everything in his power to make Franklin proud of him, and not just because they were true family, but because they cared about the same kingdom and having Franklin by his side made Nate feel like some small part of the burden he was carrying was lifted.

He finally pulled himself together, drying off his face as

fast and furiously as possible so they could both pretend he hadn't just lost it like that. But he confessed to Franklin, "I'm afraid of what happens now."

Franklin rubbed the bridge of his nose. "You found out what I've always known, didn't you? Your brother isn't fit to lead anything, and now you realize he's going to be the worst king for South Kepler, and—"

Nate blinked back some confusion. "No. That's not what—"

Franklin spoke gently. "Nate. I *know* you want Bast to be okay, but he's not the same as you. He's too high-strung. He can't take what you can. He isn't strong enough for failure. But there might still be time to fix things if you want to try. Did he make you sign anything?"

"*No*," Nate said. "What I meant is, I *didn't* abdicate, and—"

Franklin's face turned to stone, scar and all. It made Nate a little nervous, but he went on.

"—And I shouldn't have gone down there, and I don't want to be the next king, but Bast can't be. Innocent people will get hurt if he's the king. He'll use terror and power to rule. I have no idea if we can win a war against the Immortal Empire, but win or lose, I want to fight it with people who stand by me because they're loyal and we're fighting for the same thing, not because they're afraid. I don't think Bast will ever understand that."

Franklin was still a stone facade, except now there was a line of tears running down *his* face. It followed his scar, right down his cheek.

"You didn't abdicate," he repeated.

"It's *my* kingdom," Nate tried to explain. "It wasn't my first choice, but Bast isn't a better choice, and I have no idea how I'm going to do this, but no. I didn't abdicate. I told Bast the kingdom of South Kepler is mine."

"You claimed the throne," Franklin said with an almost reverent hush.

"Could we *not* put it that way?" Nate said. He decided he would take to the grave the way Franklin cried and hugged him after that, though, because some things shouldn't be written down for anyone else to see.

CHAPTER THIRTY-SIX
KEEP YOUR FRIENDS CLOSE

Training was canceled the next day, so Carina went to the infirmary and spent the day in the laboratory. She had her own lab coat now, and with Dr. McIntosh's permission, she was comparing blood sample after blood sample from people with the Immortality Virus to a blood sample she now had from her father. The only sample she hadn't yet looked at was the one labeled "V. Wellington." She was putting *that* off until the right opportunity came to ask Prince-I-Didn't-Abdicate-Nate about it.

Max found her in the lab that afternoon.

"Hey," he said from the doorway.

She removed her eye from a microscope. Max still had dark circles around *his* eyes, and she felt a little guilty for what had transpired the day before. "Hey," she said. "Did you get any sleep?"

He stepped into the lab and closed the door behind him. "I, uh, couldn't sleep."

"Thought they trained armed scientists not to need

sleep," she said lightly, hoping the tease would smooth some things over.

"Yeah, but Nate tossed and turned all night, and it kept me up."

"Sorry," she said, and she looked at the blood sample again while Max came around to check out what she was doing.

"Immortality Virus samples," he said. "All different strains?"

"Some," she said. "These are mostly mutations of the virus the Immortals who came here with Hildebrand and Godric brought, and then we have a few samples from Myles and Sister Elizabeth."

"All of whom left Earth long before I did," Max said. "You should take a sample of my blood, too. I think they called the type I got IV-2011."

"Thanks." She flipped to another slide. "I'll take you up on that."

He sat down on a stool next to her. "I am also a biologist with half a millennium of experience. I can help if there's anything specific you're trying to do with these. Anyway, I think Nate's going to be up here for a while, and Myles is ditching me to find some people he needs to make that escape vessel power up. I have nothing better to do."

"McIntosh will be thrilled," she said. "And I should introduce you to Heathrow. You might actually get along."

"With another guy you're dating?"

She didn't look up from the microscope while she said, "He's seeing someone else."

She did feel Max's hand on hers shortly thereafter. "Carina, I'm sorry about yesterday. I made a bad assumption, and I apologize if I made you feel invalidated or dis-empowered."

Now she eyed him suspiciously. "Did you talk to Miguela

about this?"

He chuckled. "Believe it or not, I have a few enlightened thoughts of my own every now and then." He brushed his thumb over the back of her hand, and it created a little tingling sensation. "The point is, it never occurred to me that you might want any of what I wanted with you yesterday."

She wanted to know what there was between her and Max, and her research could wait. "Well, what exactly *are* these things you want?" she asked as his hands brushed up her arms toward her shoulder.

He nudged down the collar of her lab coat to kiss the back of her neck. "You want me to tell you everything out loud?" he said skeptically.

She angled her neck and breathed into the feelings he was inspiring. Desired. Anticipation. A touch of lust. "Maybe not *everything*. But surely there are *some* things you can say?"

"Okay ... then ..." His lips were trailing toward her shoulder. "I want the kind of kissing that requires less clothing."

She was already helping him help her out of that lab coat. "That could be arranged."

"And more touch, too," he said. "More than we've done before. Both of us."

She turned to kiss his mouth, and also took his hands and slipped them beneath her shirt at her waist. His fingers traveled slowly along her skin. Touch was definitely on the table right now.

"Sounds wonderful," she told him.

He pulled back. "Really?"

The adoring look in his eyes—still deep blue for the moment—served as a warning for her.

"As long as you know that on Kepler, none of this stuff is grounds for committing someone to a long-term relationship or whatever," she told him. "We're just seeing how this feels."

His eyes softened on hers. "I'm Immortal," he said. "Long-term relationships are relative anyway."

Then for a while, she was lost in long, lingering kisses that spread sensation slowly from her lips through all the rest of her body. Max was a gentle lover when he wasn't anxious or desperate, which was unlike Heathrow, who was more energetic. Though it crossed her mind that she shouldn't be dwelling on the comparison. She should be more in the moment. She focused on Max, locked the door to the lab telekinetically, and said, "If it gets too cold in here—"

"Mmm-hmm," he mumbled. "I'll let you know."

"Where do you think Nate is?" Miguela asked Carina the next morning at breakfast as Carina watched Max come into the mess hall alone. "I haven't seen him this morning."

Max averted his eyes as he seemed to notice Carina noticing him. He *was* cute, in an endearingly awkward way, and she tried not to allow her face to show distress as she thought about what had happened yesterday after she'd locked that door.

"Carina?" Miguela said. "Did you see Nate?"

"No," Carina said. "Hopefully, he'll show up to training, though. Eugene's been great trying to teach me more healing skills, but it's not exactly my highest priority in terms of magic training."

Miguela craned her neck to look around the mess hall. "I know. Nate has to keep working on his magic, too. Or the next time he has to face his brother, he might not live."

Carina was committed to facing Prince-Lucky-to-be-Alive-Nate today in their first training session since he'd returned to Aurora Borealis. Still, she knew at some point before the session ended, she'd have to ask him about that blood sample. A conversation she dreaded. She hated the idea of asking Nate for anything. She stabbed her fork into her pancake. "Relax. He's not going to be *that* easy to kill."

Max hesitated as he walked up to them, then chose to set his breakfast tray next to Miguela and diagonally across from Carina. "Were you two talking about Nate?" he said.

"Yes," Miguela said.

"No," Carina said.

"Well, ringing endorsement, Carina," he said, sounding *almost* normal. "Nate would probably appreciate knowing that *you* at least don't think he's going to be as easy to kill as everyone else thinks."

"If Prince Nathanial is feeling low enough to need an endorsement from me, then we should start trying to butter up Prince Bastian now," Carina said. "Because establishing diplomatic relations with *him* is going to be a joy."

It was a joke, but Miguela didn't laugh. Nor did Max. At least Miguela could still easily look Carina in the eye, though. Max could only barely manage. Carina speared more pancake and thought that the pancakes were unpleasantly chewy today. Not what she liked in pancakes but satisfying, given her mood.

"Carina, I think we should talk about your relationship with Nate," Miguela said. "He's up against a lot already, and all of Kepler is at stake, not just South Kepler. You need to learn to get along with him. For real."

She swirled pancake in syrup. Yes. She got it. Bastian Wellington was a razor blade waiting to slit your throat if you crossed him. Nate was obnoxious, crass, obstinate, disrespectful, rash, but not an evil psychopath. There, see? She was already on her way to nearly getting along with the guy.

Ollie came in and set her breakfast tray down by Carina. "You guys talking about Nate? I hear he's here to stay until he's ready to go back to South Kepler for his coronation."

"Yes," Max and Miguela said in sync. Which was *very* weird since Carina and Max clearly were *not* in sync in any way that mattered.

"Can we not talk about Nate anymore?" Carina asked. "This is ruining breakfast for me."

"So what conversation wouldn't ruin breakfast, then?" Ollie asked.

Carina sneaked a quick look at Max, who was looking down at his food like it was moldy.

Ollie leaned back. "*Oh*," she said, and, mercifully, she started up a conversation about a letter she'd gotten from Sister Elizabeth that morning. But after Max picked up his tray to leave, Ollie leaned in and whispered to Carina, "Hey, do you want to talk about it?"

"About what?" Carina said.

Miguela rolled her eyes. "About you and Max. Um, awkward?"

Carina shoved the plate of pancakes she hadn't been able to finish to the side with her tray, leaned her head down on the table, and groaned. "It was the *worst* awkward."

Miguela, who had been taking a sip of juice right then, nearly spat out the juice with the laughter that statement apparently inspired.

"Oh, yuck." Ollie covered her hands with her eyes while Miguela continued to laugh. "You and Max? How bad *was* it? Because the way you two were not looking at each other …"

Carina winced. The answer was "terrible and incredibly disappointing." Nothing beyond kissing Max had felt good for her. *Nothing.* By the time they unlocked the laboratory door, the whole infirmary was freezing, Max seemed exasperated, and Carina felt like they'd just engaged in a botched clinical experiment they should never, *ever* repeat.

"Just give us the highlights," Miguela suggested. Then she and Ollie listened to as many details as Carina was willing to provide with increasingly horrified looks on their faces.

"What do you think?" Carina asked when she was done. "Can it get worse than that?"

"Only if you stay with him," Ollie said. "Max isn't right for you at all. There *is* no real passion there. For you, he's just a cute guy."

"A cute guy you like slightly more than you like rattycats," Miguela added.

"Damn it," Carina said. "I have to break up with him, don't I? Or preemptively break up with him or something. Because I'm not mad at him for anything. I do *like* him. I just don't think I'm truly attracted to him. Not like I thought I was."

Miguela brushed away the concern. "Rip it off like a bandage. He'll be fine."

That made it sound far easier than it would actually be. Carina moaned. "He is a *puppy dog*, Miguela. I'm going to feel like I'm scolding a puppy for piddling on a rug."

"That's close to the truth," Ollie pointed out.

Miguela snickered. "And people can get over things. Nate told me he doesn't like me that way, and I'm fine. I've been trying to let myself feel bad enough to cry, but I never make it past a couple of tears."

"Oh, Guela." Carina put on her best stricken look in an attempt to sympathize with her sister's pain. "I am *so* sorry."

Miguela pushed her breakfast tray back, too. "As *if*. You thought me dating Nate was a terrible idea."

Carina dropped the stricken look. "No. If you had wanted to date him, I'd have tolerated it. But I didn't think he saw you that way, and I didn't want him to hurt you." She considered the number of times she'd warned him about this, though, and that familiar sense of irritation Nate inspired rose up in her. "And if you need me to exact revenge on him, I can think of a lot of ways to put him in pain."

Miguela laughed hard again. "Carina, do you think you may be attracted to Nate? In a deep-down kind of way?"

Carina practically knocked over what was left of her morning hot cocoa. "No! I am not that *damaged*. Max was a *far* better choice."

"Uh," Ollie said.

"Right," Miguela said.

"He *was*," Carina said. "I have all kinds of things in common with Max. We're both nice people. We both like—" she struggled for something "—biology?"

"Nate and I are both nice people," Miguela said. "We both like history. Those are generic things to base a relationship on. Max was never going to work for you. He's Immortal, and you're Mortal. He hates rattycats. You rescued four last month. Max doesn't have any magic. You have a ton of magic. Max …"

"I *get* it, Miguela," Carina said. "Maybe we were an opposites attract thing."

"You and Max can't be opposites," Miguela said. "You aren't even on the same spectrum."

"So what? Maybe he was just your first crush," Ollie suggested. "But if you want to stay friends with him, you can't keep seeing him and you have to tell him what's going on."

Carina stood up. "I know. I better talk to him before training."

"Good luck," Miguela said. "If you need strength, remind yourself that you'll probably have to face Empress Hildebrand someday."

"As if the first step to defeating an evil empress is being able to break up with a boy," Carina said sarcastically.

"It is, for you," Miguela said, sounding far too chipper.

"And don't feel too bad," Ollie said. "He'll have forever to get over it."

Carina found Max in the barracks alone after breakfast. He smiled half-heartedly and patted the spot next to him on his bed. But breaking up seemed like the kind of thing better done sitting directly across from a guy than next to him. So, with a mental nose hold, she sat down on Nate Wellington's bed instead.

"I know," Max said. "You're here to rip out my heart, aren't you? But yesterday didn't feel right, did it?"

"Well, it wasn't … bad …" she lied.

He laughed humorlessly. "You don't have to pretend, Carina. We were both there." He leaned forward and reached for her hand. "I don't know. Maybe we're just not right for each other. I mean … do you *feel* anything for me?"

"I care about you," she said, now truthfully. "I want you to be happy. I don't want bad things to happen to you. I'm not angry at you anymore. I would appreciate your help with the research I'm doing. And I have some good memories of you from the summer. I thought we had a chance together."

He let go of her hand and sat back rather sadly. "Nah. You can't realistically date an Immortal, Princess Carina. Not for long anyway."

She thought of Heathrow, who she knew would be happy

in a casual relationship with her until either of them found a serious relationship. She'd never thought to put a timeline on *that*. "We could have dated for years before it would have mattered."

"Two or three years, maybe. That's hardly any time for an Immortal. It's better for both of us this way, Care. Maybe that's why nothing seemed right."

Carina shifted anxiously at the edge of Nate's bed. "Is that what you were *thinking* about all that time yesterday?"

Max sighed again. "Maybe at least feeling it. You have major duties and a short life to complete them in. Five hundred years from now, you'd have been a pleasant memory for me. But if I'm involved in your life, I could ruin your reputation, make it harder for your own people to trust you, make you question your relevancy, complicate everything …"

"I could have wanted a complication," she pointed out.

He met her eyes but did not ask the question she thought he was going to. *Did* she want a complication? Did she care enough about him for that?

"I'm kind of glad it ended this way," he said.

She was baffled. "You're *glad* physical incompatibility ended us?"

He snorted. "I'll tell you about my breakup with Amanda sometime. Deciding there just aren't enough sparks between you and someone you care a lot about isn't the worst way to end something romantic. Not by far. And dating a princess isn't bad for a guy like me, no matter for how long." He held his hand to his chest and affected a noble tone of voice. "I will think well of you for my entire Immortal life."

A feeling of relief found her as she decided he actually *was* going to be okay. "I'm glad you were my first boyfriend, Max," she said. "Even if you are five-hundred years older than me."

"Don't put it like *that*," he said. "That makes me sound like a pedophile. I'm only about seventeen in, uh—" He began to redden. "Maturity? In Kepler years? I'd be more like twenty-three in Earth years, and you would be closer to twenty-two, although some scientists think human maturation is different on planets other than Earth, and—" The red deepened into a cringing crimson as he seemed to catch what must have been a bewildered expression on her face. "You don't care about any of this."

The blush and the blathering were both endearing. It made her think there was hope for Max and his romantic prospects. With someone other than her. "Maybe you need to find another Immortal to date," she suggested.

"Maybe Kepler just isn't my planet for romance," he said. "But this frees me up to focus on Nate. That poor guy needs all the help he can get."

Carina could have done without that reminder. Still. "Speaking of which. Want to find Ollie and walk to the training center with us? There's something I need to talk to Nate about this morning, and I need witnesses, so everyone knows it happened later."

Max tilted his head at her. "That is surprisingly similar to something he said to me this morning about you. But does this mean we can just be friends?"

She felt that was a decent outcome. "We can be friends."

"Then you'll be happy to know Nate just lost a bet on that," Max told her. "He had several plates of fries on you eventually deciding to kill me."

She *was* happy about that.

CHAPTER THIRTY-SEVEN
KEEP YOUR ENEMIES CLOSER

Nate had something to say to the princess. He wanted to blame it on Franklin, who'd decided that Nate needed to "negotiate terms" with her about their future training sessions.

"Look, Nate. If you want to stand a chance against your brother one day, you need Carina to be willing to fight you one-on-one again, and I'm not comfortable forcing that unless she gives her express permission," Franklin had told him. "Fights with you are hard on her."

Fights with *her* were hard on *Nate*.

But truthfully, Nate thought Franklin might be underestimating the importance of an agreement from Garcia on this. Bast was a force to be reckoned with. To beat Bast in the future, Nate needed the princess to engage in *brutal* practice fights that would leave him and her burned, frost-bitten, bruised, bleeding, and probably even sometimes unconscious.

Meaning: to secure his kingdom's future, he needed to have an awkward conversation this morning with a girl who hated him, and it needed to be about how he wanted her to engage regularly in an exercise of mutual destruction. It would have been easier to ask her out on a date.

So, when Princess Carina walked into the training center with Max and Ollie, Nate was sitting on a bench, trying to steel his nerves, and Franklin was standing nearby. Carina said good morning to Franklin, then she approached the bench and, to Nate's greatest surprise, she said, "Good morning, Nate," in a polite, professional tone.

It was such a departure from their norm, it almost threw Nate off his game. But he managed to stand and replicate her tone with, "Good morning, Carina."

Good. He could be a grown-up.

He started to say, "I wanted to talk to you before we get started today," while she said, "There's something I need to talk to you about" at the same time.

Awkward. But he didn't want to risk the possibility that she would preempt what he needed by telling him she *wouldn't* train with him anymore or something, so he said, "Um, if it's okay, can I start?" Then when she nodded, he began to explain that he had decided not to abdicate, that he would be here until he returned to South Kepler, that he hoped they could continue their training together …

She gave him silence and a few confused blinks in return as he rambled. He decided he better hurry to the main point, and he said, "The thing is, Bast is going to fight me for the crown, and you are the only person on the planet who has anything close to the skills he has, so I need you to go back to one-on-one fights with me again. Which, I know I didn't make easy for you in the past, and at some point, they'll have to be even more challenging. But it can all be on your terms. You can decide when we use actual heat or cold, and when we bring in Max and Ollie to help or any of the militia or whatever. As long as we keep progressing ...”

She was staring so intensely at him that he had time to notice that her eyes were the same color brown as the bark of a thousand-year-old suckle tree after a good rain. Also, they were about a thousand years deep. He had no idea how she felt about what he was saying. It would have taken him an eternity to get to the bottom of that. He moved on to a straight-up plea.

“Look, I have *never* in my life won a fight with my brother,” he said earnestly, “and probably the only reason I even managed to leave the castle in one piece is what I learned from those water fights we had.” He could feel his ears burning, he was sweating, and he’d turned the gym too warm for everyone, but he pressed on. “So, I guess, what I’m trying to say is, this isn’t going to be fun for you, so just tell me what I have to do for you to keep working with me, because I really need you to. My, uh, kingdom needs it.”

She was going to say, “no.” That’s what he’d have said. Or she was going to make him grovel. Or worse. And there was so much tension in the hot air you’d have thought this was a hostage negotiation.

Then she pushed her shoulders back and took a big, deep breath, and Nate *felt* the tension receding as the room cooled to a more reasonable temperature. Apparently, she’d decided to take things down a notch.

“You’ve been working on that,” he said.

“Yes,” she said. “I learned it from you, though. And I expected to keep training with you if you came back, but I do think it’s a good idea to negotiate some terms.”

That wasn’t *such* a bad reaction. “What are they?” he asked suspiciously.

She glanced at Franklin, who was tugging at his scar. "First, Franklin is the best teacher I've ever had, and we both trust him. We agree that *he* is in the best position to determine what we can handle in our training exercises. We try whatever he thinks we need. If that means one-on-one fights, so be it."

A no-brainer. "That's … fine," Nate said, feeling quite cautious about how well this was going. "What else?"

She lifted her chin a bit. "You can't get chivalrous about training with me because you think I might refuse to keep working with you if you scare me or something. We both need to improve. Neither of us can do that if you treat me like I'm breakable."

That was laughable. Who had ever treated her like she was *breakable*? Hopefully not Max. If so, his buddy was a moron. "Yeah. No problem," he agreed. "No one gets better if we're *nice* to each other in training sessions."

She nodded. "Exactly. And the last thing is something I want from you, but I'm not sure how you'll feel about it."

What could she possibly *want* from him? Buckets of jewelry from the Aurelian gold mines? Some law passed about Northerners when he was king? Was she going to ban him from the stables? He was briefly concerned, but what she said next wasn't at all what he'd expected.

"I was the one with your sister when she died."

Nate's skin prickled. *She* was the one who'd made sure Vivian wasn't left lying with the dead Immortals? *She'd* put that blanket over Viv? Folded her hands?

Carina went on. "She deserved more dignity than how we left her. And we took a sample of your sister's blood before we left her there, too. Which we shouldn't have done. But we have it now, and I'd like to ask you to let us study it."

Well, the princess *was* a Northerner. It was amazing her

people hadn't taken all kinds of tissue samples. A little blood was hardly a big deal. Though Bast might have freaked out. Even though Bast had sent Vivian's blood to New Paris University Medical School himself.

"So … aren't you asking right now?" he said.

"No," she said, looking a little more flustered than he thought the princess was capable of being. "I mean. I guess I am, but I need you to give your permission in front of the Royal Society at the next meeting. As the crown prince of South Kepler. In the interest of diplomacy. Because I don't think it's right for *my* kingdom to have that sample without your express permission."

It hit Nate right then that if Icy was this concerned about a blood sample, then she *couldn't* be quite as bad as he thought. Only a human with some empathy would worry about something like that. So, maybe he would never *like* her. Maybe she was entitled and stuck up, obstinate and hard to crack. But Viv had been all those things. Bast was all that in spades. And they all could have been nicer to Carina. Or told her what was really going on. Maybe if they had, Nate's sister and Carina would have ended up friends.

Also, Princess Carina had been with Vivian at the end. Had Viv been afraid? Conscious? What were her last words? The princess could tell him exactly what had happened, and Nate thought maybe someday he'd like to know. Maybe. But for now, it was getting a little cold in the gym.

"Whatever version of the Immortality Virus my sister was infected with could put anyone with magic at risk," he said. "And all Kepler's best scientists are in the Royal Society. They should have whatever they need to study the virus. Maybe they'll find a cure and one day, it'll save my life."

"So, you're okay with us studying your sister's blood?"

she said as the temperature in the gym evened out again. "And you'll say that in front of the Royal Society?"

He shrugged. "Sure. Have at it."

Franklin was extremely pleased, and he decided Nate needed a royal uniform to attend a Royal Society of North Kepler meeting. But Nate hadn't exactly packed his old uniform, and it wouldn't have fit if he had.

When he proposed he borrow a suit from someone on the isle, Franklin rejected the idea. "No Southern Royal has been invited to attend one of these meetings in over a hundred years. You need to show up looking royal. And we know someone who can help," he said.

A few days later, one of the king's attendants took all kinds of uncomfortable measurements while Nate stood on a pedestal in Prince Eugene's room. Eugene made snarky, hilarious remarks about it from the next room over the whole time.

The new uniform—apparently made by Lizzy Dupree— arrived just in time for the meeting. It was a tricked out version of what the Southern Guard would have worn if they were having a parade: tailored black pants, black boots, and a high-collared, starched-stiff black shirt. Also, a long-tailed double-breasted coat with an inner lining that buttoned up like a vest and a maliciously pointy collar. Lizzy had all the adornments perfect: shiny gold buttons, carefully detailed seams, slightly ruffled cuffs. Red trim all over the place. Crazily ornate.

It made Nate feel over-dressed. He'd never liked wearing a royal uniform. Bast could make a uniform look good, but Nate could barely get a damned uniform on, and he nearly always discovered something later that wasn't properly tucked, buttoned, or cuffed.

"But it almost makes you look like a real prince," Max told him.

"Almost," Franklin said.

Franklin also had a new uniform, and he seemed completely comfortable in it as they made their way to the assembly building where the Royal Society was gathering. But when they walked into the auditorium, Nate was glad to be dressed so formally. None of the scientists were wearing anything more formal than a suit, but he had the immediate impression that the members of the Royal Society of North Kepler were all cut from the same cloth as the Royal Church of South Kepler's clergy. Their thoughts were equally loud, judgy, and pretentious, and the agenda he was handed—a full page, front and back, of fine text printed on very thick paper—was nothing short of ostentatious.

There were seats reserved for him and Franklin in a row of five on a stage where he was supposed to sit by Princess Carina and look royal for three hours or more. She was already there, chatting with a pudgy man who looked quite self-important, and Nate's instinct to be threatened by the princess took over the second he realized she was doing a *much* better job than him looking royal in a formal uniform. She was pulling off an even stiffer jacket, a flashy blue silk vest, boots with heels that probably made her taller than him, and slicked-back hair that kind of made him miss her normal mess of curls.

She hardly looked like the girl he'd started training with again at all. That girl was fluid with her movements, and she had facial expressions. This one was frozen to look like she could have commanded the entire mainland continent to ice over. Exactly what the princess of North Kepler should look like. But Nate decided it was Miguela's fault when it occurred to him—along with a *terrible* feeling of something that *had* to be shame rushing from his chest all the way to his toes—that Princess Carina was kind of stunning that way. Attractive stunning. He banished that thought from his head immediately. She was not *attractive*. She was icy as hell. That was his story, and he was sticking to it.

He greeted her with a polite, "Princess Carina," and she returned his greeting with an equally polite, "Prince Nathanial." Then the pudgy man—apparently the chair of the Royal Society—made a fuss about how thrilled they were that a member of the Southern Royals was taking some interest in scientific advancements and wasn't the princess just marvelous and also, had Prince Nathanial met Heathrow Princeton? Oh, come here, Heathrow, meet the prince!

A tall guy who knew the princess well enough to kiss her cheek and share a "we're all in for it now" look with her, came up on stage, shook hands with Nate, and said, "Pleasure to meet you, Your Highness." Then Nate felt embarrassed for everyone as the chair of the society clapped both Nate and Heathrow hard on the back and said, "Thank the stars, we now have enough fire in the room to prevent our princess from freezing anyone to death over an ethics violation, eh?"

If a look could have killed, the princess would have killed the guy for that. Maybe she was thinking about it, in fact, but Nate naturally threw a little heat back at the chill, and probably the pudgy man never knew what danger he was in. But *Princeton* noticed, and before he left the stage, he pulled Nate aside and said, "I don't have the magic you have, but I'm ten times smarter than you, so if you ever *actually* hurt Carina, I will find a way to kill you, understand?"

"Um, she is *my* training partner," Nate said, feeling like this was an unnecessarily vicious threat from someone who had dated the girl. Did Heathrow not *know* the princess? "She is perfectly capable of defending herself."

Heathrow looked intensely at Nate. "I didn't mean it *that* way."

Nate wanted to ask Heathrow where he'd gotten off the crazy train, but then the chair called Nate back over, and an additional amount of unnecessary chitchat occurred before everyone was finally seated. Soon, Nate found himself competing with the princess to see who could look stiffer in front of a crowd.

She won. Obviously. He had no idea how she was pulling off pretending like she cared about anything going on at that meeting, though. Because what proceeded from there was the most boring show of intellectualism Nate had ever seen. Bast would have *loved* it. *Nate* was blessed to be wearing a pointy collar or he might have fallen asleep.

Also, he hadn't understood the princess's anxiety about all this before, but he got it now. She'd fought some battle over that blood sample, and he was kind of impressed that it had mattered enough to her to take the issue up with the Royal Society.

So, when it came time for the princess to get up and talk about it, he paid attention to all fifteen minutes of the speech she'd prepared. The Northern Royals admired the esteemed scientists of the Royal Society and their commitment to knowledge. She knew how important it was to each and every one of them to uphold the *highest* ethical standards. She was immeasurably grateful to Doctor McIntosh for allowing her access to his library of blood samples, and she was personally studying every sample. This project, after all, was *absolutely critical* not only to the wellbeing of her family and all the remaining Cardinals but to anyone with magic.

Then she got to his part.

"As you all know, it was with some trepidation that I learned of our collection of a blood specimen from Queen Vivian Wellington's body after her death," she said, sounding all royal about it. "I will admit that I was, perhaps, naïve with regard to the importance of this research. However, I am pleased to have with me today, as my guest, the crown prince of South Kepler. He has consented to allow me to resolve this issue, one more of diplomacy than ethics, in front of all of you today. Prince Nathanial?"

He stood up feeling awkward and went to a table where she had an elaborate document prepared for him to sign. She pushed it toward him, looking him straight in the eye as she did it, like she was daring him to mess this up.

"Prince Nathanial, I would like to formally ask, on behalf of the entire kingdom of North Kepler and the Royal Society of North Kepler, for your permission to study the sample of blood we obtained from the late queen of South Kepler, Queen Vivian, your sister. Do you grant us that permission?"

He should have just been able to say "yes" and sign her document, but instead, he had to recite a long and complicated grant of permission in response to that. It was something that had taken him a full day to memorize, starting with a pompous, "The kingdom of South Kepler has not always appreciated the important work the kingdom of North Kepler supports in the sciences," and ending with, "But today, we are here to support a common cause. My sister's death was a personal tragedy for my family and a national tragedy for my kingdom, and we support anything that can prevent such a tragedy from happening again. The kingdom of North Kepler has my permission as the crown prince of South Kepler to study the specimen of blood obtained from my sister, the late queen of South Kepler."

Princess Carina thanked him formally and handed him a pen, and he signed a piece of paper even thicker than the agenda he'd been given. Then she presented that to some doctor, told them all how proud she was to patron the project, and *finally,* they could both return to their seats as plenty of uncalled-for applause was lavished on them.

He supposed that had been his first official act as an almost head-of-state. Could have been worse. Though under the applause, he whispered to the princess, "I have never seen anyone complicate a simple question more impressively."

She whispered back, "Just wait until Friedman gets up and starts talking about the importance of this for all science and Mortals and the whole universe."

Nate felt horrified that this wasn't over. "How long will *that* go on?"

She looked at him—actually made eye contact and everything—pointed her nose primly into the air, and said, "Long enough that we'll both need something to take our aggression out on after."

"Then are we playing with *real* fire and ice this afternoon, Princess?" he asked, now feeling curiously intrigued.

She answered with a tone of voice that almost sounded like friendly snark. "Can't think of a better time to start."

ROYAL CHURCH OF SOUTH KEPLER
PRAYER OF COLORS

Blessed are they who look upon
the heavenly light,
shot through the white wings of angels,
fluttering in divine grace.

Turn your eyes to the skies, that you may see
infinite, inky tints, sublime, subtle shades,
indigo goldenrod lavender crimson
shards of holy wonder.

Woe to those without vision,
curse those who blind themselves.
But joy to those who delight in the
shimmering colors of creation
And bask in God's eternal glow.

Until the end,
So be it.

CHAPTER THIRTY-EIGHT
THE QUEEN RESTS

Bastian was taller than he'd been the last time he needed a formal uniform. His wrists stuck out the sleeves of his old jacket. The new one was much better. He dressed carefully in it and examined himself in the mirror. The cut made his waist look slim and his chest look muscular. He was a fan of all the gold buttons and the high, pointed collar. The black contrasted nicely with his skin and made him look intimidating.

He might have to find a reason to take the jacket off later, though, because his ass looked fantastic in the slacks, and the jacket's tail covered all that. Nate would have appreciated something covering *his* butt, but that's who Nate was as a person. Bast strutted around in the shirt, vest, slacks, and boots for several minutes because he liked the look so much.

One of the new attendants poked his head into Bast's dressing room. "Your Highness, the procession will begin shortly. Your mother is waiting."

Bast took a final look at himself and straightened up his

posture. "I'm ready." He followed the attendant through the castle to the front hall. His mother never opted for a uniform, but Bast thought her sense of fashion was top-notch. Today, she was wearing a long black dress with a lace collar. Her hair was pulled into a black net, a short black veil covered her eyes, and she had a handkerchief in hand. The perfect picture of a grieving mother.

She took his hand and squeezed it hard as he came to stand by her side. "Bastian, darling, are you sure you don't want to speak at the ceremony?"

"I'm sure," he said.

"You're right. This isn't the time for you to speak. You deserve the opportunity to grieve."

As if his grief could be boxed up in an afternoon. Convenient for his mother that she could contain *her* grief to a two-hour block of time.

"And you're still certain you wish to include Nathanial in the memorial?" his mother asked as the musicians began playing. Horns signified the beginning of the procession. The castle doors opened, and light flooded the hall. Bast and Constance fell in line with their guard.

"We're still telling everyone he's dead, aren't we?" Bast said.

His mother circled her arm around his as they walked. "We could still delay with Nathanial," she said. "Doing it this way will draw more attention to your place as the crown prince. I want to make sure you're well enough for that."

Well enough. A little hint that she was monitoring every session he had with the stupid psychologist she'd brought in to make sure he was healing *appropriately*. She didn't really care if he was healing. She cared if he *looked* like he was healing.

But appearances were everything if he wanted to start

taking power back from his mother. "I see no reason to delay. The kingdom is my responsibility now. The sooner I accept that, the better."

"Of course, Bastian, dear."

He narrowly escaped a sigh, and they walked the rest of the way to the Royal Church in silence, marching through Alighieri to the official funeral drone. He'd done this once before, after his father died, but the march hadn't seemed so long walking at Vivian's side. Now that he was alone, he noticed things he hadn't before. Like how the carpet they walked on wasn't one continuous piece and how the people lining the streets looked somber but didn't cry.

The sun shone too brightly, even under cover of clouds, and the heat made the rubberized sidewalks glitter harshly. By the time they reached their destination, Bast was tired. The steps up into the church had never felt more difficult to climb. The aisle from the church doors to the elevated dais had never looked so perilous. The last time he'd climbed those steps, Vivian had been alive, bleeding out, right there on the dais. He'd launched himself up those steps that day. He couldn't even remember his feet hitting them, he'd been going so fast.

Today, it seemed to take forever simply to reach the front of the church, with the eyes of South Kepler's elite all weighing down on him. The last prince of South Kepler. The only First Degree Cardinal officially still alive. A truly terrible and inappropriate thought occurred to him. He would be expected to *procreate* now. If he didn't, he would go down in history as the final First Degree Cardinal ever to rule South Kepler. Strange the thoughts one has when trying to avoid something otherwise inevitably painful.

His mother let go of his arm at the steps to the dais,

bowed her head as if taking a moment to pray, then stepped up to kneel by the closed casket on the left. A shower of roses adorned the casket, and there was a gold plate on the end that read, "Nathanial Herschel Xavier Wellington, Prince of the Southern Kingdom of Kepler." A picture of Nate taken over a year ago was propped up on an easel so the people of South Kepler would have some way of knowing where Nate had stopped in time.

It made Nate look too young, but still, his eyes pierced into Bast as their mother kissed Nate's casket and said something Bast couldn't make out. Who knew what? It was all for show. She'd never loved Nate. Then she turned to the casket on the right, and Bast found himself thinking another inconvenient thought. This time it was about how he would also be expected to learn the ugly swordsmanship Nate had favored. Totally unnecessary. Completely gender biased. Yet, the king of South Kepler was supposed to be capable of swinging a sword around like an idiotic Renaissance man.

His mother came down the steps—he had somehow missed the moment when she'd prayed over the other casket—and she paused to set her hand on Bast's upper arm and make a properly theatrical production of wiping tears delicately from her eyes. Then she moved on to her seat in the front row and left Bast hesitating to complete his goodbyes alone.

This was it. He took one step up. Stopped. Took another step up. Stopped again. It was only six steps, and yet, it took what seemed an eternity to reach the top.

He went to Nate's empty casket first. This part he could handle. He could look at those eyes the color of swamp muck drilling into him with self-righteous judgment. Nate might return any time to seize power from Bast, but if he knew what was good for him—what was good for the kingdom—he might choose to disappear forever. Or maybe he'd be killed by some virtuous member of the Southern Guard. Whatever happened, Bast couldn't trust Nate anymore. He knelt by the casket and what he said to Nate that no one else would hear was, "Wherever you are, don't return."

Then he stood again and wobbled as he turned. Perhaps he'd knelt for too long. Perhaps he should run down those steps and away from all of this. Just like Nate. Escape and hide somewhere in the East or make a new life for himself in Gandhi, where he could bribe a plastic surgeon into mutilating his face so he would no longer be recognizable. Why not? South Kepler was a disaster. It was going to be such hard work to defeat the Immortal Empire. And Bast would be no more alone if he ran away than he would be if he stayed. He would be alone for the rest of his life. Why bother with all of this?

But he had to bother.

There was honor involved.

More importantly, a God-granted destiny.

He moved toward the other casket unwillingly.

He didn't want to look.

Which was ridiculous. He'd chartered Vivian's coffin himself, with its golden base, polished wood sides, feather-down mattress pad, silken cloth lining. He'd chosen her dress, picked out her shoes, demanded a particular hairstyle, and selected every flower. He'd wanted to minimize the extent to which anyone else put their dirty hands on her. So he'd been the one to lay her down in there himself—under his mother's close supervision, but without telekinesis—picking her up from where they had her on a table in the morgue and carrying her in his arms to her coffin.

After he'd lain her down on that silken cloth in the casket, he'd smoothed her clothes, made sure nothing was folded wrong or wrinkled. He'd arranged her hair in loose, flowing curls around her head—not too wild, but beautiful anyway. Then he'd placed one of her hands on top of the other. Her hands felt smaller than normal. It was as if she'd shrunk, and it took him several moments to realize she hadn't changed at all. It was *his* hands that had gotten longer, perhaps a little wider. Her body was dead. And that was the whole crux of it all. He was living. He could change. He hadn't stopped.

But she had.

And because of that, he was frozen now before her coffin. Not wanting to look one last time. Not wanting to see what he knew he would see. Not wanting to say goodbye.

He'd never wanted to say goodbye.

He glanced toward the rest of the church. He and his mother had been the last visitors, as was the custom. After this, the memorial service would begin. The bishop would close the casket. The pallbearers would carry it to a horse-drawn carriage. Vivian would take one more ride through Alighieri before she returned to the cathedral, where they would take her deep inside the church and lay her in that cold stone box in the memorial hall. They'd place a hard marble slab above her coffin, and he would be there to say one more prayer before he finally left her behind forever.

Though it felt more like *she* was leaving *him* behind.

There were so many people looking at him, and he could see some murmuring uncomfortably to each other. The music stopped, and the hushed voices died down. There was utter silence in the cathedral as the people watched their next king with tears streaming from his eyes. What was the prince doing? Why didn't he say his goodbyes and let them get on with the ceremony? There was only so long someone could sit on those hard benches. Only so long one could stay silent, mourning the dead, before they needed to live again.

He forced himself to look at Vivian one last time.

Vivian. The one person he had always loved. The one person he knew had always loved him. The one person he trusted. His confidante and best friend. The person who could make him laugh. The person who understood him. The person who would never have betrayed him. The person he'd have given everything to save.

Except for his own life.

So, in the end, he hadn't loved her enough, had he? Because if he had, he wouldn't have given up on her. He wouldn't have let her try to do her bullshit hero thing. He would have run toward her at the end. He would have protected her. He would have had enough magic to keep her alive a little longer. Get her back down that cursed mountain. Maybe take her North, accept help from the University of New Paris Medical School.

She might be with him now. Maybe with Nate, too. Or they might have been looking at Nate's empty casket together. Joking that their brother ought to stay out of South Kepler because it wasn't safe here for the kind of fool who didn't know when to save his own ass.

Bast knelt over her casket.

She still looked like she was sleeping and maybe dreaming of a secret he wouldn't know until he, too, had passed on from this world. Her soul, he knew, was no longer in that body. When the casket closed, *she* wouldn't truly be trapped in some dark place. She was gone from there. Right? So maybe she was watching him from somewhere else. Maybe she was feeling sorry that she'd left him here. Maybe he would be reunited with her again in some different realm one day.

But what was he going to do between now and then? And why had God refused him this *one thing* that everyone else seemed to have? A *single person* who loved him unconditionally and without any selfish reasons for doing so? Wasn't *everyone* supposed to have at least one person who would never desert them? Was it too much that he'd wanted that?

He was shaking. He couldn't get up. He closed his eyes and knew that he had to let Vivian go, but how was he supposed to do that? A sob escaped, rising out of his throat and moving through his lips. Then another, and a third. The sound echoed through the cathedral. He couldn't do it again. Three times was a grieving future king. Four times was a future king going mad with grief.

He *was* going mad with grief.

And then someone stepped up behind him. He didn't know who. It surely wasn't his mother. She wasn't good with the kind of unselfish love he needed right now. Unselfish love made you vulnerable, and too much had been taken from her already for that. Mom could only love Bast to the extent he was infallible. She might not love him in this moment of weakness. She certainly wouldn't comfort him.

But there was a hand on his shoulder anyway and another on his other arm, and it was so strange that what Bast noticed was that whoever it was—probably some member of the Southern Guard—had impeccably polished shoes. Excellent quality, too. Not just your standard boots. Those had been purchased in Gandhi.

The person helped him stand. He did it with a lift and a low, subtle, "Your Highness." Nothing else, but the message in those words from this stranger was clear. It was time to end this. Time to say goodbye. He couldn't stay longer, or every person in the church would see him break down and weep.

So he touched Vivian's face with the back of his hand, tried not to feel angry at her for leaving him, whispered goodbye to her, and the only place on his body that felt warm at that moment was where that unfamiliar hand from a stranger held his arm.

Then Bast lifted his head and allowed the stranger to walk him away from the casket, toward his seat. It was no one he knew. Not Nate coming back from the dead, nor Jax back from exile, nor Gael from wherever his mother had sent him. Just one of the guards. A tall man with glistening black hair, eyes too dark for emotion, and a set jawline. Someone who had decided Bast couldn't stay at Vivian's side anymore without embarrassing the entire kingdom.

It was especially strange that for the one moment when Bast met that man's pitch-black eyes, he didn't feel quite as alone. But then the man walked away, and the lines of the man's jaw turned out to be the last thing Bast could recall in any detail about the entire rest of the day.

Everything else was a painful blur that he went through in slow, excruciating motion. The ceremony was gibberish. The casket closing over Vivian and encasing her in the dark was a pit of hell. The walk behind the horse-drawn hearse was misery. The entry into the memorial hall of kings and queens gave Bast chills. He nearly broke down when they lowered Vivian's casket into her final home, but he managed to recite the Prayer of Colors as they put that slab over her.

His mother didn't say anything to him that evening before she retired, but Bast's room was too large for him to sleep in his own bed. Instead, he climbed the stairs to Vivian's room, a place he hadn't ever thought he'd go to again. It was cleaned out now. None of her personal effects remained. None of her books. None of her clothes. None of the trinkets she'd kept on her desk. Even the linens were brand new. But the chair she'd liked to read in was still there, so he curled into that chair and felt pain until he fell asleep too exhausted to feel anything.

The next morning at breakfast, his mother dropped a newspaper into his lap. The front page was a picture of Bast weeping as he knelt by Vivian's casket in the church.

"Good for you," his mother commented. "Mortals love to feed off other people's pain. This will go a long way for your reputation. The honorable prince, hurt so deep by the loss of his brother and sister, now taking up the heavy mantle of power."

Bast ate a piece of toast with zero appetite. He'd woken with the feeling that change had to come. "Yes, about that," he said to his mother. "My coronation is only a few years away. We need to begin planning."

"Oh, Bastian," his mother said. "You needn't fret about *that*. The security detail for your coronation will be far more stringent than—"

"I *meant* for the transition of power," Bastian said.

His mother sat back in her seat. A long smile stretched out on her face, and he thought she must be feeling some combination of pride and pain at the realization that her son was no longer going to sit back and let her handle the kingdom.

Which meant both a loss of power and also a new card

to play *if* she played the game right. Or she would be his card to play, but let the games begin.

"Does that work for you?" he asked with his most charming voice.

And she responded with her most gracious voice. "Absolutely, Bastian. We can have that conversation any time you'd like."

EPILOGUE
THE IMMORTAL EMPIRE

Lord Godric made his way from his villa in the lovely, flowering hills of Immortal Isle down the steps to his own private white sand beach, where the most beautiful thing he had ever seen was waiting for him, barefoot and wearing a colorful bikini and a sarong. Her skin was sun-kissed, her hair was sun-bleached, and her smile was the smile of eternal sunrise.

"Christian!" the Empress said. "We have wonderful news. Have you seen this?"

She handed him a copy of *The Alighieri Times*, and the front page was like an homage to the work they'd done these last fifty years or so.

Remaining Cardinal Prince Grieves Fallen Queen, read the headline, and there was a photo of the poor young prince, looking skinny and broken as he knelt between the coffins of his two dead siblings. He was alone now, with no one to protect him but that miserable bitch Constance, who Godric was especially looking forward to killing one day.

"I believe this requires mimosas," he said to Mila. Celebration was called for, after all. The destruction of the "last" so-called "Cardinal Family" was a sweet victory. The Mortal pests had been far more difficult to subdue than he and Mila had expected before they reached Kepler. If only they had submitted to Mila's rule. Certainly, the Immortal Empire ran on a strict code, but that was to control the baser instincts of their ilk. You couldn't let Immortals with their strain of the virus run amok. They'd kill each other in a few decades, and that would leave you with nothing to rule.

Mila didn't want that. Nor did he. To the contrary, all they wanted was paradise on Kepler. A perfectly oiled human civilization on a planet molded for an ideal Immortal human existence. But the Mortals had fought back against the Immortal Empire, and magic made them difficult to control.

"There's more," Mila told him as they began their breakfast on the beach under the shade of the palm trees they'd had planted here years ago. "Lady Gage returned with the spies we sent to Cerulean. The crown princess of North Kepler visited her and the other Immortals we allowed them to capture in that prison. Apparently, it broke the girl's heart to see the conditions the prisoners were living in. She asked her daddy to fix things. He *is* alive."

Obviously, any living monarchs were a problem, but in this case, the Immortal Empire had long suspected that the Northern Royals were not dead. The confirmation that they were simply more cowardly than the Southern Royals was helpful information.

"But she didn't set the prisoners free," Christian noted.

"Of course not." Mila scoffed. "The Mortals have no sense of justice when it comes to us. But we now know that the Northern Royals are hiding somewhere close to Cerulean, and *that* narrows our search."

"That much closer to exterminating the pests."

"You know I don't like that word, Christian," Mila said. "It's not as though we're trying to *eradicate* all the Mortals or even one race or caste. It's only the magic we need to eliminate. Unless we're any closer to harnessing that for ourselves? How is your most recent experiment coming?"

"With General Fordham?" Christian said. The general was definitely one of his favorite projects. Christian could admit that he had a taste for cruelty, but he only indulged when deserved or absolutely necessary. Fordham fell into the latter category, and there was nothing like working with someone admirable who refused to break.

"Has he agreed to talk yet?"

"He swears he'll die before he talks. So maybe he will. But the serum is closer than ever to perfection. We can now quell his magic abilities for a solid week."

Mila laughed, and Christian tipped back his champagne glass to drain the last of his mimosa and enjoy the perfect blue of the Keplerian sky. Once upon a time, he and Mila had wondered if they would miss Earth, but Kepler was a million times more beautiful. He leaned over to kiss his Empress then because who could resist kissing a beautiful, laughing goddess under a morning sun while drinking a mimosa on a gorgeous beach?

"One way or another, we'll have what we want soon enough," she said.

She was the most fiercely determined person he'd ever met, and he was thousands of years old. Gorgeous. He kissed her again. "I'm sure we will."

TO BE CONTINUED.

THE KEPLER DECLARATION OF MORTAL COMMITMENTS

We, the Mortal humans of the planet of Kepler, in order to pursue a more perfect and harmonious world, do hereby commit:

1. To respect life above all.
2. To be stewards of Kepler's land and resources.
3. To safeguard the aboriginal Keplerians.
4. To facilitate conflict peaceably when possible.
5. To shun the use of weapons of extreme violence, including firearms.
6. To uphold the sovereignty of nations.
7. To seek the highest standard of living for all humans on Kepler.
8. To prohibit slavery and trafficking of any human or aboriginal Keplerian.
9. To use and develop technology responsibly and purposefully.
10. To value every human as equal to another.

ACKNOWLEDGEMENTS

Something I wish I had done with *Sisters of the Perilous Heart* from the beginning is flag it clearly in the blurb as a self-published book. I hire an amazing cover designer and a copy editor who is extremely tolerant of my em-dashes to help me make the book look professional, and I rely on beta readers and critique partners to help me ensure that the story makes some sense. Otherwise, the *Mortal Heritance* series is my creation alone.[1]

As self-publishing becomes increasingly common and the quality of self-published books rises, readers like you have more choices. Self-published books aren't the same as traditionally-published books, though, especially in young adult literature. The traditionally-published young adult literature of today represents books vetted by agents and editors and published by established publishers. The writing in those books is rich, the storytelling is complex, and the themes are

---

1.   No, it is not fanfiction. I do love fanfiction, though, and I have written fanfiction about fandoms that feature elemental magic, such as the ability to produce fire or ice.

inspiring. One young adult book represents a whole team with a vision and a message. The industry is putting a much-needed spotlight on #ownvoices, too, which is wonderful because those voices have long been neglected in publishing and all young readers need to be able to find themselves in a story about a hero they can admire and relate to.

Self-published books are not vetted by gatekeepers, and as a self-published author, I do not feel my books serve the same purpose as traditionally-published books. I am a business owner, and my goal is not to educate or persuade large swaths of readers. I merely seek to entertain a niche audience with light-hearted books. Furthermore, I am not a neglected voice. I am a straight, cisgender, privileged, white female. My perspective is heartily represented in books for teens already.

This is not to say that you should not read my books or that I'm not taking myself seriously. There *is* a message I am trying to convey with the *Mortal Heritance* series. It has something to do with building the confidence you need to fail often enough to succeed (which is kind of the story of my own life). You should read my books because they are fun, the characters might stick with you, and everyone deserves an easy escape sometimes.

Still, there is a difference between literature that also entertains you and genre fiction that has a few solid literary moments. Mine are the latter, and I hope that when you are in the mood for something more deep and meaningful, you explore young adult literature written by #ownvoices authors who represent perspectives not heard often enough in young adult fiction. If you are looking for one of these literary gems, try searching the Internet for "ya books ownvoices." That's what Miguela or Bast would do, and they are intellectuals.

Now, for some thanks with regard to this book:

To Brenda Vasher (my mother) and Carol Vasher (my aunt), thank you both so much for loving me enough to get through the beta version of this book.

To Jenny at Seedings Design (www.seedlingsonline.com), who designed my cover and title page, you are such a pleasure to work with, and I love every cover you create for me more than the last.

To Graham at A Fading Street Publishing Services (www.fadingstreet.com), who is my copy editor, thank you for always being efficient and easy to work with and for tolerating my InDesign-to-Word-and-back formatting mess.

The earth, book, bishop, and knight icons were designed by Freepik. I designed the other illustrations inside the book, including the map and other icons, using Affinity Designer, Rise of Kingdom font made by vladimirnikolic, and free vectors designed by Freepik.

Finally, to all the writers I co-work with virtually, I love our community, and I am so glad to write alongside all of you and share our indie writer journeys.

~Sandra L. Vasher

ABOUT THE AUTHOR

Sandra L. Vasher is an indie writer, recovering lawyer, dreamer, consultant, blogger, serial entrepreneur, and mommy of very spoiled dog. She enjoys long drives in fall weather, do-it-yourself projects, animated movies and cartoons, fanfiction, red wine, traveling everywhere, and baking sweet and savory treats. She can often be found trying not to hunch over her computer at her favorite coffee shops in Raleigh, North Carolina. Follow her online at sandyvasher.com.

BOOKS BY SANDRA L. VASHER

Mortal Heritance
Sisters of the Perilous Heart
Kingdoms of the Frozen Dead (January 2021)

The Immortal Mistakes
Stella Rose Gold for Eternity
Lizzy Dupree and the Thousand-Year Crush
Mila Hildebrand is Forever Not Yours

Nonfiction Books
I Hear Some People Just Have Sex (An Infertil-
ity Memoir with an Ambiguous Ending)